The Best of
BETTY
NEELS

The
Marrying Kind

MILLS & BOON

CONTENTS

Romance readers around the world were sad to note the passing of **Betty Neels** in June 2001. Her career spanned thirty years, and she continued to write into her ninetieth year. To her millions of fans, Betty epitomized the romance writer, and yet she began writing almost by accident. She had retired from nursing, but her inquiring mind still sought stimulation. Her new career was born when she heard a lady in her local library bemoaning the lack of good romance novels. Betty's first book, *Sister Peters in Amsterdam,* was published in 1969, and she eventually completed 134 books. Her novels offer a reassuring warmth that was very much a part of her own personality. She was a wonderful writer, and she will be greatly missed. Her spirit and genuine talent will live on in all her stories.

Tempestuous April

CHAPTER ONE

MEN'S SURGICAL WAS QUIET—there had been two emergency admissions before midnight; a case in theatre—a rather nasty appendix—at one o'clock, and a cardiac arrest at half past two; these happenings interspersed by old Mr Gadd's frequent and successful attempts to climb over his cot sides and amble down the ward in search of refreshment. But none of these happenings appeared to have upset Miss Harriet Slocombe, sitting, as neat as a new pin, at Sister's desk, writing the bare bones of her report. She appeared to be as fresh as the proverbial daisy and would have been genuinely surprised if anyone had suggested to her that she had had a busy night. She sucked the top of her ballpoint and frowned at the clatter of plates from the kitchen where her junior nurse was cutting bread and butter for the patients' breakfasts. It was four o'clock, almost time for her, in company with Nurse Potter, to consume the tea and toast with which they fortified themselves before beginning their early morning work. Miss Slocombe removed the pen from her mouth and got up in order to do a round of her patients. She went from bed to bed, making no sound, due very largely to the fact that she had removed her shoes from her feet some time previously, and was in her stockings. The shoes stood side by side under Sister's desk, waiting to be donned again after her tea break.

She reached the end of the ward and paused by the windows opening on to the balcony, to look out into the chill gloom of the early morning. March could be dreary; especially just before dawn. She stood watching the fine drizzle and thought with pleasure of the three-week holiday she was to have in a fortnight's time…and at the end of it she would be coming back to St Nick's as Ward Sister of Men's Surgical. A rosy future, she told herself robustly, and sighed. She was twenty-four years old and pretty, with wide blue eyes, a retroussé nose and a gently curving mouth; she wore her bright blonde hair—the envy of her friends—in a complicated knot on top of her head, and her person was small, so that she looked extremely fragile. She was in fact, as strong as an ox. She had a faint air of reserve and a nasty temper when roused, which was seldom. She was liked by everyone in the hospital with the possible exception of one or two of the housemen, who had expected her to be as fragile as her appearance and were still smarting from her astringent tongue. They called her Haughty Harry amongst themselves, and when she had heard about it, she had laughed with everybody else, but a little wistfully, because she knew that with the right man she wouldn't be in the least haughty… She sighed again, and went to tuck up Mr Gadd who had, as usual, fallen sound asleep at the wrong end of the night. In the next bed to him, the theatre case opened hazy eyes and said in a woolly drugged voice,

'Cor, dang me, you'm as pretty as a picture,' and went immediately to sleep again.

Harriet smiled, a warm, motherly smile, wholly without conceit; she was aware that she was a pretty girl, but two elder sisters and three brothers younger than herself had taught her at an early age to put things in their proper perspective. She had long since outgrown her youthful dreams of captivating some young, handsome and wealthy man with her good looks; but outgrown though they might be, they had so far made it impossible for her to settle for anything less. She moved soundlessly down the ward, adjusted two drips, took a blood pressure and carefully and gently examined the two emergencies; they were sleeping soundly. She supposed that they would go to Theatre during the day. She reached the last bed and stood a moment facing the quiet ward, listening. She ignored the snores, the sighs and Mr Bolt's tracheostomy tube's faint whistle, she ignored the background sissing of the hot water pipes and the soft rhythm of the electric pump beneath young Butcher's bed—all these sounds were familiar; she knew who and what made them. It was other sounds she was listening for—a change in breathing, an unexpectedly sudden restlessness and more sinister— the quiet from a bed where there should be the small sounds of a sleeping man. Her trained ear detected nothing untoward, however, and she nodded, well satisfied, and turned to Sister's table, just as Nurse Potter, plump and beaming, edged herself round the ward door with a tray. She put it down carefully and whispered breathily,

'I made Bovril toast, Staff,' and indicated the generous pile before them. Harriet was already pouring out the tea.

'Good. I love it and I'm famished. I only hope we'll get the chance to eat it all.'

They began to munch, and presently, when their hunger was a little blunted, Harriet started to plan the morning's work.

Night nurses' breakfast was always a noisy meal—everyone talked and laughed with a false energy inspired by the knowledge that the night was over once more. The paralysis of tiredness which had crept over them in the early hours of the morning had been forgotten. Later, it would return, so that those who weren't already in bed were liable to sleep in the bath or drop off over a late morning cup of cocoa—in the meantime they were all bursting with vigour. The staff nurses sat at a table on their own; there were perhaps a dozen of them, of whom Harriet was the last to arrive that morning. Late though she was, she looked unruffled and incredibly neat and not in the least tired.

'We stayed to help,' she volunteered as she sat down. 'There's been an accident at the brickworks.'

There was an understanding murmur—the brickworks was notorious for the fact that it could always be relied upon to fill any vacant bed in Men's Surgical at all times.

She was left to make a substantial breakfast at her leisure, and not until she had poured her third cup of tea did someone ask,

'Has anyone seen the new RMO? I ought to have done—after all, I am on Medical, but all I got last night was our Mr Rugg.' Mr Rugg was young and uncertain and definitely not a lady's man. The speaker looked around the table until her eye lighted upon Harriet, who had gone a delicious pink.

'I might have known… Harry, where did you meet him?'

Harry put down her cup. 'He came on to the ward last night,' she said serenely. 'We had that cardiac arrest, remember?' She looked inside the empty teapot and put it down again resignedly. 'He's nice—good-looking and one of those gravelly voices and polished manners—' She was interrupted by a chorus of knowing groans; when they had subsided she added gently, 'He's engaged.'

A disappointed voice asked, 'How do you know? He couldn't have had time to tell you that!'

'He talked while he was making up the chart. I expect he felt lonely and wanted to talk about her. Perhaps I've got a sympathetic face,' she observed hopefully, and was greeted by a shriek of friendly laughter; her friends and acquaintances holding the opinion that anyone as pretty as Harry Slocombe needed to be nothing else. After a moment she laughed with them, privately wondering why everyone other than her own family attached such importance to looks.

A couple of hours later she was sitting up in bed reading sleepily when there was a knock on the door and a tall well-built girl came in.

Harriet put her book down. 'Sieske, you're never on at eleven again?'

The girl nodded gloomily and came to sit on the end of the bed. She was nice-looking, with a pleasant, placid face framed in pale hair which she wore in an unfashionable and highly becoming bun in the nape of her neck.

'Aunt Agnes must loathe me,' she remarked. Aunt Agnes was the Sister on Men's Medical, she had been there for unnumbered years and made a habit of loathing everyone. 'It is because I am not English, you think?'

Harriet shook her head. 'She never likes anyone. I shouldn't worry anyway, it's only another two weeks, isn't it? I shall miss you, Sieske.'

'Me you too,' said Sieske with obscure sincerity. She patted her bun with a large capable and very beautiful hand and turned solemn blue eyes on Harriet.

'Harry, will you not come with me when I go? You have three weeks' holiday; you could see much of Holland in that time—we should all be so glad; my family think of you as a friend, you know. I tell them many times of my visits to your home—we shall be highly pleased to have you as guest. It is a quiet place where we live, but we have many friends, and the country is pretty too.' She paused and went on shyly, 'I should like you to meet Wierd.' Wierd was her fiancé; after several months of friendship with Sieske, Harriet looked upon him as an old friend, just as the Dutch girl's family—her mother and father, younger sisters and the older brother who had just qualified as a doctor at Leiden—seemed like old friends too. The Dutch girl had told her so much about them that she felt that she already knew them. It would be delightful to go and stay with Sieske and meet them all—there was a partner too, she remembered; mentioned casually from time to time. Harriet searched her sleep-clogged brain for his name. Friso Eijsinck. She didn't know much more about him than his name, though. Sieske had mentioned too that he wasn't married. Harriet felt faintly sympathetic towards him, picturing him as a middle-aged bachelor with a soup-stained waistcoat. She dismissed his vague image from her mind.

'I'd love to come,' she said warmly. 'But are you sure it will be all right with your family?'

Sieske smiled. 'But of course I am sure. Already they have written with an invitation, which I extend to you. I am most happy, as they will be. We will make plans together for the journey.' She got up. 'Now you will sleep and I will write to Moeder.'

'We'll arrange it all on my nights off,' said Harriet sleepily. 'Get a day off and come home with me—tell Aunt Agnes you have to go to your grandmother's funeral.'

'A joke?' queried Sieske. She had a hand on the door but paused to look back doubtfully at Harriet. But Harriet was already asleep.

Harriet's family lived in a small west country village some forty miles from the city where she worked. Her father had had a practice there for twenty-five years or more and lived in a roomy rather ramshackle house that had sheltered his large family with ease, and now housed a growing band of grandchildren during school holidays. His eldest son had just qualified in his turn and had already taken his place in the wide-flung practice. It was he who fetched the two girls from hospital a few days later. He owned an elderly Sprite, which was always overloaded with passengers, but both girls were used to travelling in this cramped fashion and packed themselves in without demur. The country looked fresh and green after the rain, the moors rolled away into the distance—Harriet tied a scarf tightly round her hair and drew a deep breath; she was always happiest where the horizon was wide. The village looked cosy, with its thatched and cob walled cottages; the daffodils were out in the doctor's garden as they shot up the drive and stopped with a tooth-jolting jerk at the front door. The girls scrambled out and ran inside to the comfort of the shabby hall and thence to the big sitting-room at the back of the house, where Mrs Slocombe was

waiting with tea and the warm welcome she offered to anyone
who set foot inside her home. She listened to the girls' plans
as they ate their way through home-made scones with a great
deal of butter and jam, and the large fruit cake Mrs Slocombe
had thoughtfully baked against their coming. She refilled their
cups and said calmly, 'How lovely for you, Harry darling. You'll
need a passport and a photo—better go into town tomorrow and
get them settled. How will you go?'

Sieske answered, 'From Harwich. We can go by train from
the Hoek and my father will meet us at Leeuwarden.'

Mrs Slocombe replenished the teapot. 'Travel broadens the
mind,' she observed, and looked at Harriet, immersed in a map.
Such a dear child, and so unlike her brothers and sisters with
her delicate prettiness and femininity and so gently pliant until
one encountered the sturdy core of proud independence and
plain common sense beneath it. Mrs Slocombe sighed. It would
be nice to see Harriet happily married as her two sisters were.
Heaven knew it wasn't for lack of opportunity, the dear girl was
surrounded by men as though they were bees round a honey-
pot; and she treated all of them as though they were brothers.
Perhaps she would meet some nice man in Holland. Mrs Slocombe smiled happily at the thought and gave her mind to the
serious business of the right clothes to take.

They spent the rest of that evening making their plans, helped
and sometimes hindered by the advice and suggestions proffered by members of the family and their friends as they drifted
in and out of the sitting-room. Her brother William, coming
in from evening surgery, remarked with all the experience of
someone who had been to the Continent of Europe on several
occasions, 'Still at it? Good lord, Harry, anyone would think
you were going to the other side of the world instead of the other
side of the North Sea.'

His sister remained unmoved by his observations, and merely
picked up a small cushion and threw it at his head with the un-
erring aim of much practice. 'Beast,' she said affectionately.

'But it is the other side of the world to me, isn't it? I've never been outside Britain before, so any part of the world is foreign—just as foreign as the other side of the world—and everyone I meet will be a foreigner.'

This ingenuous remark caused a great deal of merriment. 'I hope,' said William, half seriously, 'that you'll remember that you are going to be the foreigner.'

'Harriet will not feel foreign with us,' said Sieske stoutly. 'We all speak English—that is, Father and Aede and Friso speak it very well, and Maggina and Taeike are learning it at school—only my mother does not speak it though she does at times understand.'

'And then there's you,' pointed out Harriet. 'You speak marvellous English.'

Sieske glowed with pleasure. 'Yes, I think I do, but then you helped me very much; it is not an easy language to learn.'

'Nor, I gather, is Dutch,' remarked Dr Slocombe dryly, 'although it doesn't sound as though Harry will need to know one word of it.'

'No, of course she won't,' agreed Mrs Slocombe comfortably. She looked across the room at her daughter and thought with maternal satisfaction what a very pretty girl she was. A great deal could happen in three weeks, whatever part of the world one happened to be in.

CHAPTER TWO

THEY TRAVELLED BY the night boat from Harwich, and Harriet, whose longest sea trip had been between Penzance and the Scillies, was disagreeably surprised to find the North Sea so spiteful. She lay in her bunk, listening to Sieske's gentle breathing above her, and wondered if she would be seasick. It was fortunate that she fell asleep while she was still making up her mind about this, and didn't wake up until the stewardess wakened them with their early morning tea. It was delightful to take turns with Sieske, to peer out of the porthole at the low coast of Holland. It looked as flat as she had always imagined it would be, and lonely as well. An hour later, however, disembarking amidst the cheerful bustle, she reversed her opinion. There seemed to be a great many people, all working very hard and apparently delighted to see the passengers coming off the boat; a larger porter took their luggage and led them to the Customs shed, exchanging pleasantries with Sieske, and thumped down their cases in front of a small rat-faced man who asked them in a surprisingly pleasant voice why they had come and what they had brought with them. Here again Sieske was useful; Harriet found that she did not need to utter a word, although she said 'Thank you' politely when she was handed her passport, and was taken aback when the Customs Officer wished her a happy holiday—in quite beautiful English.

The train snaked silently through green meadows where black and white cows, coated against the chilly wind, stood placidly to watch them flash by; there were farms dotted here and there, with steep roofs, and gardens arranged very neatly around them—the villages were dominated by their churches; Harriet had never seen so many soaring steeples in her life, nor, for that matter, had she seen so many factories, each with its small satellite of new houses close by. She didn't like them very much and turned with relief to the contemplation of a canal, running like a ruler through the neat countryside, and carrying a variety of picturesque traffic. Presently they were served coffee and ham rolls, and the two girls sat back, watching the country flash by under a blue, rather watery sky stretching away to the flat horizon. In no time at all they were at Rotterdam—Harriet watched the early morning crowds racing to work with a faintly smug sympathy. The three weeks of her holiday stretching ahead of her seemed a very long time indeed. She wondered idly what she would feel like on the return journey. Once they had left Rotterdam, the scenery became more rural, the villages lying neatly amongst the flat meadows, like cakes arranged tidily on a plate—Gouda, even from a distance, looked intriguing—Harriet wished that they might have stopped to look around, but the train went remorselessly on to Utrecht and then to Amersfoort, where they had to get out anyway and change trains. They stood on the platform and watched the express rush away towards the frontier, and then because they had half an hour to wait, they went and had a cup of coffee and Sieske spread the incredibly small Dutch money on the table between them and gave Harriet her first lesson. They laughed a great deal and the time passed so quickly that they were surprised when the train for Leeuwarden arrived and they were stowed on board by a kindly porter, who tossed their cases in after them and waved cheerfully as the train pulled out.

They still had a two-hour journey before them, Harriet settled herself by the window once more, listening to Sieske's unhurried voice and watching the subtle changing of the countryside. It began to look very like the New Forest, with stretches of heath and charming little woods; there were glimpses of houses too, not large, but having an air of luxury, each set in its own immaculate grounds. Presently the woods and heathland gave way in their turn to rolling grassland. The farms looked large and prosperous, even the cows looked plumply outsize and although there were plenty of villages and towns there was a refreshing lack of factories.

Sieske's father was waiting at Leeuwarden, a large, very tall man with thick grey hair, a neat moustache and an elegant Van Dyke beard. He had a round merry face, but his eyes were shrewd behind the horn-rimmed glasses he wore. He greeted Sieske with a bear-like hug and a flow of incomprehensible words, but as he turned to shake Harriet's hand, she was relieved to find that his English was almost as good as her own.

'You are most welcome, Harriet,' he said warmly. 'We hope that you will have a pleasant holiday with us—and now we will go home; Mother is waiting—she is most excited, but she would not come with me because everything has to be ready for you when you arrive.'

He led the way over to a BMW, and Harriet looked at it with an appreciative eye as they got in. She gazed around her as they went through Leeuwarden, glimpsing small side streets that would be fun to explore. Dr Van Minnen seemed to read her thoughts, for without taking his eyes off the road, he said, 'You shall come here, Harriet, and look around one day soon. There is a great deal to see as well as a museum of which we are very proud.'

Franeker, Sieske's home, was only a short distance from Leeuwarden; in less than twenty minutes they were slowing down past a large church and turning into the main street of the charming little town.

The doctor lived in a large house overlooking a tree-lined canal which ran between narrow cobbled streets lined with buildings from another era. No two houses were alike, except in a shared dignity of age and beauty. Harriet got out of the car and stood gaping at the variety of rooftops. She would have liked to have asked about them, but Sieske was already at the great wooden door with its imposing fanlight, and the doctor caught hold of her arm and hurried her inside behind his daughter, to be greeted by his wife. Mevrouw Van Minnen was very like her daughter and still remarkably youthful—there was no hint of grey in her pale blonde hair and her eyes were as bright a blue as Sieske's; she was a big woman, but there was nothing middle-aged in her brisk movements. The next hour or so was taken up most agreeably, drinking coffee and eating the crisp little biscuits—*sprits*—that went with it. There was a great deal of conversation which lost none of its zest by reason of Harriet's lack of Dutch, and Mevrouw Van Minnen's scant knowledge of English. Presently they all went upstairs to show Harriet her room—it overlooked the street, so that she could see the canal below, which delighted her; and although it was small it was very comfortable. She unpacked happily; it was, she decided, going to be a delightful holiday. She did her hair and her face and went downstairs to join the family for *koffietafel*, and ate her bread and cold meat and cheese and omelette with a healthy appetite which called forth delighted surprise from Mevrouw Van Minnen, who had thought she had looked too delicate to do more than peck at her food. Sieske translated this to Harriet, giggling a great deal, and then said in Dutch to her mother:

'Harry isn't quite what she looks, Moeder. She appears to be a fairy, but she's not in the least delicate; and of course it notices here, doesn't it, because we're all so big.'

'Such a pretty girl, too,' her mother murmured. 'I wonder what Aede and Friso will say when they see her.'

Aede wouldn't be home until the evening, it seemed, and no one knew what Friso was doing—he had taken the morning surgery so that Dr Van Minnen could go to Leeuwarden—he had presumably gone to his own home. They would see him later, said Mevrouw Van Minnen comfortably, and suggested that the two girls went out for a walk so that Harriet could see something of the town.

An hour later, the two of them were strolling along looking in the shop windows while Sieske carefully explained the prices. They had reached a particularly interesting display of clocks and jewellery when Sieske suddenly exclaimed, 'I forgot, I have to buy stamps for Father—the post office is in the next street. Wait here, Harry—you can practise your Dutch in this window—I won't be a minute.'

Harriet looked her fill, and then because Sieske still hadn't come back, went to the edge of the pavement and looked up and down the street. It was surprisingly busy for a small town, with a constant thin stream of traffic. She was standing on the corner outside the beautiful town hall and she watched idly as the various buses and lorries halted by her; the cars were mostly small, so that when an AC 428 Fastback pulled up it caught her attention immediately. There was a girl sitting in the front by the driver—a girl so dark that it was impossible not to notice her amongst the fair-haired giants around the town, thought Harriet; she was quite beautiful too. She turned her head and stared at Harriet with great black eyes which barely noticed her. She looked cross, and Harriet, with that extraordinary feeling that in someone else's country you can do things you wouldn't do in your own, stared back openly before transferring her gaze to the driver. He was looking ahead and she studied his profile at her leisure; it was a handsome one, with a domineering nose and a firm chin; his forehead was high and wide and his very fair hair was brushed smoothly back from it. Looking at him, she had the sudden deep conviction that they had met before; her heart started to race, she wished with all her heart that he would turn and look at her. As though she had shouted her wish out loud at him, he turned his head and she found herself gazing into level grey eyes. It seemed to her that she had known him—a complete stranger—all her life; she smiled with the sudden delight of it, wondering if he felt the same way too. Apparently he did not; there was no expression on his face at all, and she went slowly pink under his cool stare. The traffic ahead of him sorted itself out, and he was gone, leaving her gazing sadly after him; the man who had been in her thoughts for so many years; the reason for her being more than friends with the men she had met. He had been her dream; but dreams didn't last. A good thing perhaps, as quite obviously she had no part in his; indeed, he had looked at her as though she had been a lamp-post.

Sieske came back then, and said, 'Harry, what is it? You look as though you've seen a ghost.'

Harriet turned to walk beside her friend. 'No, not a ghost.' She so obviously didn't want to say any more that Sieske bit off the questions she was going to ask, and started to talk about something quite different.

Aede arrived after tea—which wasn't a meal at all, Harriet discovered, just a cup of tea with no milk and a plate of delicate little biscuits. He was like his father, tall and broad, and looked younger than his twenty-five years. He had just qualified as a doctor and was at the hospital at Leeuwarden working as a houseman, and it would be at least another six months before he started to specialize; eventually, of course, he would join his father's practice. He told Harriet these interesting facts in fluent English, sitting beside her on the comfortable sofa near the stove. He drank the decidedly cool tea without apparently minding in the least, and consumed the remainder of the biscuits. Harriet liked him; he wasn't as placid as Sieske, but he was obviously good-natured and an excellent companion. They sat around happily talking shop until almost supper time, while Mevrouw Van Minnen, looking almost as young as her daughter, sat in a straight-backed chair by her work table, knitting a sock at speed and managing to take a lion's share in the talk despite the fact that everything had to be said twice in both languages.

They sat down to the evening meal soon after seven, with a great deal of laughing and talking. Dr Van Minnen, who had disappeared soon after tea to take his evening surgery, came back in time to dispense an excellent sherry from a beautiful decanter into crystal glasses.

'Where's Friso?' inquired his wife. 'He hasn't called to see Sieske.'

The doctor answered her and then repeated his words, this time in English for Harriet's benefit. 'My partner has had to go to Dongjum, a small village a few miles from this town—an extended breech, so he's likely to be there most of the night.'

Harriet felt a pang of pity for the poor man—she had been told that he didn't live in Franeker, but in a nearby village close to the sea; he looked after the rural side of the practice while Dr Van Minnen attended his patients in Franeker.

'Is Dr Eijsinck's share of the practice a large one?' she asked Aede.

'*Hemel*, yes—and very scattered, but he's a glutton for work.'

And Harriet added a harassed expression and a permanent stoop to the stained waistcoat, and then forgot all about him in the excitement of discussing Sieske's and Wierd's engagement party, when their forthcoming marriage would be announced. It was to be a splendid affair, with the *burgemeester* and the *dominee* and various colleagues of the doctor coming, as well as a great many young people. It was fortunate that the sitting-room and the drawing-room were connected by folding doors, which could be pushed back, making one room. Harriet sat back, listening quietly and wondering which of her two party dresses she had had the forethought to bring with her she should wear. Every now and then she thought about the man in the AC 428 Fastback.

The following morning after breakfast, Harriet took the post along to the doctor in his surgery. She hadn't been there yet, but she had been told the way. She went down the long narrow passage leading to the back of the house and through the little door in the wall opposite the kitchen. She could hear a murmur of sound—shuffling feet, coughs and a baby crying, as she knocked on the surgery door. The doctor was alone, searching through a filing cabinet with concentrated fierceness. His voice was mild enough, however, as he remarked.

'Mevrouw Van Hoeve's card is here somewhere—the poor woman is in the waiting room, but how can I give her an injection until I check her notes?'

Harriet put the post down on the desk. It seemed that doctors were all the same the world over.

'I've brought your post,' she said soothingly. 'If you'll spell the name to me I'll look for the card while you see if there's anything important…'

Dr Van Minnen gave her a grateful look. 'I do have an assistant,' he explained, 'but she's on holiday.'

He sat down with a relieved sigh and picked up the first of his letters, and Harriet started to go through the filing cabinet. Mevrouw Van Hoeve was half-way through the second drawer, filed away under P-S; no wonder she couldn't be found. Harriet took it out and turned round in triumph to find that the door had opened and a man had come in; he spoke briefly to Dr Van Minnen and stood staring at her with the same cool grey eyes that she had been trying so hard to forget. She stood staring back at him in her turn, clutching the folder to her; her pretty mouth agape, while the bright colour flooded her face.

Dr Van Minnen glanced up briefly from his desk. 'Harriet, this is my partner, Friso Eijsinck.'

The Friso she had imagined disintegrated. This elegant waistcoat had never borne a soup stain in its well-cared-for life; indeed, the whole appearance of its wearer was one of a well-dressed man about town. There was no sign of a stoop either; he was a giant among the giantlike people around her and he wore his great height with a careless arrogance; and as for the harassed expression—she tried her best to imagine him presenting anything but a calm, controlled face to the world, and failed utterly.

She said, 'How do you do, Doctor,' in a voice which would have done credit to one of Miss Austen's young ladies, and this time she didn't smile.

His own, 'How do you do, Miss Slocombe,' was uttered in a deep, rather slow voice with a faint impatience in its tones. There was a pause, during which she realized that he was waiting for her to go. She closed the filing cabinet carefully, smiled at Dr Van Minnen, and walked without haste to the door which he was holding open for her, and passed him with no more than a brief glance, her head very high. To her chagrin he wasn't even looking at her. Outside, with the door closed gently behind her, she stopped and reviewed the brief, disappointing meeting. She doubted if he had looked at her—not to see her, at any rate; he had made her feel in the way, and awkward, and this without saying anything at all. She walked on slowly; perhaps he hated the English, or, she amended honestly, he didn't like her.

Sieske was calling her from the top of the house and she went upstairs and put on her clove pink raincoat and tugged its matching hat on to her bright hair, then went shopping with Sieske and her mother.

Wierd was coming that evening. Harriet spent the afternoon setting Sieske's hair, and after their tea combed it out and arranged it for her, then stood back to admire her handiwork. What with a pretty hair-do and the prospect of seeing Wierd again, Sieske looked like a large and a very good-looking angel.

There was no evening surgery that day; they were to meet in the drawing-room for drinks at six-thirty. Harriet went upstairs to change her dress wondering what she was going to do until that time. She suspected that the arrangement had been made so that Sieske and her young man would have some time to themselves before the family assembled. She was just putting the last pin into her hair when there was a knock on the door, and when she called 'Come in', Aede put his inquiring head into the room.

'Harriet? Are you ready? I wondered if you would like to put on a coat and come for a quick run in the car—there's heaps of time.'

She had already caught up the pink raincoat; it wasn't raining any more, but it lay handy on a chair and she put it on, saying, 'I'd love to, Aede. But do we tell someone?'

They were going downstairs. 'I told Moeder,' he said. 'She thought it was a jolly good idea.'

His car was outside—a Volkswagen and rather battered. Harriet got in, remarking knowledgeably that it was a good car and how long had he had it. This remark triggered off a conversation which lasted them out of Franeker and several miles along the main road. When he turned off, however, she asked, 'Where are we going?'

'Just round the country so that you can see what it is like,' Aede replied, and turned the car into a still smaller road. The country looked green and pleasant in the spring evening light. The farms stood well apart from each other, each joined to its own huge barn by a narrow corridor at its back. They looked secure and prosperous and very different from the more picturesque, less compact English farms. They passed through several small villages with unpronounceable names in the Fries language, then circled back and crossed the main road again so that they were going towards the coast. On the outskirts of one village there was a large house, with an important front door and neat windows across its face. It had a curved gabled roof and a large garden alive with daffodils and tulips and hyacinths. Harriet cried out in delight, 'Oh, Aede, stop—please stop! I simply must stare. Will anyone mind?'

He pulled up obligingly and grinned. 'No, of course not. It is rather lovely, isn't it?'

'And the house,' she breathed, 'that's lovely too. How old is it? Who lives there?'

'About 1760, I think, but you can ask Friso next time you see him; it's his.'

Harriet turned an astonished face to her companion. 'You mean Dr Eijsinck? He lives there? All by himself?'

Aede started the car again. He nodded. 'Yes, that is, if you don't count a gardener and a cook and a valet and a housemaid or two. He's got a great deal of money, you know; he doesn't need to be a doctor, but his work is the love of his life. That doesn't mean to say that he doesn't love girls too,' he added on a laugh.

'Why doesn't he marry, then?' She waited for Aede's answer. Perhaps Friso was engaged or at least in love; what about that dark girl in his car?

Aede thought for a moment. 'I don't know,' he said slowly. 'I asked him once—oh, a long time ago, and he said he was waiting for the girl.' He shrugged his wide shoulders. 'It didn't make much sense…' He broke off. 'Here's Franeker again; we're a bit late, but I don't suppose it will matter.'

Harriet smiled at him. 'It was lovely, Aede. I enjoyed every minute of it.'

He brought the car to a rather abrupt halt in front of the house and they both went inside.

'I'll be down in a minute,' said Harriet, and flew upstairs, to throw down her raincoat, look hastily at herself in the mirror and then race downstairs again. Almost at the bottom of the staircase she checked herself abruptly and continued down to the hall with steps as sedate as the voice with which she greeted Dr Eijsinck, whom she had observed at that very moment standing there. Disconcertingly he didn't answer, and she stood looking up at him—he was in her way, but his size precluded her from passing him unless she pushed by. It seemed a long time before he said reluctantly,

'You smiled. Why?' He gave her a hard, not too friendly stare. 'You didn't know me.'

So he had seen her after all. Harriet felt her heart thudding and ignored it. She said in a steady voice,

'No, I didn't know who you were, Dr Eijsinck. It was just... I thought that I recognized you.' Which was, she thought, perfectly true, although she could hardly explain to him that she had dreamed about him so often that she couldn't help but recognize him.

He nodded, and said, to surprise her, 'Yes, I thought perhaps it was that. It happens to us all, I suppose, that once or twice in a lifetime we meet someone who should be a stranger, and is not.'

She longed to ask him what he meant and dared not, and instead said in a stiff, conversational voice,

'What excellent English you speak, Doctor,' and came to a halt at the amused look on his face. And there was amusement in his voice when he answered.

'How very kind of you to say so, Miss Slocombe.'

She looked down at her shoes, so that her thick brown lashes curled on to her cheeks. He was making her feel awkward again. She swallowed and tried once more.

'Should we go into the drawing-room, do you think?'

He stood aside without further preamble, and followed her into the room where she was instantly pounced upon by Sieske so that she could meet Wierd and see for herself that he was everything that her friend had said. He was indeed charming, and exactly right for Sieske. They made a handsome couple and a happy one too. Harriet suppressed a small pang of envy; it must be nice to be loved as Wierd so obviously loved Sieske. She drank the sherry Aede brought her and sat next to him during the meal which followed and joined in the laughter and talk, which was wholly concerned with the engagement party. It was discussed through the excellent soup, the *rolpens met rodekool*, the *poffertjes*—delicious morsels of dough fried in butter to an unbelievable lightness—and was only exhausted when an enormous bowl of fruit was put on the table. Harriet sat quietly while Aede peeled a peach for her, and listened to Dr Eijsinck's deep voice—he was discussing rose grafting with her hostess, who turned to her and said kindly, but in her own language,

'Harry, you must go and see Friso's garden, it is such a beautiful one.'

Aede repeated her words in English, and then went on in the same language.

'We went past your place this evening, Friso. I took Harriet for a run and we stopped while she admired your flowers.'

Harriet looked across the table at him then and smiled, and was puzzled to see his mobile mouth pulled down at the corners by a cynical smile, just as though he didn't in the least believe that she had a real fondness for flowers and gardens. When he said carelessly, 'By all means come and look round, Miss Slocombe,' she knew that he had given the invitation because there was nothing else he could do. She thanked him quietly, gave him a cool glance, and occupied herself with her peach. She took care to avoid him for the rest of the evening, an easy matter as it turned out, for Dr Van Minnen had discovered that she had only the sketchiest knowledge of Friesland's history, and set himself to rectify this gap in her education. It was only at the end of the evening that Dr Eijsinck spoke to her again and that was to wish her good night, and that a most casual one.

Later, in her pleasant little room, she sat brushing her hair and thinking about the evening. Something had gone wrong with her dream. It had seemed that kindly fate had intervened when she had met him again, but now she wasn't so sure, for that same fickle fate was showing her that dreams had no place in her workaday world. Harriet ground her even little teeth— even though he had a dozen beautiful girl-friends, he could at least pretend to like her. On reflection, though, she didn't think that he would bother to pretend about anything. She got into bed and turned out the light and lay in the comfortable darkness, wondering when she would see him again.

CHAPTER THREE

SHE AWOKE EARLY to a sparkling April morning and the sound of church bells, and lay between sleeping and waking listening to them until Sieske came in, to sit on the end of the bed and talk happily about the previous evening.

'You enjoyed it too, Harry?' she asked anxiously.

Harriet sat up in bed—she was wearing a pink nightgown, a frivolous garment, all lace and ribbons. Her hair fell, straight and gold and shining, almost to her waist; she looked delightful.

'It was lovely,' she said warmly. 'I think your Wierd is a dear—you're going to be very happy.'

Sieske blushed. 'Yes, I know. You like Aede?'

Harriet nodded. 'Oh, yes. He's just like you, Sieske.'

'And Friso?'

Harriet said lightly, 'Well, we only said hullo and good-bye, you know. He's not quite what I expected.' She explained about the gravy stains and the permanent stoop, and Sieske giggled.

'Harry, how could you, and he is so handsome, don't you think?'

Harriet said 'Very,' with a magnificent nonchalance.

'And so very rich,' Sieske went on.

'So I heard,' said Harriet, maintaining the nonchalance. 'How nice for him.'

Sieske curled her legs up under her and settled herself more comfortably. 'Also nice for his wife,' she remarked.

Harriet felt a sudden chill. 'Oh? Is he going to marry, then?' she asked, and wondered why the answer mattered so much.

Sieske laughed.

'Well, he will one day, I expect, but I think he enjoys being a...*vrijgezel*. I don't know the English—it is a man who is not yet married.'

'Bachelor,' said Harriet.

'Yes—well, he has many girl-friends, you see, but he does not love any of them.'

'How do you know that?' asked Harriet in a deceptively calm voice.

'I asked him,' said Sieske simply, 'and he told me. I should like him to be happy as Wierd is happy; and I would like you to be happy too, Harry,' she added disarmingly.

Harriet felt herself getting red in the face. 'But I am happy,' she cried. 'I've got what I wanted, haven't I? A sister's post, and—and—' The thought struck her that probably in twenty years' time she would still have that same sister's post. She shuddered. 'I'll get up,' she said, briskly cheerful to dispel the gloomy thought. But this she wasn't allowed to do; the family, it seemed, were going to church at nine o'clock, and had decided that the unfamiliar service and the long sermon wouldn't be of the least benefit to her. She was to stay in bed and go down to breakfast when she felt like it.

Sieske got up from the bed and stretched herself. 'We are back soon after ten, and Wierd comes to lunch. We will plan something nice to do.' She turned round as she reached the door. 'Go to sleep again, Harry.'

Harriet, however, had no desire for sleep. She lay staring at the roses on the wallpaper, contemplating her future with a complete lack of enthusiasm, and was suddenly struck by the fact that this was entirely due to the knowledge that Dr Eijsinck would have no part of it. The front door banged and she got out of bed to watch the Van Minnen family make their way down the street towards church, glad of the interruption of thoughts she didn't care to think. It wasn't quite nine o'clock; she slipped on the nightgown's matching peignoir and the rather ridiculous slippers which went with it, and made her way downstairs through the quiet old house to the dining-room.

Someone had thoughtfully drawn a small table up to the soft warmth of the stove and laid it with care, for cup, saucer and plate of a bright brown earthenware, flanked by butter in a Delft blue dish, stood invitingly ready. There was coffee too, and a small basket full of an assortment of bread, and grouped together, jam and sausage and cheese. Harriet poured coffee, buttered a crusty slice of bread with a lavish hand and took a large satisfying bite. She had lifted her coffee cup half-way to her lips when the door opened.

'Where's everybody?' asked Dr Eijsinck, without bothering to say good morning. 'Church?'

Harriet put down her cup. 'Yes,' she said, with her mouth full. His glance flickered over her and she went pink under it.

'Are you ill?' he asked politely, although his look denied his words.

'Me? Ill? No.' If he chose to think of her as a useless lazy creature, she thought furiously, she for one would not enlighten him.

'Well, if you're not ill, you'd better come to the surgery and hold down a brat with a bead up his nose.'

'Certainly,' said Harriet, 'since you ask me so nicely; but I must dress first.'

'Why? There's no one around who's interested in seeing you like that. The child's about three; his mother's in the waiting room because she's too frightened to hold him herself; and as for me, I assure you that I am quite unaffected.'

She didn't like the note of mockery—he was being deliberately tiresome! She put her cup back in its saucer, got up without a word and followed him down the passage to the surgery where she waited while he fetched the child from its mother. She took the little boy in capable arms and said, 'There, there,' in the soft, kind voice she used to anyone ill or afraid. He sniffed and gulped, and under her approving, 'There's a big man, then!' subsided into quietness punctuated by heaving breaths, so that she was able to lay him on the examination table without further ado, and steady his round head between her small firm hands. Dr Eijsinck, standing with speculum, probe and curved forceps ready to hand, grunted something she couldn't understand and switched on his head lamp.

'Will you be able to hold him with one arm?' she asked matter-of-factly.

He looked as though he was going to laugh, but his voice was mild enough as he replied. 'I believe I can manage, Miss Slocombe. He's quite small, and my arm is—er—large enough to suffice.'

He sprayed the tiny nostril carefully and got to work, his big hand manipulating the instruments with a surprising delicacy. While he worked he talked softly to his small patient; a meaningless jumble of words Harriet could make nothing of.

'Are you speaking Fries?' she wanted to know.

He didn't look up. 'Yes… I don't mean to be rude, but Atse here doesn't understand anything else at present.' He withdrew a bright blue bead from the small nose and Atse at once burst into tearful roars, the while his face was mopped up. Harriet scooped him up into her arms.

'Silly boy, it's all over.' She gave him a hug and he stopped his sobbing to look at her and say something. She returned his look in her turn. 'It's no good, Atse, I can't understand.'

Dr Eijsinck looked up from the sink where he was washing his hands.

'Allow me to translate. He is observing—as I daresay many other members of his sex have done before him—that you and your—er—dress are very beautiful.'

Harriet felt her cheeks grow hot, but she answered in a composed voice, 'What a lovely compliment—something to remember when I get home.'

The doctor had come to stand close to her and she handed him the little boy. 'Good-bye, Atse, I hope I see you again.' She shook the fat little hand, straightened the examination table, thumped up its pillow with a few brisk movements, and made for the door. She had opened it before Dr Eijsinck said quietly, 'Thank you for your help, Miss Slocombe.'

'Don't mention it,' she said airily, as she went through.

The breakfast table still looked very attractive; she plugged in the coffee pot and took another bite from her bread and butter. She was spreading a second slice with a generous wafer of cheese when the door opened again. Dr Eijsinck said from the doorway, 'I'm sorry I disturbed your breakfast.' And then, 'Is the coffee hot?'

She wiped a few crumbs away from her mouth, using a finger.

'Don't apologize, Doctor…and yes, thank you, the coffee is hot.'

There was a pause during which she remembered how unpleasant he had been. The look she cast him was undoubtedly a reflection of her thoughts, for he gave a sudden quizzical smile, said good-bye abruptly, and went.

They were having morning coffee when he arrived for the second time. He took the cup Mevrouw Van Minnen handed him and sat down unhurriedly; it seemed to Harriet, sitting by the window with Sieske, that he was very much one of the family. He was answering a great number of questions which Dr Van Minnen was putting to him, and Harriet thought what a pity it was she couldn't understand Dutch. Sieske must have read her thoughts, for she called across the room.

'Friso, were you called out?' and she spoke in English.

He replied in the same tongue. 'Yes, for my sins…an impacted fractured femur and premature twins.'

Sieske said quickly with a sideways look at Harriet, 'Don't forget Atse. Weren't you glad that Harry was here to help you?'

'Delighted,' he said in a dry voice, 'and so was Atse.'

Harriet, studying her coffee cup with a downbent head, was nonetheless aware that he was looking at her.

'So you didn't get to bed at all?' asked Aede.

'Er—no. I was on my way home when I encountered Atse and his mother; I was nearer here than my own place—it seemed logical to bring them with me. I'd forgotten that you would all be in church.'

Harriet abandoned the close scrutiny of her coffee cup. So he had been up all night; being a reasonable young woman she understood how he must have felt when he found her. And the coffee—he had asked if it was hot and she hadn't even asked him if he wanted a cup. How mean of her—she opened her mouth to say so, caught his eye and knew that he had guessed her intention. Before she could speak, he went on smoothly,

'I am indebted to—er—Harriet for her help; very competent help too.'

Mevrouw Van Minnen said something, Harriet had no idea what until she heard the word *koffie*. She opened her mouth once more, feeling guilty, but he was speaking before she could get a word out.

'What is Dr Eijsinck saying, Sieske?' she said softly.

Her friend gave a sympathetic giggle. 'Poor Harry, not understanding a word! He's explaining that he couldn't stay for the coffee you had ready for him because he had to go straight back to the twins.'

Harriet had only been in Holland a short time, but already she had realized that hospitality was a built-in feature of the Dutch character—to deny it to anyone was unthinkable. Mevrouw Van Minnen would have been upset. Friso was being magnanimous. The least she could do was to apologize and thank him for his thoughtfulness.

He got up a few minutes later and strolled to the door with a

casual parting word which embraced the whole company. She
was too shy to get up too and follow him out—it might be days
before she saw him again. He had banged the front door behind
him when Sieske said urgently,

'There, I forgot to tell Friso about the flowers for Wednesday! Harry, you're so much faster than I—run after him, will
you? Tell him it's all right. He'll understand.'

Harriet reached the pavement just as he was getting into the
car. He straightened when he saw her, and stood waiting, his
hand still on the car door.

She said, short-breathed, 'Sieske asked me to give you a message. That it's all right about the flowers, and that you would
understand.'

She stood looking at him and after a moment he gave a glimmer of a smile and said, 'Oh, yes. Of course. Thanks for reminding me.'

'I wanted to—It was lucky Sieske asked me. I'm so sorry
about this morning—you know, the coffee. It was mean of me.
I don't know why I did it.' She stopped and frowned, 'Yes, I
do. You weren't very nice about me being in a dressing-gown,
but of course I understand now, you must have been very tired
if you were up all night—I daresay you wouldn't have minded
so much if you had had a good night's sleep,' she finished in-
genuously.

'No, I don't suppose I should,' he agreed gravely. He got into
the car, said good-bye rather abruptly, and was gone, leaving her
still uncertain as to whether he disliked her or not. It suddenly
mattered very much that she should know, one way or the other.

They were immersed in plans when she got back to the sitting-room. Wierd was coming to luncheon, reiterated Sieske;
they would go for a drive, she and Wierd and Harriet and Aede.
Dokkum, they decided, with an eye on Harriet's ignorance of
the countryside, and then on to the coast to Oostmahorn, when
the boat sailed for the small island of Schiermonnikoog.

They set out about two o'clock, Wierd and Sieske leading the way. It was glorious weather, although the blue sky was still pale and the wind keen. Harriet in a thick tweed suit and a headscarf hoped she would be warm enough; the others seemed to take the wind for granted, but she hadn't got used to it. It was warm enough in the car, however, and Aede proved to be an excellent guide. By the time they had reached Dokkum, she had mastered a great deal of Friesian history and had even learnt—after a fashion—the Friesian National Anthem, although she thought the translation, 'Friesian blood, rise up and boil,' could be improved upon. The others were waiting for them in the little town, and she was taken at once to see the church of St Boniface and then the outside of the Town Hall, with a promise that she should be brought again so that she could see its beautiful, painted council room.

The coast, when they reached it, was a surprise and a contrast. Harriet found it difficult to reconcile the sleepy little town they had just left with the flat shores protected from the sea by the dykes built so patiently by the Friesians over the centuries. Land was still being reclaimed, too. She looked at the expanse of mud, and tried to imagine people living on it in a decade of time; she found it much more to her liking to think of the people who had lived in Dokkum hundreds of years ago, and had gone to the self-same church that she had just visited. She explained this to Aede, who listened carefully.

'Yes,' he said slowly, 'but if we had no dykes there would be no Dokkum.' Which was unanswerable. They turned for home soon afterwards and towards the end of the journey, Aede said, 'Here's Friso's village—his house is on the left.' They were approaching it from the other side at an angle which allowed her to catch a glimpse of the back of the house. It looked bigger somehow, perhaps because of the verandah stretching across its breadth. There were steps from it leading down to the garden, which she saw was a great deal larger than she had supposed. She peered through the high iron railing, but there was no one to see. He must be lonely, she thought, living there all by himself. The road curved, and they passed the entrance. At the moment, at any rate, he wasn't lonely—there were two cars parked by the door. Aede was going rather fast, so that she had only a glimpse; but with three car-crazy brothers, her knowledge of cars was sound and up to date. One was a Lotus Elan, the other a Marcos. It seemed that Dr Eijsinck's friends liked speed. Harriet thought darkly of the beautiful brunette; she would look just right behind the wheel of the Lotus… Her thoughts were interrupted by Aede.

'Friso's got visitors… That man's cast iron; he works for two most of the time, and when he's not working he's off to Utrecht or Amsterdam or Den Haag. Even if he stays home, there are always people calling.'

Harriet watched the Friso of her dreams fade—the Friso who would have loved her for always; happy to be with her and no one else—but this flesh and blood Friso didn't need her at all. She went a little pink, remembering how she had smiled at him when she had seen him for the first time; he must have thought how silly she was, or worse, how cheap. The pink turned to red; she had been a fool. She resolved then and there to stop dreaming and demonstrated her resolution by turning to Aede and asking intelligent questions about the reclamation of land. Harriet listened with great attention to the answers, not hearing them at all, but thinking about Friso Eijsinck.

At breakfast the following morning, Harriet learned that Sieske's two sisters would be returning in time for tea. They had been visiting their grandparents in Sneek, but now the Easter holidays were over and they would be going back to high school. Aede had gone back to hospital the previous evening; Dr Van Minnen had an unexpected appointment that afternoon; the question as to who should fetch them was debated over the rolls and coffee. Sieske supposed she could go, but there was the party to arrange.

Her father got to his feet. 'I'll telephone Friso,' he said, 'he's got no afternoon surgery, I'm certain. He'll go, and the girls simply love that car of his.'

He disappeared in the direction of his surgery, leaving his wife and Sieske, with Harriet as a willing listener, to plunge into the final details concerning the party. This fascinating discussion naturally led the three ladies upstairs to look at each other's dresses for the occasion; Sieske had brought a dress back from England—the blue of it matched her eyes; its straight classical lines made her look like a golden-haired goddess. They admired it at some length before repairing to Mevrouw Van Minnen's bedroom to watch approvingly while she held up the handsome black crepe gown she had bought in Leeuwarden. Evidently the party was to be an occasion for dressing up; Harriet was glad that she had packed the long white silk dress she had bought in a fit of extravagance a month or so previously. It had a lace bodice, square-necked and short-sleeved, with a rich satin ribbon defining the high waistline. It would provide a good foil for Sieske's dress without stealing any of its limelight. She could see from Mevrouw Van Minnen's satisfied nod that she thought so too. They all went downstairs, satisfied that they had already done a great deal towards making Sieske's evening a success, and over cups of coffee the menu for the buffet supper was finally checked, for, said Mevrouw Van Minnen in sudden, surprising English,

'We are beautiful ladies...but men eat too.' She laughed at her efforts and looked as young and pretty as her daughter.

'Will it be black ties?' Harriet wanted to know.

Sieske nodded. 'Of course. We call it Smoking—their clothes, I mean.'

Harriet giggled. 'How funny, though they look nice whatever you call it.' Friso Eijsinck, for instance, would look very nice indeed...

Harriet was sitting writing postcards at the desk under the sitting-room window when she heard a car draw up outside. It was the AC 428. She watched the two girls and Dr Eijsinck get

out and cross the pavement to the front door; the girls were obviously in high spirits, and so, for that matter, was the doctor.
Harriet, peeping from her chair, thought that he looked at least
ten years younger and great fun. She returned to her writing,
and presently they all three entered the room, bringing with
them the unmistakable aura of longstanding friendship, which,
quite unintentionally, made her feel more of a stranger than she
had felt since she had arrived in Holland, and because of this,
her 'Good afternoon, Doctor', was rather stiff and she was all
the more annoyed when he said,

'Oh hullo—all alone again? I'd better introduce you to these
two.' He turned to the elder of the girls.

'This is Maggina.' The girls shook hands and Maggina said
'How do you do?'—she was like her mother and Sieske, but
without their vividness. Rather like a carbon copy, thought Harriet, liking her.

'And Taeike,' said the doctor. She was fourteen or fifteen,
and one saw she was going to be quite lovely; now she was just
a very pretty girl, with a charming smile and nice manners.
She shook hands with Harriet, then went and stood by Friso
and slipped her hand under his arm. He patted it absent-mind-
edly and asked Harriet in a perfunctory manner if she had had
a busy day, but there was no need for her to reply, for just then
the rest of the family came in and everybody talked at once
and there was nothing for her to do but to smile and withdraw
a little into the background. She looked up once and found Dr
Eijsinck watching her across the room, with an expression on
his face which she found hard to read, but he gave her no opportunity to do so, for the next moment he had taken his leave.
She heard the front door bang and his car start up, but with-
stood the temptation to turn round and look out of the window.

Wednesday came, the day of the party, and with it a Land-
Rover from Dr Eijsinck's house. It was driven by his gardener,
and filled to overflowing with azaleas and polyanthus, and great
bunches of irises and tulips and freesias. Harriet, helping to ar-

range them around the house, paused to study the complicated erection of flowers she had achieved in one corner of the drawing-room and to remark,

'I suppose Dr Eijsinck has a very large green house?'

It was Taeike who answered. 'He has three. I go many times—also to his house.'

Harriet twitched a branch of forsythia into its exact position before she answered, 'How nice.' It would be easy to find out a great deal about the doctor from Taeike, but she couldn't bring herself to do it. She asked instead,

'Tell me about your school, will you?' then listened to Taeike's polite, halting English, aware that the girl would have much rather talked about Friso Eijsinck.

Wierd came after tea, with more flowers, and sat talking to Dr Van Minnen until Sieske, who had gone upstairs to dress, came down again looking radiant. It was the signal for everyone else to go and dress too, leaving the pair of them to each other's company, to foregather presently in the drawing-room where they admired the plain gold rings the happy couple had exchanged. They would wear them until their marriage, when they would be transferred from their left hands to their right. It seemed to Harriet that this exchange of rings made everything rather solemn and binding. 'Plighting their troth,' she mused, and added her congratulations to everyone else's.

The guests arrived soon afterwards, and she circled the room with first one then the other of the Van Minnens, shaking hands and uttering her name with each handshake. A splendid idea— only some of the names were hard to remember. She was standing by the door, listening rather nervously to the *burgemeester*, a handsome man with an imposing presence who spoke the pedantic English she was beginning to associate with the educated Dutch, when Friso Eijsinck came in. She had been right. He looked—she sought for the right word and came up with eye-catching; but then so did the girl with him. A blonde this time, Harriet noted, watching her while she smiled attentively at her companion, and wearing a dress straight out of *Harpers & Queen*. In her efforts to prevent a scowl of envy, Harriet smiled even more brilliantly and gazed at the *burgemeester* with such a look of absorbed attention that he embarked upon a monologue, and a very knowledgeable one, about the various theatres he had visited when he was last in London. It was fortunate that he didn't expect an answer, for Harriet was abysmally ignorant about social life in the great metropolis, and was about to say so, when he paused for breath and Friso said from behind her,

'Good evening, Miss Slocombe...*burgemeester*.'

He shook hands with them both, and the *burgemeester* said,

'I was just telling this charming young lady how much I enjoyed "The Mousetrap"!' He turned to Harriet. 'I also went to see "Cats".' He coughed. 'You've seen it, of course, Miss Slocombe?'

Both men were looking down at her, the speaker with a look of polite inquiry, Dr Eijsinck with a decided twinkle in his grey eyes. Her colour deepened. 'Well, no. You see I live in a very small village on the edge of Dartmoor. I... I don't go to London often.' She forbore to mention that she hadn't been there for at least five years. She withdrew her gaze from the older man and looked quickly at the doctor, whose face was a mask of polite interest; all the same, she was very well aware that he was laughing at her. She opened her eyes very wide and said with hauteur, 'Even if I lived in London I think it would be unlikely that I should go to see "Cats". I'm not very with-it, I'm afraid.'

She allowed her long curling lashes to sweep down on to her cheeks for just a sufficient length of time for her two companions to note that they were real. The *burgemeester*, who was really rather a dear, allowed a discreet eye to rove over her person. He said with elderly gallantry,

'I think that you are most delightfully with-it, Miss Slocombe. I hope that I shall see more of you before you return to that village of yours. And now take her away, Friso, for I am sure that was your reason for joining us.'

There was nothing to do but smile, and, very conscious of Friso's hand on her arm, allow herself to be guided across the room. Once out of earshot, however, she stood still and said,

'I'll be quite all right here, Doctor. I'm sure there are a great many people to whom you wish to talk.' She looked pointedly through the open double doors into the dining-room, where the beautiful blonde, glass in hand, was holding court. Somebody had started the record-player; Sieske started to dance and half a dozen couples joined them. Her companion, without bothering to answer her, swung Harriet on to the impromptu dance floor. He danced well, with a complete lack of tiresome mannerisms. Harriet, who was a good dancer herself, would have been happy to have remained as his partner for the rest of the evening, but in fact it was long after midnight before he came near her again. She was perched on the bottom stair, between two of Aede's friends, listening to their account of life on the wards in a Rotterdam hospital where they were housemen. She saw him standing in the open doorway of the drawing-room across the hall, watching them. After a minute he started to cross the hall, taking care that both young men saw his approach. When he was near enough, he said smoothly,

'Harriet, I have looked for you everywhere.' He glanced at the two young men with a smile of charm and authority which brought them to their feet with a cheerful 'Very well, sir,' and an equally cheerful 'See you later' for Harriet who found herself alone on the staircase; but not for long, for Dr Eijsinck folded himself into the space beside her, taking up the lion's share of it with his bulk. Harriet was annoyed to feel a thrill of pleasure at his closeness and in an effort to ignore it, said crossly,

'You haven't been looking for me everywhere—you must have seen me dozens of times in the last hour or so. And why did you send those two boys away? I wanted them to stay.'

He stretched out his long legs. 'Yes, I thought you would,' he said complacently. 'That's why.'

Harriet's bosom heaved with an emotion she didn't bother

to define; she turned furious blue eyes to meet his lazily smiling ones. 'Well,' she uttered at length, and then again, 'Well!'

'At a loss for words?' he asked kindly, to madden her. She turned her head away, and smiled at Taeike who was wandering across the hall, and was on the point of calling her when he said softly, 'No, Harry, I want to talk to you.' His voice sounded different—firm and gentle. She looked at him and went slowly pink under the look on his face; he was smiling too—the smile was different too. He studied her for a minute and then said mildly, 'That's better; you usually look at me as though I were a rather unspeakable drain.'

She gave a little splutter of laughter at that and then frowned fiercely to show him that she hadn't meant it. 'Excepting the first time we met,' he continued, ignoring the frown. 'You looked at me then as though you were—er—glad to see me.'

She managed to look away at last, and despite the sudden thudding of her heart said steadily, 'I thought you were someone I...knew.'

'That's not quite true, is it?'

Not looking at him made it easier to regain a level head. He hadn't said that he had been glad to see her; and what about the brunette and the exotic blonde who had accompanied him that evening? And what had Aede said? That Friso had a great many girl-friends—Sieske had said it too. Harriet had no intention of being one of the many. She said in the same steady voice,

'Not quite true, no. But it answers your question well enough.'

She looked at him then, to find only amusement on his face, perhaps she had been mistaken after all. He held out a hand. 'Let's dance,' he said.

They circled the room once before he drew her out on to the verandah. The night was surprisingly mild, wind still and very dark. They stood looking out over the unseen garden; the faint clean smell of grass, mingled with the tang of tulips and the heavier scent of the hyacinths, made the air a delight. The music had stopped, to be replaced by a babble of voices until presently a new record was put on—it was 'If you go away' and a man was singing. Harriet listened to the words—they made her feel sad, even though they were only part of a song. Friso Eijsinck, very close beside her, said softly,

'You like this song.' It was a statement, not a question.

'Yes.'

'You think it is possible for a man to feel like that about a woman?'

'Yes,' said Harriet. Regrettably, her conversational powers had deserted her; perhaps a good thing, for she was having difficulty with her breathing.

'It expresses sentiments which I do not think I can improve upon,' said Dr Eijsinck thoughtfully, 'unless it is by doing this...'

She was caught, turned and held close—and then kissed. She had been kissed before, but never in this fashion. Against all common sense, she kissed him back. When she drew away he loosened his hold at once, but without releasing her, and said over her shoulder,

'Hullo, Taeike.'

Harriet, still within the circle of his arm, glimpsed her standing in the doorway for a brief moment before she turned on her heel and went inside. She had said nothing at all, but she had broken the spell; she told herself that she was glad, for she had so nearly allowed herself to be carried away. She said lightly,

'It's getting chilly—shall we go inside?' and led the way back to the drawing-room without looking at him. She was at once whisked off to dance, and Friso didn't seek her out again, only towards the end of the evening she saw his broad back disappearing through the door, and when she searched the room, the beautiful blonde had gone too.

It was while she was helping to restore some sort of order to the rooms after the last guest had gone that Harriet finally admitted to herself that she had fallen in love with Friso Eijsinck; not the perfect Friso of her dream, but this man of whom she knew nothing; who barely spoke to her, and when he did, left

her uncertain as to whether he even liked her. She stacked some
plates carefully—probably he didn't—his kiss on the verandah
had been almost certainly prompted by the sweet-smelling garden and the song…and almost as certainly he would have forgotten it by now. She wished with all her heart that she could
do the same.

CHAPTER FOUR

IT SEEMED VERY quiet on Thursday; Wierd, who was a pathologist and worked for a big drug firm outside Delft, had left early; so had Aede; neither of them would be back again for at least a week, but Sieske, sitting on the end of Harriet's bed for a rather sleepy morning gossip, told her that Wierd had suggested that the two girls should go down to Delft on Monday; he would be free in the afternoon, and it was a chance for Harriet to see something of Holland.

'Very nice,' said Harriet, 'but I'd love to poke around on my own. Would you mind? You could both meet me somewhere.'

Sieske protested at this until Harriet said, 'Then I shan't come.' She liked Sieske very much, and Wierd was great fun, but she remembered the old adage 'Two's company, three's none'. Besides, it would be good for her to go on her own. She smiled persuasively at her friend, and got her own way.

They went to Sneek in the afternoon, to visit Sieske's grandparents. Sieske drove the Mini she and her mother shared between them, with Harriet beside her, and Mevrouw Van Minnen dozing comfortable in the back. They took the narrow country roads, through small villages, each with its own church and café, and less frequently, a solitary shop, with rows of *klompen* on either side of the door and a great many advertisements in the windows for Van Nelle's tea and Niemeijer's coffee and the more familiar washing powders and Blue Band. Sneek, when they reached it, was smaller than she had expected, and very quiet. Sieske explained that the best time to visit it was during the sailing week in August, when it was packed with visitors, but it was too early in the year for the boats to be out on Sneekermeer, although the more hardy were to be found at week-ends, wrapped warmly against the wind, enjoying the luxury of an almost empty lake.

Sieske's grandparents lived close by the Water Gate, in a house as old and charming as their son's; they had, of course, been at the party the previous evening, but had gone home early. Now they settled down comfortably to mull over every aspect of the guests' clothes, views and appearance, and this naturally led to a not unkindly gossip about their various friends, and finally, over cups of tea, praise of Mevrouw Van Minnen for having arranged such a memorable evening. Harriet didn't understand the half of it, but there was a great deal to look at in the room, and Sieske translated as much as possible of the conversation, and presently old Mijnheer Van Minnen came and sat beside her, and talked, rather hesitantly, in English. He asked a great many questions and expressed surprise that she was not married, or at least engaged.

'Perhaps you will find a husband here, Harriet,' he said. She felt herself go pink under his sharp old eyes and was glad that they got up to go before she needed to answer.

Maggina and Taeike were home when they got back; they were tired and rather cross and didn't talk much, and after the evening meal they went to the small room at the back of the house where they studied their school books without the temptations of the radio or television, leaving their elders to sit and talk in desultory fashion until they dispersed, by common consent to an early bed.

The next morning at breakfast, Harriet asked, rather diffidently, if she might help in the morning surgery. 'I could look out the cards for you, Doctor, and clear up things—that's if no one minds.'

She looked round the table. Sieske, she knew, was going to the dressmakers, the girls had already left for school…she turned back to the doctor, who smiled and said, 'Yes, Harriet, you would be a real help, but you must not feel that because you do it today, that you have to do it every day.'

The waiting room was full; it was, Harriet thought, very like Out-Patients in hospital. The fact that she was unable to understand a word of what was being said made very little difference. Cut fingers and earache and varicose ulcers were the same in any language. The plump rosy-cheeked babies cried in exactly the same way as did the babies at home, and the small boys were just as bent on having their own way. The last patient came and went, and she cleared up, closed the filing cabinets and went back through the door into the house, and if she felt disappointment at not seeing Dr Eijsinck, she didn't admit it to herself.

They went to the Planetarium in the afternoon; there was no one there but herself and Sieske and the curator, who explained the complexity of nails in the little attic, and answered her questions in schoolmaster's English. She had no doubt at all that he would have answered her just as easily and fluently in French or German. They went back downstairs into the small back room where the solar system revolved, year after year, around the blue wooden ceiling. It was a small house; she imagined it centuries earlier, not very well furnished, but cosy. Like so many other houses in Holland, it became home the moment you entered the front door. But perhaps, she reflected, that only applied to the old houses she had been in; she had had no opportunity to visit anything modern and didn't particularly want to. She wondered, fleetingly, if she would be given the opportunity to see inside Dr Eijsinck's house. The possibility seemed remote.

It was the next morning, during their early morning gossip, that Sieske said, 'Let's go over to Friso's house this afternoon; Father is on call this week-end, and Mother will stay with him, and Maggina and Taeike are going to some friends. There's an old bike you can have.' She looked inquiringly at Harriet, who said, in a neutral voice,

'That sounds fun, but won't he mind?'

'He won't be there; it's his week-end off, and he said something about going to The Hague.'

Harriet said slowly, through an aching disappointment, 'I'd love to go.' It would, after all, be something, just to see his garden.

They set off after lunch, laughing a good deal, for the bicycle which had been found for Harriet was an old-fashioned model, with high handlebars and a saddle to match. She felt like Queen Victoria at her most dignified until she nearly fell off when she idly back-pedalled. She had quite forgotten that was how the brakes worked.

There was a narrow paved path running beside the road to the village; for the exclusive use of cyclists, it made the journey much less hazardous for Harriet, who felt a keen urge to veer to the left. The path was uneven, and dropped a couple of feet into a ditch on its other side, so it was just as well that she had no traffic problems; besides, there was a great deal to look at and exclaim over. The April sun was warm and in its light the countryside looked as though it had been newly painted; only the sky was still a remote, pale blue, and the wind, the ever-present wind, chilled everything it touched. Harriet, despite her thick polo-necked sweater and slacks, shivered, to be warmed by the sight of the iron gates of Friso's house, their gilded spear-headed tops shining in the sun, and standing invitingly open. The drive was short and straight, to end in a generous sweep of smooth gravel before the front of the house before it divided, to disappear round either corner. Sieske led the way to the left-hand fork. Harriet, following more slowly, surveyed the solid front door, with its imposing knocker and beautiful fanlight, and longed to get off her bike and go inside. There were three long windows before she reached the corner; she could just glimpse their draped pelmets and rich, heavy curtains; the windows continued along the side of the house too, and there was a small stone balustraded stair disappearing to a basement she could not see.

Sieske had disappeared and Harriet found her standing on the vast gravelled space behind the house. She had propped her machine against the stone balustrade which separated it from the garden below, and Harriet put hers carefully beside it and turned to look her fill. The verandah she had seen from Aede's car ran the full width of the house behind them, a fine tracery of wrought iron, with wide floor-length windows opening on to it from the house, and a delicate stair leading to the gravel, from whose centre another stone stair led to the garden. It was a perfect example of Dutch formality; an exact rectangle enclosed by a yew hedge clipped to perfection, filled with a geometrical design of flowers in carefully matched or contrasting colours bordered by green velvet turf. There was a rectangular pool in its centre, with a flagstone path running around it, and a group of small stone children ringing a small fountain as its focal point. Harriet leaned comfortably over the stonework, looking at it all, and said at length,

'If I lived here, with this garden, I should never want to go anywhere else so long as I lived,' and then flushed pinkly in case Sieske misunderstood. Apparently she hadn't, for she said merely,

'Yes, it is beautiful, and old too. Friso's ancestor, the one who built the house, made the garden—it's not been changed since.' She turned away and said, 'Let's go and find Jan—he's the gardener—and tell him we're here.' She led the way along a narrow path at right angles to the house; it had turf borders and dense shrubbery on either side.

'This leads to the greenhouses,' explained Sieske. 'I'll go on ahead, shall I, and then come back for you.'

Left alone, Harriet slowed her steps. It was warm and sheltered and very quiet. The path curled and curled again and then divided. She took the left-hand fork and came almost immediately into a small open space, with a potting shed in one corner with a wheel-barrow outside it. Friso Eijsinck was sitting on its handle, filling a pipe. He got to his feet and said 'Hullo,' in a quite unsurprised way, and smiled at her so that her heart thumped against her ribs and she could barely muster breath to say 'Hullo' too, and then stupidly, 'You're in The Hague.'

'I changed my mind,' he said easily. 'Come and sit down.'

'Sieske's gone to speak to your gardener.' She had retrieved her breath; all the same, she thought she would stay where she was. 'I hope it's convenient…we didn't think you would be home, Doctor Eijsinck.'

Her voice sounded stiff even to her own ears, as it apparently did to her listener's, for he said invitingly, 'Try calling me Friso, and stop playing at Haughty Harry with me. I'm not a carefree young houseman, you know—you're quite safe.'

She stared at him, beautiful eyes blazing beneath knitted brows, her mouth slightly open while she sought for words. 'Well,' she managed, 'of all the…you…you…' A thought struck her. 'How did you know about Haughty Harry?' she demanded.

He said smoothly, 'Your fame went before you. Sieske painted a very true picture of you—I should have recognized you anywhere.' He patted the other handle of the wheelbarrow. 'Come and sit down.' She did as she was bid this time, and he said, 'That's better; I do dislike saying everything twice.'

She asked at once, for she had to know, 'Did you know who I was—I mean that day I was waiting on the pavement…'

'Yes, of course. And you recognized me, didn't you, although you didn't know me.'

She scuffled her feet in the soft earthy ground and wondered exactly what he meant. She would like to know. She had opened her mouth to ask when Sieske's voice, quite close, called, 'Harry, where are you?' She appeared beside them before they could reply and said comfortably,

'There you are—how nice that you found Friso; I stopped to look at these orchids of yours, Friso. They're gorgeous.'

She sat down on the wheelbarrow handle which he had vacated, and he went to sit on a chopping block. It was typical of the man, thought Harriet, that he contrived to look well-dressed in an open-necked shirt and corduroys and Wellingtons. He looked up and caught her eye, and she said in a hurry, 'Oh, do you grow orchids? How interesting,' and was sorry she had spoken, for he immediately began to talk about paphiopedilums and odontoglossums, only pausing to say, 'But of course you would know all about them, Harriet.'

She gave him a level look and said flatly, 'No. I just like gardens.'

'Ah, yes, of course,' he remarked blandly, and got to his feet. 'And I shall be delighted to show you this one.'

They set off, the three of them, shortly to be joined by two dogs, who appeared silently from the shrubbery and padded along, one each side of the doctor who was leading the way. 'J. B.,' he introduced the bulldog with a casual wave of his hand, and when Harriet said 'Hullo, J. B.', the noble animal gave her a considered glance and plodded on. His canine companion was, however, of a quite different character; due perhaps to his peculiar appearance. He seemed to be all tail, with a long thin body and a small pointed foxy face with eyes of melting softness. He watched his master eagerly and when the doctor said 'This is Flotsam' danced around Harriet with a great show of good fellowship. 'Nice dog,' said Harriet, 'but what a funny name.'

'Yes, isn't it?' remarked Sieske, 'but it's just right, you see, because Friso found...' she was quietly interrupted.

'Shall we go round the Dutch garden first? It's by far the best thing to see.'

They wandered around, taking their time, especially Harriet, who was inclined to go off on little trips of her own to get a closer view of anything which might have caught her eye. Her enthusiasm was shared by Flotsam who behaved as though he

was seeing everything for the first time and was enraptured
by it; Harriet bent down and pulled gently at a long feathery
ear—he really was an unusual-looking dog, not at all the sort
of animal she would expect to find. Her thoughts were interrupted by Friso saying,

'Sieske, would you go into the house and tell Anna to have
tea for the three of us—I'll take Harriet to see the garden room
and we'll join you in a few minutes.' He had been strolling along
with an arm flung around Sieske's shoulders, but withdrew it
now, and gave her a gentle push. 'If your mother is expecting
you home you can telephone her at the same time.'

Harriet watched her friend disappear in the direction of the
house, and then, because Friso was staring at her, burst into
speech.

'A garden room? It sounds delightful. Where is it? Do we go
the same way as Sieske?'

She should have held her tongue, for he came very close and
took hold of her hand and kissed her, very lightly, on her cheek,
then said, laughing a little, 'No, we go down here,' and drew her
along a very narrow path burrowing itself through the shrubbery. It was surprisingly short and ended opposite the small
stone stairs she had passed earlier in the afternoon. They went
down it, still hand in hand, with the dogs close at their heels,
and Friso opened the thick wooden door on to a room lighted
by a row of little windows under the verandah. It was dim and
cool inside, with rows of shelves along its whitewashed walls,
piled with a comfortable clutter of flower pots, seed trays, balls
of string and watering cans. There was a heavy wooden table
against one wall and a variety of shabby basket chairs, plumply
upholstered and well cushioned. Along the other wall there was
a stone trough full with a great variety of ferns, their scent delicious and faintly damp.

Harriet looked around her. 'It's nice,' she said slowly, 'to
be here, on a warm summer day, arranging the flowers for the
house…' She stopped and blushed, for she hadn't meant to say

that at all, but Friso said smoothly, as though he hadn't heard, 'My mother used to bring me here when I was a very small boy. I sat and watched her while she filled the vases; she did it very well.'

Harriet looked up and met his calm grey eyes, her own holding the question she didn't like to voice; he answered it as though she had spoken. 'She's in Curaçao, with my young brother; he's Medical Superintendent at the hospital there. He's been married for a couple of years and they had a little girl a few months ago; my mother went to the christening.' He went on deliberately, 'I also have a sister. She's married too, and lives in Geneva.'

Harriet bent down and tickled Flotsam's chin, then said uncertainly, 'I'm glad you have a family.'

'Now why should you say that?' he wanted to know. She found herself telling him about the stained waistcoat and the stoop and the harassed expression, then peeped at him to see if he was laughing, and was surprised to find that he wasn't. 'And were you sorry for me?' he asked gravely.

'Well, yes,' said Harriet, and he went on, 'But not any more.'

'No.' She felt foolish and a bit cross, mostly with herself. 'How can I be sorry for you when you have a lovely home and a family and a gorgeous car,' she paused, 'and—and beautiful girl-friends.'

He gave a great shout of laughter, and she said with a certain peevishness, 'I'm glad you find it amusing,' and started to walk towards the door, but he got there first and stood in front of it, blocking it entirely, looking down at her, smiling.

'You're beautiful too, Harriet. Shall I add you to my collection of girl-friends?'

She stood very still, waiting for the feeling of anger which didn't come; only a sudden wish to burst into tears followed by the urgent desire to toss off some lighthearted reply. For the life of her, she couldn't think of one, and was still desperately searching when he said gently, 'I'm sorry, Harriet—I had forgotten that you aren't like anyone else.' He opened the door and whistled to the dogs, 'Let's have tea,' he said in a perfectly ordinary voice.

They entered the house from the verandah. The room, she supposed, was the drawing-room; it was very large and high-ceilinged, the walls were painted white and intricately gilded, there was a great crystal chandelier hanging from the centre of the ceiling, and miniature ones spaced along the walls. The floor-length curtains were of deep rose velvet, fringed and braided and elaborately swathed; they matched the carpet and the cut velvet of some of the chairs and the enormous couches on either side of the hooded fireplace, but the remainder of the easy chairs and the window cushions were covered in a pale chintz, which somehow turned the rather formal room into a very habitable one. Harriet had stopped just inside the French window; it wasn't the sort of room to be walked through unheeding, but Friso said briskly,

'This is the salon—drawing-room you would say, I think. We always have tea in the small parlour—it's cosier.'

He led the way to a door set in the wall and opened it for her to go in. The room was indeed small and cosy compared with the rather grand room they had just left; it was panelled in some wood Harriet didn't recognize and was carpeted in a rich claret colour which was echoed in the brocade curtains at the windows. There were several high-backed, winged chairs, and a couple of William and Mary tallbacks flanking a sofa table. Harriet saw that they were all old, beautifully cared for, and used constantly. Sieske, who was curled up in a chair by the small fireplace, put down the magazine she was reading.

'I told Anna that we would ring for tea'—she waved a hand at the small table beside her, already burdened with plates of biscuits and tiny iced cakes and paperthin sandwiches; apparently Friso liked more than a cup of tea in the afternoon. He walked across the room now, and pulled the old-fashioned bell rope, at the same time saying,

'Sit down, Harriet,' and took a seat himself near Sieske and asked her, 'Are you going to Delft in the Mini?'

Sieske put down her magazine.

'Yes. Oh, Friso, will you come too—I mean, we could all go in your car.'

He hesitated before he replied, so that Harriet was filled with a sudden excitement that he would, then he said coolly, 'Sorry. I'm pretty sure to be busy, and there's the baby clinic in the afternoon.' He stretched out his vast person, so that he filled the not inconsiderable chair he sat in, and started to talk about nothing at all, and continued to do so, most entertainingly, all through tea. They got up to go presently, and Harriet reflected that he hadn't suggested that she might like to see at least some of his house. But he made no such suggestion, nor did he mention another visit, but walked to the gates with them and said *'Tot ziens'* in a casual way, which was, she had already gathered, the Dutch way of saying 'See you soon'. They were some yards from the gate when he bellowed something at Sieske, who looked over her shoulder and shouted back. Harriet would have liked to look back at him too, but she recognized her limitations as a cyclist; to risk falling flat on her face would have ruined a not altogether successful afternoon. She said to Sieske, who was beside her again, 'He sounded as though he was swearing great oaths!'

Sieske laughed. 'Dutch is perhaps a little difficult. Friso merely said that he would call for us tomorrow morning and take us to church.'

Harriet rang her bell for no reason at all. 'Not me?' she asked.

'Yes, of course, you. You and me. Mother will stay in case there are calls for Father. I do not know about Maggina and Taeike; I suppose if they want to come, they can.' She fell to talking about the garden, and Friso's name wasn't mentioned again.

Harriet dressed with care the next morning. Her thin wool dress and coat were almost new and a delicious shade of almond

green. They became her mightily; so did the silk turban with its
ends tied in a jaunty knot in the nape of her neck; her shoes were
good ones and matched her gloves and handbag. She applied
Miss Dior with thoughtful care and surveyed herself in the long
mirror between the windows; even her critical eye approved of
what it saw. She nodded at her reflection and went downstairs;
the desire to impress Dr Eijsinck with the knowledge that she
was no penniless dowd working powerfully within her. Sieske
was in the sitting-room, telephoning Wierd; she looked up as
Harriet went in, raised her eyebrows and made a feminine sound
of appreciation, echoed by Maggina and Taeike, who appeared,
hatted and gloved, in the doorway.

Sieske had rung off and was about to speak when the front
door was opened by a powerful arm and Friso joined them. He
gave them a collective good morning, bestowed a brief disin-
terested glance on Harriet, much as a man would look at yesterday's newspaper, and disappeared in the direction of the surgery.
He reappeared a moment later, agreed casually to Taeike's urgent request to sit by him in front, and opened the door; as they
filed through, he said, feelingly, 'Great heavens, four of you!'
There was laughter from the Van Minnens and a polite smile
from Harriet; after all, he had suggested it, hadn't he? The ill-
conceived idea that she should cry off with a splitting headache
was wrecked at birth by his compelling hand helping her far
more carefully than was necessary, into the car.

The church was large, too large for the size of the village,
but nonetheless surprisingly full. Dr Eijsinck's pew was in the
very front; it had elaborately carved ends which bore his name
written in copper plate on a little white card fixed into a brass
holder. He stood, completely at ease, while they all filed past
him. Taeike had hung back, but had had to go in first, looking
sulky; Maggina went next, then Sieske, who took Harriet's hand
and tugged it gently. The doctor settled himself in the remaining space; there seemed to be a great deal of him at such close
quarters. He found the hymn for her in a beautiful leather-bound

book he produced from a pocket, while Sieske explained about not kneeling and sitting down to sing and to pray. Harriet felt faintly confused, especially as she wasn't attending very much to Sieske. How could she, with Friso sitting beside her?

Even though she didn't understand a word of the service, she enjoyed it. The doctor and Sieske took care to point out how far they had got in the incomprehensible book she held as she sat between them, listening to Sieske's pretty voice singing, and to the doctor's deep one, booming its way unselfconsciously through the hymns. The sermon was long, but the *dominee*, an enormous white-haired man with a compelling voice, fascinated her. She had the impression that he was haranguing the congregation about their misdeeds, but a cautious glance around showed nothing but rows of guiltless faces—either they hid their feelings well, or he was unnecessarily stern. But whatever he was his voice was beautiful; it rolled around the church, helped by the magnificent sounding board above his head, and she wished she understood him.

She had been warned beforehand about the two collections; she had her two *guldens* ready as the elders advanced down the aisle, but then her eye caught the notes in the doctor's hands—they were almost hidden, but she thought that they were for ten *gulden*. She looked at Sieske, but she was bending over to pick up a glove. The doctor's enormous hand took her bag from her, extracted the two *gulden* pieces, and put one in each of her hands. He said nothing, but he smiled, his grey eyes twinkling, so that she found herself smiling back at him. Just for that moment they seemed to have known each other for ever.

It seemed that they were to go back to Friso's house after church; a few people were coming in for drinks; it was all very like life in the village at home. Harriet followed the others through the main door into the tiled hall, and allowed a small neat man with a wrinkled face to remove her coat and take her gloves, and then shook hands with him when Maggina introduced him as Wim without explaining who he was. He didn't follow them into the drawing-room, so presumably he was the manservant Aede had mentioned. She lingered for a moment at the door; she would have dearly liked to have explored the hall and the doors on either side of it, and still more, the carved staircase curving up to the floor above. There were a number of portraits on the walls too. She turned reluctantly to encounter the vast expanse of the doctor's waistcoat, and spoke to it with a hint of apology. 'I was just looking at the hall. It's rather— rather beautiful.' She blushed fiercely; even to her own ears the remark had sounded pretentious. 'Not that I know anything about it,' she added, inadequately, making it worse.

He stood aside for her to enter the room and said politely, 'I'm glad you like it. Come and have a glass of sherry,' and ushered her across the expanse of carpet to where the others were sitting. She had barely taken two sips when the door opened again, and the *dominee* came in, followed by several other people who apparently were on terms of good friendship with Friso. Harriet shook hands with them rather shyly, and was relieved when they immediately spoke in English, showing a kindly interest in her which she found very pleasant, if surprising. She was passed from one to other little group until she fetched up by the *dominee*, who asked a great many questions in quite perfect and beautifully spoken English, and only interrupted himself when the lantern clock on the wall beside him struck the hour in a delicate faraway fashion. 'So late!' he exclaimed, 'I must go, but with regret. We must meet again before you return, Miss Slocombe.' He engulfed her hand and shook it so that the bones protested and went away, to be replaced at once by an elegantly dressed little woman, who wanted to know, surprisingly, if Marks and Spencer were still selling those rather nice quilted dressing-gowns...she had bought one on her last visit to London; she would certainly get another if they were still available. Harriet, who did a good deal of her own shopping there, was able to give her the news that they were, and the ab-

sorbing topic of clothes kept them happily occupied until there
was a general movement of departure.

Harriet found herself going through the door with the doctor,
hazily uncertain as to how this had happened; she had thought
that she was surrounded by other people; they appeared to have
melted away. They paused on the step outside, watching everyone sort themselves into their cars. There was another car
there now, a dark blue Bentley, with Wim sitting in the driving
seat. She said without much thought, 'Is that your car, too, the
Bentley?' She glanced up at him, to encounter a cool glance
from the grey eyes.

'Yes. Wim will take you back. I'm sorry that I cannot, but
I have guests for luncheon.' He put his hands in his pockets,
lounging against the side of the door. 'By the way,' he said, 'you
look very smart—I'm much impressed. But then I was meant
to be, was I not, Harriet?'

She took her glove off, and then put it on again with care;
her voice shook only a little when she replied, 'How detestable
you are! I hope I shan't see you again, Dr Eijsinck.' She started
to walk towards the car, and he walked with her.

'You're a shocking liar,' he remarked cheerfully. He saw them
all into the car, ignoring Taeike's still sulky face, then put his
head through the open window next to Harriet.

'I should have asked you to lunch, Harriet, then you could
have met the brunette.' He grinned at her. Before she could
think of an answer the car had started.

'What did he mean?' asked Taeike sharply. Harriet was far
too busy with her own thoughts to notice the edge of the girl's
voice. 'Oh, it was just a joke,' she said carefully, and fell to talking about the various people she had met.

CHAPTER FIVE

THEY SET OFF for Delft the following morning, shortly after breakfast; a meal during which each member of the family had added his or her quota to the list of sights that Harriet simply had to see. She wrote them down in her neat handwriting with a pen borrowed from Dr Van Minnen, on a leaf torn from his pocket-book. It was a lengthy list by the time she had finished it; she looked up to make some laughing remark and encountered Taeike's stare from the other side of the table. For a brief, unbelieving second Harriet thought she saw hate in the pretty little face, and then told herself she was mistaken as Taeike's face broke into a sweet smile as she said in her deliberate English, 'I hope you have a lovely day, Harriet.'

They went over the Afsluitdijk, Sieske sending the Mini racing along its length while she pointed out the opposite coast and explained about the *dijk*. Harriet listened and looked at the quiet water lapping at the *dijk*'s edge, and watched the birds pottering along between the stones of the *dijk* itself. It was all very quiet and peaceful. There were very few cars, and those tore past them, their only aim to get to the other side as quickly as possible. They went through the giant sluices and were on dry land again; pretty enough, but not to be compared with Friesland. She told Sieske so, to have her remark greeted with delight.

'You speak like a true Friesian,' she glanced sideways at Harriet. 'I believe you like my country, do you not?'

'Very much,' said Harriet. She was thinking of Friso Eijsinck.

'And the people?' went on Sieske.

'I like them too,' said Harriet. She went pink and turned a flurried attention to the landscape, which unfortunately hardly merited any comment, so she fell back on the safe and ever-engrossing topic of her friend's wedding, and if Sieske thought that the subject had been changed rather suddenly, she gave no sign.

They had plenty of time. Wierd was to meet them after lunch, and it was barely half past nine when they reached the further shore. Sieske decided to take the by-roads across the *polders*; it would give Harriet a chance to see the new farms the Government had built on the reclaimed land. The country was neat and orderly and new to the point of bareness, but the farms looked prosperous and well cared for, but presently they left the *polders* behind and in due time reached Broekop-Langendijk, much more to Harriet's liking, for it was nothing but a complex of canals criss-crossing in all directions, held together by a great many bridges. The canals were alive with a number of small boats and an occasional large one—to her enchanted eye it looked like the backdrop to some gigantic musical show. Sieske, who knew the way very well, crossed the main road just above Alkmaar and took the road to the dunes until it emerged on the other side of the Velsen tunnel and they were back on the main road again. But now there was a great deal to see; the bulb-fields were showing their colours, not perhaps at their perfection, but nonetheless a delight to the eye. Harriet gazed at everything in sight and never stopped asking questions, which Sieske, her eyes on the road, answered with great good nature and in some detail.

They parked the car in a narrow cobbled street in Delft; its bonnet hanging precariously over the canal beside it. Harriet eyed the quiet water below; the car wheels were only a few inches from the edge—but apparently everyone parked in the same manner; it made more room, Sieske explained. They strolled to the market place, and found a tiny coffee shop behind a pastrycook's, and drank their coffee and made their plans.

'I wish you'd come with us this afternoon,' said Sieske for the hundredth time.

Harriet shook her head. 'I'd love to potter off by myself if you don't mind, Sieske. I'll meet you for tea—only write down the name of the café.'

Presently they wandered off, standing to gaze at canals and bridges and old houses, of which there were a great many; until they stopped for lunch in the courtyard of a small restaurant next to the Prinsenhof Museum. Here they parted, Sieske to meet Wierd, Harriet to explore the museum so conveniently close by. Her afternoon went too quickly; there was no time to see even half the things on her list because she idled along one street after the other, each one looking more like something out of Grimm's Fairy Tales than the last; even the sight of the inhabitants in modern dress didn't quite disillusion her. She became hopelessly lost, which didn't matter at first until she glanced at her wrist-watch and knew that she was going to be late for tea. She was forced to show the name of the café Sieske had written down for her to the only person in sight, a short thick-set man coming towards her on the opposite side of the narrow cobbled street—he wore a semi-nautical cap and an oil-stained shirt, its buttons strained to bursting point across a powerful chest. She addressed him, absurdly, in English. 'Excuse me, but would you tell me how to find this café?'

She smiled at him and thrust the piece of paper under his nose. He read it very slowly, addressed her cheerfully, unintelligibly and at some length, and caught her arm in a massive paw. She trotted along beside him, having rather a job to keep up in her high heels and wondering if perhaps she had been a little foolish. Supposing he hadn't understood? She looked around and recognized nothing at all. They seemed to be going up and

down a great many streets, each of them exactly like its fel-
lows. She tugged his arm so that he stopped, showed him the
paper again and felt relieved when he smiled hugely, showing
some terrible teeth, and caught hold of her arm again, walking
faster than ever. They turned a corner and she heard the hum
of traffic and presently saw the main road before them. They
came to a halt and he pointed to her left and smiled again. Harriet decided that he was rather nice and wished she could have
thanked him in his own language. She managed a *Dank U* and
remembered the packet of English cigarettes in her handbag.
She pulled them out to offer him, then shook his hand because
everyone shook hands in Holland and it seemed the polite thing
to do. Before she turned the corner again she turned round and
they waved to each other like old friends. The café was very
close, she could see Sieske and Wierd looking rather anxiously
in the opposite direction. Sieske turned round and saw her and
said with her usual calm, 'There you are. We were wondering
what had happened.'

Harriet told them as they sat over their tea, and they laughed
a great deal and ate a number of cream cakes because they
looked so delicious and Wierd was anxious that they should.
Afterwards they walked slowly back to the car and on the way
Harriet stopped to buy postcards so that Sieske and Wierd could
say good-bye without her there to watch. By the time she had
caught up with them they had reversed the car on to the road
and she felt a secret relief that she hadn't been sitting in it; it
would be so easy to accelerate into the canal instead of revers-
ing. She got in and they went slowly down the street, waving
to Wierd as they went, and then out of the town and on to the
motorway. It was still quite early, just after five, and they were
ahead of the great surge of traffic which would pour on to the
roads after the day's work. They made good time, not stopping
to dawdle and look at the view as they had done in the morning; they were half-way across the Afsluitdijk and it was almost
eight o'clock when Harriet saw the AC 428 coming towards

them, very fast. Not so fast, however, that she was plainly able to see Friso Eijsinck wave a careless gloved hand as they passed. The black-haired girl beside him stared straight ahead of her and took no notice at all. Sieske said placidly, 'That was Friso.'

'Yes,' said Harriet in a calm voice which quite hid her own astonishment at the feelings their encounter had stirred up. 'What sort of fish do they catch in the Ijsselmeer?'

She had asked that question already on the way to Delft that morning. She was conscious of Sieske looking at her before she replied. 'Eels, mostly. Do you know who that girl was?'

'No,' said Harriet, 'and I'm not in the least interested.'

'No? Well, I suppose not. But you fit into everything so well here, I keep forgetting that you're not going to stay.' She slowed down to go through the outskirts of Harlingen. 'There's no reason why you should be interested in people you may never see again.'

Harriet swallowed and said carefully, 'No.' She felt like bursting into tears, which she told herself was very silly of her. Instead she said too brightly,

'It was fun today, but I like Friesland. Does Wierd know yet where he'll be working after you're married?'

It was a red herring which lasted until they reached home.

They were all sitting round the table eating the meal Mevrouw Van Minnen had made the rest of the family wait for, when the front door was opened and closed again with a thud followed by silence. Harriet dissected her chop with all the care of a young surgeon performing his first operation. Only one person shut the door like that, and only one person, despite his size, walked so lightly that it was impossible to hear him. She had got her breath nicely under control by the time the door opened and Friso walked in. He returned a cheerful *Dag* to the chorus of greetings, and added, presumably for her benefit, 'Hullo.'

She looked up briefly and said 'Hullo' before returning to her chop, while Taeike jumped up and made room for him at the table, and Maggina ran to get a fresh plate and Mevrouw Van

Minnen made haste to serve him. He sat down beside Taeike, ruffling her hair as he did so, and accepted his supper with every sign of content. Harriet passed him the pepper and salt and when he asked, 'Did you have a good day in Delft?' replied in a composed voice that yes, she had enjoyed herself immensely.

'What did you see?' he wanted to know, making short work of a chop. She told him, and watched his eyebrows lift. 'Why,' he remarked, 'you didn't see the half!'

She would have been content to let it rest at that, but Sieske told him laughingly that Harry had gone off on her own and got herself lost, and would doubtless have missed her tea altogether if it hadn't been for the good offices of the man in the semi-nautical cap. Harriet sat silently waiting for him to laugh, but instead he looked annoyed, and said in a critical tone which had the effect of infuriating her,

'You should know better than to wander off on your own like that.'

Her beautiful eyes shone very blue through the narrowed lids, but she said mildly enough, 'I'm not a child, Dr Eijsinck, and I have a tongue in my head!'

He shot an amused glance across the table. 'In many ways you are a child,' he observed, 'and you forget that the tongue in your head is a foreign one.'

She sat staring at him, longing to pick a quarrel, but with the Van Minnen family laughing and talking around them, it was impossible to do so, and he knew it. Instead she said with false meekness,

'I daresay it was very stupid of me—I fear my education was sadly lacking, for I can only speak my own language.'

'Now you have made me out to be a pompous ass,' he protested, amidst the general laughter—but not quite general, Harriet noted. Taeike frowned and protested too with a look of fury on her pretty face, and as soon as she could make herself heard, begged Friso to help her with her homework.

'But I'm tired out,' he said, looking exactly the reverse. 'I've not had a minute to myself since Sunday luncheon.' He caught Harriet's eye and grinned wickedly. 'You'll bear me out, will you not, Harriet?'

She felt her cheeks grow warm. He had no right to talk to her like that, just because she had known who was lunching with him then, and had seen him taking the girl home—presumably—more than twenty-four hours later. She said in a quiet little voice, despite the tell-tale cheeks,

'Why, certainly, Doctor Eijsinck. I'm sure you have very little time to yourself, but I daresay you like it like that. Though I can't say that you look very tired.'

She didn't smile at him, but at Taeike instead, who, however, didn't smile back. Harriet wondered why she was upset and then forgot about it as Friso pushed back his chair and spoke laughingly to Mevrouw Van Minnen, then pulled Taeike to her feet. 'Ten minutes, and not a second more,' he said as they went towards the door.

He was back in the drawing-room, playing chess with his partner long before Sieske and Harriet had cleared the table and carried the supper dishes into the kitchen for the daily maid to deal with in the morning. The two men sat, wrapped in a companionable silence and a great deal of smoke from their pipes while Mevrouw Van Minnen sat at her pretty little rosewood worktable, stitching at her gros-point. The two girls joined her and fell to discussing their plans for a trip to Amsterdam. There were relatives there, it would be easy to stay a night, even two. It was unthinkable that they should allow Harriet to go home without seeing something of the capital. There were the lesser but nevertheless interesting attractions of Leeuwarden to be sampled too, but Aede would take care of that, said Sieske; he planned to take Harry off for the day when next he was free.

She went away to fetch the coffee and presently returned with the tray; her return coincided with the chess game ending in stalemate, and the reappearance of Maggina and Taeike, very cheerful now that their homework was done. They sat around drinking the delicious coffee, arguing as to what Harriet should and should not see when she went to Amsterdam.

'And what does Harriet wish to see?' inquired Dr Eijsinck, who had said very little until that moment.

'Canals and old houses and flower stalls and one of those street organs,' she answered promptly, then added hastily for fear of decrying their kindness, 'and all the other things you have suggested as well.'

Dr Van Minnen laughed. 'At that rate, you will need to spend the rest of your holiday in Amsterdam, and that we cannot allow.'

Dr Eijsinck didn't get up to go until the two younger girls had gone up to bed.

'Will you all come over tomorrow evening?' He looked at Mevrouw Van Minnen and then turned to his partner. 'Any calls can be put through for you.' He had spoken in Dutch and was answered in that language before he turned to Harriet and said with casual friendliness,

'Everyone is coming over to my place tomorrow evening for dinner—naturally you are included in the invitation, Harriet.'

She thanked him politely, surprised to glimpse a look on his face which belied the formality of the words. She was even more taken aback when he added, 'Have you done any sailing, Harriet? I'm free after midday tomorrow; I wondered if you would like to come on the Sneekermeer—I've a boat there.'

She felt her heart race, which was absurd…he doubtless wanted a crew, and there was no one else available. 'What sort of boat?' she asked cautiously.

He looked surprised. 'A Sturgeon.' He had answered readily enough; probably he thought she had asked out of politeness. She forbore to mention that her three brothers, when not engrossed in cars, found solace in boats and when there had been no one else around, she had crewed.

'I'd like that very much,' she said finally.

He nodded briefly. 'Good, I'll fetch you about half past one.

Wear something sensible and warm; you can bring a dress and change at my place.' He nodded again, and a minute later she heard the gentle roar of his car.

She didn't sleep very well, thinking about him. She had already realized that she was becoming obsessed by Friso Eijsinck; if she wasn't careful, she would lose her head over him completely, and what, she asked herself bitterly, could be sillier or more useless than that? The knowledge that she was past preventing this sorry state of affairs anyway added to her misery. She lay forlorn in bed and didn't bother to wipe away the tears trickling down her cheeks. They were still wet when she finally went to sleep.

He came for her at half past one the following day. She had done as she had been told and as well as slacks and a sweater had borrowed a pullover of Sieske's—its polo neck hugged her ears and the sleeves had to be rolled up, but it would be warm. She had borrowed a pair of the right sort of shoes from Maggina, too. Her hair hung in a shining plait over one shoulder and she hadn't bothered with make-up, only lipstick. Experience had taught her that men who ask girls to crew don't particularly mind what they look like, as long as they can handle a tiller and don't fall overboard. She went out to the car, a silk jersey dress over one arm, and a pair of shoes and a handbag in her hand. Dr Eijsinck, looking, if that were possible, larger than ever in an Aran sweater, took them from her and put them in the back of the car and said with faint surprise, 'Is this all you have with you?'

It was Harriet's turn to look surprised. 'Should I have brought something else?' she inquired.

He opened the door of the car for her to get in. 'Hairpins and things,' he hazarded.

'In my bag. My hair comes down if there's much wind, and then it's a nuisance.'

He had settled himself beside her and started the car. 'So you have sailed before.'

She glanced sideways at him and he returned her look with a bland one of his own. She said with a little air of apology, 'I've sailed with my brothers during the holidays. Dinghies mostly, and only when there wasn't anyone else around who could do it better.'

He laughed. 'Your opinion of yourself is a low one, Harry, yet I imagine that you do most things well.'

They had left the town behind, and were making their way across country towards Sneek. He drove fast but never carelessly and she supposed that he would handle a boat in the same efficient way. She felt absurdly elated by his compliment, although upon reflection it was the sort of remark that one could safely make to a schoolteacher or someone similar…but of course, she was something similar. Nurses and teachers did the same work, the one for the mind, the other for the body. Her spirits, which had begun to rise a little after her bad night, sank to new depths. He said with disconcerting perception, 'I didn't mean to make you sound like an elderly schoolteacher.'

She smiled ruefully. 'All the same, I'm a not so young nurse—that's much the same sort of thing.'

'How old are you?' he asked.

'Twenty-four.'

'With a successful career before you, so I hear. Surely it would suit you better to marry?'

The question was thrown at her carelessly; he sounded like the head of the family giving a poor relation some good advice. She lost her temper. 'Only if I can marry for money,' she said in a tight little voice. 'I don't care what the man's like just so long as I have a great many clothes and furs and jewels…' She stopped, appalled at the awful lies she was telling him. Her flash of temper had gone.

He said in a shocked voice, 'That's not true, I simply don't believe you.' He pulled the car into the side of the road and turned to look at her. 'Well?' he asked.

She felt her face redden, but said at once, 'Of course it wasn't true. You made me angry.' She didn't explain why. 'I don't care tuppence if my husband has any money or not. I don't think money is the most important thing in life...' Her face flamed anew. 'I'm sorry,' she said awkwardly, 'I forgot. Sieske said you were very rich. I didn't mean to be rude.'

He laughed with genuine amusement. 'Yes, I am, and although it's nice to have most of the things I want, I agree with you, money isn't important. I should be quite happy without it.'

She smiled. 'Oh, yes, I know. At least I...' she faltered, 'I think you are that kind of person.'

He started the car again. 'As I said before, Harriet, you aren't like anybody else.'

He flashed her a smile of such tenderness that her breath forsook her and by the time she had regained it they were approaching the outskirts of Sneek and she was able to plunge into a great many questions about the town, all of which he answered with great patience, not looking at her, so that she was unable to see the laughter in his eyes. But they held no mockery, only the lingering tenderness.

The boat was a beauty. Harriet inspected her with the thoroughness that was part of her nature, and when he asked her, half laughing, if she approved of it, said seriously,

'She's beautiful. I hope I shall do all the right things.'

He laughed, tossed her a yellow inflatable waistcoat and said,

'Put that on for a start, in case I throw you overboard in a fit of rage.'

She did as she was told. 'Do you have rages?' she asked.

He was busy with the sail and looked at her over his shoulder.

'Occasionally,' he conceded, 'but don't worry, I don't feel one coming on today.' He was smiling, and she smiled too, feeling suddenly happy. The sky was blue, filling slowly with little puffs of cloud; the boat danced gently under her feet. Why was it, she wondered, that being in a boat was like being in another world?

They went down the waterway to the lake with the wind behind them and set course for the opposite shore, sitting side by side in the cockpit with Harriet at the tiller. There were perhaps half a dozen boats sharing the Sneekermeer with them, and none of those near. They talked about boats and gardens and inevitably, hospital, and then boats again.

'I love those big curved boats with prows,' said Harriet, pointing to one.

'A *botter*,' he explained. 'I've got one—it's in the boatyard being repainted. I don't go out in her often though, only when there are half a dozen of us—it's a family boat; very safe, and ideal for children. When I marry I shall pack my entire family on board and sail away for several weeks at a time.'

She looked away from him and said in a quiet voice, 'That sounds nice,' and then, to change the subject, 'Are they seaworthy?'

She got to know quite a lot about him that afternoon. He was not a man to talk much about himself, but by the time they turned for home she had a pretty good idea of his background and likes and dislikes. And she, hardly realizing it, had talked too—about her family and her work and the elderly pony she still rode when she went home. They didn't talk so much on the way back, for there was more to do and it took longer too; tacking into the wind. They could have used the engine, but Friso told her that he only used it to take the boat in and out or if he was pressed for time. The sky had clouded over; the small clouds that had looked so harmless an hour or so earlier had joined themselves together, swallowing the blue above them. The wind had freshened too, but Harriet wasn't cold; her cheeks were gloriously pink, and her eyes shone, and although the wind had ruffled her hair, the thick plait still lay neatly over her shoulder. She looked round once to find Friso staring at her, his grey eyes brilliant. She put a hand up to her hair and asked,

'Is there something the matter?'

His eyes held hers. 'No,' he said, his deep voice suddenly harsh. 'You're beautiful, Harriet. You must have been told that many times before.'

When she didn't answer, he went on sharply,

'You do know you're beautiful?'

Harriet turned from the contemplation of a pair of swans flying with swift grace towards the reeds at the lake edge.

'Yes,' she said composedly. 'I should be stupid if I didn't—just as you would be stupid or a hypocrite if you didn't admit to your own good looks. But you're neither, and I don't suppose you give it a thought. Well, neither do I.' She grinned like a little girl. 'You should see my sisters; they're really beautiful.'

He chuckled. 'You disarm me, Harriet. Tell me about them.'

'They're married; Diana has three boys; Rosemary has a girl and a boy.'

He trimmed the sail. 'Older than you?'

'Oh yes. I'm in the middle—my brothers are younger than I.'

She altered course a little in obedience to his nod. 'I was to have been a boy. Henry after my grandfather...'

'Ah, now I know why you're called Harry. It couldn't be a more unsuitable name. You are...very much a girl.'

His steady gaze met hers across the boat. It needed a great effort to look away from him and a still greater effort to control her breath. She swallowed back the wave of excitement which threatened to engulf her and said the first thing which came into her head.

'I suppose you are much older than your...' she stopped. 'I mean, are you the eldest?' She had gone a little pink and went pinker when he laughed and said, 'Yes, but I'm not as elderly as your tone implies, although I'm ten years older than you.' He added outrageously to make her gasp, 'I prefer my girl-friends to be at least ten years younger than myself.'

She said, 'But I'm...' and stopped herself just in time. If she should disclaim any desire to be one of his girl-friends he was quite capable of agreeing with her most readily. After all, she wasn't; at least… Instead she said, 'There's a great deal of cloud. Do you suppose it will rain before we get back?'

His smile was gently mocking. 'Ah, the weather. Such a safe subject,' and proceeded to sustain a conversation on the subject which lasted, on and off, until he brought the car to a standstill outside his house door. His knowledge of the elements, in their every aspect, appeared to be a profound one; Harriet's ears buzzed with facts about cumuli, low pressure and humidity. She had answered suitably when comment had been called for, because she was by nature a nicely mannered girl, but as she got out of the car she gave him a speaking glance and then almost choked when he said silkily, 'It was you who wanted to talk about the weather, Harriet.'

He walked round the car to where she was standing and threw a massive arm around her shoulders. She stood very still under it, her heart thumping, and was conscious of deep disappointment when all he did was to urge her forward, up the steps to where Wim was waiting at the open door. Inside, he released her, saying merely,

'Letje will take you upstairs. You'll want to change. The others will be here in half an hour or so.'

She left him standing in the hall and followed the soft-footed, smiling Letje up the stairs; at least she was going to see something of the house.

CHAPTER SIX

THE ROOM SHE was ushered into was at the side of the house, overlooking the path she had walked along with Friso. She stood at the window looking down at it and sighed without knowing it before turning away to study her surroundings. They were charming. The room was, by her own standards, large, and furnished in the Empire period—the bed, dressing-table and wardrobe were mahogany and vast; they shared a patina of well-cared-for age. In any other, smaller room they might have been overpowering, but here they were exactly right; set off by a skilful scattering of small satin-covered chairs with buttoned backs and elaborately pleated skirts. There was a sat-inwood writing table under the window and a work-table in Japanese lacquer, very small and dainty. A little round table with piecrust edge stood companionably by one of the chairs, bearing a bowl of spring flowers; they smelled with a faint fragrance and made the room seem lived in, although she guessed that it was seldom used. There were portraits on the walls too—rather austere gentlemen in wigs or high cravats, according to their period; their wives—presumably their wives—looked soberly down at Harriet from heavy frames, their dim rich silks setting off the magnificence of their meticulously painted jewels. She thought she detected a fleeting resemblance to Friso in some of the faces; he had certainly inherited their austerity of looks upon occasion. She realized all at once that she had been wasting time and went into the adjoining bathroom and turned on the taps. She would have to hurry.

She was putting on her lipstick when there was a tap on the door and Sieske came in.

'Harry, did you have a good time?' She eyed her friend critically. 'How nice you look—that's a lovely dress.' She went and sat on one of the little chairs and Harriet put away the lipstick and looked down at herself.

It was a pretty dress; a soft gold-coloured sheath, patterned with honeysuckle; she had felt rather guilty when she had bought it, for it had cost a lot of money; now her feeling was one of satisfaction. Without doubt it did something for her. She hoped that Friso would share her opinion.

It seemed he did not, for beyond a laughing reference to her seamanship as he offered a glass of sherry, he addressed her in only the most general of terms throughout the evening. The oyster soup, the fillets of sole Maconaise, the saddle of lamb— even the sweet—some frothy confection of marrons glacés— Anna's own invention—were dust in her pretty mouth.

She allowed none of her true feelings to show, however, and laughed and talked with the faintly shy air which she had never managed to overcome. Whenever the opportunity presented itself, she surveyed her surroundings. The dining-room was large and square and in the front of the house; its walls were panelled with a wood she couldn't identify; it was furnished with the massive round table at which they sat. It had been made to accommodate a dozen guests at the least, but now the ribbon-back chairs had been reduced to a paltry seven. The sideboard, large and splendidly simple, took up most of one wall, and all around them were more portraits of bygone Eijsincks, their painted eyes watching each morsel of food she ate. She looked away from a particularly haughty old gentleman with sidewhiskers and encountered Friso's lifted brows. He looked so like the portrait that she averted her gaze and applied herself to her dinner.

They sat after dinner in the salon, drinking their coffee and something richly potent and velvety from delicate liqueur glasses. Harriet, sharing one of the sofas with Maggina, was content to listen, for the most part, to the conversation around her—the easy, not too serious talk of old friends. She longed to explore the room thoroughly, to pick up the china pieces lying about and examine them and run her hand down the thick velvet folds of the curtains. Everything was so very beautiful. She checked a sigh, looked up and caught Friso's eye upon her again.

It was soon after this that the front door knocker suddenly reverberated through the house, not once, but half a dozen times, to cease as suddenly, presumably upon the opening of the door. Everyone had stopped talking to listen to the faint agitated voice from the hall, and every head turned as Wim came in, moving somewhat faster than was his wont, and bent to speak quietly in his master's ear. He had barely finished what he was saying before the doctor was on his feet. He said something in his turn to Dr Van Minnen in a crisp voice totally unlike his usual slight drawl, so that gentleman got to his feet and started for the door. Harriet, seething with curiosity, was forced to sit quiet while he spoke to Mevrouw Van Minnen too. It wasn't until he was on the point of leaving them that he spoke to Sieske. He sounded like a general giving orders and he didn't wait to see if they had been understood. The two younger girls he ignored.

Sieske got to her feet and started to follow him from the room, saying over her shoulder, 'Come on, Harry. There's a car in the canal—they don't know yet who's in it—they'll bring them here. We have to get the surgery ready.' She led the way across the hall and opened a door under the staircase and switched on the light. Harriet, close on her heels, saw that the surgery was roomy, with a door at the other end of it, presumably leading to a side entrance. She went straight across the room and opened the door and found a light switch there too, which shone on to the drive running alongside the house. She had no idea how much time they had; Sieske, who knew her way around, was busy with the oxygen cylinder, fitting on the tube and mask and putting the catheters ready. Harriet began to clear what furniture there was away from the centre of the room; they would want all the space they could have if they had to do any resuscitation. She found a notepad and pen, and several pairs of scissors which she took from the well stocked instrument cabinet in one corner. There were some syringes and needles there too; she took those as well and cleared a space on the doctor's desk and arranged them neatly where they could be got at in a hurry. She wasn't sure that the doctor would approve of the way she had piled his papers and swept them to one side. In her experience, doctors in general practice preferred to work at a desk cluttered with unread circulars, cryptic notes on the backs of envelopes, electricity bills, samples of pills, snapshots of their loved ones and a great variety of official forms. It seemed to her that Friso's desk ran true to form. She said without turning round,

'Has anyone telephoned the police and the ambulance?'

'Wim,' replied Sieske. She had her head in a wall cupboard. 'There's plenty of Savlon; I'll put some into a couple of gallipots and dilute enough to fill a jug. Someone's sure to need cleaning up.'

Harriet nodded to the back of her friend's head, 'Blankets?' she asked.

'Wim,' said Sieske, emerging. Harriet flew across the hall in search of him, encountered him coming through a door beyond the stairs and remembered too late that she didn't know the word for blankets. She stopped before him and said hopelessly, 'Blankets, Wim.' And he said, 'Yes, miss, I have them here.' He indicated a pile of them beyond the door and began to pile them into her arms; when he thought she had enough he said, 'I'll bring the rest, miss.' She went back across the hall, thinking that it was just like Friso to have a servant who spoke English when required. It was quite good English too.

She piled the blankets neatly on to the doctor's chair, and Wim went away again, presumably to fetch more. There were sounds of feet coming along the drive and a moment later Dr Van Minnen and another man came in carrying a man between them; he streamed water, his clothes plastered with mud and weed; his face was white, his eyes closed. They put him carefully on the floor and Dr Van Minnen dropped down on his knees beside him while his helper squelched his way out again. Sieske was already on the other side of the prone figure, but Harriet wasted no time in watching her, for Friso had come in through the door carrying an elderly woman. He laid her down with the same care as the others had used and Harriet rolled the unconscious form expertly over into the prone position, turned the limp head gently to one side and swept a hand into the mouth, but the woman's teeth were her own; there was no danger there. She swept the sopping arms above her patient's head, and then sank back on her heels and put her hands on the small of the woman's back.

'I see you know what you're about,' said Friso from above her, and was gone. It was hard work, but worth it; for after a few minutes she felt the first faint movement in the body beneath her hands; she persevered and was rewarded by the faint tinge of colour in the white cheeks, before long she saw the slight fluttering of the woman's eyelids. She stopped her efforts long enough to catch at a still flaccid wrist and check the pulse; it was weak but steady. Harriet straightened her back and found Mevrouw Van Minnen standing by her, holding a blanket. They wrapped the woman in it between them and began to remove her wet clothing, beginning with her shoes. But Harriet had barely unlaced one of them when there was a commotion at the door again and Friso came in with a half-grown boy. He gave one brief glance in Harriet's direction and said, 'Leave the woman to Mevrouw Van Minnen and come here. I've emptied his lungs.'

He laid the boy down and Harriet saw at once that they wouldn't be able to turn him over because of the wound in his chest. It wasn't a large wound, but a circular depression, oozing with a gentle persistence. Someone had opened his jacket and shirt, probably to see where he was hurt. She snatched up a wad of gauze and covered it, then took another piece of gauze and opened the boy's mouth to catch and hold his tongue. Friso had peeled off his jacket and she saw that he was soaked and as muddy as the boy he had brought in. He knelt down behind the boy's head, caught his arms above the elbow and started artificial respiration. It wasn't an ideal state of affairs, for the chest wound needed urgent attention, but still more urgent was the task of getting the boy to breathe again.

'Let go his tongue,' said Friso, and started the kiss of life. Released, Harriet got to her feet and started to collect swabs and dressings; there would have to be an anti-tetanus injection too, as well as one for gas gangrene. She went back to the boy, told the doctor what she had done, asked, 'Shall I give them both now?' and at his nod, possessed herself of scissors and began to cut the wet sleeve open.

It was wonderful when the boy started to breathe—he was shocked and severely injured—it was hard to know just how severely until he could be got to hospital, but at least he was alive; all three of them were alive. She got the oxygen and fixed it up and set about cleaning the wound. She had just about finished when a great many people arrived at once—the police, who came in quietly and got busy with notebooks and quiet questions, and the ambulance men with their stretchers. The man and woman were conscious now and able to answer the few essential questions which were put to them, the boy lay quiet, his breath fluttering, his face bluish-white. Dr Eijsinck, using a sharper tone than Harriet had ever heard before, but not raising his voice at all, said something—sufficient to cause the boy to be lifted carefully on to a stretcher and borne away without further ado. She heard the ambulance a moment later, its sing-song warning sounding loud on the night air, moving fast along the road. His mother and father followed him a few minutes later, leaving the rest of them standing in a welter of discarded blankets, stray fragments of wet clothing, used swabs and a good deal of weed and mud. Wim, who, Harriet suspected, had been doing a great deal in an unobtrusive way, was already collecting blankets, but when Dr Eijsinck said, 'Coffee, I think, Wim,' he relinquished the task to Mevrouw Van Minnen and went away. Sieske had her head in the cupboard again, putting back what she had taken out. Harriet turned to the desk and began to clear away the small paraphernalia—swabs, scissors, gallipots— she cleaned them all in turn and returned them where they belonged, then returned to restore the desk to its original state of ordered chaos. She had picked up an old copy of the *Lancet* and was trying to remember if it had been under the blotter or with a pile of circulars she had swept aside, when Friso, who was conferring with Dr Van Minnen and the policemen, broke off the conversation long enough to say, mildly,

'Don't bother, Harry. My desk needed a clean-up anyway.'

She put the *Lancet* down thankfully and went to fold blankets with Mevrouw Van Minnen—they had them tidy just as Wim came back and informed them, in two languages, that coffee was in the salon, and the two young ladies were anxious for news. 'The gentlemen,' he added, 'will take their coffee where they are.'

Maggina and Taeike fell upon them when they reached the salon, slightly aggrieved that they had not been allowed to help but nevertheless curious to hear what had occurred. The three ladies spent a pleasurable half hour answering their questions, repairing their make-up and drinking a great many cups of coffee, and deploring the muddy state of their shoes and stockings. Harriet glanced down at her own dress and saw the little blobs of dried mud and pieces of weed and here and there, small specks of blood. The dress, she thought regretfully, would never be quite the same again. The two doctors came in presently—the police had gone and the men had changed into dry clothes, Dr Van Minnen rather precariously rigged out in a shirt and trousers of Friso's. He lowered his rather portly frame into a chair, remarking that he must have put on weight for everything was so tight. His homely little joke relieved a little of the delayed excitement and tension and when Wim appeared with a tray on which was a tall silver jug and some glasses the atmosphere lightened considerably. Harriet took a sip of the frothy yellow liquid, and found it to be warm. It was only after she had swallowed that she discovered it to be extremely fiery as well. She choked a little, and Friso, who had sat down opposite her, raised an eyebrow at her and asked, 'Do you like it, Harriet? It's Cambridge Punch, from a very old English recipe, and a splendid pick-me-up.'

She took another cautious sip; it really was very nice. 'What's in it?' she asked.

'Eggs, milk, brandy and rum.' He smiled suddenly and kindly at her. 'Just what you need after all that excitement. You worked like a beaver; thank you, Harry.'

There was really nothing she could say—'Not at all' would sound ridiculous—so would 'It was a pleasure.' She smiled shyly and took another sip and felt the rum and brandy combine to give her a pleasant glow inside.

Everyone was suddenly talking at once again, and he didn't speak to her again. It was only when they were on the point of leaving that he asked her, 'Do you like my home, Harriet?'

He had her hand between his own and showed no sign of relinquishing it. She looked up at him. 'Yes, Friso, very much.'

'As I had hoped,' was all he said. She fell asleep that night still wondering what exactly he had meant.

CHAPTER SEVEN

AEDE TELEPHONED THE next morning; he would be free on the following day, he explained, so how would Harriet like to spend it with him in Leeuwarden. She agreed readily, suppressing the thought that if she did so, she would be unable to see Friso, always supposing that he came to his partner's house. She thanked Aede with a false enthusiasm and went to find Sieske.

When she awoke the next day, it was to find the sky shrouded in high grey cloud, and by the time Aede arrived to fetch her, another lower layer of cloud was scudding in from the sea, blown by a wind which whined and whistled around the housetops. The road to Leeuwarden looked bare and sad; the country on either side unprotected.

'It's very flat,' said Harriet. 'The sea could rush in.'

Aede laughed comfortably. 'You forget our dykes; they do not break so easily—it would need an earthquake or a bomb; besides, there are always men watching.'

It was a comforting thought; Harriet turned her attention to the city outskirts, and forgot the weather. They were driving down a rather dull road which led to a roundabout surrounded by modern buildings, then suddenly they were in the old city—there was nothing dull about the canal they crossed to enter the bustling, shop-lined street, bisected by a much bridged canal. The shops were modern, but above them rose a variety of old roofs, which Harriet found enchanting, but when she begged Aede to stop, he said,

'Lord, no. Not here. We'll go and have coffee and leave the car at the hotel; then we can walk around.'

At the end of the street, past the old Weigh House, he turned into an even busier street, crossed the canal again and stopped outside a pleasant hotel overlooking a square. They got out, and before they went inside. Aede took her arm and turned her round.

'This is our most important statue,' he explained, and pointed towards a pedestal upon which stood a cow. 'Our prosperity.' he said simply. 'We owe it to our cows.'

They drank their coffee in the hotel, sitting in the window of the café overlooking the busy square, talking leisurely about the happenings of the previous week.

'Did you enjoy Delft?' Aede asked.

Harriet nibbled the little sugary biscuit which had come with her coffee. 'Very much—I got lost.' She told him all about it and he laughed and then said, 'But you should be careful, you know, you're a foreigner—you must never go off on your own again.'

'That's what Friso said.'

'Did he? Well, yes, naturally.' He stopped abruptly, and Harriet knitted her brows, trying to make sense of this remark. Why should it be natural for Friso to be concerned about her? She pondered it briefly and then went faintly pink as a possible solution struck her, to be at once cast down by Aede's next words.

'What I meant was, Friso would have said that to any pretty girl.' He frowned, hunting for words. Harriet achieved a creditable smile.

'Aede, what a nice compliment! And now do tell me what we're going to do first.'

He responded to this conversational red herring with an obvious relief.

'How about the Museum—the Friesian Museum? We could walk there and pick the car up later.'

They set off, back over the canal, driven to walk at a furious pace by the ferocious wind. The sky seemed lower and blacker than ever, but at least it wouldn't rain until the wind died down.

They walked along arm in arm, talking comfortably. 'Where's your hospital?' asked Harriet.

Aede waved a careless arm. 'Over there. Just outside the town. It's new, not completed, in fact, but there's plenty of work just the same.'

He went on talking about it until they reached the museum, which had once upon a time been a private mansion and still contrived to look like one. The curator was large and white-haired and spoke scholarly English in a gentle voice. Harriet thought that Friso would look something like him in twenty years or so. The train of thought set up by this idea was broken only by Aede's quite dramatic description of Great Pier's achievements in the sixteenth century. Judging by the size of the sword she was called upon to examine this Friesian hero must have been a giant even amongst his own giant-like race. They stayed a long time, going from room to room; sometimes the curator joined them for a few minutes, but most of the time Aede painstakingly led her round; he seemed to be enjoying it as much as she. It was almost two o'clock when they got back to the hotel for lunch, and the wind showed no signs of abating. Now there were short flurries of rain—they decided to stay in Leeuwarden for the rest of the day, and in spite of the worsening weather, they prowled happily up and down the narrow lanes, looking at the old, small houses, while Aede pointed out their architectural points, and when Harriet at length had had her fill, they strolled in and out of the shops, where she bought presents to take home—silver teaspoons and Makkum pottery, and tobacco for her father. They had forgotten all about tea and presently they went back to the hotel again and sat over drinks and then ate a leisurely meal before going back to Franeker. The countryside looked even more desolate in the heavy dusk; the road stretched before them, shining wetly. Harriet was glad when they stopped outside the cheerfully lighted house in Franeker. It was pleasant to sit quietly, talking about their day with the rest of the family, and drinking Mevrouw Van Minnen's excellent coffee. The howling wind and rain beating on the windows seemed curiously unreal heard from the comfort of the sitting-room. Aede got reluctantly to his feet after a time and went of, cheerfully enough, back to his hospital in Leeuwarden. After he'd gone, the rest of them sat around, still talking.

'Friso's on call,' remarked Doctor Van Minnen. 'I hope he won't need to go out tonight.'

Harriet remembered his remark when she was lying in bed, listening to the storm. She wondered if anyone bothered to see that Friso had a hot drink and took off his wet clothes when he went out on a bad night. She worried about it for quite a time until her common sense told her that he had servants enough to look after him. He didn't look in the least neglected. She turned over, thumping her pillow with an unnecessary violence, and told herself that she was a fool, and after a little while went to sleep.

She awoke the next morning to a sudden fierce clap of thunder. The wind had apparently gathered strength from the night hours; so had the rain. She turned from the unpleasing prospect outside as Sieske tapped on the door and came in. She was already dressed and offered the information that she would have to go to Sneek after breakfast. Oma wasn't well—she would have to take the Mini and see what was the matter.

'I'll not ask you to come with me, Harry,' she said. 'Not in this weather. Father has gone to Leeuwarden—he's anaesthetizing at the hospital today. Do you mind being at home with Moeder?'

'Me?' asked Harriet. 'No, of course not. I shall air my Dutch.'
She was putting up her hair and her mouth was full of pins; she
said indistinctly, 'Isn't there a surgery here today?'

Sieske uncurled herself from the bed. 'No. Friso sees Father's
urgent cases when he's at the hospital; but he doesn't come
here.' She didn't look at Harriet. 'He just does the visits.' Harriet didn't speak, so after a minute she went on, 'I've been listening to the news—the wind's done quite a lot of damage and
there's a little flooding locally—It's the spring tide, you know,
and the wind blowing from the north-west at the same time.'

They went downstairs to breakfast.

The morning passed slowly; Harriet and Mevrouw Van Minnen had an early lunch—there wasn't much else to do and it kept
their minds off the dismal scene outside. Sieske had telephoned
from Sneek, and although she had made light of it, they gathered that she had had a very unpleasant journey. It was shortly
after that the telephone went dead. They were in the sitting-
room, improving Harriet's Dutch when they heard a car coming
wetly along the street. It stopped; brakes squealing, outside the
house, and Mevrouw Van Minnen, who had gone to look out
of the window, said, '*De jeep van Friso*,' which remark Harriet
was well able to understand. She got up and went to the window
too. Why had Friso come? But it wasn't Friso who got out and
ran up the steps to peal the bell with a desperate urgency, but a
young man who was a stranger. He stood in the hall, dripping
over the carpet, talking to Mevrouw Van Minnen. He spoke as
though he was repeating a lesson learned by heart, and when he
had finished, she nodded calmly and stood thinking. At length
she turned to Harriet.

'Friso calls help. Calls for Sieske—baby.' She paused, frowning in deep concentration. Harriet snatched up her writing pad
and pen and held them out. Mevrouw Van Minnen nodded and
smiled and proceeded to draw a pair of forceps. Harriet had no
difficulty in recognizing them; so Friso wanted to do a forceps
delivery—he'd want the Minnett's gas-air portable; she had

seen it in Doctor Van Minnen's surgery. Not to be outdone by
Mevrouw Van Minnen's basic English, she said, '*Ik ga*.' She
turned to go to the surgery—she knew exactly what she would
need to take with her—but Mevrouw Van Minnen put a hand
on her arm and said painstakingly,

'Dyke break. Much water.' She held a hand a foot or so above
the floor, and looked hopefully at Harriet, who made a frustrated sound which changed to a crow of triumph as she remembered the dictionary on the sitting-room table. With its
invaluable help and some lucky guesswork, she possessed herself of the fact that there had been some sort of accident to the
sea dyke above the patient's house; a small area was under water.
She would have liked to know more, but there simply wasn't
time—Friso was waiting.

She was ready in ten minutes. She had put on slacks and
a sweater and borrowed an anorak and boots from Taeike's
wardrobe. The needed equipment stood in the hall while the
messenger swallowed coffee; he had said very little after his
one long speech, now he muttered something to Mevrouw Van
Minnen, shouldered the Minnett's and opened the door. The
Land-Rover seemed a haven of refuge after the few seconds'
walk from the house. Harriet sighed soundlessly with relief
and hoped that the journey was to be a short one. In this she
was disappointed. Once out of the little town, they headed, as
she knew they would, for the coast. It was slow progress in the
teeth of the gale and the rain lashing down to flood the wind-
screen as though there were no wipers working, but in time
they reached Tzummarum, which straddled the coast road. Harriet looked hopefully at her companion, and above the wind
he shouted something at her and shook his head. Clearly, they
had further to go.

It was at St Annaparochie, several kilometres further, that
he turned off the road, and into a country lane winding past
the church, straight to the sea. Perhaps in good weather it had
a passable surface, but now it was covered in a wet sand which

had turned to mud. Clear of the village, Harriet could see the flooded *polder* land with the sea dyke behind it. Her companion waved a vague arm towards the sea and, for the first time, smiled at her. She concluded that they were almost at the end of their journey, and sure enough, after a further five minutes of skidding and sliding in the mud, he drew up.

Harriet couldn't see anything at all when she first got out. The wind took her breath and the rain lashed her face with such frenzy that she was half blinded. She held on to the Land-Rover with all her might, and presently was able to take stock of her surroundings. The dyke was closer now; it looked undamaged, but in the distance, where it followed the curve of the coast, she could make out a great many figures moving what looked like a dragline; there was a pile of what might have been wreckage, but it was too far off to see. She transferred her gaze to the cottage under the dyke—it was already under water as far as its low window-sills, as was the larger house only a few hundred yards away from where they had stopped. She became aware that the man was beside her, and without a word, she picked up one of the bags and started down the small slippery path behind him. It led them to what she supposed was a field when it was dry; it was now boot-high in water, and was obviously going to get deeper as they proceeded. She sloshed along in her companion's wake, her thoughts intent on keeping her feet at all costs.

It was when they were level with the first house that she stopped. She had heard a faint whine, but when it wasn't repeated, she supposed that it was the wind, but after a few more steps she stopped again. The wind was whining; but this wasn't the wind. In the little yard behind the house there was a large ruffiany dog, up to his belly in water, and fastened securely to the wall by a stout rope. The man had gone past it with barely a glance; Harriet guessed that he was too worried about his wife to think of anything else; she would get no help from him, nor would he stop. It would only take a minute. She put her hand into the pocket of her slacks and withdrew the sort of all-purpose knife that all boys carry. It seemed a surprising thing for the delicate-looking and ultra-feminine Miss Slocombe to have about her person, but as she had once sensibly observed, it was only common sense to be equipped for any eventuality. She put the bag she was carrying on the top of a convenient wall and went over to the dog, selecting the strongest blade as she did so.

The man didn't look round until they were at the door of the cottage. Harriet stood quietly while he gave vent to his feelings. She gathered they weren't happy ones, and when he made to wade back towards the dog beside her, she put a protective hand on the shabby head pressed against her knee, and said, 'No. He stays here with me. I'll not leave him to drown.' She spoke with an air of authority which he could understand, even though her words were unintelligible. She walked past him, her hand on the beast's head and, still muttering, he pushed the door open and they went inside. The passage was small, with a door on either side and a narrow steep stair between; the water was already lapping the lower steps. They stood, the three of them, listening to the ceiling creaking under Dr Eijsinck's tread. He called out something as he came, and in a moment his long legs, encased in gumboots, appeared on the stairs. He stopped just above the water, staring at them. After a long silence he said in a cold voice to make her shiver,

'You! Why in heaven's name have you come here? I asked for Sieske…even if she couldn't come, surely someone could have been found.'

He looked so fierce that Harriet clutched the dog's fur harder and it whimpered softly. She said 'Sorry' and patted its dirty head. It gave her a moment to bottle up her rage, when she spoke her voice was as quiet and level as usual.

'Sieske's in Sneek. There's only her mother at home—and me. There was no time to find anyone else.' She swallowed returning rage. 'May I remind you that I am a nurse?'

He didn't appear to hear her. His eyes were on the dog. It stared at him with its yellow eyes, red tongue hung between terrifying teeth. Dr Eijsinck laughed softly, and with genuine amusement.

'Do tell me, Harriet, why have you brought this dog with you?'

She explained and added, 'Please don't let that man turn him loose. He's cold and wet and hungry.'

He didn't answer her, but turned to the man and said something and the man growled a reply. 'Come upstairs then, since you are here, and bring that damned great beast with you.'

Upstairs was an attic, one corner of which had been boarded up to form a bedroom. Harriet peeled off her soaking anorak, bade the dog sit down and not stir and started to unpack the bags with a practised hand. The patient was dozing fitfully—worn out, she supposed. Friso was washing his hands in the little tin basin on the chest which was pushed against one wall. Without turning round, he asked,

'You understand Minnett's?'

Harriet tied the tapes of the gown which she had had the forethought to include in one of the bags, and started to lay out the things Friso would need; they were each packed in sealed packets, ready for use. She was trying, unsuccessfully, to forget the look of anger on his face when he had seen her—he had looked at her quite differently when they had gone sailing, and later that evening too…she brushed the thought aside and answered his question in a civil voice which betrayed nothing of her real feelings.

'Yes, Doctor, I do know about Dutch rules. In England, provided the patient has been previously examined and pronounced fit by the doctor, the midwife may administer gas-and-air analgesia from a Minnett's apparatus without supervision. I am a midwife,' she added unnecessarily.

He had his back to her, and in any case, she didn't look up from loosening the packs so that he could withdraw their contents with a sterile hand. He spoke softly. 'My good girl, are you presuming to teach me the rules?'

Harriet took a very small blanket out of one of the bags and laid it handy, ready for the baby.

'Certainly not,' she said briskly. 'I merely wish to reassure you.'

She squeezed her small person past his bulk and went to the head of the bed; the patient was awake. Harriet took her hand and smiled and nodded at her, waiting patiently for Friso to explain to the woman what had to be done.

The baby was a boy. Harriet wrapped him in the blanket with all the care of a saleswoman wrapping a valuable parcel, and gave him to his tired, happy mother, whose pulse, she noted, was too rapid. She told Friso, wondering if he would snub her again when she told him that she had brought two vacolitres of five per cent saline with her. He made it easy by telling her that the woman would have to go to Leeuwarden as soon as she could be moved.

'She'll need a transfusion, and this is no place for her at the moment.'

Harriet agreed soberly and mentioned the vacolitres, suffering a mixture of relief and disappointment when all he said was,

'Good girl—let's have one up, shall we?'

It only took a few minutes, then Friso called something through the half-open door and the man came in, smiling and faintly uneasy at the sight of his wife. Harriet took off her gown, listening with half an ear to the unintelligible talk, until Friso said, 'Coffee outside. We'll leave them for a bit.'

The dog was sitting where she had left him in a corner of the attic. He whined gently and wagged a stumpy tail, and she went and sat down beside him on the floor, leaving Friso to fetch two mugs of coffee from a table which also held a small paraffin stove and a collection of pots and pans and crockery. There was a box too, full of food, doubtless swept in haste from a downstairs cupboard. Furniture had been stacked neatly along one wall of the attic. Harriet wondered about the carpets.

'Will they get compensation?' she asked, accepting her coffee. Friso put a pan of water down in front of the dog, who drank with pathetic gusto, then fetched two chairs and, as an after-thought, an end of bread from the table. They sat side by side, watching the animal dispose of the unappetizing meal with a relish highlighted by a display of awesome teeth and rolling eye.

'Yes, but not at once. Don't worry about that. It'll be seen to. Drink your coffee, then we can give Mevrouw Bal a cup and get things cleared up.' He took his watch out of a pocket and put it back on his wrist. 'It's almost six; the tide will be high at half past seven—we shall have to stay here.' He got up and went to peer out of the small window set in the attic wall.

Harriet drank her coffee, reserving the last of it for the dog. He licked the bowl hopefully long after no drop remained, then edged nearer to her so that she could put an arm round his mat-ted woolly shoulders. She addressed Friso's back. 'How long shall we be here?'

He shrugged broad shoulders. 'Most of the night at least, I should suppose. Once the tide's on the turn they can get on with repairing the breach. If the ambulance can get through as far as Bal brought the Land-Rover, it'll be easy enough. While we're making his wife comfortable, he must go back to St Annaparo-chie and get the police to contact the hospital—they'll send an ambulance as soon as it's possible.' He turned round to look at her. There was no sign of anger in his face now; she wasn't sure of his expression, but there was something in it which embold-ened her to ask, 'Why were you angry when I came?'

He came and stood in front of her, very close, so that he ap-peared even taller and broader than he was. 'Why do you sup-pose?' His voice was dry.

'Well,' she said carefully, 'I suppose you were disappointed because it was I and you were afraid that I wouldn't be able to help you or understand the Minnett's or—or make myself use-ful. I know,' she added mournfully, 'that you haven't got much of an opinion of me.'

'I was not aware that I had even offered an opinion of you—if you must know, I find you an excellent nurse, a woman of great good sense, and a beautiful and utterly charming companion. My anger was the result of my fears for your well-being, my dear—my very dear Harriet.'

He walked away as he spoke and she heard him talking to the couple in the bedroom, and a moment later Mijnheer Bal came out and went downstairs, and Friso put his head round the door and asked her to bring his patient a cup of coffee. His voice sounded so ordinary that she fancied that she must have imagined all that he had just said. But there was no time to think about it—she did as she was bid, and then, while Friso made shift to pack away the equipment, she washed the mother and bathed the baby and set the little room to rights, and when there was nothing more to do, she went back into the attic, feeling shy. Friso apparently did not share her feelings, for all he said was,

'Finished? Can you open a few tins and warm something up for all of us to eat?'

Her practical nature took over, giving the shyness no chance. She said, 'Yes, of course,' and went to inspect the untidy pile of odds and ends on the table. From these she selected a number of tins and was pouring their contents into an iron pan she had providentially found in the clothes basket when Friso said, 'Need any help?' and strolled over to stand beside her. He eyed the neatly opened tins. 'Naturally, you carry a tin opener with you,' he murmured blandly. 'I should have known.'

Harriet looked apologetic. 'Well, not always, but I've a knife I usually carry around.'

'Ah, yes. With a corkscrew and that small instrument for digging stones out of horses' hooves.' His voice was grave, but he was laughing at her, though she didn't dare to look up and see. She said 'Yes,' rather shortly, and then, 'You're in my way. And we're running short of water.'

He picked up a kettle and a bucket and went obediently down

the stairs. She could hear him wading about down below, and presently he began to whistle; the small domestic sound made everything very normal; she salted her pot-au-feu, unable to see it through sudden tears. She put down her spoon and brushed them away angrily, not sure why she was crying.

It was more than an hour before Bal returned; by then the contents of the pot were giving off a delicious aroma. Harriet had given Mevrouw Bal her supper and tucked her up once more with the baby and had then turned her attention to the dog, who had devoured a generously filled bowl of stew with such speed that there had been nothing to do but to give it, rather guiltily, a second helping. There was plenty in the pot anyway, and she had reason to be glad of this when Mijnheer Bal returned and Friso, who, between visits to his patient, had been on foraging expeditions of his own, joined them. The two men emptied their plates with almost as much speed as the dog had done; she gave them more and went on eating her own smaller helping. 'When did you last have a meal?' she inquired.

Friso looked up. 'Last night. I went to a case early this morning and didn't stop for breakfast—came straight on here. I should think Bal is in like case.'

He said something to the other man, who shook his head and then laughed, and then made, for him, quite a long speech. Friso translated.

'He didn't have any breakfast either; but he says he's glad you came, because your cooking is very good.' He got up and put the plates on the table, and when she started to get up, said, 'No, stay where you are, I'll get the coffee. You deserve a rest.' While he was doing it, he said over his shoulder, 'The police have sent a man in to Leeuwarden; the telephone is still out of order.' He glanced at his watch. 'The tide will be on the turn soon, they should be able to reach us within the next hour or so.'

He poured the coffee and gave her a mug. He said on a laugh, 'I never dared to hope that you were a good cook too.'

She met his twinkling eyes with a composed air and a racing heart, hoping that her hot cheeks would be attributed to her efforts over the little stove. They weren't.

'You're lovely when you blush,' he added.

She drank her coffee in a dream, then, after taking a look at Mevrouw Bal and the baby, went to heat water for the washing up. It took some time and she filled it in by gazing out of the window at the weather, which hadn't improved at all. The two men sat silent, puffing at their pipes with an air of not wishing to be disturbed—in any case, she could think of nothing worthwhile to talk about. She wandered over to the stairs and looked down and exclaimed 'Oh!' in a rather thin voice before she could stop herself. The water had risen—not just a few inches; the stairs were two-thirds covered. The water was dark and still and menacing. She drew back with a shudder and felt the reassuring touch of Friso's hands on her shoulders.

He said placidly, 'It won't come any higher; the tide's on the ebb. They'll be able to start repairing the breach, and this will all be pumped dry in no time at all. This weather can't last much longer.'

She twisted round to look up at him. He looked weary and he badly needed a shave, but the calm of his face wasn't superficial; it went deep inside him. She had been frightened, but now she felt safe. She said so and he raised his eyebrows quizzically. 'That's an illusion,' he said comfortably, 'because of my size. If I had been a small man, you might not have felt so safe.'

Harriet drew a deep breath. 'You're wrong,' she said steadily. 'I should feel safe with you whatever your size.' And in the same breath, 'The kettle's boiling.'

The police arrived first. Two large quiet men, who reflected Friso's calm. They came quietly up the small staircase in their heavy rubber boots and their waterproof coats, saluted the doctor as an old acquaintance, and listened wordlessly to what he had to say. Harriet had been sitting on a pile of blankets with the dog, smelly but warm, beside her. She listened to Friso's quiet voice too—it sounded assured and completely confident; just to hear it was happiness. She caught his eye and smiled, her mouth curved delightfully, her blue eyes shone; she had forgotten the past and the future; the present was enough, here with him.

He stopped what he was saying and looked back at her, not smiling, his face impassive. In a moment he finished talking to the men and spoke to her in English.

'Harriet, I should like you to meet two good friends of mine—Mijnheer Kok and Mijnheer Wijma.'

She scrambled to her feet, and the dog too, and shook the enormous hands held out to her. The dog grinned toothily and blinked at the men with bright eyes. '*De hond*?' queried Constable Kok. She couldn't understand what Friso was saying, but he could see from the expression on the policeman's face that he accepted the explanation. The men laughed and Bal, who was at the window, stopped his laughter to point and say something to Friso. 'The ambulance,' he said over one shoulder, and Friso nodded to her, said, 'See to Mevrouw Bal, will you?' and smiled.

They had already taken down the drip, and Harriet had readied her and the baby for the journey as far as possible; but she went at once to make sure that there was nothing more that needed to be done, and in a minute or two, Friso asked, 'May we come in?'

She held the baby while they lifted his mother on to the stretcher and strapped her firmly on to it. When they were ready, Friso said, 'Let me have him.' She saw that he was wearing a windcheater, and strove to speak in a matter-of-fact voice. 'You're going with the patient.' It was a statement of something she had really expected.

He tucked the baby into the crook of his arm and stood while Harriet covered the small creature carefully with the plastic tablecloth she had luckily found earlier in the evening, leaving the solemn sleeping face uncovered.

Friso said quietly, 'Stay here until I come. I'm going to see them safely into the ambulance. Bal will go with them, and the ambulance men, of course. Kok or Wijma will bring me back.'

She nodded, but couldn't forbear from saying, 'The water looks very deep.'

'Well, we don't have to walk, you know. They've got a couple of boats.'

She hadn't thought of that, and smiled her relief. 'I'll be tidying up,' was all she said, and watched them make their cautious way downstairs. It was quiet when they had gone, but she had the dog.

She had everything to rights by the time she heard him returning. The dog's deep growl ceased as he heard Friso's voice, and when he climbed the stairs, it wagged its tail, watching him with hopeful yellow eyes. Harriet said nothing, but in answer to her inquiring look the doctor said cheerfully,

'They'll be in Leeuwarden and tucked up in bed before we're home ourselves. Let's be off.'

She stood silently while he passed the bags and the Minnett's box to the waiting men below, then obediently started down the stairs, the dog breathing hotly at her heels. The water had ebbed, but not much; she had no idea how deep it was and she had no opportunity of finding out, for Friso was suddenly there and she had been picked up and carried to the boat. The wetness of his jacket damped her cheek, but she could feel the steady beat of his heart beneath it and nothing else mattered; she could have stayed in his arms for ever. Apparently the doctor had no such thought. He dumped her unceremoniously in the boat and then turned to help the dog, who was paddling gamely alongside. It stood between them, and shook itself, making them all a great deal wetter than they were already, then sneezed loudly before curling itself up at Harriet's feet, smelling dreadfully of wet fur.

The wind was dying down at last, although the rain was coming and going in mean little squalls. They climbed the slippery path back on to the road, and the three men fetched the bags and then pulled the boat up on to the dyke. The policemen yawned hugely, grinned and said, 'Till tomorrow,' and went along to their car. The dog, without being asked, had got in with the paraphernalia in the back of Friso's Land-Rover. Harriet sank into the front seat—it wasn't all that comfortable, but after the attic, it was bliss. Friso didn't talk—for one thing the road was in a shocking condition and needed all his attention, and for another Harriet guessed that he was very tired. The police car stopped in St Annaparochie and the policemen waved gaily as they went past, for all the world, she thought, as though they were all going home from some party. They were almost at Friso's house when he spoke.

'What do you intend to do with this animal?' he inquired. She detected amusement in his voice and it provoked her to answer more sharply than she intended.

'Look after him, of course. His owners—if he ever had any—don't seem to want him. I shall find him a good home.'

'Most commendable,' observed the doctor smoothly, 'but I doubt if Mevrouw Van Minnen will—er—welcome him as a member of the household, even for a short stay. He's a farm dog, you know, with a reputation for fierceness and a lamentable habit of biting people he doesn't like.'

Harriet didn't answer at once. Then, 'You—you don't think anyone would like him for a pet?'

'Decidedly not.' He was very positive.

She sat silent. 'You wouldn't like to have him, would you?' she said at last. 'He'd be nice company for J. B. and Flotsam.'

She knew it was a forlorn hope, for hadn't he just said that no one would want the poor beast?

Friso slowed down to enter his gateway. 'You know,' he said gently, 'I think perhaps that's a good idea.' His voice gave her no inkling of the probable dog-fights which lay ahead of him.

He pulled up in front of the door, there was a light on in the hall, she could see his face in its gentle glow.

'Oh, Friso, thank you. I'll come and see him.'

She saw him grin. 'Rather a long journey from England, I fancy. You'll have to rely on my good nature and regular bulletins from Sieske.'

She looked away. Once she had gone, he would add her to his list of other, perhaps forgotten girls. The thought hurt, but there was nothing to do about it. She said, determinedly cheerful,

'I know he'll be happy with you. I'm very grateful. Thank you for being so kind.' She was unable to keep the relief from her voice. 'I'm sure you won't regret it.'

If she had hoped for wholehearted agreement on his part, she was doomed to disappointment, for he said nothing, but got out of the car and came round and helped her out without breaking his silence, unless she chose to count the low whistle he gave to the dog, who answered it by clambering over the back of the Land-Rover and coming to stand by them, shivering.

The door opened before Friso could reach for his key. Anna was in the hall, looking large and motherly in a voluminous dressing-gown. She started to talk at once, and although Harriet couldn't understand a word of it, she was lulled by the sympathy in her voice. She had been helped half out of her jacket when she stopped suddenly.

'But I must go back to the Van Minnens.'

'At one o'clock in the morning? I asked the police to call up one of their men in Franeker with their walkie-talkie—he'll take them a message; he will have delivered it by now and everyone will have gone to bed, knowing that you are safe.'

Wim had appeared silently, and the doctor handed him the soaking coats and said, 'Sit down,' to Harriet and started to pull off her boots. 'Ah, yes,' he went on, 'the dog.' He explained at some length, speaking Fries, because Wim and Anna preferred it. They made sympathetic sounds when he had finished, and

Wim went away and returned presently with a large towel with which he started to dry the dog.

'Shall I do that?' asked Harriet. 'After all, it's because of me that he's here.'

'Wim likes dogs,' Friso answered shortly, 'so does Anna. You can be sure that he will be dried and fed and bedded down in greater comfort than he has ever known in his life before. You are going to have a bowl of Anna's famous onion soup and then you're going to bed.'

He pulled her to her feet, and smiled down at her, and for a moment Harriet forgot that she would be going away in a few days and would never see him again, and that the future was lonely and hopeless. She smiled back at him, her heart in her eyes.

She sat in the small sitting-room where they had had tea, and drank her soup. Friso had some too, and Anna went silently to and fro, watching eagle-eyed that she ate it all up. Afterwards she sat in a gentle stupor. 'That soup was wonderful,' she murmured. 'I feel as though I've had a glass of brandy,' and sat bolt upright in her chair when Friso said,

'You have. Anna's onion soup is something rather special. She puts in cheese and fried bread and pours brandy over them, then adds the soup. Anna is worth her not inconsiderable weight in gold.'

He got up and took her bowl away and gave her a cup of creamy coffee. She drank it, wondering what he had thought of the stew he had eaten in the cottage. She very much doubted if Anna used anything in tins—it must have tasted terrible to someone who liked his soup made with brandy... As though she had said it all out loud, he went on, 'But I never tasted anything better than that stew this evening.'

It was silly to feel so elated. She allowed herself to be led upstairs by Anna, wrapped in a dream induced by brandy and sleepiness, and the mixture of excitement and fright which she had had to hold in check all the evening. Under Anna's motherly eye, she bathed, donned the proffered nightgown and got into bed, to fall asleep within seconds.

CHAPTER EIGHT

SHE AWOKE TO a pale watery sunshine and sat up in bed and took stock of her surroundings. It was a pretty room—the sort of room the daughter of the house might have had, she supposed. The furniture was eighteenth-century and allied with a pink and white Toile de Jouy. Presently she got out of bed and went to look out of the window. The room was at the back of the house, overlooking the little fountain in the formal garden; even under the half-hearted sky it was a charming sight. She went back to bed, stopping on the way to look at herself in the triple mirror on the dressing-table. She frowned as she studied the nightgown—it was silk, real silk, and trimmed with a great deal of lace. It was just a little too big for her, although a perfect fit for the stunning blonde who had come to Sieske's party—it would probably fit the brunette too, thought Harriet viciously. She got back into bed, a prey to a variety of thoughts, none of them pleasant, and all of them becoming rapidly more and more exaggerated. It was a good thing when a strapping girl with beautiful eyes and lint-coloured hair brought in her morning tea. There was a note on the tray in Friso's handwriting. She read the untidy scrawl. 'Breakfast in half an hour' was all it said.

He was in the hall with the three dogs when she went down.

J. B. and Flotsam were standing belligerently on either side of him, eyeing the newcomer with ill-concealed dislike.

'Hullo, Harry,' said Friso. 'Have you a name for your friend? If so will you call him over to you?'

She didn't need to call, for the dog had heard her step on the stair and turned to prance on clumsy paws to greet her. She saw that he had been bathed and combed, and carried all the signs of a dog recently well fed. He sat down beside her, facing the other dogs. She put a hand on his head and he grinned. He belonged.

'I thought Moses would be a good name—the water, you see.'

Friso smiled. 'A splendid name. J. B. and Flotsam will think he's yours; they're more likely to accept him in that case. Shall we go and have breakfast? I've a surgery in half an hour. I'll take you back afterwards.'

He opened a door she hadn't been through before—the room beyond was small, its one big window overlooking the front drive. It was furnished in the style of Biedermeyer—the walnut chairs glowed with polish, as did the heavy side table. There was a peach-coloured cloth and napkins on the breakfast table, palely echoing the heavy curtains drawn back from the window. Breakfast, Harriet noted, as she took the chair Friso held for her, was served in some splendour and calculated to tempt the most finicky appetite. Which hers was not. She poured the coffee and handed Friso a cup and went scarlet when he said, 'You slept well? You must have found my sister's nightgown rather on the large side—she's a big girl, and you, if I may say so, are not.'

Before she could stop herself she blurted out, 'It was your sister's? I thought…' and then, appalled, added, 'I—I beg your pardon.'

His grey eyes held hers across the table. He said evenly,

'Now I wonder what other idea you could possibly have had in that pretty little head of yours?'

She was saved from replying to this unanswerable question by a slight fracas between the dogs. J. B. and Flotsam had

edged towards Moses, and were now each side of him, showing
their teeth, and he, who could have made mincemeat of them
both, was obviously restraining himself from doing just that.
He was, after all, something of a guest and despite his tramp's
appearance, retained half-forgotten canine manners. He showed
his own teeth in warning, then dropped his lip meekly in company with the other dogs, while Friso called them to account,
which he did in a tone of voice which brooked no disobedience.
Peace restored, he apparently forgot that he had had no reply to
his question, for he began at once to tell her about the accident
on the dyke—a foreign plane, off course, had crashed and ex-
ploded. What with the damage and the high tide and the gale,
it had triggered off the chain of events which had led them to
spend so long at the cottage under the dyke. They finished their
meal, with Friso talking with a casual ease which lulled her into
believing that she had imagined the anger in his eyes. He looked
at his watch at length and said, 'I must go—' then got up and
pulled the embroidered bell rope by the carved open fireplace.
'Anna shall take you to the sitting-room—if you could amuse
yourself there for an hour or so.' His glance fell upon Moses.
'Perhaps you had better take him with you.'

She curled up in a large armchair in the sitting-room, the
dog beside her, and leafed her way through a variety of glossy
magazines, but for once their contents couldn't hold her attention. She got up and wandered around, looking at the books,
which seemed to be in a variety of languages, and studying
the portraits on the walls. An hour seemed a very long time,
there was still five minutes of it left by the carriage clock on
the mantelshelf when she opened the door leading to the salon
and went in. There was plenty to see here—a glass-topped table
on slender legs, displaying a collection of small silver, a great
glass-fronted William and Mary china cabinet, its shelves filled
with plates and cups and bowls and little figures. She examined
everything slowly, picturing Friso living here, surrounded by it
all, his ancestors staring down at him from their heavy gilded

frames. She turned her attention to these now, and was standing before a full-length portrait of a haughty-looking young woman in a yellow crinoline when the door opened and the doctor came in.

'You didn't mind me coming in here?' Harriet wanted to know.

He closed the door gently behind him and leaned against it. 'No,' he said, 'my house is yours, my dear Harriet.'

She turned back to the portrait, feeling her cheeks warm. He had called her that once before—his dear Harriet—his very dear Harriet. Perhaps it was just a way of talking… She looked rather beseechingly at the owner of the crinoline.

'My great-grandmother,' said Friso from behind her. 'A haughty piece—like you.'

She turned without thinking, and found herself within a couple of inches of his excellently tailored waistcoat. She tilted her head the better to make her point. 'I am not haughty,' she said indignantly.

'Let us put it to the test,' he said suavely. It was no use to try and free herself, for he had her fast by the shoulders. She saw him smile before his mouth came down on hers.

'And now tell me exactly what you meant at breakfast.'

She had been floating between heaven and earth—now her dream was doused with the cold water of reality, and because she was an honest girl, she didn't pretend not to understand him.

'It was unpardonable of me, and it was not my business.'

His hands tightened on her shoulders, but he was looking over her head with a curious intentness at his great-grandmother's chilly stare.

'You are sure that it's not your business, Harriet?'

She gulped back all the things she wanted to say. She would regret them bitterly later, and worse still, Friso would regret them too. Far better for them to remain the good friends they had become despite their frequent tiffs; there were only four days left now. She said with a casual friendliness which cost an effort, 'Of course I'm sure. Your friends—girl-friends—aren't my concern, but I hope you find one soon who will make you forget all the others.'

He had strolled over to the window, and stood with his hands in his pockets, his back to her. 'But I have.' He sounded flippant, and she was quick to hear it. She achieved a laugh. 'Until the next one comes along—I'll get my things, shall I, if you're ready to go?'

She didn't wait for a reply but went quickly upstairs to the charming room she had so happily slept in. As she passed the mirror she gave herself an angry look. 'What a fool you are,' she told her image, and blew her delightful nose with a violence calculated to check the tears she longed to shed.

They went in the Bentley. Friso was going on to Groningen after he had been to see Mevrouw Bal and the baby and he hadn't much time.

'This old girl gets me there and back with time to spare,' he explained.

Harriet observed, 'How nice,' in a hollow voice. It seemed like sacrilege to refer to a Bentley 'T', by Mulliner Park Ward with a registration number barely a year old, as an old lady.

He gave her a quick searching glance. 'Don't worry about Moses,' he said, and his voice was so kind that the tears ached in her throat. 'You'll see him again, you know.' He slowed down to thread his way through Franeker. 'He and Wim are good friends already and he'll be company for us all around the house.'

He drew up outside Dr Van Minnen's house, and dropped a hand over her clasped ones on her knee. 'Thank you for your help last night, Harry. We would have been in a pretty pickle if you hadn't turned up.'

Harriet turned and looked at him; her eyes looked enormous and very blue. 'I'm glad I was able to help, though I am sure you would have contrived something even if no one had come.' There wasn't time to say more, for the front door had been flung open and Mevrouw Van Minnen and Sieske were standing there waiting to welcome them. They all went inside, everyone talking at once and contriving to translate for Harriet as they went. Friso had just finished a rather brisk account of the night's happenings, when Dr Van Minnen came in from his surgery and demanded to have the whole tale again. More coffee was poured, and Friso began his tale once more, but this time in Fries, sitting comfortably back in one of the great armchairs, smoking his pipe, as though he had all day in which to do nothing. Harriet, watching him covertly, thought what a tranquil man he was; he never appeared to hurry, but she supposed that nothing would stop him doing something he had made up his mind to do.

Before she could look away he turned his head and stared across at her and suddenly smiled as though he had made a pleasant discovery. She caught her breath and heard Sieske say, 'Harry, wake up. Those two will talk shop for hours. I'm sure Friso left a great deal out—start again and tell us everything from the beginning.'

It took some time, for Sieske had to translate as she went along, and Mevrouw Van Minnen asked a great number of questions. She had only just finished when Friso got to his feet and said, 'Well, I must be off.'

He lifted a hand in general farewell and when he got to the door called to Sieske to go to the car with him; there was a medical journal he wanted his partner to have. They went out of the door together, and Harriet, who was sitting by the window, could see them standing on the pavement deep in conversation. She turned her back; he hadn't even bothered to smile at her when he went. She didn't look up when Sieske returned either, but went on trying to decipher the morning paper's headlines.

'Friso's taking us down to Amsterdam tomorrow.' said her friend, 'and he thinks he'll probably come and fetch us home again too.'

Harriet was up early the next morning and spent a great deal of time on her face and hair. She would be wearing the green outfit again, not, she told herself, because she would be seeing Friso, but because she was going to Amsterdam and wanted to look as nice as possible. She went down to breakfast, smelling deliciously of Fête. Everyone else was already at table, and as she slipped into her seat there were appreciative sniffs. Dr Van Minnen, deep in his morning paper, glanced over the top of it.

'You're both dressed to kill, I see,' he observed mildly. 'And very nice too.' He smiled at his daughter and Harriet. 'I wish you both a good trip—enjoy yourselves.'

He looked at his watch, drank his coffee and folded his paper neatly. On his way to the door he stooped to kiss his daughter's cheek, waved to Harriet, and disappeared surgerywards. Maggina and Taeike got up too, grumbling that they should have to go to school while everyone else had fun. Taeike said slowly, 'Do you think Friso would take us to Leeuwarden first, before you go?'

Sieske gave a little snort. 'Whatever next! Why should he? It's hard enough for him to find the time to take us as it is.'

'Then why does he?' asked Taeike rebelliously. 'You could quite well go by yourselves.' She went out, banging the door behind her, and Sieske said in answer to Harriet's questioning eyebrows, 'It's all right, she dotes on Friso—you see, she's known him most of her life and hates to be left out of anything he does.'

Harriet would have liked to pursue the subject, but there wasn't time. She went upstairs and put on the fetching turban picked up her handbag and overnight case and ran downstairs again in time to see Friso come in the front door. Her heart jumped and raced so that her breathlessness wasn't entirely due to the stairs. He stood in the hall, impeccably dressed and very assured, and his 'Good morning, Harriet' was coolly friendly, only as she got nearer she could see how his eyes twinkled. 'How very glamorous,' he observed. 'Enough to steal my heart, if you hadn't already done that.'

She blushed and looked uncertain, almost, but not quite, sure that he was teasing. It was fortunate for her peace of mind that Sieske and her mother came out of the dining-room and he turned, just in time to receive Sieske's nicely proportioned but not inconsiderable weight in his arms.

'Friso! You are a dear to take us—I telephoned Tante Tonia and she says you must stay to lunch. You will, won't you? I said you would.' She gave him a slow sweet smile. 'We shall be there long before midday, and you'll have time enough.'

He gave her an avuncular hug. 'I see that you have got it all arranged, you scheming girl! Poor Wierd,' he added in mock horror. 'Has no one warned him of your true nature?' He gave her a gentle push. 'Go and fetch your things. Harriet's sitting here like Patience on a monument.'

Harriet drew her brows together. 'That's quite inapt,' she said tartly, 'for I'm not smiling at grief, nor am I turning green and yellow.'

He gave her a mocking smile. 'My apologies to you and Shakespeare, my dear girl. You're neither green nor yellow, and I'm quite prepared to take your word for it that you're not smiling at grief—if you say so.'

Harriet inclined her head slightly, looking, she hoped, remote, but it was lost on Friso, who went to the stairs to bellow at Sieske to hurry herself up and then started talking to Mevrouw Van Minnen in Fries, with a casual apology over one shoulder for doing so. Harriet had the darkling thought that Friso might not be best pleased at taking them to Amsterdam—she would have dearly loved to find out who had suggested it in the first place, but Sieske came racing down the stairs and into the car, and there was no chance to say a word to her. She wasn't sure how she came to be sitting beside Friso; but there was Sieske, sitting in the back of the car, reading a letter from Wierd which she hadn't had time to open, and here he was inquiring if she was comfortable. She said, 'Yes, thank you,' in a meek voice, and he let in the clutch.

He took the route over the great dyke across the Ijsselmeer, and kept up a gentle flow of conversation that needed little answering. Harriet listened to his slow deep voice with its faintly accented English, and tried to imagine what life would be like when she went back to England, and there would be no Friso. It did not bear thinking about, but of one thing she was sure, she would dream no more. She sighed, and stifled the sigh as he said, 'You wretched girl, you're not listening to a word I'm saying; I could have saved my breath.'

'I did hear, indeed I did, but a thought came into my head.'

He was looking straight ahead. 'A very sad thought, I take it.'

'Well, yes. I'm sorry, I'm not very good company.' She peeped at his profile. It looked stern; then he turned and smiled before she could look away and she found herself smiling too.

He said, 'You are at all times a good companion, Harriet, and the only one I want.'

She stared at him, the colour washing over her pretty face. He was looking ahead again. She longed for him to turn his head so that she could see his eyes, although common sense told her that he was unlikely to do so while driving the car past a huge trans-Europe transport at sixty miles an hour. When next he spoke it was over his shoulder to Sieske. 'We'll stop at Hoorn, shall we? We can have coffee at that place over the Weigh House—unless you can think of anywhere you'd rather go.'

Sieske deliberated with her usual placid charm and said, 'Yes, that would be delightful, and if there's a telephone there I'll ring up Wierd—he's going to try and come over to Amsterdam the day after tomorrow.' She subsided into a happy silence, clutching Wierd's letter.

The café over the Weigh House was delightful; it had somehow caught the atmosphere of the little town. Harriet peered out of the window and was quite prepared to agree with Friso when he said that Hoorn hadn't changed very much in the last three hundred years. Presently Sieske went away to telephone.

'How's Moses?' asked Harriet, very conscious of Friso's calm stare across the little table.

'Eating me out of house and home. Oh, don't worry, he'll be

worth his keep—I'm sorry for anyone who tries to get into the house uninvited. The three of them would confound the enemy, tear him limb from limb and bring me the pieces in triumph. I think he misses you.'

The softness of Harriet's heart was reflected in her face.

'I shall miss him too,' she said regretfully. She was about to say something else when she caught the doctor's eye. Something in his face set her pulse hurrying. His voice sounded different too.

'And if I tell you that I shall miss you a great deal more than Moses, what will be your answer, my dear Harriet?'

She didn't say anything, because she was unable to think of the right words, but she felt her happiness bubble up inside her and smiled; not just with her mouth, but with her eyes too. A small sensible voice inside her head was reminding her that she was in grave danger of joining the luscious blonde and the beautiful brunette, and possibly a number of other young ladies on his list. She turned a deaf ear, for none of them seemed real; only she and Friso were real, staring at each other across the table's width. He smiled. 'You may have cautioned your tongue to remain silent, but you're quite powerless to stop your eyes saying what they want to.' He stretched a hand out to take hers and hold it fast; it was firm and cool and his touch sent a tingling up her arm. Sieske came back and he made no effort to release her, and the pink in her cheeks deepened, but her friend, after one swift glance, started a rather involved explanation of Wierd's plans to meet them.

'He's arranged everything,' she said happily. 'You'll be worn out with sightseeing, Harry, but it's your only chance.'

Harriet avoided Friso's eye. 'You're a dear to arrange it all, Sieske, and I know I shall love it. Never mind if it's a rush, I'll have plenty of time to sort it all out when I get home.'

'You won't, you know,' said Sieske. 'You'll be far too busy being a ward sister; your head will be full of cutdowns and operation cases and getting the off-duty worked out to please everyone.'

Harriet sighed. 'I'd forgotten. But I'll have off duty and days off.' Sitting there, with Friso's hand over hers, the future looked singularly uninviting; after all, Friso hadn't really said anything to alter it. She cast around desperately for another topic of conversation.

'That reminds me,' she said, and the relief of having thought of something showed on her face, 'I wanted to ask you something.' Her glance in Friso's direction was so fleeting that she quite failed to see the look of amusement on his face. 'You and Mijnheer Bal were talking in that attic and you recited something and he joined in, and you said that if I reminded you, you would explain it to me.'

She tried, with no success at all, to withdraw her hand and felt his fingers tighten. 'Ah, yes. Our ancient Friesian oath; you know it, of course, Sieske.' He started to speak in his own tongue, rolling out the incomprehensible words in his quiet slow voice. When he had finished Harriet said, 'There were two English words—ebb and flood.'

'That's right—our language has a certain similarity to your own. I'll translate it, though it won't sound so splendid. I imagine the men who first uttered it were tough, but they lived in tough times. It goes something like this. "With five weapons shall we keep our land, with sword and with shield, with spade and with fork and with the spear, out with the ebb, up with the flood, to fight day and night against the North-king and against the wild Viking, that all Friesians may be free, the born and the unborn, so long as the wind from the clouds shall blow and the world shall stand".'

Harriet said quietly, 'I like it.' She repeated, '"So long as the wind from the clouds shall blow"—that's for ever.'

'We are a persistent race; we do not give up easily, nor do we let go.' The grey eyes bored into hers. 'For ever is a long time—

loving is for ever, too. So long as the wind from the clouds shall blow. Remember that, my dear Harriet.'

She stared back at him. How could she forget, and what exactly did he mean? And now she would probably never know, for he had released her hand and was paying the bill, and telling Sieske that if they wanted to powder their noses they had better hurry up.

For the rest of the journey the talk was of places and things and the world in general. She took but a token share in the conversation while she tried to remember everything that Friso had said, and in consequence became so bewildered that she had to be told twice that they had reached the outskirts of Amsterdam. Tante Tonia had a flat on the Weesperzijde. The houses were tall and narrow with basements and steps up to their front doors; on the other side of the street was the Amstel river, its broad surface constantly ruffled by the laden barges chugging one way or the other—a fact which, to Harriet's way of thinking, more than compensated for the basements. The street was quiet too, trams ran along the main street at the end, it was true, but their noise was quite drowned by the constant, hooting on the river and the peculiar thumping noise of the diesel engines on the barges.

Friso stopped half-way down and told them to go on ahead while he got their bags. They mounted the steps and Sieske pressed the second bell in the gleaming row of bells, each with its little visiting card, at the side of the door. The door gave a click and opened, and they went up the precipitous staircase to the first floor.

Tante Tonia was waiting for them—she was like her sister, but in a large, cosy fashion. Mevrouw Van Minnen was what was commonly called a fine figure of a woman, Tante Tonia was frankly plump, with grey hair severely drawn back from a face whose eyes were still a bright youthful blue; and held only lines of laughter. She greeted them warmly, speaking a fluent, ungrammatical and dreadfully muddled English which none-

theless lost none of its sincerity. The girls were bustled into the
sitting-room where Oom Jan repeated the embraces and made
them welcome in an English as pedantically correct as an old-
fashioned textbook; but he broke into Dutch as he caught sight
of Friso in the doorway, leaving his wife, after exchanging
greetings with the doctor, to carry off her guests to the room
they were to share.

Ten minutes later, they were sitting round the square table in
the comfortable old-fashioned dining-room. Harriet had combed
her hair and done things to her face; she settled herself in the
chair opposite Friso, conscious that she was looking her best,
and that she had used just sufficient Fête to surround herself
in a tantalizingly faint cloud of perfume. She saw Oom Jan's
nostrils twitch appreciatively and caught Friso's eye across the
table. He was smiling, but she didn't smile back, for she dis-
cerned a mocking twinkle in his gaze; she gave Oom Jan her
full attention and ate a good lunch and tried to pretend, without success, that Friso wasn't there. It was a relief when they all
went into the sitting-room for coffee, but the relief was tempered
by her knowledge that he would get up and go at any moment.
He did in fact do just that, much sooner than she had expected.
She watched him say his goodbyes with a sinking heart and
listened to his plans to fetch them in two days' time stifling a
strong desire to go back with him to Franeker. The time was
so short—she would see him once, perhaps twice before she
left. Her gloomy thoughts were interrupted by his cool voice.

'Come down to the door with me, will you, Harriet?'

She got up wordlessly and followed him out of the flat down
the steep stairs. He opened the door and they stood on the top
step in the sunshine and because she could not bear the silence
any longer she said,

'Please give my love to Moses.'

'Of course. Why did you scowl so at luncheon?'

Harriet examined the pink nails of one hand, and said un-
truthfully,

'I did not scowl!' and added, 'You were laughing at me.'

'But you have a most endearing habit of making me laugh at you. Didn't you know that?' He possessed himself of one of her hands. 'Shall you be glad to see me when I come to fetch you?'

She looked at him then. He wasn't laughing at her now; his grey eyes were tender and sparkling, but his face was grave. She said equally gravely, 'Yes, I shall be glad to see you again, Friso.'

He kissed her on the mouth with a gentleness she hadn't expected of him. 'Dear Harriet. You still remember the Friesian oath?'

She was still a little breathless from his kiss. 'Yes.'

'Good. So long as the wind from the clouds shall blow—my dear.'

He was gone. She stood on the steps and waved, then went back upstairs, to present to the people waiting there a face transformed by happiness.

CHAPTER NINE

THE NEXT DAY was a cataclysm of sound and colour, historical buildings, museums and canals. Harriet, sitting beside Sieske in one of the boats touring the canals of the city, craned her pretty neck to see everything, while her ears tried to take in the information offered in Sieske's soft slow voice, Tante Tonia's quick, much louder one, and Oom Jan's precise English, spoken with such deliberation that he was inevitably describing some subject already dealt with by his wife and niece. Harriet nodded agreeably to each piece of information and concentrated on Oom Jan who appeared to know his Amsterdam like the back of his hand. Back on dry land, a brisk altercation, conducted in the friendliest of terms, took place. The ladies, naturally enough, considered that the shops were a vital part of the sightseeing programme, whereas Oom Jan, who detested shopping with females, urged a visit to the Rijksmuseum, followed by a look at the Mint Tower and the Begijnhof Almshouses. He was, of course, doomed to failure. Sieske pointed out in her calm way that the Mint Tower was at the end of the Kalverstraat, where all the best shops were, and that it would be the easiest thing in the world to turn aside half-way down this fascinating thoroughfare and spend a little time in the Begijnhof, which was a mere stone's throw from it. It was a happy solution, for the ladies left their escort to browse in a bookshop, and spent an agreeable half hour window-shopping, before allowing him to lead them to the Begijnhof. Harriet was delighted with the peaceful little place; it seemed incredible that anything so quiet could exist for centuries in the heart of the bustling city. She wanted most desperately Friso to be there too, so that she could tell him how she felt. Her mouth curved into a happy smile at the thought of seeing him again. The fact that she was leaving in two days' time wasn't important any more; all that mattered was what Friso would say to her before she went...

Via the Mint Tower, they crossed the Munt Plein and took coffee in the comparative luxury of the Hotel de l'Europe, so that they could watch the unending traffic on the water; and then made their leisurely way down the Leidseweg towards the museum. It was cool inside the big rooms, and they wandered through their vastness, gazing at a seemingly unending vista of paintings. It was almost one o'clock by the time they had finished, and when Oom Jan suggested lunch in the museum restaurant they lost no time in following him through the big glass doors and allowing themselves to be led to a table by the window. The food was good; soup—real soup, not out of a tin; Wienerschnitzel with tiny peas and potatoes creamed to incredible smoothness, and a sweet composed largely of whipped cream. Harriet devoured it all with a healthy appetite and obediently drank the glass of wine she was offered. Presently, relaxed and revitalized, they started to plan their afternoon.

'The Palace,' said Sieske, 'and probably you'll see one of those street organs you asked about.'

Harriet smiled at her friend, thinking what a dear she was; she was going to miss her when she got back to hospital. She dragged her thoughts away from the future; time enough to do that in two days' time.

'No good,' said Tante Tonia, 'the Palace isn't open today—we'll have to fit it in tomorrow. What about diamonds?'

It was a happy thought. The afternoon passed quickly, for

after a visit to Van Moppes' diamond showrooms, they walked down some of the narrow streets lining the canals, peering into the small shop windows of countless antique dealers. They took their tea in a very small room behind a pastrycooks', where the cakes were so various and rich that Harriet was quite unable to choose for herself and ate her way happily through a rich confection of chocolate and cream and nuts which Sieske assured her was delicious; she would have eaten a second of these confections if her host had not looked at his watch and declared that if they didn't go home that minute they would be late.

'What for?' they asked, but he laughed and refused to say, merely exchanging a conspiratorial smile with his wife. It wasn't until they were sitting down doing justice to various cold meats and an enormous bowl of salad that he answered their question.

'I have seats for the Stadsschouwburg—The Netherlands Opera Company are performing *Tosca*.' He smiled, well pleased with the girls' delight and they finished the meal in a little rush of excitement, which augured well for the success of the evening. And success it was—the theatre was bright with lights and pleasantly crowded. Their seats were a little to the side of the circle with an excellent view of the stage. They settled themselves comfortably and whiled what time there was before the curtain went up by studying the audience and discussing what they would do when Wierd arrived the following morning. He would have to go back about tea time, but Sieske was determined to make use of him and his car. A short trip, she thought, before lunch at Scheveningen. Harriet agreed happily to everything suggested. Friso was to come after tea; until then she didn't mind in the least what she did. The curtain rose, and she became absorbed in the music, and perhaps because she was so much in love herself, almost burst into tears as the tragic story unfolded itself.

It was fortunate that the interval intervened and Oom Jan whisked them all away to the foyer to drink something dark red and velvety in a glass, which had the immediate effect of mak-

ing her feel very cheerful indeed, but later caused her to feel
more and more sad at the complications the people on the stage
were forced to endure. But by the time the opera was finished
she had quite recovered her volatile spirits and was delighted to
be taken to a café for coffee before going back to the Weesperzijde, to go to bed and sleep almost immediately, while listening to Sieske's soothing voice from the next bed, still plotting
and planning for the next day.

The sun was shining when they got up. It was still early by
the time they had had breakfast, but they had barely finished
their coffee when Wierd arrived. Sieske went downstairs to meet
him, and Harriet wondered if she would have the chance to do
the same when Friso arrived that evening. The thought made
her smile, so that Wierd wanted to know if it was Amsterdam
that made her look so happy. She said seriously,

'Amsterdam is lovely, but Friesland is beautiful.' She looked
dreamily out of the window, not seeing the street outside, but
Friso, busy with his patients, and only turned round when she
heard Sieske say,

'Well, you're going back this evening, Harry. But now Wierd
wants to take us to the Keukenhof gardens.' She slipped an arm
into that of her fiancé. 'And then perhaps Den Haag—and we
can eat at Saur's.'

'That'll be nice,' Harriet said. Indeed, she had only a slim
idea as to what the Keukenhof was, and didn't much care, but
if it was a pleasant way of passing a day, that was all right. She
went to get a jacket and her handbag, wondering if 'evening'
meant just after tea or quite late. She wanted very much to ask
Sieske if Friso had a surgery to take before he came to fetch
them, but she felt shy of talking about him, even to Sieske. She
mooned about, doing unnecessary things to her face and hair,
and was quite surprised when Sieske put her head round the
door, and asked, her usual placidity ruffled, 'Harry, what do
you do? You have to fetch only your jacket and bag, and it is
already ten minutes.'

Harriet was opening and shutting drawers in a guilty fashion. She turned a rather pink face to her friend, and said,

'I'm sorry, I was thinking about—'

She stopped herself in time, and ended tamely, 'Just thinking.' She looked so contrite that Sieske smiled at her.

'It will be beautiful in the Keukenhof, Harry; it is like Friso's garden, but many hundred times larger.' She went over to the mirror and poked at her pretty hair, missing Harriet's sudden vivid blush.

There was another delay occasioned by Tante Tonia, who gave a good many well-meaning instructions as to how they could reach the Keukenhof in the shortest time and the most suitable method with which to explore it when they got there. When they finally reached the car, Wierd said, speaking in his careful English, 'We have the time to go along the little roads, if you would like, Harry.'

Harriet, sitting in the back and watching a very long, very thin barge glide down the Amstel, agreed very readily to this plan. The motorways were wonderful if you need to get from here to there in a hurry, but it seemed that today there was no need of that. They drove through the ordered incomprehensible confusion of Amsterdam's traffic into the comparative quiet of Amstelveen, where they turned off on to a road running along the top of a dyke, which had the double attraction of Schipol on one side of it, and a canal on the other. Harriet, anxious to miss nothing, craned her neck to look at everything her companions felt she should see and listened to Wierd while he gave her a potted history of the Haarlemmermeer Polder. He did it very well, only she did wish that he wouldn't use such long and difficult words—it couldn't be because he wanted to air his English, because he wasn't that sort of man at all. Her ears rang with strange Dutch names from long ago, and detailed accounts of windmills and steam pumps and their uses, as well as a great many useful and interesting facts which Sieske slipped in from time to time. It was a relief to reach Aalsmeer where they stopped for coffee, and explained to her why they weren't going to stop there for her to see the flower auction. 'It'll take a long time to see it properly,' Sieske pointed out, 'and then we should have to hurry round the Keukenhof if we're going to The Hague as well. When you come to visit us again—' she blushed faintly, 'Wierd and me—we can come.'

Harriet said, 'Yes, of course,' and smiled, mostly at her own secret thoughts—perhaps Friso would be with her.

They left Aalsmeer by the same road so that Harriet could have a glimpse of the lake, then Wierd turned down what he described as a local road, bisecting the *polder*, until they came to another canal with its accompany road, which in due time led them to Lisse and the Keukenhof.

Harriet hadn't quite known what to expect, certainly not the blaze of colour which met her eyes. They got out of the car, and Wierd said, 'No plan, I think? Just to amble?'

Harriet was only too delighted to agree, having already ambled in several directions just to make sure that everything was real. It was surprisingly quiet and free from people; the coachloads and bus tours, said Wierd, would come about lunch time. They wandered up and down the paths and along the edge of the water, where the flowers grew as though nature had put them there and not astute bulb-growers with an eye to getting big orders. The water was criss-crossed with little rustic bridges; they were half-way over one of these when Harriet's eye was caught by a group of people coming towards them from the other side. Well in advance of the others walked a smallish figure, escorted by a tall man, talking animatedly. They were very close to Harriet when she realized who it was. She looked round rather wildly for Sieske, who had stopped with Wierd to hang over the bridge to watch the fish. They were standing with their backs to the balustrade, looking unconcerned, as were the few people opposite them. All anyone had done, as far as she could see, was to move back as far as possible to make a little more room. She did the same thing herself a bare moment before Queen Beatrix walked past, flashing a pleasant smile as she went, followed by the members of her entourage, struggling manfully to keep up the pace. When they had gone, and the small brisk figure was no longer visible, Harriet joined the others, open-mouthed.

'That was Queen Beatrix,' she said.

'That's right,' Sieske's voice was as calm and unhurried as ever it was. 'She comes here because she loves to look at the flowers too, but she does not care to make an occasion of it—she prefers that we do not stare or gather to watch her.'

'Oh? Well, I'm so glad I've seen her. She looked charming and just as a queen should look—she smiled at me too. Who was the man with her?'

Wierd answered. 'That would be the Directeur of the Keukenhof, and the people with her are the members of her household.'

'She walked very fast,' commented Harriet. 'The people at the back were almost running.'

'Our Queen,' said Wierd a trifle pompously, 'is a very energetic person—she is also much loved by her people.'

Harriet saw that he was slightly hurt and very much in earnest. She said hastily, 'I'm sorry if I sounded if I was criticizing the Queen. I didn't mean to. I like and admire her very much and I'm very happy to have seen her.' She smiled at her two friends. Meeting the Queen seemed a sort of good luck symbol for the future…she sighed on a sudden little glow of happiness and asked,

'Those tulips over there by the trees—they're gorgeous. What are they called?'

Sieske followed her gaze. 'Kaufmanniana,' she murmured knowledgeably. 'Gluck, I think. Is it not so, Wierd?'

He nodded. 'Yellow and carmine—Friso has some in his garden; you will have seen them?' He looked inquiringly at Harriet, who to her vexation felt her cheeks grow hot at Friso's name. But she answered coolly enough, 'So he has, by the pool.' Her words conjured up such a clear picture of herself standing on

Friso's verandah with Friso beside her that for a moment she forgot where she was.

Sieske gave her a long considered look. 'You will see them again,' she said positively, and Harriet, certain of it too, flashed a smile that caused Wierd to say, 'How very happy you look, Harriet. It is as though you are in...' He didn't finish his sentence, for his future bride had given him an unseen but none the less extremely painful kick on the shin with a well-shod size seven. Rendered speechless with pain, he caught her warning eye; but his drastic reminder had been unnecessary, for Harriet had not been paying attention anyway. She had caught sight of a bed of yellow hyacinths she had admired in Friso's garden. She searched her memory. 'City of Haarlem,' she said dreamily, and smiled again at nothing at all, not noticing the understanding glances her companions exchanged as they started to stroll along beside her.

'If you come this way,' suggested Wierd, 'there are some daffodils—jonquils. If you remember Friso has them naturalized beside that little path between the glasshouses and the house.'

Of course she remembered. Friso had kissed her by the potting shed and they had walked down that same path together. The three of them stopped by the sweet-smelling bed; its fragrance made memory even more vivid. She beamed at Wierd. 'What a lovely day this is being,' she breathed.

It had turned fine, with a well-washed sky and pale sunshine, which despite its lack of warmth held a promise of summer. It was pleasant amongst the flowers and the newly leafed trees. The storm and flood seemed distant and vague, like some half-forgotten news she had read a long time ago. But it was only three days. Time, she discovered, had very little meaning for her, only in relation to the amount of it she had to spend away from Friso. She no longer cared about the blonde, or the brunette, nor for that matter any other girl he most certainly had known at some time or other. She was a victim of her own dream, and she didn't care.

They got to The Hague in time for lunch. Harriet had felt a sharp disappointment as they passed through its suburbs, they were so remarkably unforeign, but as they got nearer the heart of the city, she could find no fault with it, by the time they had found somewhere to put the car and walked up Lange Voorhoust, she was quite enchanted with it.

Saur's was fun too. They went downstairs to the smart, expensive snack bar, crowded with young people like themselves eating delicious bits and pieces. Harriet left the ordering to Wierd and was surprised when he asked if she was hungry. She said simply, 'Yes, of course,' then added hurriedly, in case he was short of money, 'But a sandwich will do.'

He looked horrified. 'I ask only because you are so small a person and perhaps eat only a little.'

Sieske giggled. 'Harry eats like a horse,' she eyed her friend's fragile form. 'No one know where it all goes to, for she always looks the same. If you order the same for her as you intend to order for us two outsizes, she'll eat every crumb of it.'

When the food came, her sapient remarks were completely justified. It seemed the restaurant was noted for its seafood. Harriet ate her way happily through everything put before her. She had imagined that, like so many lovesick women, she would have lost her splendid appetite, instead of which she was enjoying it all very much. It was after two o'clock by the time they had finished, and when she noticed the time, her heart gave a little leap at the thought that there were only a few hours before she would see Friso.

Naturally enough, after this pleasant interlude, the girls found it imperative to do a little window shopping. They admired the hats—unpriced in Van Dooren's window; speculated as to the cost of the fur coats in Kulme's, and were only dissuaded from going into La Bonneterie to inquire the price of an enchanting organza dress by Wierd, who pointed out that unless they intended to spend the rest of the day looking at clothes, which, he pointed out reasonably, were obtainable anywhere and probably far cheaper than in s'Gravenhage; it was high time they were on their way to Scheveningen.

Their combined efforts to make him see the silliness of his remarks about clothes being the same anywhere lasted until they reached the car, and, as far as they could see, had no success at all.

The sea looked cold; slow, pale blue waves rolled in steadily on to the wide sands. The three of them walked along the sea front, the wind tangling their hair; it had a nip in it which made them step out briskly. They admired the hotels lining the broad road, and gazed at the famous pier, then turned back to walk the other way so that Harriet could see the fishermen's wives in their costume. She wished she had brought her camera; instead, she bought a great number of postcards; it was amazing what a lot of people there were to whom she hadn't sent this proof of being abroad. They went back to the car at length, discussing where they should have tea. Sieske's quiet persistence won the day and Harriet found herself back at The Hague, taking tea amidst the Victorian splendour of Maison Krul. It was a leisurely little meal and inevitably the talk was of the wedding. When they at length got up to go, Wierd decided to go back to Amsterdam on the motorway. 'I don't know what time Friso is coming,' he said, 'but I don't suppose he'll want to wait around, and I must get back myself.'

They shared the motorway with a horde of other drivers, all presumably competing in a Le Mans of their own. Wierd apparently shared their ambition, for he did his best to out-Jehu them; it seemed with some success, for as they reached the outskirts of Amsterdam, he looked at his watch and announced with quiet pride that he had knocked off three minutes of his previous record. Harriet, who was a tolerable driver herself, applauded his efforts, and acquitted herself so well in the ensuing conversation that he confided to Sieske afterwards that for a foreigner, her friend Harriet was a very sensible girl, as well as being pretty, if you happened to like small women. Sieske smiled at him fondly and said nothing. She was very fond of Harry, and she liked everyone else to like her too; they almost always did.

It was still quite early as they rounded the last corner into the Weesperzijde. There were already a great many cars parked along the side of the street, none of them Friso's Harriet felt disappointment like a physical pain take possession of her. The faint hope that he had parked somewhere else and was in the flat waiting for them was quickly dispelled when they arrived at the top of the stairs and found Tante Tonia standing at her door. Quite a few minutes were wasted while she wanted to know if they had had a good day and had the weather been fine and what did they think of the Keukenhof this year. When, after what seemed like hours to Harriet, they went into the sitting-room it was to find it empty. She went a little pale, fending off a premonition that something, somewhere, had gone wrong. Her dismal thoughts were cut short by Tante Tonia asking her if she was tired. 'For you look rather white. It is perhaps good that you do not return to Franeker this evening.' She smiled at them both, a bearer of what she thought was good news. 'Friso telephoned—he regrets that he cannot come for you. I am to tell you you will be fetched tomorrow morning, after breakfast.'

Harriet felt a little better. It was a bitter disappointment, but tomorrow morning wasn't far off. He must have been called out on a case or got held up in some way. Being a doctor's daughter, she was able to think of half a dozen causes which could upset the best laid plans. She cheered herself up with this reflection, and resolutely ignored a niggling doubt at the back of her mind that there was something...

It was half-way through the evening meal that she found herself wondering if he would telephone, and apparently Sieske had thought the same thing, for when Oom Jan suggested a walk and a cup of coffee, she asked if there was anyone to take a message if they were out.

'But why should he telephone again?' asked Oom Jan reasonably. 'He has already said what he had to say, and tomorrow morning you will go home.'

There was no argument against his logic. They fetched their coats, and accompanied their host and hostess down the stairs and out on to the pavement, where they turned their faces towards the imposing pile of the Amstel Hotel. It was a pleasant evening, cool and windy, and the Amstel, still loaded with traffic, reflected the evening sky and gave a glow to its surroundings. They turned the corner and went over the bridge and past the hotel. Harriet had a good look at it as they went slowly past. It looked remote and welcoming at the same time; she thought that she would like to stay there and wondered if she ever would. They crossed the Amstel again and turned their steps towards the centre of the city, and Tante Tonia and Oom Jan argued equably as to which was the best place to have coffee. They settled for the Haven restaurant, which was thirteen floors up and afforded a fine view of the whole city, so that Harriet almost forgot how unhappy she was and spent a delightful hour picking out landmarks under the others' guidance. They had drinks as well, and a great many sorts of tiny savoury biscuits to nibble. She had advocaat and enjoyed it very much.

Surprisingly, she slept all night, although her last troubled thoughts had been of Friso. He hadn't telephoned while they had been out; there was no need to do so this morning. It was the first thing that she thought of when she awoke—that he would be coming in a few hours' time. She lay in bed, impatient of the clock, and at last got up earlier than usual on the pretext of writing another batch of postcards; it was better than doing nothing. Sieske woke up after half an hour or so, stretched and yawned and lay watching her friend. 'I shall miss you very much, Harry,' she said at length. 'Just because you are going back to England our friendship does not end, you understand?'

Harriet put down her cards—it was a dull job, anyway—and said with emphasis, 'Of course not, Sieske. You'll both be over to see us as soon as you can, won't you?'

'First you will be here, Harry, for you will be bridesmaid at my wedding.'

'So I shall,' said Harriet briskly. 'And that's only a month or two away. I must book my holidays.'

She paused. Hospital, that small world of its own, seemed unimportant. If—no, when she went back, it would absorb her ruthlessly and become her way of life again.

She jumped visibly when Sieske said idly, 'I wonder why Friso didn't come yesterday. It must have been something serious to keep him. He told me that he would come.' She turned a vague gaze upon Harriet. 'Did he not say so to you also?'

Harriet found her tongue. 'Yes, he did. I—I wondered too.'

Sieske got slowly out of bed and wandered around the room in search for her stockings. 'Well,' she remarked cheerfully, 'we'll soon know, for he'll be here after breakfast.'

The remark threw Harriet into a fever of activity. The cards were forgotten; she padded along to the bathroom on urgent feet, decided that her nails were in need of a manicure, and having put her hair up with extraordinary care pulled it all down again, declaring that she looked a complete fright. Throughout this exhibition of nerves on her part, Sieske had continued to dress herself without haste, making appropriate soothing noises at intervals, and contriving to get her down to the breakfast table not more than five minutes late. As they were leaving the bedroom she stopped in the doorway and looked back over a shoulder. 'He feels exactly the same as you do, Harry. At least, I'm almost sure he does—I've known him a long time.' She smiled into her friend's suddenly pink face and led the way to the dining-room.

For once, Harriet's splendid appetite had failed her, she sat at the table watching the minute hand crawl around the clock's face, making a roll last a very long time, and talking so much that no one noticed that she wasn't eating; but how could she eat when she was so happy? They had finished at length and the two girls were standing at the window when a car drew up in front of the house. It was neither the AC 428 nor the Bentley, but Dr Van Minnen's BMW.

'It's Father,' exclaimed Sieske, and then, 'And Maggina and Taeike.' She sounded puzzled, but went at her usual unhurried pace from the room. Harriet stayed where she was by the window, fighting a childish desire to burst into tears of disappointment, and what was worse, a growing unease. She tried not to look too eagerly at the doctor as he came into the room, and fancied that he looked uneasily at her, although he sounded as cheerful as usual.

'Good morning, Harry. You see we have all come to fetch you home. The girls are free today, and months ago I promised that I would take them to see the Dam Palace, and here we are. We shall drink coffee first, eh?' He looked at his sister-in-law. 'And then we will spend a little time at the Palace before we go back to Franeker. You will like that?' He added carefully, 'Friso regrets that he could not come.'

She ignored that and said, 'The Palace? How lovely.'

Her voice sounded full of false enthusiasm in her own ears, but apparently no one else thought so, for the talk went on uninterrupted around her and lasted right through coffee and their good-byes and during the car ride to the Dam Square.

It was while they were inside the Palace that Harriet found herself standing with Taeike at one end of the windows. They were in one of the salons and had turned their backs upon the glories of its Empire furniture and yellow brocade, to gaze at the bustle of the city all around them. Harriet was struggling to carry on a conversation without much success, for Taeike was proving a difficult companion, and Harriet's efforts were not perhaps as wholehearted as they might have been, for her mind was full of Friso. There was something wrong—very wrong; he could have telephoned or sent a note by Dr Van Minnen. He had done neither. They had parted the best of friends—more than friends, for there had been a promise of something more than friendship between them. She gave her head a weary little shake and asked a completely unnecessary question about the street organ in the square below. Her question wasn't answered, instead, Taeike said, 'Friso takes Vader's surgery this morning.'

The niggling doubt in the back of Harriet's mind resolved itself into something icily tangible, sending chilly fingers down her spine to make her shiver. She said merely, 'Oh?' and waited.

'Yesterday I saw him.' Taeike looked sideways at Harriet, who met the look with a credible smile.

'Did you? I expect he was busy.'

'No, he was at home, and not busy at all. I know why he did not wish to come yesterday.' She hesitated, struggling with her English. 'It is secret.'

'Then we shouldn't talk about it, should we?' said Harriet crisply, longing to do just that. 'Just look at all those pigeons!'

Taeike ignored this obvious red herring. 'It is secret, yes,' persisted the Dutch girl. 'But I think not for you, for you go away tomorrow—and I think also that you do not tell secrets if you say that you will not.' She eyed Harriet shrewdly. 'And you will not tell, not even to Friso, that you know?'

The icy fingers had gone, leaving a hard cold lump in her chest. So there was something…the sooner she knew the better. 'Very well,' she said cheerfully. 'Although I think you should have told Friso first; and I can't understand why you should want to tell me.'

It had cost an effort to sound cheerful, but when Taeike reiterated, 'You promise you will not tell—and that you will not say to Friso that you know?' she answered readily, 'I promise that I won't say a word.'

She smiled at the pretty face beside her; after all, it was hard to keep a secret when you were little more than a child. She braced herself against bad news. Perhaps Friso had to go away—or could he be ill? She discarded the thought as ridiculous; Friso was so obviously never ill.

'He is going to be married,' said Taeike.

Harriet was looking at the street organ. She would, she knew,

remember every detail of it until the day she died. It was playing
'The Blue Danube'; the strains of music came faintly upwards
through the closed windows—a tune she had always liked. It
seemed a very long time before she heard her voice say, 'Is he?
But why is that a secret? Most—most people marry.'

She steeled herself to look at Taeike as she spoke, and was
puzzled at the expression on her face. It could have been pity,
mixed with a kind of speculation. Harriet turned her head again
and looked out of the window again, without seeing anything
at all of what was going on outside.

'You like Friso.' It was a statement, not a question.

Harriet closed her eyes and became aware that the pounding
in her ears was the pounding of her heart. She didn't want to
believe a word of what Taeike had said, but at least she would
have to hear her out. She said evenly, 'Yes, I do. You do too,
don't you, Taeike?'

The girl beside her lifted her head proudly. 'I have known
Friso since I am little—always we are friends; therefore you
understand why he tells me. He says to me, I do not see Harriet again—she is too nice; too—too *deftig.*' Taeike used a word
which Harriet recognized as meaning dignified and respectable
and decorous. 'You are not, he says, a flirt, but a good friend.
He wished to tell you of his marriage, but he knows that you
like him...' She stopped, and then said softly, 'I'm sorry, Harry.'

Harriet went on looking out of the window at nothing at all.
She knew now how people felt when they died of shame, because it was happening to her too. She clutched her handbag
very tightly because she wanted something to hold on to. She
had to think clearly, but it had become difficult to think at all.
There was a question she had to ask, too.

'Taeike, Friso could have told me this himself.'

The pretty little face was sympathetic. 'Yes, that is so. But
perhaps he thinks that as you go away for ever tomorrow, it is
nicer—kinder for you like this.' She frowned. 'He has only to
say that he is too busy...you see?'

It made sense in a horrid sort of way. Harriet swallowed the
unpalatable truth. Her dream had shattered around her, and really she only had herself to blame; what had been a couple of
weeks' friendship for Friso she herself had glorified into something much more serious—and he had been the one to see it.
But why had he said the things he had? She tried to think about
it and concluded that it wasn't until after he had said them that
he had realized that she wasn't just having fun with a holiday
flirtation. She couldn't bear to think about it any more; it was
a relief to see the rest of their party advancing towards them,
for she realized that further conversation, such as it was, was
quite beyond her.

CHAPTER TEN

THE REST OF the day was unending. Harriet had the sensation of
listening to her voice and watching her own actions as if they
were those of a stranger, but apparently her behaviour was entirely normal, for no one made any comment; she supposed that
she was saying and doing the right things. Fortunately there
had been a great deal to talk about in the car on the way back
to Franeker and she had joined in the chatter with a feverish
animation that she hoped would drown her other feelings. This
hadn't been the case, of course, but at least it had prevented her
thinking any more about the conversation in the Palace. They
got back for a late lunch, rendered even later by the number of
questions and answers which Mevrouw Van Minnen asked and
received. Harriet went to her room afterwards on the pretext of
packing, something that she could easily do in a few minutes,
but she wanted to think. Just half an hour by herself and she
might be able to sort out the situation, for to accept it without
a struggle seemed to her to be very poor-spirited. She put her
case on the bed and began half-heartedly to empty a drawer,
but she had barely had time to open it before there was a knock
on the door and Aede's voice asking if he might come in. She
called to him in a falsely cheerful voice and summoned up a
welcoming smile as he opened the door.

'Aede, how nice to see you again. Have you got the day off?'

'No. Urgent family business,' he laughed. 'Father told me about your adventure at Bal's cottage. What an experience to have on holiday! Did you mind very much?'

'Mind? Oh, no. I was frightened, but there was so much to do.'

He crossed the room and stood looking down into the street. 'I heard all about Moses too. Friso told me; he thought it most amusing.' He seemed to notice the case for the first time. 'What are you doing?'

Harriet picked up a handful of tights. 'Packing.'

'Now? It'll only take a few minutes surely, and you can do it this evening or even tomorrow morning. I've got the car and I don't have to be back until six o'clock or thereabouts. Let's go for a run and you can bid a temporary good-bye to Friesland. You're coming over for Sieske's wedding, aren't you?'

'Of course.' As she said it, she wondered how she would be able to avoid returning. She would hate to miss her friend's wedding, but she didn't want to see Friso... Yes, she did want to see him; but not with another girl. She smiled at Aede, which encouraged him to say with some awkwardness, 'I'm thinking of getting engaged myself—a girl I met in medical school; so you'll have my wedding to come to too. Not yet, of course—in a year maybe. Now, are you coming out?'

Harriet tied a scarf over her hair and picked up a cardigan.

'Yes, I'd love to, and you must tell me all about your girl.'

They went downstairs and found Sieske in the hall, and stood talking for a minute or so, Harriet wasn't paying much attention to what was being said, nor did she see the understanding look the brother and sister exchanged.

Aede didn't ask her where she wanted to go but went straight out of the town towards Leeuwarden, and rather to her surprise, right through it and on to the Groningen road. It was a broad motorway, but the country on either side was delightful, green and placid. Just looking at it had the effect of calming Harriet so that presently she found herself listening with real interest to Aede's plans for the future.

After half an hour he turned off the road and started to make his way back in the direction of Leeuwarden through a series of small country lanes.

There weren't many villages, nor were there many people.

'Milking time,' said Aede, and pointed out the clusters of cows gathered round the milking machines in the fields.

'Where will you live when you marry?' Harriet asked.

'Franeker. Eventually I shall take over from Father, you know. In the meantime there is plenty of work for the three of us. I shall enjoy working with Friso, he's a good chap. We shall be passing his house in a minute or two. Would you like to stop?'

Harriet said, 'No, thank you,' in a quiet voice. If Taeike had been wrong and there had been a misunderstanding, she had no doubt that Friso would discover it and put it right; if not, she would make no move. For the hundredth time she tried to remember if she had said or done anything. She could think of nothing, only that she had let Friso see her feelings.

'Here it is,' said Aede, and there it was indeed. Friso's house, looking lovelier than ever in the spring sunshine. He slowed down as they passed, but she scarcely noticed that as she searched the grounds for a sign of life. There was no one to be seen, but as they rounded the corner and passed the gates, a dog barked.

'That's Moses,' she said. 'I—I thought I should see him before I went home.'

Her companion negotiated a milk float drawn by a plodding horse which had no intention of giving up the crown of the road.

'I don't see why you shouldn't. Did Friso say so? He did? Then you will, Friso is a man of his word, come what may.'

This remark had the effect of making her feel a little more cheerful, they arrived back at the house almost gaily, and the gaiety lasted through her good-bye to Aede and the unexpected influx of the doctor's friends who had come to wish her Godspeed, and stayed for drinks. The *burgemeester* and the *dominee* arrived within a few minutes of each other, and in turn, engaged her in conversation. Neither of them mentioned Friso. Behind her smiling attentive face, she struggled to think of some way of introducing him into the talk, but she was given no chance, for the *burgemeester* talked about a production of 'She Stoops to Conquer' which he had seen at Chichester the previous year, and the *dominee* discussed the art of making jam, of all things. Friso had never mentioned Chichester to her and she had strong doubts as to whether his knowledge of jam-making had ever reached more than a theoretical level. Without changing the subject in a most noticeable manner, she could see no way of dragging his name into the conversation. It was left to the beautiful blonde who had arrived without Friso to utter his name. Harriet had found herself in a corner with the elegant creature, where they carried on a strictly basic conversation about clothes—a safe subject for women in any language. Harriet admired her companion's white mini-dress; there was little of it, but what there was was superbly cut.

'Dior?' she hazarded vaguely, anxious to please the beautiful creature and feeling strangely incapable of jealousy towards her. After all, she had arrived with an escort of two young men whom she had treated with a great deal more warmth than she had shown Friso. She couldn't be the girl he intended to marry. Harriet checked the thought sternly. Thinking about it could come later.

The blonde smiled. 'You like? Italy. My uncle buys for me.' She waved vaguely in the general direction of the room before them. There were several gentlemen who could have been her uncle; it didn't seem worth the trouble of finding out, however. Harriet decided to abandon the subject anyway; she was searching feverishly for a topic that could be dealt with easily in simple English, when her thoughts were brought to a stunned halt by her companion. 'Friso is silly,' she pronounced. 'He will not come with us. He says he is busy. That is not so—' she shrugged her shoulders. 'He sits alone—with dogs.' Her tone implied that she had no opinion at all of a man who sat with dogs in preference to taking her out. She looked at Harriet with interest. 'You are red; very red. Not well, perhaps?'

'I am warm,' said Harriet faintly. 'The room is warm, are you not warm?' She stopped, aware that she sounded like a Latin grammar. She was having trouble with her breathing too. She said in an urgent voice,

'Friso is ill?'

'Ill? Huh!' The small sound obviously meant the same in both languages. 'Friso is never sick,' the girl laughed gaily. 'You do not know him well, or you would not ask.'

Harriet sighed. 'No,' she agreed in a small voice, 'I don't think I do.' She was glad to be borne away by the curator of the Planetarium to give him her opinion of Friesland and Franeker in particular. It prevented her thoughts from straying.

It was late when she went up to bed. Long after the last guests had gone, they had stayed up talking, and she had watched the clock, willing it to slowness in case Friso should still come. But he didn't, and when at last she was in bed she had to admit to herself that she wasn't going to see him again. Taeike had been right, after all. There was no question of him coming in the morning. Her train left Leeuwarden at half past seven, the doctor would drive her to the station to catch it; no one in their senses would come calling at six o'clock in the morning. She lay thinking about him and her lovely ruined dream, too unhappy to cry.

She fell asleep just before dawn, so heavily that Sieske had to shake her awake. She went down to breakfast, her pretty face without colour and so woebegone that Mevrouw Van Minnen thought that she was in no condition to travel, and suggested that she should postpone her journey.

Harriet begged her not to worry. 'I'm always like this before I go on a journey, aren't I, Sieske?' She added mendaciously, 'I feel marvellous.'

Sieske gave her a long look across the table and said comfortably, 'Yes, Harry dear.' She turned to her mother and explained at length.

Harriet wondered exactly what she was saying, but whatever it was, it convinced Mevrouw Van Minnen, who nodded and smiled, apparently satisfied. Maggina and Taeike had come down too, not to eat their breakfasts, it was too early for that, but to say good-bye. Sieske was going to the station anyway— she would have gone the whole way to the Hoek if Harriet had not firmly declared that she could manage the trip very well by herself.

Harriet finished her breakfast and went upstairs to get the presents she had brought from England and had saved until this moment—Blue Grass cologne for Mevrouw Van Minnen, tobacco for the doctor, undies for Sieske which she had admired when they had gone shopping together in England, and wisps of nighties for Maggina and Taeike. She offered her gifts shyly and begged everyone not to open them until she had gone, but Taeike would not wait. She tore her parcel open with all the impetuosity of youth and stood staring at the pretty trifle, then looked quite wildly at Harriet, who said gently, 'I do hope you like it, dear. You are so pretty.'

'Thank you, Harry. It's beautiful.' She covered it carefully with its tissue paper. 'You think I am pretty?'

'Yes, I do. When you are quite grown up I think that you will be lovely.'

Taeike's eyes filled with tears. She held out her hand, barely touched Harriet's fingers, and dropped it to her side again. 'I must have my bath. Good-bye, Harry.' She didn't look at her at all, but went quickly out of the room, her parcel under one arm. If there had been more time, her strange conduct might have caused comment, but Mevrouw Van Minnen was answering the telephone, and the doctor was already on his way to fetch his car. Maggina said good-bye too and Harriet and Sieske went upstairs to fetch their hats and coats. Harriet was ready first and

went downstairs, where she stood by the window in the sitting-
room, waiting for the car. She could just see the small alleyway
which housed the garage the doctor used. The bonnet of his car
was nosing out into the street just as another car flashed past
it and drew up with a harsh squeal of brakes at the front door.
It was the AC 428, and Friso and Moses got out of it. Harriet
whispered, 'Friso, oh, Friso!' but remained rooted to the spot,
regrettably aware that she should be formulating some plan or
other to meet the situation. Instead she watched him cross the
pavement and mount the two steps to the door with Moses at
his heel. He did this unhurriedly and she had time to note that
he was quite collected in manner, and, despite the early hour,
presented an immaculate appearance. She turned her back on
the sight of him and faced the door. She could hear his deep
voice mingled with the laughing protestations of Mevrouw Van
Minnen, accounted for, no doubt, by the presence of Moses.
She glanced at the Friese clock on the wall; it was almost time
to go. She was picking up her handbag when the door opened
and Friso and Moses came in. She longed to run to him, but
instead she said brightly,

'Hullo, Moses,' and the beast pricked his ears at her voice
and shambled across the room to lean against her, looking up
into her face with every sign of pleasure in his own ugly one.
She flung her handbag down again and gave him a hug, and
said from the safe vantage point of his furry shoulder,

'Hullo, Friso. Thank you for bringing Moses.'

He hadn't moved from the door, but stood watching her, an
expression she couldn't read upon his face. But when he spoke
his voice was friendly enough.

'I said that you should see him before you went back to England, did I not? I saw no reason to break my word.'

She would have liked to have contested this statement. Had
he not said that he would come to Amsterdam to fetch them
home? She opened her mouth to say so, then closed it again because the look on his face had become all at once forbidding and

arrogant and she had the uneasy feeling that if she attempted
to cross verbal swords with him now she would come off much
the worse. She said instead,

'Is he good? I hope he'll be happy.' She pulled an ear and
Moses licked her hand. She had to admit that a miracle had
occurred since he had become a member of Friso's household.
His rough coat shone with brushing, he held his stump of a tail
with pride, and he had already begun to fill out; even his teeth
looked less fearsome. As if aware of her scrutiny, he grinned,
blinked his small yellow eyes and licked her again.

She said soberly, 'I shall miss him,' to be chilled by Friso's
cool voice, 'That would hardly be possible after such a short acquaintance.' He stared at her. 'In any case, I am sure that Sieske
will give you news of him when she writes to you.'

So Taeike had been right after all! She lifted her chin and
smiled across at him. It had been delicately put, but she was as
capable of taking a hint as the next one. 'I'm sure she will. I
shall look forward to hearing about him.'

She saw him look at the clock, and said quickly before he
could say it,

'I have to go. I've had a lovely holiday, you have all been so
kind.' She paused because she could hear her voice wobbling
and that would never do. She hadn't realized until that moment
that tyrannical convention was forcing her to say all the right
and proper things, while she wished to say only what was in
her heart.

Friso put out a hand and she prevented herself just in time
from putting her own out when he said,

'Shall I have the lead? Just in case Moses wants to follow
you.'

She gave the dog a final hug and put the lead into Friso's
outstretched hand, carefully not touching it. Her chest ached
with the tears she was determined to hold back. She reached
the door and he stood aside and let her go past. With her hand
on the handle she forced herself to face him. Even then she

would have said something, but his detached, faintly mocking air was discouraging. Alas for her dream! She swallowed, and said merely,

'Well, good-bye, Friso. I hope…' She stopped, not at all sure what she did hope.

Friso's mouth twisted in a wry smile.

'Well? What do you hope, Harriet? Health, wealth and happiness, I suppose.' His usually quiet voice had a nasty edge to it.

They were standing close to each other, the dog between. She could see the little sparks in his eyes and knew that he was angry. She said,

'Yes, that is what I truly hope for you, Friso,' and this time she didn't care how much her voice wobbled. She wrenched the door open and whisked through, intent on getting away before the ache in her chest dissolved into tears. She heard Moses whine, but Friso didn't wish her good-bye.

CHAPTER ELEVEN

MEN'S SURGICAL HAD been busy all day; theatre cases, admissions from Casualty, a cardiac arrest in the middle of ward dinners. Harriet came back from her seven o'clock supper and started her final round. The nurses were clearing the ward ready for the night; filling water jugs, tidying away the papers and bits of string and old envelopes and orange peel which had accumulated since the afternoon. She went round slowly, looking carefully at each patient and stopping to chat with most of them. Old Mr Gadd, perceptibly weaker, but still demanding cups of tea at unsuitable times, kept her talking for several minutes. It was almost eight o'clock when she finally reached her office and sat down to fill in the Kardex for the night staff. She got up again almost immediately and opened the window, for it was a lovely May evening, and warm. She had been back two weeks from Franeker—it seemed like two years, and very long years at that. She sat down again, not attempting to work. Her desk was very neat and tidy; she looked at it and reminded herself that this was what she had wanted more than anything else—a ward sister's post. Now she had it, and it no longer appealed to her in the least.

It was a pity, she told herself roundly, that she had ever gone to Franeker and become so unsettled. She glowered at her blotting paper and saw Friso's face clearly upon it, and when she shut her eyes to dismiss it, he became even clearer beneath her lids. She sighed, opened them again and began to write. She had always supposed that hearts broke quickly, but it seemed that it was a slow, painful business. The door opened behind her, and without looking round, she said,

'Please pass me Mr Moore's chart, Nurse.' She studied it for a minute. 'Will you take his BP and pulse? They're due at eight.' Mr Moore was the cardiac arrest, recovered now, but needing constant care. The nurse said, 'Yes, Sister.' The door closed behind her and Harriet went on writing, concentrating fiercely. Presently the door opened again, and she asked,

'Well, Nurse?' and turned her head and smiled from a face which had, since her holiday become both pale and thin.

The nurse made her report, wondering, as a great many other nurses were wondering, what Haughty Harry had been up to while she was away. She was just as kind and sweet and hardworking as she had always been, but everyone agreed that she had somehow lost her sparkle.

After the nurse had gone, Harriet sat at her desk, doing nothing, waiting for the night staff to come on duty, her thoughts busy with the day's work. It had been as all the other days, and yet not entirely satisfactory. She tried to put a finger on the cause of her disquiet and couldn't. It was true there had been that terrible moment when Mr Sellers, one of the consultants, had arrived unexpectedly, and come upon her doing nothing, and on the desk before her a sheet of paper with Friso's name written upon it a dozen times, because just to write it had made him seem less hopelessly far away. Mr Sellers had looked at her handiwork without appearing to do so and then asked,

'Settled down, have you, Sister? No regrets? Can't think why a pretty girl like you should want to wear an apron and cap instead of marrying.'

She had gone a slow painful scarlet and made some silly remark about a career, and he had laughed kindly, and said,

'What, no young man in Holland?' Her denial had been far too quick and hot; she realized that now. And Matron—Harriet knitted her brows in puzzlement. She had done her usual ward round, but instead of the formal, gracious leave-taking at the ward door, she had hesitated and made the astonishing request that Harriet should make out the next two weeks' off duty and send it down to the office forthwith. What was more she had been requested to make up the mending book and the instrument and stationery books too, none of which was due for another week. Matron had offered no explanation and Harriet had supposed at the time that it was some new scheme she hadn't known about—she was, after all, new to her job. All the same, if she hadn't known it to be a ridiculous idea, Matron had behaved exactly as though she expected her new ward sister to be on the point of leaving. Harriet wriggled uneasily on her chair, remembering Matron's query as to whether Staff Nurse Wilson was completely reliable. Perhaps Wilson was to be offered a ward—but there was none vacant. Quiet steps on the stairs heralded the night nurses. Harriet, glad to have her thoughts interrupted, opened the Kardex, and turned to greet them.

Half an hour later she was at the hospital entrance, waiting for William. She had two days off—it would be nice to go home and potter around the house and garden, and perhaps help her father in the surgery. Her thoughts, never far from Franeker, went back to the morning when she had been helping Dr Van Minnen and Friso had come in. She closed her eyes the better to remember every small detail, so that her brother, who had just arrived, had to shout from his car to attract her attention. She got in meekly and said, 'Sorry, William, I didn't see you.'

He slammed the door shut for her. 'That's all right, old girl. My fault—I'm late.'

Harriet nodded understandingly, knowing from a lifetime of living in a doctor's household that it was no use expecting punctuality for meals or appointments or birthday treats...

broken bones and babies and diabetic comas saw to that. She asked with real interest,

'Anything nasty or just backlog?'

'Backlog,' he said shortly. They had to wait at the traffic lights and he turned to look at her. 'How's things with you? You look whacked.'

She replied suitably to this brotherly observation and lapsed into silence as he weaved a way through the city and out on to the road towards the moors. Indeed, she was silent for most of the journey, but as her brother was fully occupied in describing the charms of a particularly interesting girl he had met while he had been on a course in Bristol; it went unnoticed. Only as he drew up with his usual jolt and gave a telling note on the car horn to signal their arrival to the family did he remark,

'You're peaked. You must be sickening for something.'

Harriet made haste to deny this. 'Of course I'm not, William—I told you, I'm just tired.' There was an edge to her voice; he heard it and frowned. She was his favourite sister and she wasn't at all her usual serene self.

She used the same excuse for her mother, who, however, wasn't so easily satisfied with her explanation.

'Harriet told me she was tired,' she mused as she and her husband were getting ready for bed. 'She's never tired—not that sort of tired,' she added obscurely. 'And you're not going to tell me that she finds her job too much for her.'

Her husband yawned. 'I had no intention of telling you anything, my dear, but our Harry has certainly lost her zest for life. Anaemic, perhaps?'

Harriet's mother gave him a withering look. 'Anaemic!' she snorted. 'She's in love, of course. She looked like this when she came home from her holiday and everyone said it was the journey. It's that partner in Franeker—that Dr Eijsinck. She mentioned him in every letter, but she's not so much as breathed his name since she came back.'

'Couldn't you ask her?' queried the doctor.

His wife paused in her hair-brushing. 'No, dear. She'll tell me if and when she wants to.' She started brushing again with unnecessary vigour. 'Poor little Harry!'

The village street looked very pleasant as Harry strolled along on her way to the village stores, the following afternoon. It was warm and sunny, and at that hour of the day, when the children had gone back to school and their mothers were still tidying up after dinner in their cosy thatched cottages, it was very quiet indeed. The late spring sunshine beat down on her neatly piled hair, turning it to an even brighter gold; she was wearing a sleeveless knitted dress, the same pale pink as the washed walls of the cottages, and she looked prettier than ever despite her dismal feelings. There was no one in Mr Smallbone's shop; only Mr Smallbone himself, standing behind his polished counter. It was dim inside and smelled pleasantly of biscuits and coffee and, more faintly, of cheese. She put her basket down on the counter in front of him and he took off his glasses and beamed at her and said in his creaky old voice,

'Good afternoon, Miss Harriet. Home again, I see.'

He always said that, ever since she had gone to hospital to start her training, and as always, she smiled and said, 'Yes, Mr Smallbone. Days off again. I've brought Mother's order.' She waited while he went through the small ritual of writing the name and address in his order book in a large crabby hand. This done, he put the pencil down, reached under the counter and brought out a tin of chocolate biscuits and proffered them with an air of long custom—which indeed it was; she could remember Mr Smallbone's biscuits back through the years. She took one now and started to nibble at it the while she started on her list. They were debating the type of bacon she should purchase when she heard the shop door open behind her. Mr Smallbone looked over her shoulder and said, 'Good afternoon, sir,' and Friso's voice answered him.

Harriet had no breath in her body and her heart was thumping madly. She looked unseeingly at the side of bacon Mr Smallbone was holding up for her inspection, then cautiously turned her head and stared unbelievingly. She closed her eyes and opened them again; Friso was still there. Her heart had got into her throat, making it hard for her to speak. She swallowed it back and managed, 'Friso,' in a dieaway voice, and then, 'It is you, isn't it?'

'In person, my dear girl. And how is Miss Slocombe? Are you enjoying your new status as Ward Sister?' He studied her carefully with a faint smile. 'I can't say it's improved your looks. Maybe it isn't your true vocation in life, after all.'

She had been feeling pale, but this remark brought a fine flush to her cheeks, and because she felt uncertain she said rather crossly,

'If that's all you came to say, you can go away again!'

She turned her back on him, although it cost her an effort to do so, and said loudly to Mr Smallbone, 'I'll take the small back, I think, cut on number seven.' And heard Friso say, just as though neither Mr Smallbone or the bacon had been there, 'No, it is by no means all I came to say, and I have no intention of going away.'

Mr Smallbone finished writing about the bacon and looked up, not at her but over her shoulder at the doctor. He said nothing, but his blue eyes twinkled as he took the list from her unresisting hand, laid it tidily in the order book, and came from behind his counter to cross the shop to the door, where he turned the 'Open' sign to 'Closed', pulled down the old-fashioned linen blind and turned the key in the lock. With the faintest glimmer of a smile at them both, he walked back again, opened the lace-curtained door at the back of the shop and disappeared behind it. In the utter silence which followed, his voice could be heard—a faint dry murmur, followed by an unmistakable chuckle. Harriet still had her back to Friso, but when he said quietly, 'Turn round, Harriet,' she did so. After all, she couldn't stand for ever with her back to him. She did it reluctantly, though, holding her shopping basket in front of her like a shield. There was a loose strand of cane in the handle, and she began twisting it and untwisting it; it was something to do. She watched Friso, wondering what he would say, and was conscious of disappointment when he remarked casually,

'I've been to see your parents.'

She thought about this for a moment; there seemed no suitable answer, so she said 'Oh?' in a cool voice, which, despite her efforts, held a small tremor. She said 'Oh' again in a quite different voice, however, when he thundered, 'Leave that damn basket alone and attend to me, Harry!'

He was, she saw, quite exasperated and very tired. The sight of him so made her want to cry, but crying was something she had done a great deal of in the last two weeks, and she had no intention of starting again.

He smiled suddenly and tenderly and the tiredness vanished.

'Let's get one thing clear,' he said firmly. 'It's you I shall marry, my pretty.'

'But how can I be your pretty?' She had lost control of her voice and was appalled to hear it spiral into a near-wail.

'Ah, yes,' he interposed, 'I should have explained, but seeing you again has emptied my head of all good sense.' He walked towards her, coming so close that she was forced to tilt her head back to see his face. His great arm folded around her to crack her ribs with its strength.

'This first,' he said quietly, 'for I have no more patience.' He bent and kissed her mouth with a tender fierceness that blotted out the ache in her ribs. 'My dear darling,' he said presently, 'I've loved you since we first met—I fell in love with you five weeks ago when I saw you in Franeker, standing on the pavement staring at me with your great blue eyes and smiling.'

'Did you really?' asked Harriet with interest. 'You looked at me as though I were a lamp-post!' She was prevented from enlarging upon this nonsensical idea by the simple expedient of being kissed again—something which proved so satisfactory to them both that there was quite a pause before Friso said,

'I couldn't quite believe that I had found you at last.'

'But you drove away.'

His eyes were dancing, though he answered gravely enough.

'Against my inclination, my lovely girl—luckily common sense prevailed. You see I was pretty sure who you were; I knew that I should see you again—and soon. I could hardly leave Roswitha in the middle of Franeker while I...'

'Roswitha,' said Harriet rather sharply. 'The brunette—the beautiful brunette...'

'The *dominee's* daughter—occasionally I give her a lift in the car. She works in Alkmaar.'

'And the beautiful blonde—the one at Sieske's party?'

'The daughter of an old friend—I had to bring someone, you know.' He was laughing at her until she said, 'Oh, Friso, dear! Please explain. Taeike told me you were going to be married.' She looked at him, appalled at her muddled thoughts which somehow had to be voiced. She had her mouth open to speak when he put a gentle finger on her lips.

'No, listen, my dear love, listen to me. You shall scold me later if you wish. I promise that I will be meek.'

She was between laughter and tears. 'Friso, you're never meek!'

'Am I not? In that case, I daresay we shall quarrel a great deal when we are married—that is, if we can find the time, for I shall have my patients and you will have the children.'

She felt his arms tighten and sighed deeply, a sigh of pure content. 'Shall we go sailing in your *botter*?' she asked. 'You said once that it was very suitable for children.'

He said, his deep voice full of laughter, 'I can see that, what with quarrelling and sailing and bringing up children, we are going to lead a very busy life; although there will be time for other things—such as this.' He bent his head again, and for the moment at any rate, Harriet forgot all about the *botter*. Rendered breathless, she nevertheless managed to repeat, 'Please explain, Friso. I've been so unhappy.'

'It was Taeike—and I blame myself; for it should never have happened. You see, dearest, I have known her since she was a toddler and to me she was—is still a child. But she's fourteen, you know, and has her mind full of dreams and fancies—' he paused. 'She saw that we loved each other and she tried to stop us. When you were in Amsterdam she came to see me—she told me that you were going to marry someone in England, she showed me a snapshot of you both. I had no reason to disbelieve her. It could have been true, for sometimes you behaved as though you couldn't stand the sight of me, and I had let you see that I cared, but I had to be sure that you felt the same way.' He stopped and kissed the top of her head in a contemplative manner. 'I learned the whole a few days after you left; she told me then that she had told you a similar story, but she likes you very much, Harry, and she couldn't bear to make us unhappy any longer.' He chuckled. 'It was a snapshot of your brother, by the way.'

'Poor Taeike,' said Harriet, in a voice comfortably muffled in his shoulder.

'She'll get over it, darling—already has, for I told her that when she would be old enough to marry me I should be as old as her father. I fancy I shall be looked upon in the light of an uncle in future.'

Harriet reached up and clasped her arms around his neck. 'None of it matters, does it?' she said. They smiled at each other and then drew apart; the faint squeak of the door sounded almost apologetic.

Mr Smallbone peered at them with a conspiratorial air. 'The afternoon trade,' he murmured.

Friso loosed Harriet. 'Of course,' he said, and went and changed the sign round again, pulled up the blind and opened the door on to a small group of puzzled and slightly indignant housewives. He smiled at them with charm, so that they smiled back, mollified, their ill-feelings forgotten. He ushered them into the shop and went back to stand by Harriet. He looked across the counter at Mr Smallbone, and said loudly enough for everyone there to hear him.

'Thank you for your kindness, Mr Smallbone. Perhaps we can repay it in some small part by inviting you to our wedding—tomorrow morning at eleven. In the church, of course.'

He took Harriet by the arm and led her out of the shop amidst a sudden outbreak of excited talk. Outside in the road she stopped and peeped up at him, and said almost timidly,

'Friso, dear Friso, you can't mean eleven o'clock tomorrow.' Her voice wavered. 'The hospital—my work—Mother and Father—no clothes...' her voice faltered and rose to a squeak. 'The licence!'

He tucked her arm rather more firmly into his. 'I don't think I've forgotten anything,' he said with calm. 'My dear love, why do you suppose it took me so long to come to you?'

They started to walk down the road, between the cottages. Harriet felt her hand taken and held in Friso's own. It all seemed impossible, but if he said that everything had been arranged... they would be together for always. As though he had read her thoughts, she heard him say, 'Remember our Friesian oath, darling? I told you then that loving is for ever.'

* * * * *

Last April Fair

CHAPTER ONE

MRS GREGSON'S ELDERLY VOICE, raised in its never-ending vendetta against the nurses making her bed, penetrated throughout the entire ward; it even penetrated Sister's office, so that its occupant rose from her work at her desk with a sigh, opened the swing doors and made her way down the long ward to where her troublesome patient lay. She was a very pretty girl, tall and slim and nicely curved in her navy uniform. She had corn-coloured hair, cut short and swinging around her neck, with a fringe over her blue eyes and a nose which tilted very slightly above a softly curved mouth so that despite her twenty-six years she reminded anyone meeting her for the first time of a small eager girl wanting to be friendly with everyone.

She reached the bed just as its occupant, sitting in a heap in the middle of it clutching a blanket round her frail person, drew breath to begin on a fresh round of abuse. 'Yer ter leave them blankets,' she shrilled, 'me bed's fine—it don't need making.'

'And what is our Doctor Thorpe going to say when he comes presently and finds you in that untidy heap?' Phyllida Cresswell's voice was quiet and quite unworried by Mrs Gregson's tantrums.

''E won't saynothin', 'e'll be too busy looking at yer pretty face.'

Phyllida wasn't in the least put out. 'There you go again, making up stories. You just wait until I tell his wife!'

Mrs Gregson cackled happily. 'Just me little joke, Sister dear, though you mark my words, some feller'll come along one day and run orf with yer.'

'It sounds exciting,' agreed Phyllida. 'And now how about this bed?'

'Well, if yer say so...'

Phyllida smiled at the old lady, smiled too at the two student nurses and started off down the ward again. It was a good thing that Philip Mount was the Surgical Registrar and rarely came on to her ward; Mrs Gregson's sharp eyes would have spotted that they were rather more than colleagues within minutes. Phyllida frowned slightly. Philip was getting a little too possessive just lately. It wasn't as though they were engaged. Her frown deepened; perhaps it would have been better for them both if they had been, although she couldn't remember that he had ever suggested it, merely taken it for granted that one day they would marry. And he was a good man; there weren't many like him, she knew that; not particularly good-looking, but well built and pleasant-faced and rarely bad-tempered, ready to make allowances for everyone—she wasn't good enough for him and she had told him so on several occasions. But he had only laughed at her, refusing to take her seriously.

She went back into her office and sat down at her desk again and picked up the telephone. There was the laundry to warn about the extra sheets she would need, the dispensary to argue with over the non-arrival of a drug she had ordered, the office to plead with for the loan of a nurse because one of her student nurses had gone off sick—she sighed and lifted the receiver.

The day went badly, with no nurse to replace the one who had gone off sick, two emergencies, Doctor Thorpe's round and him in a nasty temper and not nearly enough clean linen returned from the laundry. Phyllida, a sunny-tempered girl, was decidedly prickly by the time she went to her midday dinner, a state of mind not improved by her friends wanting to know why she was so ratty, and made even worse by one of her friends demanding to know if she had had words with Philip.

'No, I have not,' she declared crossly, and thought suddenly that a good row with him would be better than his even-tempered tolerance when she was feeling ill-humoured. She added rather lamely: 'I've had a foul morning and Doctor Thorpe was in one of his tetchy moods; the round took for ever.'

The talk became general after that and presently, back on the ward, she regained her usual good nature so that Mrs Gregson stopped her as she was going down the ward to say: 'That's better, Sister dear. Black as a thundercloud yer've been all morning.' She grinned, displaying impossibly even false teeth. 'We ain't such a bad lot, are we?'

Phyllida had stopped to lean over the end of her patient's bed. 'You're the nicest lot of ladies I've ever met,' she assured her.

Mrs Gregson nodded, satisfied. 'Going out this evening?' she wanted to know.

Phyllida said that yes, she was and she still had a lot of work to do as she went on her way. She and Philip were going to have dinner with his elder brother and his wife. They lived in Hampstead in a pleasant house; privately she found them a dull couple with two dull children, but they seemed content enough and she had, upon occasion, detected a gleam of envy in Philip's eye at the sight of their comfortable home with its neatly kept garden, well-behaved dog, gleaming furniture and shining windows. She frowned a little as she bent to take her newest patient's blood pressure. It wasn't that she didn't like cleanliness and order and furniture polish, but somehow there was too much of it. She thought with sudden longing of her own home, an old rambling house in a village near Shaftesbury, standing on high ground so that it creaked and groaned in the winter gales and captured all the summer sun there was on its grey stone walls. Her father was the village doctor with a practice scattered miles in every direction and her mother ran the house with the help of old Mrs Drew who was really past it, as well as coping with the large untidy garden, two dogs, a variety of cats, an old pony and some chickens and over and above these such of her four children who might happen to be at home, and they usually brought friends with them.

It was late March, thought Phyllida, neatly charting her findings; the daffodils would be out and the catkins, and in the wilder corners of the garden there would be violets and primroses for the picking. She had a week's holiday due to her, only a few days away now. The thought cheered her enormously and she felt guilty at the relief of getting away from Philip for a little while—perhaps while she was at home she would be able to make up her mind about him. And really, she chided herself as she went from bed to bed, with a nod and a word for the occupants, there should be no need of that. He was a splendid man, generous and honest and thoughtful—he would make a perfect husband. He would be dull too. She wiped the thought from her mind as unworthy and concentrated on his good points so that by the evening when she went off duty she was almost eager to see him.

She took extra pains with her face and hair as she changed out of her uniform and then poked around in her wardrobe. She had clothes enough, for unlike many of her friends she had no need to help out at home, but now she dragged out one dress after the other, dissatisfied with them all, until, pressed for time, she got into a grey wool dress with its matching long coat, tied a bright scarf round her neck, caught up gloves and handbag and skipped down the austere staircase of the Nurses' Home. Philip was waiting in the hospital yard. That was another nice thing about him; he never kept her waiting and he never grumbled if she were late. She smiled widely at him as she got into the elderly Rover he cherished with such care.

'I've had a foul day, Doctor Thorpe was as sour as vinegar and they sent up two chest cases. What about you?' she asked.

'Oh, quite a good list, one or two tacked on, of course, but

Sir Hereward was in a good mood.' He turned to smile at her. 'Shall we go to Poon's?'

Phyllida didn't really like Chinese food, but she agreed at once. Poon's was well away from the hospital and not expensive, and although Philip wasn't mean, he hadn't anything other than his salary. They drove through the City, cut into Long Acre and into Cranbourne Street and turned into the Charing Cross Road. There was a good deal of traffic as they turned into Lisle Street and found a parking meter, and the restaurant was crowded too. Phyllida sat down at the corner table found for them and let out a long contented sigh.

'This is nice. I love my work, but it's good to get away from it. I've got a week's holiday in a few days, too.'

'Going home?' Philip was studying the menu.

She chose sweet and sour pork before she replied. 'Yes.' She gave him a questioning look.

'I've a couple of days owing to me...' His nice face beamed at her across the table.

'Then come down for them. I'm going on Sunday evening—when can you manage to get free?'

'Wednesday—until Friday midnight. Your mother won't mind?'

Phyllida laughed. 'You know Mother, she loves a house full—besides, she knows you well enough to hand you a spade and tell you to dig the garden—a nice change from whipping out appendices!'

They spent a pleasant evening together, although thinking about it afterwards, Phyllida had a feeling that they had both been trying too hard; trying in a self-conscious way to turn their rather vague relationship into something more tangible. She couldn't think why, not for herself at any rate. She was fond of Philip but she was almost sure that she didn't want to marry him, and yet her sensible brain told her that he was so right for a husband.

She lay awake for a long time thinking about it and then

overslept so that her breakfast was a scrappy affair of tea and toast, and for all the good her sleepless night had done her, she might just as well not have given Philip a thought, and indeed she had no time to think about him at all during the morning. She still had no student nurse to replace the one who had gone off sick and one of the three remaining nurses had gone on holiday. She took the report with outward calm, had a few succinct words with Linda Jenkins, her staff nurse, picked up the pile of post for her patients and started off on her morning round, casting a practised eye over the ward as she went. They might be short-staffed, but the girls were managing very nicely; the beds were being made with all speed and those ladies well enough to get up were being settled into the armchairs arranged at intervals down the long ward, a scheme intended to encourage the convalescent ladies to get together and enjoy a nice chat among themselves. Phyllida had discovered long ago that they became so interested in swapping their illnesses that they forgot to grumble at their own aches and pains, the awful food, the tepid tea, the unfeeling nurses... None of which was true, but she quite understood that they had to have something to gossip about. She paused now by a group and listened to Miss Thompson, a pernicious anaemia who ruled the new patients with a rod of iron since she had been in and out of the ward for years now, describing the operation her sister-in-law had just had. Miss Thompson had the bloodcurdling and quite inaccurate details of it so pat that Phyllida's lovely eyes almost popped out of her head. When Miss Thompson paused for breath she asked drily: 'Did she recover, Miss Thompson?'

She knew that she shouldn't have asked the question; now she would have to listen to a long-drawn-out blow-by-blow account of the unfortunate lady's return to health and strength. She passed around her letters and began a mental assay of the off duty for next week while she stood patiently. When Miss Thompson had at last finished, Phyllida, mindful of hurt feelings, merely remarked that some people had remarkable experiences, admonished the ladies to drink their mid-morning coffee when it arrived and went on her way. She recounted it all to Linda over their own coffee later and chuckled her way into a good humour again, so that when she thought of Philip during a rare few minutes of leisure later that day it was with mild pleasure at the idea of him spending a couple of days at her home.

She only saw him once before she started her leave, and for so short a time that they could only exchange a brief remark as to when he would arrive. She still felt pleased about him coming, but her pleasure was a little dimmed by his matter-of-fact manner, and his 'See you, then' was uttered with the briskness of a brother. True, they had encountered one another in the middle of one of the busiest corridors in the hospital, with nurses, porters and housemen milling up and down, but, thought Phyllida, suddenly annoyed, 'if he loved her as much as he said he did, he could surely have looked at her with rather more feeling?' She left the hospital the following evening, glad that she hadn't seen him again.

She drove down to her home in the neat little Vauxhall Astra, a present from her parents on her twenty-first birthday, five years ago, and although she could have afforded to exchange it she had never felt the need; it went well and she understood it as well as she would ever understand any car. She fastened her seat belt, gave a last glance at the rather grim hospital behind her and drove out into the busy street to meet the London traffic.

It took her quite some time to get out of London and on to the M3, but she was a good driver and not impatient. Once on the motorway she sent the small car racing along and at its end, took the A30 to Salisbury. It was almost empty of traffic by now and she made good time to the town, working round it to the north and picking up the A30 again on its further side. She was on home ground now and although it was getting on for ten o'clock, she didn't feel tired. Just short of Shaftesbury she turned off on to the Tisbury road and then turned again, going through pleasantly wooded country and climbing a little on the winding road. Over the brow of the hill she slowed for a minute. The lights of Gifford Ferris twinkled at her almost at its foot, not many lights, for the village was small and off the main road. But it was by no means isolated; there were other villages within a mile or two on all sides; any number of out-lying farms and main roads to the north and south. Phyllida put her foot down and sent the car scuttling down the hill and then more slowly into the village's main street. It had a small market square with a stone cross in its centre, a handful of shops around it besides a comfortable hotel, and at the top of the hill on the other side one or two old stone houses. She stopped before one of these and jumped out, but before she could reach the door it had been flung open.

'Your mother's in the kitchen, getting your supper,' observed her father placidly. 'Nice to see you, my dear—did you have a good trip?'

She kissed him soundly. 'Super—almost no traffic once I'd left London. Something smells good—I'm famished! I'll get my case...'

'Run along and find your mother, I'll bring it in. The car will be all right there until the morning.'

Phyllida walked down the long narrow hall and opened the kitchen door at its end, contentedly sniffing the air; furniture polish, the scent from a bowl of hyacinths on a table, and fragrant cooking. They spelled home.

Her mother was at the scrubbed table in the middle of the room, cutting bread. She looked up as Phyllida went in, dropped the knife and came to meet her. 'Darling—how lovely to see you, and how nice you look in that suit. There's watercress soup and mushroom omelette and buttered toast and tea, though Father says you're to have a glass of sherry first. He'll bring it presently.' She returned Phyllida's hug and added: 'Willy's here just for a few days—half term, you know.'

The younger of her two brothers appeared as her mother spoke, a boy of fourteen, absurdly like his father, with tousled hair and an air of never having enough to eat. He bore this out with a brotherly: 'Hi, Sis, heard you come, guessed there'd be food.'

She obligingly sat down at the table and shared her supper while their mother cut bread and wondered aloud how many more meals he would want before he settled to sleep.

'I'm growing,' he pointed out cheerfully, 'and look at Phylly—she finished growing years ago and she's stuffing herself.'

'Rude boy,' observed his sister placidly. 'How's school?'

Her father came in then and they sat around, all talking at once until Willy was sent off to bed and Phyllida and her mother tidied the kitchen, washed up and went to the sitting room with a tray of coffee.

It was a pleasant room; long and low-ceilinged and furnished with some nice pieces which had been in the family for generations. There was comfort too; easy chairs drawn up to the open fire, a vast sofa with a padded back and plenty of small reading lamps. Phyllida curled up on the sofa, the firelight warm on her face and dutifully answered the questions with which her mother bombarded her. They were mostly about Philip and cunningly put, and she answered them patiently, wishing illogically that her mother didn't seem so keen on him all of a sudden. She had been vaguely put out after Philip's first visit to her home by her mother's reaction to him. 'Such a nice young man,' her parent had declared, 'and so serious. I'm sure if you marry him he'll make a model husband.' It hadn't been the words so much as the tone in which they had been uttered, and ever since Phyllida had been worried by a faint niggling doubt at the back of her pretty head; a model husband sounded so dull. But this evening she could detect no doubt in her mother's voice—indeed, her parent chattered on at some length about Phyllida's future, talking about the wedding as though it were already a certainty.

Phyllida finished her coffee, observed rather tartly that no one had asked her to get married yet and when her mother remarked that she had understood that Philip was coming to stay for a couple of days, pointed out very quickly that it was only a friendly visit—it made a nice restful change after his work at the hospital. Mrs Cresswell agreed placidly, her still pretty head bent over some embroidery, and presently Phyllida went to bed.

Being home was delightful—pottering in the garden, helping her mother round the house, going for long bike rides with Willy, helping in her father's surgery. Phyllida relaxed, colour came back into her London-pale cheeks, her hair seemed more golden, her eyes bluer. Her mother, looking at her as she made pastry at the kitchen table, felt certain that Philip would ask her to marry him when he came.

She was right; he did, but not at once. He wasn't a man to rush his fences, and it wasn't until the morning of his second day there that he suggested that they might go into Shaftesbury for her mother and do some shopping, and Phyllida, called in from fetching the eggs from the hen-house at the end of the garden, readily agreed. She had been glad to see Philip when he had arrived, but not, she confessed to herself, thrilled, but they had quickly slipped into their pleasant, easygoing camaraderie and he was an undemanding companion. She put a jacket on over her slacks, combed her fringe, added a little more lipstick and pronounced herself ready.

Shaftesbury was full of people and cars; it always was, probably because it was a small town and built originally on top of a hill and its shops were concentrated in two main streets. They had done their shopping, chosen a variety of cakes from the fragrant bakery hidden away in an alley where the two streets met, and sat themselves down in the buttery of one of the few hotels for a cup of coffee before Philip made any but the most impersonal remarks.

'Wouldn't you like to leave hospital and have a home of your own?' he wanted to know.

Phyllida chose a bun, not paying as much attention as she

should have done. 'Oh, yes,' she said casually, 'I'd love it. Have a bun?'

'Then why don't you?'

She looked up then, suddenly realizing what he was going to say. 'Don't, Philip—please…'

He took a bun too. 'Why not? You must know that I want to marry you?'

'Yes—well, yes, I suppose I did, but not—not urgently.'

He was a very honest young man. 'If you mean I'm beside myself with impatience to get married, you're right. But I've given the matter a great deal of thought lately and I'm sure you're the wife for me; we know each other very well by now and I'm more than half in love with you.' He smiled at her across the table. 'How about it, Phylly?'

She knew that she was going to say no. Perhaps, she thought desperately, she had never intended to say anything else, but it was going to be hard to say it. For one thing, she was strongly tempted to accept Philip's matter-of-fact proposal. They would live together happily enough, she would take an interest in his work and he would be a kind and considerate husband, of that she was sure. She would have a pleasant enough life with enough to live on, a nice home, friends of her own sort and children. She would like several children; only she had the lowering feeling that Philip would want a neat little family of a boy and a girl. He would be a splendid father too and the children would be good, obedient and reasonably clever. In fact, life wouldn't be what she had dreamed—a vague dream of a man who would sweep her off her feet, treasure her and love her and never on any account allow her to wear the trousers, and more than that, would fill his house with a brood of healthy, naughty children.

She sighed and said gently: 'It wouldn't work, Philip.'

He showed no rancour. 'Why not? You must have reasons.'

She frowned. 'I like you very, very much—I think for a while I was a little in love with you, but I'm sure that it's not enough.'

She looked at him with unhappy blue eyes. 'I'm sorry, Philip—and I don't think I shall change my mind.'

He said calmly: 'You're in love with someone else?'

'No. Oh, no, no one at all, that's why it's difficult…you see, you're so right for me. I respect you and admire your work and the way you live, and I like being with you, only I don't want to marry you.' She added miserably: 'It would be such a mistake, and the awful thing is I don't know what I want.'

Philip finished his coffee with the air of a man who wasn't in the least defeated. 'I'm not taking no for an answer,' he told her quietly. 'I won't bother you, but I'll wait.'

'But it won't be any good.' She looked like an unhappy little girl, her short upper lip caught between her teeth, her eyes enormous under the fringe. She felt suddenly peevish. If she could get away, right away, he would forget her because he didn't love her, not with the sort of love which just didn't want to go on living without her—he might even fall in love with someone else quite quickly. It struck her then that he was the kind of man who didn't need to love like that; he was a calm, even-tempered man and too much love would choke him. When he only smiled and offered her more coffee she didn't say any more, for what was the use?

Philip didn't allow her refusal to make any difference between them. He spent the rest of the day with her, treating her with the same good-natured affection that he had always shown her. He went back to London that day after tea, saying all the right things to her mother and father and reminding Phyllida cheerfully that they would be going to the Annual Dance at the hospital together two days after her return: 'Though I'll see you before then,' he had assured her.

She watched him go with mixed feelings; real regret that she didn't love him and a faint touch of temper because he seemed so unmoved about her refusal—or was he so sure that she would give in? The thought made her even more peevish.

The moment he was out of sight her mother remarked: 'Well, dear, are you going to marry him? I'm sure he must have asked you.'

Phyllida hadn't meant to say anything about it—not just yet anyway, but she perceived now that her mother would go on gently asking questions until she got an answer.

'Yes, he did, and I said no.'

'Oh, good.' Mrs Cresswell took no notice of her daughter's surprised look. 'He's a very nice man, darling, but not your sort.'

'What is my sort, Mother?' Phyllida didn't feel peevish any more.

Her mother washed a tea-cup with care; it was old and treasured like most of the china she insisted on using every day. 'Well, he doesn't have to be handsome, but eye-catching, if you know what I mean, the sort of man who would take command in a sticky situation and know just what to do—and not let you have your own way unless he thought it was good for you.'

'A bigheaded tyrant,' suggested Phyllida.

'No, dear, just a man who would never take you for granted; take great care of you without you ever knowing it, and know exactly what he intended doing with his life—and yours, of course.'

'A paragon. Mother, I never knew you were romantic—does Father know?'

'He married me,' observed her parent placidly. 'What will you do about Philip? I mean, you can't help but see him often, can you?'

Phyllida had piled the tea things on to a tray, on her way to putting them away in the carved corner cupboard in the sitting room. 'I hadn't thought of that,' she said slowly. 'It would be sense to leave, I suppose.'

'Well, think about it, darling.' Her mother spoke briskly. 'It could be done easily enough.'

Phyllida gave her a faintly mocking look. 'Mother, you have no idea...'

'No, dear, but things can always be done, however awkward, if only one applies oneself to them.'

Nothing more was said after that. Phyllida went back to London two days later, reluctant to give up a job she liked and go through all the fuss and bother of finding another one—and outside London, she supposed gloomily.

She didn't see Philip until the evening of the dance; indeed, she had taken care to keep out of his way, going to great lengths to avoid their usual meeting places, keeping one eye on the ward door in case he should come to see a patient referred for surgery.

But she had to see him again eventually. They met in the entrance hall, shortly after the dance had started, he very correct in his black tie, she prettier than ever in a pearly grey chiffon dress and silver slippers.

Her hullo was a trifle awkward, but Philip didn't seem to notice. He took her arm, asked her where she'd been during the last two days and suggested that they went into the big lecture hall, decorated for the occasion, and danced. It wasn't until they had circled the place at least twice that he asked: 'Had second thoughts, Phylly?'

'About what?' And then, despising herself for the remark: 'No, I haven't, Philip, and I'm not going to—truly I'm not.'

He laughed down at her. 'No? Shall we wait and see? We meet most days, don't we, so it won't be a case of "Out of sight, out of mind"—you're very used to me being there, aren't you?'

She met his eyes. 'Yes. You mean you'll wear me away like water on a stone.'

'Nicely put, although I wouldn't describe you as stony. You'll change your mind.'

Perhaps it was because he looked so smug and sure of himself that she resolved then and there to look for another job. She didn't say anything though, but danced the night away, mostly with Philip but with all the other men she knew as well. She enjoyed herself too; tomorrow was time enough to think things out.

She hadn't got much further by the following evening when she came off duty. It had been a busy day with several of her patients not doing as well as she had hoped, so that she felt too depressed to do more than take off her cap and put her feet up on the sofa in the Sisters' sitting room. She closed her eyes the better to think and then opened them again as the door opened and Meg Dawson, Surgical Ward Sister and one of her closest friends, came in. 'There's a phone call for you, Phylly—your mum.'

Phyllida had taken her shoes off as well. She padded down the passage to the phone box at its end and picked up the receiver. Her mother's voice, very youthful still, sounded very clear. 'Phylly? Father wants to talk to you.'

Phyllida was surprised; she and her father got on splendidly, but he was a busy man, not given to telephone conversations unless they concerned a patient. She said cautiously: 'Yes?'

Doctor Cresswell didn't waste time. 'You mentioned leaving, Phylly—if you do, there's a job going in about three weeks' time.'

A sign from heaven, thought Phyllida childishly. 'I could leave then—I've still another week's leave due, so I'd have to work three weeks notice…' She knew that her father was nodding his head even though he didn't speak. 'What sort of job?'

'A patient of mine until I referred her to Sir Keith Maltby— I attend her parents too. A girl of eighteen with erythroblastic leukaemia—I wasn't called in until she had been ill for some time, sent her straight to Sir Keith who got her into hospital; she was there two months, had several courses of cytotoxic drugs and has improved considerably, gained weight, taken an interest in life. Her mother came to see me today, says Gaby has set her heart on going to somewhere sunny—they want to take her on a short cruise—Madeira and the Canaries, but they want a skilled nurse to keep an eye on her and recognise the signs and symptoms if she should have a relapse. All expenses paid, and fare of course, and a decent salary—about three weeks, they think. Of course you realise that Gaby hasn't very long to live. Sir Keith agrees with me that she should be allowed to do what she wants within reason—her parents are wealthy, fortunately. It would get you away, my dear, if that's what you want.' And when Phyllida didn't answer: 'I could arrange for you to see these people—the name's de Wolff—they've booked for a cruise leaving on April the sixth, that's not quite four weeks away.'

Phyllida heard herself say that yes, she would like to meet the de Wolffs and that provided they liked her, she would be prepared to take the job. 'I've a couple of days off, but not till the end of the week, that would be too late to give in my notice—look, Father, I'm off at five o'clock tomorrow and on at one o'clock the next day. I'll drive down in the evening, see them in the morning and drive straight back—I can just do it provided they'll make an appointment early in the morning.'

'Splendid, my dear. I'll see to it and ring you back.'

So she found herself the next day rushing off duty, racing into her outdoor things and driving as fast as traffic permitted out of London. The appointment was for half past nine on the following morning and to save time she was to go to the de Wolffs' house, as it was on the London side of Shaftesbury and she could drive straight on back to work after the interview. She hadn't told anyone about it and she hadn't seen Philip. She had toyed with the idea of going to the office and giving in her notice that morning, but there was always the chance that the job wouldn't turn out to be what she expected. She got clear of London at last and belted for home.

CHAPTER TWO

MRS CRESSWELL WAS waiting with supper, and her father came from his study to talk to Phyllida while she ate it. 'Gaby's a nice enough girl, poor child—difficult at times, I gather from her mother, but it has to be remembered that she's very ill. She has no idea how ill, of course, although her parents have been told. Not that they've accepted it well; they simply cannot believe that a girl of eighteen can die. They're both energetic, social types and can't understand why Gaby isn't the same.'

Phyllida carved another slice of her mother's home-baked bread. 'You don't like them,' she stated flatly.

'I wouldn't go as far as to say that, shall I say that I regret their attitude towards illness and death—two inconvenient states they simply refuse to recognise, but I'm glad they're so eager to take Gaby on this trip. Sir Keith tells me it's only a question of three months or so.'

'Oh, Father, how awful—isn't there anything at all to be done?'

He shook his head. 'You know that yourself, my dear. Thank heaven it's extremely rare—other forms of leukaemia have a much more favourable prognosis these days.'

Phyllida left home after breakfast the next morning, to drive the few miles to the de Wolffs' home. She joined the main Salis-

bury road presently and then turned away on to a country road
leading to Berwick St John, and after another mile came upon
the house she was looking for. It was Edwardian, much gabled
and ornamented with beams and plasterwork in an attempt to
make it look Tudor. It was large too, spick and span as to paint-
work and altogether too perfect for her taste. She thought with
sudden nostalgia of her own home only a few miles away and
so very different, its ancient oak door almost always open, its
mullioned windows wide, with curtains blowing a welcome.
There were no curtains to be seen here and no open windows.

She got out, crossed the gravel, so smooth that she felt guilty
treading on it, and rang the bell. The man-servant who opened
the door matched the house exactly; correct; unwelcoming and
without any warmth. He begged her to enter, ushered her into
a small panelled room furnished with expensive, tasteless furniture, and went away.

Both Mr and Mrs de Wolff entered the room a moment later,
bringing with them an air of brisk efficiency and charm. They
bade Phyllida seat herself, and without any preliminaries, proceeded to put her—as Mr de Wolff observed—in the picture.
'You shall see Gaby presently,' promised Mrs de Wolff, and
smiled charmingly at Phyllida. She was a handsome woman, in
her forties but not looking it by reason of exquisite make-up and
beautifully cut hair, and a casual tweed suit which must have
cost a great deal of money. She smiled a lot, thought Phyllida,
and she quite understood what her father had meant when he
had told her that neither she nor her husband wanted to accept
the fact that Gaby's illness was a terminal one.

'The specialist takes a grave view, of course,' said Mr de
Wolff, teetering on his toes before the fireplace, like the chair-
man of a board meeting, 'but we're both so healthy ourselves
we take a more optimistic view. This little holiday should do
her the world of good, and she's so keen to go.'

'You will notify the ship's doctor of her illness?' asked Phyllida, 'and I should want her medical notes with me so that they can be referred to if necessary.'

Mrs de Wolff frowned, and just for a minute all the charm had gone, but it was back almost at once. 'Of course we'll see to all that, Miss Cresswell, you can safely leave us to arrange everything just as it should be. We shall consult Sir Keith, of course—such a pity that he's in Scotland, otherwise you could have gone to see him, but I'm sure your father has told you all there is to know about Gaby.' She got to her feet. 'Would you like to see her now before you go? We do so hope you'll come with us, but it's for you to decide of course.'

She crossed the room and rang the bell and when the unsmiling manservant came, asked him to let Miss Gaby know that she was wanted in the morning room.

The first thing Phyllida thought when she saw Gaby was how very pretty she was, small and slim to the point of thinness and far too pale, with a cloud of dark hair to match her dark eyes. This thought was followed at once by a second one, that the girl looked far more ill than her parents had made out. She seemed a docile little creature too, replying meekly to her mother's remarks about how much she wanted to go on holiday with them, and what she intended to do. But she offered no remarks of her own, although she smiled at Phyllida and went on smiling when her father said that she was a spoilt girl and had everything she could possibly want. He sounded very pleased with himself as he said it, and Phyllida wondered if he had stopped to think that having everything one wanted wasn't much use if one wasn't going to be alive to enjoy it.

She stayed for another half an hour, asking questions as discreetly as possible as to her duties. It would be mostly companionship, she gathered, and the giving of Gaby's medicines and pills, as well as a number of small routine tasks—temperature and pulse and blood pressure and making sure that her patient slept well. She rose to go presently, reiterating that she would want the case notes with her, and reminding the de Wolffs that

the ship's doctor would have to be informed. Gaby had gone
with some small excuse so that Phyllida could speak openly
now. A little uneasy because of the de Wolffs' casual attitude
towards their daughter's illness, she said gently: 'You do know
that Gaby is very ill? I know it's hard to believe—and you're
quite happy about her making this trip?'

Mrs de Wolff's charming smile slipped again. 'Quite happy,
Miss Cresswell,' she said with finality. So Phyllida left it at
that, only staying to arrange to meet them all on the morning
of the sixth.

'We shall be driving up,' explained Mr de Wolff. 'We'll pick
you up at the hospital, that will be the easiest way, I think.'

They wished her goodbye, and the manservant ushered her
out into the chilly March morning. She had driven for ten minutes or so when she said out loud: 'Well, they could at least have
offered me a cup of coffee!'

She reached Salisbury by continuing along the same country
road from the de Wolffs' house, stopping on the way to have the
cup of coffee no one had offered her, and once through Salisbury she made for London without waste of time.

At the hospital she had the leisure to change into uniform,
write out her resignation and present herself at the office. The
Senior Nursing Officer was considerably astonished, but in the
course of her long and successful career she had learned when
not to ask questions. Beyond expressing a sincere regret at Phyllida's decision to leave, she said nothing other than to wish her
a successful future and advise her to give the office due warning as to the exact date of her departure.

'You have a week's holiday still, Sister Cresswell, and I expect you can arrange to add your days off to that. I shall have
to appoint someone in your place, but in the meantime I think
that Staff Nurse Jenkins is quite capable of carrying on. Do
you agree?'

'She's very good, Miss Cutts, and the patients like her. The
nurses work well for her too.'

'In that case I see no reason why she shouldn't apply for the post.' Miss Cutts nodded kindly in gracious dismissal.

Phyllida, speeding to the ward, felt intense surprise at what she had done. Probably if she had stopped to think about it, she would have decided against leaving, but now it was done she felt relief as well. She still had to see Philip and explain, but she would bide her time and choose the right moment for that.

But the matter was taken out of her hands. He came on to the ward to take a look at a suspected duodenal ulcer which would probably need operation, and instead of leaving at once he followed Phyllida to her office, shut the door behind him and asked her quietly: 'What's this I hear about you leaving?'

'Oh, dear—so soon?' She turned to face him across the small room. 'I only saw Miss Cutts half an hour ago and I haven't told a soul—I was going to talk to you about it, Philip.' She pushed her cap away from her forehead. 'Not now, though—I've heaps to do.'

'You're off at five o'clock? I'll meet you at Tony's at half past six.' He went away without another word, leaving her to wonder for the rest of the day if she had made the mistake of her lifetime. Even now, if he overwhelmed her...she wondered at the back of her mind if he felt strongly enough about her to do that. With a tremendous effort she dismissed the whole thing and attacked her work; there was enough of that to keep her mind off other things; the duodenal ulcer not responding to medical treatment; Mrs Gregson springing a mild coronary upon them; the young girl in the corner bed with undulant fever, so depressed that no one knew what to do next to get her cheerful again, and the sixteen-year-old anorexia nervosa next to her, taking precious time and patience with every unwanted meal...

Tony's was a small unassuming restaurant within five minutes' walk of the hospital and much patronised by the doctors and nurses. Phyllida arrived punctually and found a table for two by one of the windows. There was no view, only the drab street outside, and she sat staring at it until Philip slid into the seat opposite her.

His 'Hullo—shall we have the usual?' was uttered in his normal calm way and when she nodded: 'And now what's all this nonsense about leaving?'

'It's not nonsense, Philip. I've given Miss Cutts my notice and I leave in three weeks' time—just under, as a matter of fact. And I've got a job.'

Just for a moment his calm was shaken. 'A job? So you'd arranged it all some time ago?'

'No.' She explained carefully and added: 'I'm sorry, Philip, I like you very much, I told you that, but the best thing to do is for us to stop seeing each other.'

He said with faint smugness, 'You're afraid I'll wear you down.'

She stared at him, her blue eyes clear and honest. 'I don't know,' she told him earnestly, 'but if you did, it wouldn't be right.'

The waitress brought them the soup of the day and Phyllida studied it as though it was something of vital importance. Presently she said: 'It's difficult to explain, but when I marry I want to be so in love with the man that nothing else matters; there'd be no doubts and no wondering about the future and where we'd live or how.' She looked up from her soup and gazed at him from under her fringe.

'And you don't feel like that about me? Phylly, grow up! You're living in a fairy tale—there's no such thing as that kind of love, only in romantic novels. I'm surprised at you, I thought you were such a sensible, matter-of-fact girl, with no nonsense about you.'

Phyllida picked up her spoon and gave the Heinz tomato a stir. That was the trouble, she thought silently, he'd got her all wrong. She was romantic and full of nonsense; he had confused the practical, sensible young woman who ran the medical ward so efficiently with her real self, and looking at him now, she could see that he still thought it.

He was half way through his soup by now. 'Well, trot off if you must,' he told her cheerfully, 'and come back when you're ready. I daresay I'll still be here.'

She sat silently while the soup was replaced by pork chops, frozen peas and a pile of chips which might have daunted any girl but her, who ate like a horse and never put on an inch. When the waitress had gone again, she said patiently: 'I'm not coming back; this job is only for three weeks—I don't know what I'll do after that.'

It annoyed her that he still looked complacent, but to say more wasn't going to help. Deeds, not words, she told herself silently.

'What is this job?' he wanted to know.

She told him, and being an opportunist, picked his brains. 'I don't know a great deal about it—I've never seen a case, though I've nursed one or two lymphoblastic leukaemias and they did rather well.'

'This one isn't likely to—it's rare, so rare that there aren't enough statistics, but it's a terminal illness, I'm afraid. Have you got the notes yet?'

'No. Sir Keith Maltby has been looking after her, but he's in Scotland. Father will get the notes from him, though, he's already telephoned him about it. He doesn't object to Gaby going on this cruise—he says she can do what she likes provided her parents understand that the moment she shows signs of deterioration they must get her to hospital or fly her back without delay. The ship's doctor will have all the facts; Mr de Wolff has undertaken to see about that. There's plenty of money, I believe, so there's no reason why anything should go wrong from that side of it.'

As she spoke, she wondered uneasily why she didn't quite believe what she was saying. Perhaps because she had taken a faint dislike to Mr and Mrs de Wolff—quite an unfounded one, based entirely on his brisk attitude towards his daughter's illness, and his wife's calculated charm. Phyllida gave herself a mental shake, agreed with Philip that it would be interesting to see Madeira and the Canaries even if her chance to do so might be limited, and then applied herself to responding suitably to his unshakable friendliness.

It remained unshakable too for the next few weeks, and she felt guilty because she was unable to feel regret at her decision, largely because Philip made no secret of the fact that he expected her to come running once she had brought Gaby back home again.

'Any ideas about the next job?' he asked her airily. 'A bit difficult while you're away, isn't it? It'll mean an enforced holiday while you find something to suit you and then go after it. You might not get it either.' He sounded so satisfied that she could cheerfully have thrown something at him.

Leaving the ward was harder than leaving Philip, she discovered; she had grown fond of it during the last few years; it was old and awkward to work in and there were never enough staff, but she had loved the ever-changing succession of patients, and some of those, like old Mrs Gregson, were so upset at her going that she had promised that she would come and visit them the moment she got back from the cruise. Unthinkingly she had mentioned that to Philip and been furious with herself for doing so when she saw the knowing little smile on his face, smugly sure that she was making an excuse to return to the hospital and see him. She managed not to see too much of him, though, going home for her days off so that she might collect Gaby's notes and listen to her father's sound advice, as well as root around in her bedroom to see what clothes she should take with her. It would be warm for most of the time and last year's summer dresses looked depressingly dull. She decided to travel in a jersey suit and the silk blouse she had bought in a fit of extravagance, pack some slacks and tops and buy one or two things in London.

There was a nice selection of cruise clothes; her modest list lengthened as she went along the rails. In the end she left the shop with a new bikini, three cotton dresses, sleeveless and light as air, and because they were so pretty, two evening dresses, one in pink crêpe with not much top and a wide floating skirt, and the other of white organza. She wasn't sure if she would have the chance to wear them, but there was no harm in taking them along. She already had a flowery-patterned long skirt and several pretty tops to go with it and a couple of short silky dresses from last year.

She packed her bags, arranged to have the rest of her luggage sent home, bade goodbye to her friends at a rather noisy party after the day's work, and retired to bed, but not to sleep at once. There was too much to think about—Gaby and her treatment and the still vague disquiet because she didn't know too much about it, although the notes were comprehensive enough and her father had primed her well. Presumably the ship's doctor would keep a close eye on her patient, and after all, her parents would be there. Slightly reassured, Phyllida allowed her thoughts to turn to Philip. She had contrived to bid him good-bye at the party, with people milling around them so that there was very little chance to say much. She had tried to sound final, but he hadn't believed her. It was annoying and she worried about it, getting sleepier and sleepier until she nodded off at last.

She left the hospital in some state, for the de Wolffs arrived for her in a chauffeur-driven Cadillac; it took up a lot of room in the forecourt and Phyllida, turning to wave to such of her friends who had managed to spare the time to look out of their ward windows, saw their appreciative grins. She got in beside the chauffeur after a final wave and caught Mrs de Wolff's eye. It didn't look in the least friendly and she wondered why, but she smiled at Mr de Wolff, and spoke to Gaby, who answered her eagerly and with encouraging warmth. Phyllida, a charitable girl who seldom thought ill of anyone, supposed Mrs de Woolff had had a trying time getting ready for their holiday. She settled herself in her seat, resolving to do her best to see that Gaby wasn't only well looked after, but kept amused too, so that her parents could enjoy themselves too.

They arrived at the dock with only a very short time to spare before embarking—done deliberately, Mr de Wolff explained, so that there would be no delays for Gaby in getting on board. Phyllida took her patient's arm as they walked slowly up the gangway, for Gaby looked exhausted, then followed the steward up to the Sun Deck. They were to share a de luxe cabin and she looked around her with deep satisfaction; she was used to the normal comforts of life, but this was luxury. She sat Gaby down in a comfortable chair, noted with satisfaction that their luggage was already waiting for them, and took a quick look round.

The cabin was large, even for the two of them, with beds widely spaced, a comfortable sofa, a table and two easy chairs. The window was large and the lighting well arranged and the adjoining bathroom all she could have wished for. It only needed a pleasant stewardess to offer to unpack for them to complete her satisfaction, but she declined this service and asked instead if they could have a tray of tea, for Gaby looked as though she could do with something of the sort. It was barely midday and Mr de Wolff had told her they would be going to the second sitting for their meals, still an hour and a half away; ample time to unpack, check unobtrusively that Gaby was fit to go to the restaurant, and try to get to know her better.

They drank their tea without interruption. The de Wolffs hadn't appeared; probably they realised that Gaby was tired and needed to rest. Phyllida unpacked for both of them, not bothering her patient to talk. After lunch she would search out the doctor, show him the notes and ask for any instructions he might care to give her. Gaby could rest on her bed in the meantime. The girl looked fagged out and Phyllida frowned a little; the job was full of uncertainties and Gaby was a very sick girl. She wondered again if it had been wise of her parents to allow her to come on the cruise and then conceded that if the girl had set her heart on it and had so little time to live, they were only doing what any loving parents would want to do. It was a pity that Sir Keith hadn't seen Gaby for some weeks, but the de Wolffs had said that he had agreed to the trip, so it must be reasonably safe for Gaby to go. Phyllida dismissed her gloomy thoughts and started to chat quietly, hanging away her patient's lovely clothes as she did so.

They shared a table with Mr and Mrs de Wolff at lunch, both of whom dominated the conversation, talking animatedly about the places they were to visit, the various entertainments on board and how splendid it all was for Gaby, who ate almost no lunch, replied docilely when she was spoken to, and attracted a good many admiring glances from the surrounding tables.

Phyllida did too, although she wasn't aware of it; she was too concerned about her patient.

The meal was a leisurely one, passengers serving themselves from a long buffet of cold meats and salads, arranged in mouth-watering abundance. Gaby's parents didn't seem to notice that she was drooping with fatigue, so that Phyllida took affairs into her own hands and when the steward brought the coffee, excused both herself and Gaby, whisked her to their cabin, tucked her up on her bed, and went in search of the doctor's surgery.

It was three decks down, adjacent to a small hospital. The doctor was at his desk, a young man with a pleasant open face, talking to the ship's nurse. Phyllida took a dislike to her on sight and felt that the feeling was reciprocated; she didn't like heavy make-up and brightly tinted nails on a nurse, nor did she fancy the hard blue eyes and tight mouth in what should have been a pretty face. However, her errand wasn't with the nurse. She introduced herself briskly, stated her business and waited for the doctor to speak.

He looked bewildered. 'But I haven't heard...' he began. 'I've had no information about this Miss de Wolff. Perhaps you'll tell me about her, Miss—er—Cresswell.'

It took a little time, although she gave the information concisely and without personal comment. When she had finished he said thoughtfully: 'Of course I'll look after her and do every-thing in my power to help. You say she's entered a period re-mission? Then it's quite possible that she'll be able to enjoy this cruise, to a limited extent, of course—and return home at least none the worse. May I keep these notes and study them? I'll see that you get them back. Perhaps if I were to call and see Miss de Wolff...this evening, or later this afternoon after tea?'

Phyllida agreed. 'I thought we'd have tea in the cabin and then dress without hurrying.'

'Very wise. I think you should suit your activities to her mood. You say she insisted on coming on this holiday?'

'Well, yes, so her parents told me—perhaps it was just a flash in the pan; she's not shown anything but a—a kind of docile acceptance.'

The doctor rose to his feet. 'Would you like me to talk to her parents?'

Phyllida considered. 'If when you've seen her you think it necessary, yes, please.' She hesitated. 'They seem to think that this cruise will put her on her feet again. They can't accept...'

'I know—it's hard for people to realise. Miss de Wolff has no inkling?'

'None that I know of, but I don't know her very well yet. I'll tell you if I think she has.'

They parted in friendly fashion and Phyllida started off down the long corridor taking her to the other end of the ship, to be overtaken almost at once by the nurse.

'I thought I'd let you know that you'd better not expect too much help from me,' she began. 'I have quite a busy time, you know, and I have to be on call round the clock.'

Phyllida stopped to look at her. 'That's OK, I'm sure you must be pretty busy. I don't expect I'll need any help, thanks all the same.'

The other girl gave the suggestion of a sniff. 'If you need any advice...' she began.

Phyllida's large blue eyes flashed. 'I expect I'll be able to cope,' she said gently. 'I've been Medical Ward Sister at St Michael's for four years.' She smiled widely, added 'goodbye' and went on her way, her blonde hair flying round cheeks which were a little pinker than usual, by reason of her vexation.

The doctor was very good with Gaby, matter-of-fact and friendly, taking care not to alarm her by questions which might give her reason to think. And afterwards, on the pretext of fetching some pills in case Gaby felt seasick, Phyllida went back to the surgery.

He said heavily: 'Well, Miss Cresswell, if she'd been my daughter I'd never for one moment entertained the idea of her coming on a trip like this, however much she'd set her heart on it. And she's not wildly enthusiastic about it, is she? Is she spoilt? She didn't strike me as being so.'

Phyllida shook her head. 'I don't think so. She's very quiet and agrees with everything her parents suggest.' She didn't add the unspoken thought that Gaby appeared to be in considerable awe of her parents and anxious, almost painfully so, to please them.

'Well, I'll have a word with them and take a look at her each day. You'll come to me at once if you think it necessary, won't you?'

Phyllida felt better after that, and after due thought went along to the de Wolffs' cabin. It surprised her to discover that they were put out over her visit to the doctor. 'There was really no need,' declared Mrs de Wolff sharply. 'Gaby is a little tired, but otherwise she's recovering very well. We don't want ideas put into her head.'

'I don't think anyone will do that, Mrs de Wolff—after all, she's been under a doctor for so long now, she can't find it strange if the ship's doctor pays her a visit.' She turned to Mr de Wolff. 'I thought you were going to tell him about Gaby— he knew nothing at all about her.'

'I considered it unnecessary.' Mr de Wolff spoke pompously and looked annoyed. 'After all, if Sir Keith gave his consent to this cruise, I hardly suppose that we lesser mortals need to interfere.'

Phyllida went pink. 'I have no intention of interfering, Mr de Wolff, but Gaby has a severe illness and you asked me to look after her and I intend to do so. How long ago is it since Sir Keith Maltby actually saw her?'

Her employer went a rich plum colour. 'That's beside the point, Miss Cresswell. All we ask is that you carry out your duties.'

Phyllida drew a calming breath. She was wasting time; he had no intention of telling her. 'Where would you like us to meet you before dinner?'

She heard his sigh of relief. 'Oh, in the Neptune Bar—about eight o'clock.'

Gaby seemed better when Phyllida got back to their cabin, and became quite animated over the choice of the dress she should wear. She decided on a plain, long-sleeved blue silk sheath, for no one would dress on the first night at sea, and Phyllida put on one of last year's dresses, a very plain one; she considered it made her look just as a nurse out of uniform should look.

The evening went off very well after all. The doctor had introduced himself to the de Wolffs in the bar, offered his services should they be required and went away before the two girls arrived, and if Gaby didn't eat a good dinner, at least she seemed to be enjoying herself. All the same, she went quite willingly to bed when Phyllida suggested it, and Phyllida, quite tired out, went too.

The days formed a pleasant pattern; they breakfasted in their cabin and then spent a leisurely morning sitting on deck, and if Phyllida regretted not being able to join in the deck games and wander off to chat to some of the other passengers, she didn't admit it, even to herself. It worried her that they saw so little of Gaby's parents, who seemed to think that meeting their daughter at lunch and dinner was sufficient, nor did they express anxi-

ety over her condition or ask Phyllida how she was progressing.
Luckily the weather was calm and getting warmer, so that by
Sunday morning they were able to wear cotton dresses and lie
in the sun for a time. It was while they were doing this that the
doctor joined them for their mid-morning beef tea and Phyllida, in a casual voice masking her worry, mentioned Gaby's
headache. 'Quite a troublesome one,' she added lightly, 'it just
doesn't go away.'

'Ah, yes—one of those sick headaches, I expect,' observed
the doctor, taking his cue smartly.

Gaby nodded listlessly. 'Yes, I was sick in the night—Phylly
had to get up—that's why I feel so dozy now.'

The doctor didn't stay long, and presently, while Gaby slept,
Phyllida went in search of him. 'Do you think it's infiltration of
the meninges?' she asked anxiously. 'My father told me about
that. Should I tell her parents? She seemed so much better—
we haven't done much, but she was beginning to eat a little and
take an interest in things.'

'Where are her parents?'

'They play bridge a good deal of the time and they've made
a good many friends.'

'They don't see much of Gaby? Not enough to notice if she's
better or worse?'

'No.'

'I'll have a word with them if you like, and I'll have another
look at her later on. I don't like the headache and sickness, it
may possibly be what you suggest.'

By the evening Gaby was worse, the headache was persistent
now and so was the sickness, and she had become irritable, so
that nothing Phyllida could say or do was right. And when the
doctor came to see her just before dinner he looked grave. 'I'm
going to advise you to disembark at Madeira,' he said. 'There's
a good hospital there, and while I don't think she needs to go
there at the moment, if you were to stay in an hotel she could
be moved quickly. Better still, her parents could fly her back

home straight away. I don't think she should stay on board, we haven't the facilities.'

Phyllida nodded. 'You'll see Mr and Mrs de Wolff? Shall I say nothing to Gaby until it's all arranged?' She paused. 'I shall have to pack.'

'Yes, of course, I'll go and see them now.'

She went back to the cabin and sat down with a book. Gaby wasn't sleeping, but she didn't want to talk either. It was half an hour before Mrs de Wolff opened the door and came in.

'Well, here's a fine state of affairs!' she exclaimed angrily. 'All our plans changed just because Gaby feels a little under the weather! Still, the doctor knows best, I suppose. My husband's radioed for rooms for you both at Reid's Hotel and we'll see you safely there tomorrow before we get back to the ship.'

Phyllida stared at her. 'But aren't we all going ashore?'

'Good heavens, no. We've planned it all nicely—we shall go on to the Canaries and pick you up on our way back next Saturday. Gaby will be better by then. We've talked to the doctor, so you have no need to worry, Miss Cresswell. We feel confident that you can look after Gaby very well until we return—it's only five days and we simply can't miss any of this cruise and there's no need for us to do so. Besides, we've been looking forward to it for some time.'

She went and peered down at Gaby. 'You do look a little pale, darling. You'll feel better on dry land, I expect, and you girls can have a few days' fun on your own.' She patted Gaby's head and Phyllida saw the girl wince. 'We'll leave you plenty of spending money.'

When she had gone Gaby said wearily: 'Mummy always thinks that if she gives me enough money everything will be all right.'

'I expect you'll enjoy it just as much as being on board ship,' said Phyllida soothingly. 'Now, I'm going to pack our things, and suppose we have dinner here this evening? You choose what you'd like to eat and get a long night's sleep. Now I'm going to take these books back to the library.'

She went to see the doctor too, and he wasn't in the best of tempers. 'I've made it plain to Gaby's parents that she's extremely ill and possibly heading for a relapse, and I suggested that you should all fly back from Madeira tomorrow, but they won't hear of it—told me that if the specialist considered her fit enough to take a holiday that was good enough for them, that we're probably over-anxious. They agreed readily enough to Gaby going ashore with you—said they'd pick you up at the end of the week. Are you at all worried?'

'I'm in a flat spin,' confided Phyllida. 'Anything could happen, couldn't it? And here we are, thousands of miles away from home and her parents refusing to face up to her being ill. Do you think she'll be all right? I'll take the greatest care of her.'

'If she keeps quiet and with you to look after her she might get over this bad patch, but she really needs to be flown home and taken to hospital, but her parents utterly refuse. They say that this has happened before and she's always got over it.' He sighed. 'At least Mr de Wolff has all the particulars of her case and I've written a covering letter; he's promised to deliver it himself at the hospital and arrange for a doctor to call and see Gaby—probably tomorrow in the evening or the following morning. We shall be back here on Saturday and if Gaby is no better, I'll do my best to persuade her parents to fly her back.'

Phyllida agreed. The doctor had done all he could, she would have the hospital close at hand and a doctor, so perhaps she need not worry too much. Gaby's father had said that these little relapses, as he called them, had occurred before and Gaby had always pulled through with a little extra care. But there were a number of drugs she should be having—perhaps they would have them at the hospital in Funchal. Phyllida didn't quite trust Mr de Wolff's casual view of his daughter's condition, but she had to take his word for it. She packed for them both, saw Gaby into bed for a good night's sleep and went to bed herself.

There was no hitch in the next day's plans. Gaby was cheerful, and after a good night's sleep seemed better. They went ashore just before lunch, went straight to the hotel and lunched there with Gaby's parents before they rejoined the ship. Their goodbyes were brief; they didn't look back as they left the hotel.

Phyllida and Gaby had adjoining rooms overlooking the gardens going down to the sea, with the swimming pools and tennis courts at their edge. They were spacious and airy and Phyllida made her patient comfortable in a long chair on the balcony before unpacking once more and then going to see about meals. When she got back Gaby was sitting up, looking quite animated, watching the guests in the pools. 'I'm going to like it here,' she declared, and looked happy for the first time, 'just with you. We don't need to do anything, do we? I mean, go on excursions or shopping? Daddy gave me some money to hire a car, he said we could tour the island, but I'm not keen, are you?'

'Not a bit,' lied Phyllida. 'I'm all for being lazy. And by the way, Doctor Watts from the ship wrote a note to one of the doctors at the hospital here asking him to pop round and see you this evening or tomorrow, just in case there's anything you need.'

Gaby hunched a shoulder. 'I wish people didn't fuss so. I'm quite all right if only I didn't have this head-ache.'

'Well, that's why he's coming, I expect; if it's no better he'll be able to prescribe some different tablets. Would you like to stay up here for tea? Or we can have it on the terrace—it looked super and there's a lovely view.'

Gaby settled for the terrace and presently they went downstairs and found seats in a shady corner, and Gaby, Phyllida was pleased to see, enjoyed her tea, talking quite animatedly about her clothes and the boutique they had stopped to look at in the hotel's foyer.

The rest of the day passed pleasantly. They dined at a small table by themselves, but several people around them stopped to speak and Gaby, once more in a happy mood, preened herself in their admiring glances. Phyllida went to bed happier than she had been since the cruise started. Gaby might not be better physically, but she was a whole lot happier. The thought that it was because her parents weren't there crossed her mind, but she dismissed that as unlikely. They gave Gaby everything; she had more clothes than she ever could wear, lovely jewellery, and every luxury that money could buy. She was almost asleep when the notion that Gaby had everything but real love and interest from her parents came into her head. She could have wept at the sadness of it.

Gaby felt so well the next morning that she put on one of her prettiest sun dresses and lounged by one of the swimming pools while Phyllida swam around, but as the day became warmer they moved back to the terrace, ate their lunch there and only went back to their rooms so that Gaby might rest. But they went outside again for tea and stayed there until dinner time, when Gaby changed her dress for a rather too elaborate silk one, but she looked so happy that Phyllida told her that she looked a dream and would turn all heads. Which she did. As they said goodnight later, Gaby said sleepily: 'It's been a lovely day—I'd like to stay here, just with you, Phylly, for ever and ever.'

Phyllida dropped a kiss on the pale cheek and made some laughing reply before she went to her own room.

Gaby was awake and sitting up in bed when Phyllida went in the next morning and she left her to have her breakfast and went downstairs to have her own, wondering if it would be a good idea to suggest that they might take a taxi to the Country Club and sit there for an hour or two before lunch. She didn't hurry over her meal. Gaby didn't like to be disturbed until she had finished her breakfast; it was almost ten o'clock as she got up from the table. She went back upstairs, pausing to speak to some English guests on their way out. When she knocked on Gaby's door there was no answer; probably she was reading and hadn't heard. Phyllida opened the door.

Gaby wasn't reading. She was lying back in bed, unconscious.

Phyllida drew a startled breath, pulled herself together in seconds and went quickly to the bed. The first thing she did was to press the bell, the second to feel for Gaby's pulse, so faint and threadlike that she had difficulty in finding it. Her breathing was so light and shallow that she had to bend down in order to check it. No one had answered the bell, so she rang again, took the tray off the bed, pulled the pillow into a better position and when there was still no answer to her summons, ran to the door. Something must be done, and fast, if it were to be of any use.

CHAPTER THREE

PHYLLIDA WASN'T A girl to panic, but now she had to get a tight hold on herself, making her mind work sensibly when all she wanted to do was scream for help and leave everything to someone else. This wasn't hospital, it wasn't even England; she knew no one, she wasn't even sure where the hospital was. Gaby was desperately ill—worse than that, Gaby was going to die. Somehow or other she would have to get a message to her parents, find a doctor, get her to hospital. Phyllida took another look at Gaby, lying so still in her bed, and went downstairs as fast as she could, running across the foyer to the reception desk.

There was no one there. She banged the bell and was angry with herself because her hand shook, and when no one came she couldn't stop herself crying in a shaky voice: 'Oh, please won't someone come?'

'Will I do?' asked a voice behind her.

It belonged to a very tall, powerfuly built man with what she immediately decided was a face she could trust, though at that moment she would have trusted a snake.

'Yes,' she didn't hesitate. 'I'm looking after a girl—she's desperately ill and her parents are cruising round the Canaries—I don't know exactly where they are. I need a doctor, now, this instant, and she should be in hospital. She's going to die if something isn't done quickly!'

He put a large firm hand on her arm. 'I'm a doctor, shall I take a look? Do you speak Portuguese?'

'No, but they speak English here, only there isn't anyone.'

'Coffee time. Shall I have a look at this girl? Your patient, is she?'

Phyllida nodded. 'Please. I'll give you an idea…' She started up the stairs fast, talking as she went.

She hadn't doubted that he was a doctor. He examined Gaby with careful speed while Phyllida stood beside him, watching.

There was a great deal of him and he was handsome too, with a patrician nose, a firm mouth and blue eyes beneath lazy lids. His hair was so fair that she wasn't sure if it was grey or not. He straightened up presently and looked at her. 'You're right, I'm afraid—I'll get the hospital, I happen to know someone there. There's nothing more to be done. You know that, don't you?'

'Yes. What shall I do about her parents?'

'When did they go? This girl's been dangerously ill for some time—surely they were told?'

'Yes, oh, yes. But they said that Gaby wanted to go on this cruise so badly and that's why I'm here, so that I could look after her. She got worse on our way here and the ship's doctor advised us to come ashore with her—he wanted us to fly home, but her parents wouldn't consent. They didn't want her to go to the hospital either…they wouldn't admit that she was ill, I did tell them, but they wouldn't listen. They came ashore with us and then went back on board—and that was the day before yesterday. They told me not to worry about an address if I should need them, they said it wasn't necessary, but I could radio the ship, couldn't I?'

His blue eyes hadn't left her face. 'Don't they love the girl?'

'I—I…it's hard to say; if they do it's not the kind of love most people have for their children—they gave her everything, though. They wanted to get away; her mother hates illness.'

They were in the foyer now and he had a hand on the telephone by the still deserted desk. He lifted the receiver, dialled a number as she spoke and spoke in his turn.

'They'll be here in a few minutes; you'll go with her and stay. I'll get a message to her parents. May I have their name?'

It didn't enter her head to argue with him. 'I'll get her things together and mine too. The name's de Wolff and they're on the *Blenheim*, going to Lanzarote and then Teneriffe and Las Palmas—they're expected back on Saturday.'

'Too late. Now go and get ready. I'll see you later.'

Packing furiously in Gaby's room, one anxious eye on her patient, Phyllida paused for a second. She didn't know the man's name; he might not have been telephoning the hospital, he might just disappear as suddenly as he had appeared; perhaps the ambulance wouldn't come. She shut the case with hands which still shook and then uttered a sigh of relief as she heard steady feet coming down the corridor towards the room.

She should have known better, she chided herself as she got out of the ambulance at the hospital. Her new-found friend was waiting at the entrance with a nurse and doctor and two porters. He wasted no time on greeting her, said merely: 'Follow us,' and led the procession along a corridor, past several wards and into a small room beyond them. Here Gaby was put to bed by Phyllida and the nurse while the two doctors talked together. Once she was asked if she had any notes about her patient and paused to fetch them from her case.

'They were given to me in case the ship's doctor wanted them,' she explained, 'and when he'd read them he pointed out that he hadn't the facilities for Gaby should she become worse. He couldn't understand why she had been allowed on the cruise in the first place. Nothing was said about her being ill when the cruise was booked, he was sure of that. Mrs de Wolff had told me that Gaby was expected to live for another year at least, perhaps longer, but she must have been mistaken.'

The two men nodded and after a minute of reading the big

man said: 'She's recently completed her fifth course of chemo-theraphy—Daunorubicin and Cytosine.' He glanced at Phyllida. 'Had she started the course of cytoreduction?'

'No, I understood it was to be started when we got back.'

'Well, it's too late to do anything about that now.' He handed back the notes. 'I've sent a radio telegram to the *Blenheim*; we should get an answer very shortly. And now that we know the name of the hospital where she has been treated, we can tele-phone them.' He paused at the door. 'You'll stay here.' His com-panion went ahead of him and he turned to say: 'My name is van Sittardt—Pieter van Sittardt.'

'Mine's Phyllida Cresswell.'

'We'll be in the building, ring if you want one of us—we'll be back.'

She was left with the unconscious Gaby and nothing to do but worry as to whether she had neglected to do something which might have saved her patient. Common sense told her that she hadn't; she had done exactly what she had been told to do. Moreover, she had warned Mr and Mrs de Wolff repeat-edly that Gaby wasn't improving. They had taken no notice of her—indeed, she suspected that they had thought that she was being fussy and self-important. Or perhaps they hadn't wanted to know. And they couldn't have delivered the letter from the ship's doctor at the hospital…

Gaby looked beautiful lying there. She might have been asleep, only her pallor was marked and her breathing so light that it was hardly noticeable. It was inconceivable to Phyllida that her parents could have gone off so lightheartedly, knowing, as they surely must have done, that Gaby was very ill indeed. Tidying the already tidy bedcovers, Phyllida wanted to cry.

Gaby died two hours later and it was half an hour after that when the message arrived from her parents.

They would fly back on the following morning.

Phyllida had looked dumbly at Doctor van Sittardt when he had come to tell her. For once her self-possession deserted her and she was uncertain what to do. In hospital there was a fixed procedure, followed to the letter, but here, miles from home with no one to turn to, it was altogether a different matter.

But there was someone to turn to—Doctor van Sittardt. He suggested that she should return to the hotel and return again after breakfast the next day. 'You've had nothing much to eat, have you? I'll meet you in the bar at half past seven and we'll have dinner together.'

'Yes—well—thank you, but there's...'

'I'll deal with anything that comes up, if you will allow me. There are certain formalities, and her parents aren't here.'

'You're very kind.' Phyllida studied his face and saw its impersonal kindness, and because it was such a relief to let someone else cope, she had agreed, gone back to the hotel, bathed and changed and gone down to the bar to find him waiting for her. She was glad then that she had put on the blue-patterned crêpe and taken pains with her face and hair, for he was wearing a white dinner jacket—and very elegant too, easily the most attractive man there; on any other occasion she would have enjoyed the prospect of an evening in his company, but now she kept remembering Gaby. A shadow crossed her pretty face as he reached her and he said in a friendly, brisk voice: 'Now, Phyllida, no regrets. It was inevitable, and you did everything possible.' He took her arm and found stools at the bar. 'What will you drink?'

He talked about everything under the sun and never once mentioned the day's happenings. Neither did he tell her much about himself; he was staying at the hotel for a day or two and then going to visit friends, Dutch people who lived permanently on Madeira because of the wife's health, but that was all. By the end of the evening Phyllida still didn't know where he lived or anything about him save his name.

Not that there was any need to know, she told herself as she got ready for bed. After tomorrow they weren't likely to see each other again, as she would be going back with the de

Wolffs to England and another job. She frowned at her reflection as she sat brushing her hair. Was this perhaps a sign that she should accept Philip after all? If it was she felt remarkably reluctant to take any notice of it. Philip, in the last few hours, had become strangely dim.

She slept soundly, although she hadn't expected to, and went down to breakfast, expecting to see the doctor. There was no sign of him and she ate hurriedly and then made her way in the early morning sunshine to the hospital, and met him at the entrance.

He gave her a businesslike good morning and turned her round smartly. 'I was coming to fetch you from the hotel, but since you're here we may as well go.'

'Go?' she looked at him without understanding.

'To the airport—to meet Gaby's parents.'

'Oh—yes.' She went pink, ashamed that she hadn't thought of that for herself; she should have hired a car to meet them.

The doctor went on placidly: 'I think that perhaps if there are two of us? It's a painful thing to have to do on one's own.'

She gave him a grateful look and got into the rather ramshackle car beside him and he set off without waste of time, travelling east from Funchal to the airport some twenty kilometres away. Half way there Phyllida said: 'I'm scared, having to tell them—you won't leave me, will you?'

His hooded eyes glanced sideways at her pale face. 'No. Tell me something, have the de Wolffs got money?'

She gave him a startled look. 'Well, yes, I think so. He owns several factories and has a big house in the country as well as a London flat. Why do you want to know?'

'It will help when it comes to making arrangements presently.' He overtook a bus with inches to spare. He said quietly: 'Even if I had been a pauper I would have chartered a plane as soon as I'd had that message yesterday.'

'So would I—I expect they feel terrible.'

They didn't have to wait long at the airport. The twice-weekly plane from Las Palmas arrived on time, and within a few minutes the de Wolffs were coming towards them. Mr de Wolff began speaking as soon as he was within a few yards. 'What's all this?' he demanded. 'I hope it's not a wild goose chase. I didn't telephone—no point. Luckily there was a plane leaving this morning, and heaven knows it's been inconvenient.'

And Mrs de Wolff added petulantly: 'Such a rush, and we've had to leave our luggage on board...' She paused and looked at Phyllida. 'What's wrong with Gaby this time?'

'She's dead,' said Phyllida, breaking all the rules of hospital training; bad news should be broken to relations in as gentle a way as possible...but it didn't matter, for the de Wolffs reacted just as she had feared they would. 'Why weren't we told sooner?' and 'I want to know what went wrong!'

It was here that the doctor took over; smoothly but with an edge to his cool professional voice. 'You were told. I sent a radiogram yesterday, asking you to get in touch with the hospital at once. Gaby was desperately ill—I told you that too. And nothing went wrong.' The edge had become a cutting knife. 'She received devoted care from Miss Cresswell and everything that could be done in the hospital was done.'

Phyllida looked at them both, searching for signs of grief, and could find none. Perhaps they were stunned; too shocked to feel anything. She said quietly: 'Doctor van Sittardt most kindly came to my aid yesterday...'

'Surely you knew what to do? We engaged you as a trained nurse.' Mrs de Wolff's voice rose sharply.

'Perhaps I haven't made myself clear,' said the doctor, his voice without expression. 'There was nothing to be done. Gaby was already a very ill girl. You knew that?'

Mrs de Wolff threw him an angry glance. 'Well, of course— the doctors told us she would die, but not as soon as this.'

'If she had stayed in hospital, or even quietly at home,' observed the doctor, carefully noncommittal, 'her life might have been prolonged for a short time.'

'We needed a break, we'd already booked on this cruise.' Mr de Wolff answered for his wife. 'We thought it would do her good, make her forget she was sickly.' He looked away from the doctor's stare and added uncomfortably: 'It isn't as though she were our own daughter. We adopted her when she was a baby—she was a gay little thing when she was a child, but she grew up so quiet and dull.'

The doctor didn't reply to this, neither did Phyllida, and after a moment Mr de Wolff said irritably: 'Well, we'd better go to the hospital, I suppose.'

He and his wife got into the back of the car and Phyllida settled herself beside the doctor, trying not to hear Mrs de Wolff grumbling behind her. 'I shall have to have this dress cleaned,' she complained, 'this is a dreadful car.' And then: 'I suppose we'll have to arrange to have Gaby taken back home, otherwise people might think it strange.'

Phyllida sat very upright, staring before her, her eyes wide so that she might stop her tears. Not that it helped; they tumbled silently down her cheeks and she wiped them away with a finger, stealing a glance at her companion to make sure that he hadn't noticed. He was staring ahead too, driving a little too fast, his mouth grim. He hadn't seen, she thought with relief, then went a slow red as his hand, large and cool, came down on hers and gave it a comforting squeeze. But he didn't look at her.

She wondered afterwards how she had got through that morning. Sorrow, regret, shock she could have coped with, but neither of the de Wolffs needed sympathy. Reluctantly they had conceded, in the face of the doctor's firm statement, that Phyllida had done all that she had been able to do, but they expressed no gratitude, only plunged briskly into the problems facing them, and when she asked them when she would be returning to England they told her that they would all fly back together in a few days' time, so that when Doctor Sittardt wanted to know if her future was settled, she was able to tell him that she would be leaving with the de Wolffs.

   She helped Mrs de Wolff pack up Gaby's things after breakfast the next morning while Mr de Wolff was at the airport,
making final arrangements, and when Mrs de Wolff suggested
quite kindly that she might like to have a swim in the hotel pool
before lunch, she went gladly, quite touched by her employer's
consideration.

   The water was warm and the sun shone. Phyllida swam lazily
for a while, lay in the hot sunshine for a while and then went
to dress ready for lunch. From her bedroom window she saw
the *Blenheim* lying on the other side of the harbour; she would
be sailing shortly and they should all have been on board by
now, going home. Phyllida sighed, slipped into a cotton dress,
brushed her hair smooth and went downstairs. Mrs de Wolff
had told her to wait for them in the bar, and she chose a table
in a corner and found herself wishing that the doctor had been
there to keep her company. She hadn't seen him since they had
left the hospital on the previous day and by now he would be
with his friends. She occupied her time thinking about him because it wouldn't help anyone to think about Gaby and it was
hard not to do that when she was on her own. It surprised her
presently to find that she had been there for more than half an
hour and, vaguely uneasy, she asked one of the barmen if there
was a message for her and then, at his positive 'No', went to the
reception desk and asked the same question.

   She was surprised when she was handed a note, but not un-
duly alarmed. Something must have prevented Mr de Wolff
from returning from the airport and probably his wife had gone
out there to meet him. She opened the envelope and wandered
out on to the terrace to read her letter. It was very hot now and
the sea was a deep blue under the cloudless sky. The *Blenheim*,
she noticed idly, was edging out of the harbour.

   The letter was brief but its message was clear enough; the
de Wolffs, their arrangements made at the airport concerning
Gaby, had decided to sail home on the *Blenheim*. They were
sure that Miss Cresswell would understand and she could fol-

low in her own good time, taking whichever route she preferred. A cheque covering her fees was awaiting her at the Fred Olsen offices in the town.

Phyllida sat down abruptly on a stone bench and reread the letter. No mention was made of a return ticket. She supposed they had forgotten it; they must have also forgotten that there wouldn't be another boat for a week, and although there were two flights a day to England they went via Lisbon and would doubtless cost a good deal of money. And she hadn't a great deal of that with her; enough to buy presents and small necessities for herself, but she very much doubted if that and the cheque they had left for her would be enough to get her back home. And what about the hotel bill?

All thought of lunch escaped her. She went back to the reception desk and asked about the bill and heaved a sigh of relief to find that it had been paid, but only until the following day. She told the clerk that she would be leaving then and went to get her handbag. She was halfway down the hill to the town when she remembered that it was Saturday and the shipping office would be closed. The only thing to do would be to visit the Tourist Office and find out about hotels.

And when she got there it was to discover that they had shut for the afternoon siesta. At a loss, Phyllida wandered down the Avenida Arriaga and into the Jardim de Sao Francisco and sat down under the trees. There weren't many people about in the heat of the day although there was plenty of traffic, providing a background for her thoughts.

Good sense was taking over from the feeling of panic she had been struggling to ignore. It should be easy enough to find a small, cheap hotel for a couple of nights and surely her money would stretch to a flight home on Monday—perhaps the night flights were cheaper if she could get on one. And once she was back in London everything would be all right. She could cash a cheque at the bank, telephone home; go home. She closed her eyes and leaned back against a juniper tree.

'They were a little concerned about you at the hotel,' remarked Doctor van Sittardt quietly as he sat down beside her. He put out a hand and pushed her gently back as she started up. 'You left rather suddenly without your lunch.' He glanced at her. 'The clerk mentioned a letter.'

He obviously expected an answer and Phyllida realised that he was exactly what she needed—vast and calm and reassuring. She managed the shadow of a smile, dug into her handbag and handed him Mrs de Wolff's note. 'I always thought,' she observed in a small voice, 'that I was a capable person, able to cope with things when they went wrong, but it seems I'm not. I rushed straight out of the hotel to get a cheaper hotel and book a flight back to England on Monday, but of course everything's closed for the weekend or until four o'clock. So I thought I'd come here and think things out.'

He had been reading while she spoke, now he glanced up, his blue eyes studying her steadily from under their heavy lids. 'I suspected something like this would happen; if they could dismiss Gaby's death so easily they weren't likely to treat you any differently. I should have warned you, but as you say, you are a capable girl, quite able to cope.'

Phyllida nodded, her teeth clamped together to stop the trembling of her mouth. He thought her able to take care of herself and was doubtless thankful that he wouldn't have to put himself out any more on her account. All right, she would look capable even if it killed her!

'Well now,' went on her companion blandly, 'shall we go and have lunch, or would you like a good howl first? It's very pleasant here and not many people about, and I'll lend you my shoulder.'

Phyllida unclenched her teeth and let out a tiny wail. 'Oh, however did you guess? And you've just said I'm so capable!' She made herself sit up straight. 'But I'm all right now, really I am—it was having a surprise... Do please go and have your own lunch, I'm not hungry.'

He said patiently: 'I guessed because I've sisters of my own to plague me, and however capable you are, you have to let go sometimes. A drink is what you need, and a meal. You can weep to your heart's content afterwards if you still want to.'

He swept her to her feet and walked her briskly, despite the heat, back towards the heart of the city. Down a narrow side street he stopped in front of a small restaurant, its tables spilling out on to the pavement, its interior dim and cool. He must have been known there, for they were given a table in a corner by an open window and offered a menu.

'Sercial, I think, before we eat,' said the doctor, glancing at her still pale face. 'It's very dry but splendid before a meal. We'll have Malmsey afterwards. This is a fish restaurant, but if you don't like fish, there's chicken or omelettes.'

'I like fish.' Phyllida took a gulp of her Madeira.

'Good. We'll have *bifes de atum*—that's tuna steaks—and sweet potatoes in fritters and *pudim Mareira* to follow.'

'What's that?'

'A caramel flan with Madeira sauce. Very nice.'

She took another sip and began to feel better. 'You know Madeira well?'

'I come here from time to time.' And that was all he had to say, so that to break the silence she said awkwardly:

'It looks very beautiful. I must try and come back one day and explore.'

He didn't answer at once; the fish had come and she eyed it with pleasure, her appetite sharpened. It wasn't until they had made inroads into the delicious food that he spoke. 'How much money have you?'

She paused, her fork half way to her mouth. 'Oh, enough, I think. I'll find a small hotel until Monday and book a flight home then.'

'Do you know how much the fare is?' He mentioned a sum which made her catch her breath.

'That's the return, I expect,' she said hopefully.

'No, single. I think you should stay with my friends until the next ship calls on its way back to England.'

'Oh, but I couldn't—that's a week…besides, the fare…'

'I'll telephone their head office. The de Wolffs paid for your round trip, didn't they? So unless they've claimed a refund, your passage is already paid.'

Relief almost choked her. 'Oh, I hadn't thought of that. I can stay here until it comes—I'm bound to find an hotel.'

He finished his fish and leaned back in his chair. 'Phyllida, if you were me and I were you, would you offer to help me? And expect me to accept?'

'Of course I would!' She had spoken before thinking and he smiled.

'Well, that's all I'm doing. My friends will love to have you; Metha is rather crippled with arthritis and will enjoy your company.'

'Yes, but I can't…'

'We'll go back to the hotel presently and pick up your things and I'll drive you out there. I'll give them a ring while you're packing.'

She said weakly: 'But supposing they don't want me to stay? They don't know me.'

'How could they when they haven't met you?' he asked reasonably. 'Ah, here is our Madeira pudding—they do it very well here. There are some excellent restaurants in Funchal and quite a few scattered round the island. We must take you to some of them before you go back.'

They had almost finished their pudding when he asked: 'Do you want to telephone your family?'

She swallowed the last delicious morsel. 'Well, they're rather—I think they might worry; I thought a letter. If I send it today?'

He shook his head. 'No good, the *Blenheim* will get there long before the letter. Were you going straight home?'

'Yes.'

'Then telephone. You could say that plans have been changed and you'll be back a week later.'

The waiter brought two glasses of Malmsey and the doctor ordered coffee. Phyllida, who could think of no reason for disputing his suggestion, agreed.

They went unhurriedly back to the hotel presently, and she went up to her room to pack her things, leaving the doctor to tell the receptionist and telephone his friends. When she went down half an hour later, he was sitting on the terrace, his feet on a chair, reading an old copy of the *Telegraph*. There was a tall glass at his elbow, half full, and as he got to his feet he waved to a waiter and ordered her a drink. 'I'm drinking lager, but I've ordered you a lemonade and lime. Will that do?'

'Yes, thank you.' She sat down opposite him and he lounged back in his chair again.

'The de Meesters—my friends—are delighted to have you for as long as you like to stay. They want us up there for tea.'

'Do they live far away?' she asked.

He waved vaguely towards the mountains which swept up and away behind the town. 'No—in a village about five kilometres to the north—Monte. It used to be the island's capital and it's full of lovely old houses. There's a magnificent church too.'

He finished his drink and stretched out again, and Phyllida had the impression that if she hadn't been there he would have closed his eyes and had a nap. She sipped her own drink, relaxing under his casual calm, knowing that he didn't expect her to make conversation. When she had finished he sat up, all at once brisk. 'Right, did someone bring down your luggage?'

She nodded. 'Yes, it's at reception.' She hesitated. 'You've been very kind, Doctor van Sittardt.'

He smiled, a warm slow smile that transformed his rather austere good looks and made her feel safe and secure. 'The name's Pieter.' He got to his feet and stretched out a hand and pulled her out of her chair. 'Let's go and see if that car will start.'

The little car was certainly shabby, but there was nothing

wrong with its engine. They went slowly through the town and then into the Rua 31 de Janeiro, and presently turned right into the Rua do Til. The drive might have been only five kilometres, but it was uphill all the way, and Phyllida, who had seen nothing of the island, was enchanted by the scenery as they climbed steadily up into the mountains. The doctor slowed down from time to time so that she could take it all in—the towering grey heights, the little green meadows tucked between them, with eucalyptus, mimosa and juniper trees, the small red-tiled houses, and from time to time a luxurious modern villa. He pointed Monte out to her before they reached it, to one side of the road, cloud hanging above it, its houses, and church clinging to the summit. The houses on its outskirts were modern, white-walled and red-tiled like the farms and each with its trailing vines and bougainvillea, with wisteria and the blue of the jacaranda trees adding splashes of bright colour. But once in the centre of the small place, they were back in the eighteenth century, for its square was lined with balconied houses of great age, overshadowd by the church and the mountains around them. The doctor turned the car down a narrow side street and then turned again through a wide arched gateway leading to a paved courtyard, enclosed on three sides by grey stone walls pierced by high narrow windows and with a massive door in its centre.

He stopped the car and leaned across Phyllida to open her door. 'We're here, and in case you find it rather forbidding, it's much nicer inside.'

The door was opened before they reached it by a small dark woman who smiled gravely at them and led the way across a wide dim hall to a door at one side. She flung this open, said something to whoever was inside, and stood back to let them pass.

The room was dim too with dark panelled walls and a plain white ceiling. The floor was tiled and covered by thin rugs in lovely colours and the furniture was dark and massive. There were two people in the room, a man and a woman, and the man got up at once and came towards them, his hand held out.

'Welcome, Miss Cresswell. You cannot know how glad we are to have you as our guest.' He engulfed her hand in his and beamed down at her. He was almost as tall as Pieter van Sittardt but inclined to stoutness, with a pleasant rugged face and fair hair already receding from a high forehead. 'You will forgive my wife if she doesn't get up.' He held her hand still and led her across the room to where a youngish woman was sitting in a high-backed chair. She was still very pretty with fair hair and dark eyes and she was dressed with great elegance. Only her crippled hands gave away the fact that she was an invalid. But that was forgotten when she spoke.

'I shall not call you Miss Cresswell,' she declared in a pretty voice. 'Phyllida is such a pretty name—mine's Metha,' she nodded towards her husband, 'and he is Hans. It is lovely to have you and I am so happy—these two talk about their work all the time and do not care for clothes.' She lifted a face to Pieter who bent to kiss her cheek.

'I should hope not indeed,' he declared, 'but you and Phyllida can talk to your hearts' content. I expect you miss the children.'

Metha nodded. 'Oh yes, very much—but now I have Phyllida and shall speak English all the time so that I will be occupied all the time and be happy.'

She smiled at Phyllida. 'You do not speak Portuguese, or Dutch?' and went on in a satisfied voice: 'No? That is splendid for me, for I shall improve my English and teach you a little besides.'

The solemn-faced woman brought in tea then, tea in a pot, Phyllida saw with pleasure, and plenty of milk in a jug, as well as a plate of little cakes and sugary biscuits. 'We like our tea,' explained Metha, 'it is for us a pleasant hour of the day, just to sit and talk.'

And very pleasant it was, Phyllida agreed silently, and how very at home Pieter looked, stretched out in one of the heavy

tapestry-covered armchairs. It was evident that he was a friend
of long standing but all the same, they all took care to include
her in their talk, touching lightly on her reason for being there
and then ignoring it to talk about Madeira and their life there.

Metha did most of the talking in her pretty English with
her husband joining in frequently, only Pieter van Sittardt remained almost silent, looking, Phyllida decided, almost too
lazy to open his mouth.

The pleasant little meal came to its leisurely end and Phyllida was taken upstairs by the solemn woman, who led the way
along a corridor to a room at the back of the house, with a balcony overlooking a small paved yard with a fountain in its centre. Phyllida heaved a sigh of pure pleasure at the sight of it;
things could have been so much worse—a small hotel and the
worry of wondering if her money would hold out and business
of getting a ticket for home. She would have to see about that
on Monday morning; she couldn't impose on her new friends,
whatever the doctor had said.

She unpacked and hung her things away, took a shower,
changed her dress and went downstairs again.

CHAPTER FOUR

THERE WAS ONLY one occupant of the sitting room as she entered, the doctor, lounging back in a great armchair, his enormous feet on a convenient coffee table. He appeared to be asleep, but he wasn't, for he was on his feet before she had taken two steps into the room.

'Hullo,' he smiled disarmingly at her, 'the others will be down directly. Metha said I was to give you a drink.' He pulled forward a chair and she sat down. 'Have something long and cool; they dine rather later than we do at home.'

'Thank you.' Phyllida went on hurriedly: 'I've not had the chance to thank you properly for everything you've done—you've been simply super.'

'I think that we agreed that you would have done the same for me?' He dismissed her thanks with casual ease. 'Now, this drink—how about a Pimms with not too much gin?'

He mixed the drink, handed it to her, poured himself a whisky and sat down again. 'Metha thinks it might be fun if we drove round a bit tomorrow and showed you the sights. She wants you to see Cabo Girao—that's a very high sea cliff to the west of Funchal. It's a pretty drive there and afterwards we might go on to Ribeira Brava, it won't be crowded yet—we might even swim, but Metha's a bit shy of going into the water if there's anyone about. Hans carries her in; he swims on his back and takes her with him.'

'She's so pretty and young.' Phyllida's eyes searched her companion's face. 'Isn't there anything to be done?'

'Not much, I'm afraid. She had acute rheumatoid arthritis after the second child was born; she doesn't have much pain now, but it's left her with limited movement. She's a wonderful person, never complains and always looks so serene and marvellously turned out. She and Hans have the kind of marriage one hopes for and seldom achieves.'

'Are you married?'

He smiled slowly. 'No, I've always considered myself to be a dedicated bachelor. However, I think it very likely that I shall change my mind; there's something very appealing about a wife and children to comfort my old age.'

She looked a question, not quite daring to ask it.

'And I'm thirty-nine.' He glanced at her from under heavy lids. 'You, Phyllida? Are you married, divorced, engaged or having what I believe is called a close relationship with some lucky man?'

'Oh, I don't believe in that,' declared Phyllida. Her blue eyes met his candidly. 'And I'm not married or divorced.' She added after a pause: 'Nor engaged.'

'Thinking about it?' he asked lazily.

She shook her head. 'Not any more—it was just—well, we sort of slid into supposing that we might get married later on and then I discovered that I didn't love him at all, only liked him very much.'

'Now it's so often the other way round with me,' murmured the doctor. 'I fall in love with a girl and then discover that I don't like her.'

She wondered what kind of girls he fell in love with and then told herself that it was none of her business. All the same she was trying to think of a way of putting a tactful question or two when Metha and Hans came in. Metha was walking with two sticks, but she looked so pretty and happy that it went almost unnoticed; besides, she broke into lively chatter as soon as she was in the room.

'We'll have dinner in half an hour and then have coffee on the terrace,' she declared happily. 'It's such a beautiful evening and the sunset is always a delight. Phyllida, come over here and sit with me and tell me where you bought that pretty dress. There are one or two good shops here, but not very much choice. Twice a year we go to Holland for a visit and I do as much shopping as I can while we're there, but you know what men are; you put on a hat and they say: "that's fine, dear", and there you are saddled with something hideous, suitable for an aunt!'

They all laughed and Phyllida looked across at the doctor and found him staring at her, his eyes half shut, as usual. She pinkened faintly; he would think her horribly unfeeling to be enjoying herself so much, with Gaby…

He had read her expression unerringly. 'Now, Phyllida!' He shook his head at her and smiled so kindly that she had the sudden urge to run across the room and bury her face in his shoulder and howl her eyes out. But she wasn't given the chance; he went on: 'Why don't you two girls do some shopping tomorrow afternoon? We could go to Cabo Girao in the morning, lunch at Camara de Lobos at that nice place—the Riba Mar, isn't it?— and drop you both off at that boutique you go to in Funchal, Metha. Come to that, we'll park the car and come with you.' He grinned at Phyllida. 'I might even buy you a hat.'

The dinner was delicious, although Phyllida wasn't sure what they ate most of the time, and she was too shy to ask. The two men ate hugely, leaving most of the talking to the two girls and keeping their glasses filled with a light table wine which was presently replaced by Malmsey which they drank with their coffee.

It was still warm on the terrace and the view over the mountains and down towards Funchal and the sea was breathtakingly lovely in the late evening. The talk was quiet now, an effortless flow which Phyllida found very soothing. Presently the doctor got up and came over to where she was sitting. 'Come to the end of the terrace,' he suggested, 'we can see the sunset from there and with any luck you'll see the green flash.'

She got up willingly. 'What's that?'

He shrugged huge shoulders. 'I'm not sure—it sometimes follows a Madeira sunset.'

The back of the house overlooked a sloping garden which in turn led to a banana plantation, sweeping down to the ravine far below, and on the other side the mountains towered, but the valley between allowed them a clear view of the sun, setting in a blaze of colour. It was all so beautiful and Phyllida, looking at it, found to her horror that she was on the verge of tears. She muttered: 'Oh, poor Gaby, not to be able to see all this.'

A great arm was flung across her shoulders. 'There's no one but us,' he told her gently. 'Have your cry, my dear, you'll feel better for it.'

She sucked in her breath like a little girl. 'It's all such a waste,' she stopped to sniff, fighting the tears still, 'and I can't see why.'

'My dear child, I say that every day in my work, but I don't expect to be given the answer.' He turned her round so that her head rested comfortably on his chest and stood patiently while she sobbed, and presently he said: 'Feel better? Turn round, the sun's just going down.'

They stood together, his arm still round her, and watched the sky deepen its colour, and then as the sun sank from sight, they saw the green flash.

'That's something you can tell your friends about when you get back to the hospital.' He had fished a handkerchief from a pocket and handed it to her and she was mopping her face.

'I'm not going back. I—I left St Michael's just before I came on this trip.'

'Want to talk about it?' His casual voice invited confidence. She hadn't realised how much she had wanted to talk to someone; it all came tumbling out and when she had finished: 'And the awful thing is I'm sure—at least, I'm not sure, but I think I may have made a frightful mistake; Philip's so—so safe.' She added quickly: 'I'm boring you.'

'No, you're not, and if I might offer my opinion for what it's worth; the frightful mistake would be if you were to marry Philip.'

He looked down at her thoughtfully, his eyes almost hidden under their lids. 'I think you're a girl who needs to marry for love and nothing else—you don't have any doubts if you love someone, you know.'

'I know you're right. I'm just being cowardly about looking for another job—all those forms to fill in and the interviews and then getting to know everyone.'

'In your English you say: "Don't cross your bridges until you come to them". Such a wise piece of advice. Why do you not take a holiday?' He gave her shoulder a brotherly pat. 'You have a family?'

She found herself telling him about her home, her mother and father and Willy who was going to be a doctor like his father, and Dick who was in his last year at a veterinary college and Beryl, just twenty, who was at Bristol University. 'I think I will have a holiday,' she finished, 'just for a couple of weeks while I make up my mind where I want to go.'

'A splendid idea. And now as to the immediate future. I find that I shall be going back with the next ship too; we shall be fellow passengers, and in the meantime we may as well enjoy ourselves here. Metha and Hans love having guests and I know that she longs for more female company at times. Besides, we're an excellent excuse for sightseeing—she has a passion for picnics, too. When the children are on holiday she can arrange one every day, but they're in Holland and Hans is away all day she's very much alone. He's on holiday at the moment because I'm here.'

'It sounds wonderful, but are you sure—I mean, I just can't stay here for a week...'

'Metha would be heartbroken if you didn't. Besides, with you here, we can slope off on our own.'

Phyllida laughed a little. 'Of course, if you put it like that, I haven't any choice, have I?'

'None whatever.' He turned her round and deliberately studied her face in the twilight. 'Tears all gone? Good, we'll join the others, shall we? They'll want to make plans for tomorrow.'

They took her to Cabo Girao the following day, driving back to Funchal and along the coast road, climbing all the way, with the sea below on one side, and a scattering of villages on the other. There were flowers everywhere; nasturtiums, wisteria and echium jostled for a place, with jacaranda trees making great splashes of colour next the bougainvillea, and every wayside cottage and villa had a garden crowded with every sort of flower. Phyllida craned her pretty neck in her efforts to see everything which was being pointed out to her, sitting beside Pieter who was driving his friend's Mercedes, with Hans and Metha in the back.

'There's a dragon tree!' exclaimed Metha, and Pieter slowed the car so that Phyllida should get a good view of it before racing on, still climbing.

The cliff, when they reached it, was spectacular, but she was glad of Pieter's arm round her shoulders as they hung over the rail to stare down to the sea far below, and she was secretly relieved when they rejoined Metha in the car and drove down to Camara de Lobo, where they had lunch, and then, while Hans and Metha stayed on the restaurant's terrace, the doctor took Phyllida for a stroll on the beach to get a closer look at the gaily painted boats. Phyllida scuffed her sandalled feet happily in the shingle and wished the day would last for ever; it didn't seem possible that she had known her companion for such a short time; he was like an old friend, easygoing, goodnaturedly answering her questions, treating her like a sister. She stopped to examine a shell and wondered why she didn't really want him to treat her with such offhand ease. Yet, after all, they were only acquaintances, brought together by circumstances, and once she was back in England she wouldn't see him any more. She stole a look at him, meandering along beside her. He was already deeply tanned, so that his hair looked like silvered straw, and his eyes, when he bothered to lift the lids, were a quite startling blue. His face seemed haughty in repose, but that was because his nose was large and arrogant and his mouth firm. He was indeed a handsome man. He looked sideways at her, catching her unawares, and she went red and looked away quickly. But when she made to walk a little apart from him he caught her hand and didn't let it go. 'Enjoying yourself?' he wanted to know.

'Oh, yes, it's super. I didn't expect to see anything of Madeira, you know.'

'We'll take the toboggan ride tomorrow—that's something everyone does when they come here. We'll go early before the tourists arrive.' He stopped to look at her. 'Can you swim?'

'Not very well, but I like it.'

'Good. We'll go to Ponta de Sao Lourenço, that's the only sandy beach there is. We can take Metha, of course, because there'll be no one much there and she can go in the water. We'll go over the Poiso pass and through Santo da Serra; it's a pretty run, you'll like it.'

'It sounds lovely, but I do have to go to the shipping office and collect my cheque and see about going back.'

'I hadn't forgotten. You and Metha can spend ten minutes in a boutique—it'll be open—and Hans and I will go and get your money and see about a sailing.'

'I can't bother you…'

'I'm not in the least bothered, I have to get a passage for myself too.'

'Oh, yes—of course.' She gave her hand a little tug and his grip tightened ever so gently.

'You haven't been around much, have you?' His voice was as gentle as his fingers.

She knew what he meant. 'No, I suppose not, there's not a

lot of time for a social life—one comes off duty tired and only longing to kick off one's shoes and make a pot of tea. I used to go out more often before I met Philip.'

'You didn't go out with him?' He sounded surprised.

'Well, yes, of course—I meant we didn't go dancing or to shows or anything like that, just to a restaurant for supper or to his brother's house.'

There was no expression on her companion's face. 'It sounds cosy.' His voice was dry and she gave another tug at her hand.

'No, leave it where it is. You're a pretty girl, Phyllida, you should have your chance to play the field, meet people, and by that I mean men of your own age. Who knows if you go into the wide world and fall in and out of love a few times, you may go back to your Philip after all.'

She didn't fancy the idea somehow. Philip seemed far away, belonging to another world. The thought crossed her mind that it might be fun to fall in love with Pieter. Just a little, of course; he was a very attractive man and doubtless he had a girl at home. It was a pity that she didn't know him well enough to ask him; it struck her that he had asked her a great many more questions than she had done of him. Not that it mattered, he was a chance encounter...

She reminded herself of that several times during the day; just to be on the safe side, but it was a little difficult. Hans was a chance encounter too, but with him it didn't seem at all the same.

But she enjoyed herself, spending a pleasant half hour with Metha in the boutique, looking at bright cotton dresses and beautifully cut bikinis. She didn't dare buy anything, though.

The men came back presently and Pieter handed her an envelope. 'If you sign the cheque, I'll go across to the bank and get it cashed,' he told her. 'Have you any traveller's cheques with you?'

'No—they said I wouldn't need any money because they would be paying me. I've a few pounds, though, as well as some money I brought along just in case—it's not much, though.'

She opened the envelope. The cheque was for the exact number of days she had worked for the de Wolffs. No one had thought of her expenses, but all the same there would be enough to get her home now provided she didn't spend more than a pound or two in Madeira. She slid the cheque back into the envelope and Pieter, who had been talking to the others, turned round. 'You won't need any money for your fare,' he told her casually. 'They checked with their head office and you've been given a ticket—on the boat deck, a single cabin. The ship sails at two o'clock on Saturday.'

'And now you don't need to save your money,' interpolated Metha, 'we shall go right back into the boutique and you shall buy that Indian cotton sun-dress—and I think I shall buy one too.' She beamed at the men. 'And you, my dears, may come with us.'

They went in together and the shop owner surged forward, produced a chair for Metha and whisked Phyllida away with an armful of dresses over her arm. The one she had liked, a vivid blue tied carelessly on the shoulders and with a deep scooped out neckline, was a perfect fit. Urged by the shop lady, she went back into the shop from the tiny fitting room and showed herself to the three of them. 'Beautiful,' said Metha at once. 'Smashing,' declared Hans, who prided himself on his up-to-date English, and: 'You'll need a bikini to go underneath that,' observed Pieter lazily.

So she bought a bikini too and for good measure a wide-brimmed straw hat, and while she was trying it on, the doctor, who had been prowling round on his own, came back with a silk dress flung over his arm. It was a delicate green patterned with the faintest of pinks.

'Try that on too,' he begged her. 'We're going dancing to-morrow.'

Which seemed a good enough reason for doing just that, and finding it to be a perfect fit, buying it too.

They spent the evening at the de Meesters' house and after

dinner the doctor took Phyllida for a stroll round the little town and then up the path through the park to the church, and as they walked round its dim coolness he told her about Nossa Senhora do Monte, whose bejewelled statue held pride of place on the high altar.

'Rather lovely, isn't she?' he said very quietly. 'I'm not a Catholic myself, but she stands for a great deal to many people living on the island—they come each year, thousands of them, to see Our Lady of the Mountain.'

They strolled back presently through the cool evening and then once more indoors, spent the rest of the evening playing a noisy game of Canasta.

They went swimming the next day, but only after the doctor had kept his promise to Phyllida and taken her on the toboggan ride. He drove her away from Monte, up into the hills beyond, with Hans beside them, so that he could drive the car back to his house. It was still early and there weren't many people about. Leaving Hans and the car they took a narrow path which brought them out on to a cobbled lane where the toboggans were waiting, each with two men, dressed in their uniform of white suits and straw hats.

The journey took perhaps five minutes, the toboggan sliding at speed over the ridged cobbles, guided by the two men. Phyllida found it a bit alarming, especially on the frequent hairpin-bends, but it was fun too and she had Pieter to hang on to. 'You've done it before,' she gasped, half way down.

'Lord, yes—half a dozen times.' He didn't add with a girl, but she guessed that. 'Enjoying it?'

She nodded, her silky hair flying round her head, her eyes sparkling like a child's. 'But I'd hate to do it on my own.'

'I don't think there's any fear of that.'

The ride ended by the church they had visited on the previous evening, and tourists were already going in and out of its doors, stopping to examine and buy the embroidered handkerchiefs laid out neatly on large trays carried by the local man.

But they didn't stop, going down the path again and back into the town and the de Meesters' house.

'Just time to put on the sun-dress,' remarked the doctor as they went inside, 'and don't forget the bikini!'

It was an hilarious day. Phyllida, lying awake at the end of it, went carefully over every minute of it. Pieter had driven the car, taking them up into the mountains through the kind of scenery she thought she would never see again, over the Poiso Pass, through the charming countryside past the golf course, tucked away on a small plateau and, she had considered, a bit inaccessible, and then on to Canical which she hadn't much cared for; it was dominated by a whale oil factory and looked forlorn. It was from here that they had to walk; not far, as it happened, for Pieter took the car to the very edge of the sand dunes which led to the beach. They had a light wheelchair with them for Metha and Pieter carried the picnic basket and no one hurried. The beach was almost deserted and the men went back to the car for airbeds, a huge sun umbrella, a basket full of tins of beer and lemonade and armfuls of cushions. Phyllida, remembering picnics at home—potted meat sandwiches and a thermos— got quite goggle-eyed at the lavishness of the food; delicate little sandwiches, potato fritters, cold, accompanying *espada* fish, cold chicken, tomato salad—there was no end. She had eaten a bit of everything with a splendid appetite and washed it down with lemonade. And it hadn't been hot, there had been a breeze from the sea and the water had been surprisingly cool. She had taken off the sun-dress rather shyly because there really hadn't been much of the bikini, but the doctor had barely glanced at her, and once in the water she had forgotten her shyness and after a few minutes close to the beach, she had struck out bravely, heading out to sea. She'd heard Metha laughing as Hans towed her through the water; Pieter she hadn't seen, not until he appeared beside her, swimming with no effort at all.

'They catch whales here,' he told her.

Phyllida, the kind of swimmer to sink like a stone at the least alarm, let out a small scream, swallowed a good deal of water and gurgled so alarmingly that the doctor flipped her over on to her back and slid an arm beneath her. 'When I said here,' he had pointed out unhurriedly, 'I meant some miles out to sea.'

He was paddling alongside her, looking at the sky. 'If you've finished spluttering, let's go back. Do you think you're strong enough to hold Metha up on one side, I'll hang on to the other. Then Hans can go for a swim.'

They had done that, with Metha, her thin arms on their shoulders, between them. It hadn't been quite like swimming, but it was the next best thing, and no one, unless they had looked very closely, would have known the difference; the water helped, of course, allowing her more movement, and Pieter acted just as though she were doing it all by herself. He was nice, thought Phyllida sleepily, and he had been even nicer that evening. True to his promise he had taken her down to Funchal after dinner, to the Hotel Savoy, where they had danced, watched the folk dancing and then danced again, and on the way back to Monte, at two o'clock in the morning, they had stopped at a noisy, dimly lit street café and had coffee and brandy.

Monte's narrow streets and old houses had been dark. The doctor stopped the car soundlessly and got out to open her door and then the house door. There was a lamp burning in the hall and the old house had seemed not quite real in the utter silence. She had thanked him for a lovely evening and wished him goodnight, and for answer he had caught her arm and walked her through the house to the terrace beyond. 'You can't go to bed before you've seen the view,' he had told her, and taken her to the very end of it.

It wasn't quite time for the dawn, but the sky to the east was already paling, and turning at the touch of his hand she had seen the dark outline of the mountains and the even darker ravines and beyond them the lights still burning in the outskirts of Funchal.

'All the years I've wasted in London,' she had said, talking to herself.

'Not wasted—and not so many—you can always make up for lost time.'

She had said: 'I'm not likely to come here again—not for a long time.' She didn't suppose that he had to worry overmuch about money and although she wasn't exactly poor, her salary hardly ran to the kind of holiday she was enjoying now. She turned away and gone back indoors and he had followed her, locking the glass doors after him. In the hall, at the foot of the stairs, she had said again: 'Thank you, Pieter,' and would have added a few conventional remarks to round off their evening, but she didn't have the chance. He had kissed her then—she turned over in bed and thumped her pillows, remembering it. She had been silly to think that it might be fun to fall a little in love with him. It wouldn't be fun at all, it would be disaster—a dead end affair with him bidding her a cheerful goodbye when they got to London, forgetting her the moment her back was turned. It had been an unexpected holiday, she reminded herself, and as so often happened on holiday, one met someone one rather liked and enjoyed a casual, short-lived friendship. She closed her eyes on this sensible thought; she was almost asleep when she remembered that Pieter had told her that she looked beautiful in the new dress.

After that the days flashed by, filled by picnics in beautiful remote spots and a drive to Ponta Delgada on the north coast, over the Eucumeada Pass, where they had stopped so that Phyllida might feast her eyes on the magnificent view from its top, and they had lunched at the hotel close by before driving on through the mountains. She would have liked to have stopped again, there was so much to see, but as Pieter explained, the roads were winding and precipitous and it wasn't always possible. Not that he seemed to mind the hazards; he drove with nonchalant ease whether they were going uphill, downhill or round hairpin bends which made her glad she wasn't driving.

And that evening they had gone dancing again, only this time he didn't kiss her goodnight.

Saturday came too soon, she bade Metha and Hans goodbye with real regret for it seemed as though they had been lifelong friends, and then stood aside while the doctor made his own farewells, brief and cheerful, before he took her arm and hurried her on board.

Their cabins were next door to each other and very much to her taste, roomy and comfortable and spotlessly clean. She would unpack at once, she decided, but she had scarcely opened her overnight bag before the doctor thumped on her door. 'They'll wait on the quay until we leave,' he explained. 'We'd better go on deck.'

So she went with him, to hang over the rail and shout to Metha and watch the last-minute buying and selling going on round the little stalls set up alongside the ship, while Pieter lounged beside her, not saying much, watching her intent face with a half smile.

Once they had sailed Phyllida went back to her cabin to unpack. They wouldn't get back until Wednesday morning and she would need some clothes—evening clothes especially. She decided on her long evening skirt and a pretty top to go with it, put everything else tidily away and went along to the lido.

The doctor was there, sitting at a table by the swimming pool, a drink at his elbow, deep in a Dutch paper he had bought in Funchal before they sailed. She hesitated, wondering if she should join him; they weren't exactly travelling together, only fellow passengers. She started back the way she had come, only to be halted in her tracks by his: 'Hey, where are you off to?'

She approached the table slowly as he unfolded his length and pulled out a chair for her. 'Well,' she said carefully, 'I just thought we're only fellow passengers, not travelling together, if you see what I mean. You wouldn't want me hanging round your neck like a millstone.'

'Wouldn't I? Get this clear, love, I'm a shy man, I don't know

a soul on board and I intend to cling to you like a limpet.' He
added: 'During waking hours, of course.'

He was teasing her, she knew that, so she laughed back at
him.

'Well, I don't know anyone, either. Only you must tell me if
I'm in the way.' She grinned suddenly, at ease with him once
more. 'I saw the most gorgeous blonde just now—she really
is lovely.'

He lifted lazy lids and she blinked under his intent look. 'I
must chat her up, I'm partial to blondes. Do point her out.'

'She doesn't need pointing out,' remarked Phyllida with
something of a snap, 'you'll see her easily enough for yourself.'

He didn't answer her, only asked her what she would like
to drink.

They went down to tea presently and then played Bingo, getting very excited when they nearly won, and then going along to
the shop to browse around, buying postcards she would never
send and a huge tin of toffees for Willy, who would appreciate
them far more than anything foreign and unedible.

She was almost dressed when Pieter tapped on her door before dinner. 'Come in,' she called, 'I'm trying to find an evening bag.'

He sat down on her bed, watching her while she searched
through the drawers and at length found what she wanted. He
took up so much room in the cabin that it seemed to shrink as
she stepped carefully backwards and forwards over his big feet
before sitting down beside him to change things from one bag
to the other.

He watched her lazily. 'You look very nice—we'll dance
later, shall we?'

She nodded, finished what she was doing and got to her feet.

'The bar, I think,' he suggested, 'but let's go this way; I've
an urge to play the fruit machines.' He handed her a handful
of silver. 'Split fifty-fifty whoever wins.'

Phyllida had never played before. She had wanted to on the

voyage out, but she had never had enough time to herself—besides, she had been afraid that she might lose too much money. She won two pounds now and screamed with delight. 'Here's your money, and your half of the winnings. Now you have a go.'

He won nothing and presently she cried: 'Oh, do stop, you won't have any money left—do have some of mine.'

He declined. 'My luck's out—let's go and have a drink, we can play later if we want to.'

The bar was crowded, but they found seats in a corner and bent their heads over the next day's programme. 'I don't think I'll go to the keep fit class,' said the doctor seriously, 'and definitely not the fancy dress—how about deck quoits and a nice long lie in the sun doing nothing?'

Phyllida agreed happily. And that was how they spent their days, swimming in the pool before breakfast, playing some deck game or other after breakfast and then lying side by side doing nothing, not even talking. Phyllida found it singularly restful; the sea was calm, even in the Bay of Biscay, and the weather stayed fine, although as they neared their journey's end there was a decided nip in the air, which made sweaters a necessity, and when they got too chilly, Pieter pulled her to her feet and made her play table tennis. They danced each evening too; the only fly in the ointment was the blonde girl. They had a table for two in the centre of the restaurant and the girl was seated close by in the doctor's direct line of vision. She was an eyeful, Phyllida decided vexedly on their first evening, and she couldn't compete with the white crêpe dress, cut low and with a long gored skirt which twisted and twirled as the girl walked the length of the restaurant. She had piled-up hair, dressed in a careless riot of curls and crowned with a tiny cap sporting a curling feather which curved round one cheek—absurd on anyone else, but on this girl, devastating. The doctor had studied her at length and with no expression.

'I told you I wouldn't need to point her out,' said Phyllida.

He gave her one of his bland looks. 'Oh, I do see exactly what you mean, love—she's a knock-out.'

She had agreed with chilly enthusiasm.

As far as she knew, he hadn't looked at the girl again that evening, nor the next morning. It was after lunch when he told her that he was going down to the purser's office, and strolled away.

He was still gone an hour later, and with nothing to do, she remembered that she had to press a dress for the evening. She was on her way to the ironing room when she saw them standing near the purser's office, deep in conversation. The girl was leaning back against the wall, her hands on either side of her, pressed against it, a beguiling attitude calculated to show her figure off to the best possible advantage. She was looking up at the doctor with a look which Phyllida had often tried before her looking glass, without much success because she had always giggled. She sped on down to the deck below, sure that she hadn't been seen, did her pressing and hurried back. They weren't there when she reached the purser's office.

She hung up the pink crêpe—really it had been a waste of time fussing with it, the doctor wasn't going to notice, was he? not with that creature making eyes at him—and bounced out of her cabin and back to the deck, to be waylaid at once by a young man with a lot of teeth and pebble glasses who asked her eagerly if she would like to use his binoculars. There was nothing to see, but she agreed with an enthusiasm which encouraged him to offer her a drink. It was nearly tea-time and not really warm enough for a cold drink, but he looked so anxious to please that she accepted a lemonade and stood at the rail with him, drinking it while he told her all about his job—something vague in the City.

She wasn't sure when she first felt that they were being watched; after a moment or two she looked round cautiously. Behind them, lying in a chair with his feet up, was the doctor. He grinned as she turned a shoulder to him.

She finished the drink slowly, aware that it was four o'clock and everyone was going down to tea, and trying to decide whether she should stay where she was and wait for Pebble Glasses to invite her to share his table, or excuse herself, ignore the doctor, and have tea on her own.

She knew that she was being childish and silly, which made it more difficult to decide. Luckily it was decided for her; the doctor tapped her smartly on the shoulder, smiled with charm at her companion and wanted to know if she was coming to pour his tea for him. Short of saying no, she wasn't, there had been nothing she could do about it. Out of earshot of Pebble Glasses he had observed placidly: 'Paying me back in my own coin, Phylly?'

'I don't know what you're talking about.' She tried to sound dignified, which was quite wasted on her companion, who sat her down in a quiet corner and fell to examining the plate of cakes on the table between them. Only when he had done this to his satisfaction had he said: 'empty as a hot air balloon.' He looked at her, smiling faintly. 'What a pity—such beauty, and nothing—just nothing between the ears.' He sighed: 'But I found it interesting from a medical point of view.'

His voice was so silky that she shot him a suspicious glance. 'I don't believe it.'

He hadn't appeared to hear her. 'Now you, love, have good looks and a good brain to go with them—you'll make someone an excellent wife one day.' He added wickedly. 'Was Pebble Glasses all you could find?'

It had been impossible to be grumpy with him after that.

Phyllida packed with great regret before dinner on their final evening; she had been to the purser's office and got herself a seat on the coach which would take any passengers who wished up to Victoria Station, but she hadn't told Pieter. And he for his part hadn't said a word. She supposed that they would say good-bye after an early breakfast and she would never know where he was going. Somewhere in England? Holland? She had no idea.

They were watching a spirited entertainment after dinner

when he said in a tone which brooked no denial: 'I've arranged for a car to be at the dock. I'll drive you home.'

She had been surprised at the delight which swept through her.

'But it's miles away…'

'Three hours run at the outside.'

'Well—but don't you want to go home?'

His smile told her nothing. 'I've two or three days to spare, I should enjoy the drive.'

Which really didn't answer her question.

CHAPTER FIVE

DISEMBARKING FROM THE ship at Millwall Dock was smoothly efficient and swift. Phyllida found herself and her baggage on the road outside the dock with hundreds of others, only whereas they were getting on to a fleet of coaches, taxis or relatives' cars, she had been led to a corner and told to stay there while Pieter went to look for his car. He was back inside five minutes, driving a Ford Scorpio, and long before the buses had revved up their engines he had stowed the luggage, popped her into the front seat, got behind the wheel and driven away.

It was still barely nine o'clock in the morning and the traffic in the East End was dense; it got worse as they approached the city, but the doctor didn't allow that to irritate him, he kept up a gentle flow of talk weaving in and out of the traffic unerringly so that presently Phyllida asked: 'Do you know London well? You drive as though you did.'

'I come here from time to time. I'm aiming for the M3, I think it'll be best if we cut straight through, don't you, and cross the river at Chiswick. We can stop in Richmond for coffee, and what about Salisbury for lunch? Isn't there a place called the Haunch of Venison?'

'Yes, but I'm sure Mother would give us a late lunch, there's really no need...'

He shot her a quick smile. 'Oh, let's have a last lunch to-gether, shall we?—Perhaps your mother will be kind enough to invite me to tea.'

It was while they were drinking their coffee in Richmond that Phyllida suddenly realised that she hadn't thought of Philip for days. She looked across at the doctor, scanning the headlines of the *Telegraph*, and thought how nice it was that they could sit together like this without making conversation because they felt that they should. Every now and then he read out some item which he thought might interest her, but he made no special ef-fort to capture her attention; he might have been her brother. She wasn't sure whether to be annoyed about this or not. Upon due reflection she thought not, for although they hadn't known each other long they had an easy friendship, quite at ease with each other and enjoying each other's company. But that was all; he had never shown any signs of interest in her as a person. Indeed, the blonde on board had come in for more attention...

She frowned into her coffee. She wasn't a vain girl, but she was aware that she had more than her share of good looks and although she had no sophistication to speak of, someone had told her once that she was a wholesome girl. She had quite liked it at the time, now she wasn't so sure; she didn't think that Pieter would be interested in wholesomeness—he had, she considered, an experienced eye. She sighed and he put the paper down at once. 'Sorry—my shocking manners. Let's go.'

It began to rain as they started off again and by the time they got to Salisbury it was a steady downpour. But the Haunch of Venison was warm and welcoming; they ate roast beef and Yorkshire pudding and treacle sponge afterwards, and accom-panied this nourishing meal with a bottle of claret. It was still raining when they got back into the car, and as they drove through the dripping countryside Phyllida felt a pang of disap-pointment that the first sight of her home should be marred by a grey, wet day. But her companion didn't share her view. As they went down the hill to the village and she pointed out her home on the opposite rise, he stopped the car to have a look.

'Early Georgian?' he asked.

'Partly. There's a bit at the back that's Queen Anne. It's a pity it's wet.'

'It's beautiful—rural England at her best.' He looked at her. 'Excited?'

She nodded. 'I always love coming home. I don't think I ever enjoyed living in London. I like pottering in the garden and going to the village shop and walking miles. That must sound very dull.'

She was surprised when he told her: 'I live in the country myself—not as lovely as this, but beautiful in a placid way. No hills like these.'

He started the car again, driving slowly now, and stopped again outside her home.

He was an instant success. Her mother, pottering around the window boxes along the front windows, turned at the sound of the car, crossed the narrow strip of pavement and peered through the window at them.

'Darling, how lovely, and you've brought someone with you.' She beamed at the doctor and added: 'How very nice,' because his smile held such charm.

He got out, opened Phyllida's door and when she had embraced her mother and introduced him, said in his placid way: 'I'm delighted to meet you, Mrs Cresswell. I hope it's not inconvenient…?'

Mrs Cresswell's smile widened. 'It's the nicest surprise, and how kind of you to drive Phylly home. Come in, I was just going to get the tea. There are rather a lot of us, I'm afraid.' She glanced at Phyllida. 'Willy's home again, he's been very under the weather, poor boy, and Beryl's home for a few days—so's Dick—half term,' she added vaguely, 'or whatever it is they have at these places.'

She paused to take a good look at her elder daughter. 'Darling, you're nice and brown, but you look—well—come inside and tell me about it.'

She glanced across at the doctor standing quietly by. 'There's something, and you'll know about it too, I expect. Come into the kitchen while I get the tea; the others won't be in for a bit. Willy's gone with Father on his visits and the other two went over to Diggs' farm.'

Mrs Cresswell had the happy knack of putting people at their ease and making them feel at home. The doctor was offered a seat at the kitchen table, given a pile of scones on a dish, a plate of butter and a knife, and asked if he would split and butter them. Phyllida, sitting opposite, making sandwiches, was surprised to see how handy he was; as far as she could remember he hadn't done a hand's turn at the de Meesters' house, although of course there he hadn't really needed to.

Her mother was taking a large cake from its tin. 'Well, darling?' she looked questioningly at Phyllida. 'Or shall Doctor—no, I shall call you Pieter—talk about it?'

Phyllida started to spread the sandwiches. 'Gaby died. We were put ashore at Funchal because the ship's doctor was worried about her and thought she ought to go home or into hospital. The de Wolffs left us at an hotel and went on with the ship. I—I found her unconscious and Pieter got her into hospital and fetched the de Wolffs back, then he took me to stay with some friends of his until there was another ship.'

Her mother received this somewhat bald statement calmly. 'Very distressing—poor Gaby, and poor you, darling. We have to thank Pieter for a great deal.' She glanced at the doctor's impassive face. 'Phylly, be a dear and run down to Mrs Brewster's and get some more cream—we haven't nearly enough for these scones.'

And when the door had closed behind her daughter: 'Neither my husband nor I will be able to thank you enough, Pieter. And now the child's out of the way, will you tell me exactly what happened?'

He sat back in his hard chair, his hands in his pockets. After a moment he began to tell her in his calm way, not taking his eyes from his listener's face. When he had finished Mrs Cresswell said again: 'Thank you, Pieter—just to say that isn't enough, but I don't know what else… Will you tell my husband when he comes in? After tea while we're washing up.' She added: 'Those wretched de Wolffs, what I'd like to do to them!'

The doctor nodded without speaking and then with his eyes on the door behind her: 'I can see that you're an excellent cook, Mrs Cresswell. Can you cook, Phyllida?'

'Of course she can,' Mrs Cresswell took her cue smartly. 'I taught her.' She took the cream from Phyllida and emptied it into a china dish just as the front door banged shut. 'Beryl and Dick,' she lifted her voice. 'We're in here.'

She had just finished introducing everyone when Doctor Cresswell came in too and it all had to be done again. 'And now we all know each other,' said Mrs Cresswell happily, 'let's have tea.'

It was a noisy meal with everyone talking at once, asking questions of Phyllida and not really listening to the answers, which was just as well, for she was quieter than usual. But they supposed her to be tired after her journey, although once or twice her father was on the point of asking her a question, but the doctor had intervened smoothly each time. It wasn't until the meal was over and Mrs Cresswell marched everyone into the kitchen to help with the washing up, bestowing a speaking glance at her husband as she did so, that Doctor Cresswell, left with his guest, observed: 'I gather there is something I should know. Am I right?' He got up. 'I think if we went to the study—Willy stayed out to tea, but he'll be back at any time—we might get interrupted here.'

His guest told him exactly what he had told Mrs Cresswell but without any glossing over of the harsher bits. Doctor Cresswell heard him out without comment.

'Poor little Gaby. I'll go and see the de Wolffs tomorrow.

I'm deeply indebted to you for looking after Phylly and doing what was best for Gaby. And these friends of yours, I should like their address if I may, so that we can express our thanks to them as well.'

He got to his feet. 'You'll stay the night, of course—longer if you can manage it.'

'I should be delighted; I still have a few days before I need to go back.'

'Then spend them here. Do you suppose that Phylly wants to talk to me about this?' Doctor Cresswell's nice open face crinkled into a smile. 'We're the greatest of friends and I don't want to force her—perhaps she'd rather wait...'

'I think she would like to tell you herself. She was very upset about it, although she did everything possible in the most difficult of circumstances.'

'She shall drive me on my morning rounds.' Doctor Cresswell led the way into the hall and across it to the large, airy sitting room. 'Are you a G. P. like myself or do you specialise? I gather from the talk at tea that you live in the country...'

In the kitchen her mother said to Phyllida: 'Of course Pieter will stay the night. Beryl, run up and make sure that the cubbyhole is just as it should be.'

Beryl giggled: 'Mother, isn't he a bit big for it? Hadn't he better have the room next door? Phylly and I can make up a bed in no time.'

Mrs Cresswell nodded to her younger daughter, as dark as Phyllida was fair, small and pretty too. 'Of course, dear, he is rather big, isn't he—he might be a bit cramped.'

Phylly finished drying the tea things. The cubbyhole was kept ready for Willy's friends from school or the younger nephews and nieces. She smiled at the idea of Pieter trying to fit his bulk into the narrow bed. 'Very cramped,' she agreed. 'I'll come now, Beryl.'

They all sat down to supper later, and Willy, who should have been in bed because he still wasn't quite fit, somehow managed to persuade his mother that he was well enough to stay up. It was a nice old-fashioned meal, with cold meat and pickles and potatoes baked in their jackets smothered in butter, and a very large rice pudding with cream and raisins for afters. Phyllida watched Pieter a little anxiously, remembering the delicious food they had had on Madeira and on the ship, but she need not have worried. The doctor consumed a vast supper with every sign of content and enjoyment.

Going upstairs to bed later, it struck her that she had exchanged barely a dozen words with him during the whole evening, although his goodnight had been as friendly as it always had been. Tomorrow, she promised herself, she would find out when he was going.

Only she didn't. True, they met at breakfast, but by the time she had helped with the washing up and made the beds, her father was calling for her to drive him on his morning round, and Pieter and Beryl were at the other end of the garden, picking the rhubarb from under its forcing bucket, ready for one of her mother's super pies.

'I've heard it all from Pieter,' her father told her as they started off down the hill, 'but I'd like to hear it again from you, Phylly.'

It was a relief to talk about it, she felt better when she had told him about it, and better still when her father said: 'You did all you could, you have no reason whatsoever for blaming yourself. Put it behind you, my dear. Have you thought what kind of job you want?'

She hadn't; somehow she hadn't been able to put her mind to thinking about her future and she said so.

'Then take a holiday,' advised her father.

They got back a little late for lunch, and found the doctor in the kitchen, sitting in one of the old Windsor chairs by the Aga, his long legs stretched out on the rag rug at his feet. Willy was there too and Dick as well as Beryl and her mother. They looked as thick as thieves.

Everyone turned to look at her as she went in, and it was Dick who said: 'Hi, Phylly—we've hatched a simply super scheme.' He grinned round at the doctor, who was standing, staring at nothing. 'You tell her, Pieter.'

She looked at them in turn. Their expressions reminded her forcibly of Meg, their elderly spaniel, when she hoped for a biscuit, all except the doctor, who looked half asleep. Phyllida sat herself down on the edge of the table, picked up a raw carrot from the dish and began to crunch it, and asked: 'Well?'

The doctor sat down again. He looked quite at home in the rather shabby old kitchen, just as though he had been a family friend for years. 'I have been talking to your mother about the flowers in Holland at this time of the year. Bulbs, you know, fields full of them and a rather special park where one can go and see them all growing in a charming setting. I live quite near the bulb fields and I wondered if she might like a brief holiday so that she might see them for herself—Willy would come too, of course,' he sounded very bland, 'a few days' holiday might set him up ready for school again. Only there is one snag; Willy and I would like to go fishing and we don't feel that we can leave your mother alone while we fish, and as I'm told that if she accompanied us she would only remove the hooks from the fishes' mouths and throw them back into the water, I feel that it would be hardly conducive to our enjoyment.' He contrived to sound sad. 'She would be lonely.' He gave Phyllida a long look. 'We wondered if you would consider joining the party?'

It was a neat trap and she wondered which of them had thought it up. 'I must look for a job.'

The doctor's voice was all silk. 'You did tell me that you might take a holiday first.'

She bit into the carrot. 'Father...' she began.

He answered smoothly. 'We did—er—discuss it vaguely yesterday evening, after you had gone to bed.'

The trap had closed and she was amazed to find that she felt nothing but pleasure at its closure. All the same, she wasn't a girl to give in tamely. 'How will Father manage?' She looked at her mother.

'Beryl will be home for at least another two weeks—she doesn't get her exam results until then and the job she's after depends on those—she might just as well be here, and she'll love to look after him, and Dick can come down for the weekends.' Her mother smiled so happily that Phyllida, peering at her from behind her fringe, knew that she couldn't disappoint her; she didn't have many holidays.

She said quietly, 'I'd love to come. When?'

There was a kind of concerted rush towards her, while her family, all talking at once, told her. When they paused for breath, Pieter said from his chair: 'In three days' time, if that suits everyone?'

Phyllida was sure that by everyone, he meant her; the rest of them would have already agreed happily to anything he might have suggested—even her father, who had just walked in, exclaiming: 'Well, is it all arranged? It's most kind of you, Pieter. My wife is a great gardener, nothing will give her more pleasure, but I do hope you know what you're taking on—three of them—you're sure you can house them all?'

The doctor answered him gravely. 'Oh, yes, I think that can be done. I hope you'll allow them to stay as long as possible—ten days? Two weeks?'

Willy looked anxious. 'If we're going fishing, two weeks would be super—I mean you have to work as well, I suppose?'

'I suppose I do,' he was gravely assured.

So Phyllida spent a good deal of the next two days unpacking and packing again, helping her mother to do the same, and going through Willy's wardrobe. Which left Beryl free to entertain the doctor, for Dick had gone again. She made a success of it too, judging by the way she made him laugh.

They left after breakfast to catch an afternoon Hovercraft from Dover, seen off by Doctor Cresswell, Meg the spaniel, an assortment of cats and Beryl, looking fetching in a large apron.

She had flung her arms round Pieter's neck as she wished him goodbye and given him a hug and begged him to come back soon, and he had said something softly to make her laugh and kissed her soundly. Phyllida wondered why she was going and not Beryl. It should have been the other way round.

Their journey was a pleasant one, with a stop for an early lunch and a great deal of talk, mostly on Willy's part, concerning the joys of fishing, until they reached the Hovercraft, when he switched to engineering. Neither topic interested the two ladies of the party; they listened with one ear to make sure that Willy wasn't being rude or cheeky and carried on a desultory chat about clothes, the chances of Beryl remembering that her father couldn't stand lamb cutlets at any price, and what sort of presents they would buy to take back with them. But once on board, the conversation became general while they drank coffee and ate sandwiches and listened to their host explaining the rest of the journey to them.

It was well into the afternoon by now and it seemed that they still had a fair distance to go. They would land at Calais, travel up the French coast into Belgium and from these cross over into Holland at Sluis, then take the ferry to Vlissingen and from there drive all the way to Leiden on the motorway. He lived, explained the doctor, in a village bordering one of the lakes a mile or so from that city.

'Handy for your work, I expect,' chatted Mrs Cresswell. 'Do you have beds in a hospital there?'

'In Leiden, yes, also in den Haag.'

'Ah, yes,' said Mrs Cresswell knowledgeably, 'Leiden's a medical school, isn't it?'

So now we know, thought Phyllida, a thought peevishly, all this while and never a hint as to exactly where he lived—to her, at any rate.

They were actually disembarking at Calais when she wondered about the car. They had left the one he had hired in England and she hadn't given it another thought. She glanced round her and the doctor answered the question she hadn't asked. 'It's waiting for us, it should be over here.'

It was—a Bentley, not a new model, but a much cherished fifteen-year-old motor-car, sleek and gleaming and powerful. There was a man standing by it, a corpulent, middle-aged man, with a bald head and a round, cheerful face. The doctor spoke to him, shook his hand, and waved to a porter to load the luggage. The man had gone before that was finished and the doctor installed his guests without saying who he was.

'Such a nice car,' observed Mrs Cresswell, 'and what a lot of room!'

'Yes, I think so too—I've had her for a long time now and she suits me perfectly. She has a good turn of speed, too.'

Which proved to be the case. They went so fast through France, Belgium and then into Holland that Phyllida was hard put to it to know just where they were. Only as they crossed on the ferry to Vlissingen was there time to pore over a map while they drank coffee in the bar on board, and then she didn't take it all in, there was so much to see from the deck.

The spring evening was turning to dusk under a wide cloudy sky as they took the road northwards; Bergen-op-Zoom, Rosendaal, Dordrecht, by-passing them all, so that there was nothing to see of the actual towns. But there were plenty of villages, with their great churches and neat clusters of houses, and in between, wide water meadows striped with canals. Phyllida, sitting in the back with her mother, looked about her with interest. It was so very different from Madeira, from England even, but she liked it—it was calm, placid country and only as they skirted the bigger towns was she aware of factory chimneys and bustling industrial areas. It was nice when the doctor turned off the motorway on to a secondary road which took them across country to join another motorway just south of Leiden. He left this too after a few miles to turn down a country lane, brick built and with a canal on either side of it. They were back in the country again and presently she could see water; a

wide lake stretching away into the dusk. The road ran beside
it for some distance until they reached a village. 'Leimuiden,'
said the doctor. 'The next one is Kudelstaart; I live just half
way between them.'

There wasn't a village when he slowed the car presently, just
a group of houses and cottages and a very small church, and
then a high brick wall pierced by wrought iron gates, wide open.

The sanded drive was straight and quite long and the house
at the end of it was so unlike anything that Phyllida had expected that she gave a gasp of surprise. It was a large square
building, painted white, with single-storey wings on either side,
connected by short covered passages. Its orderly rows of windows and all the ground floor ones were lighted, illuminating
the great front door with its elaborate decoration of plasterwork
picked out with gilt.

'How very grand,' observed her mother, who had a habit,
sometimes embarrassing, of saying what came into her head.
'I'm quite overwhelmed—it's a good thing it's almost dark,' she
added obscurely. But her host understood, for he assured her:

'It's not in the least terrifying, even in broad daylight, and
I'm told it's wickedly inconvenient to clean.'

Willy hadn't said anything, but now, as they stopped on the
sweep before the door, he observed: 'I say, what a super place
for a holiday—I'm glad I came!'

The doctor laughed and got out to open doors and usher
his guests out of the car, and by then the house door had been
opened too and a welcoming light streamed out to meet them
from the hall beyond.

There was a tall thin woman standing just inside, looking
so exactly as a housekeeper looked that there was no mistak-
ing her; dressed severely in a dark grey dress, neat greying hair
pulled back into a bun, a sombre face; but when she smiled she
wasn't sombre at all, and she was delighted to see the doctor,
who flung an arm round her as he introduced her.

'This is Lympke, my friend and housekeeper. She doesn't

speak English but I'm sure you'll manage to understand each other. Her husband, Aap, who brought the car to meet us, will be here presently and he speaks it very well.'

He swept them all inside, through the wide hall and a pair of arched doors into a high-ceilinged room of vast proportions. It had wide windows at one end and at the other there were a few shallow steps which led to another, much smaller room, lined with books. The furniture was exactly right for its surroundings; glass-fronted cabinets filled with silver and porcelain, splendid wall tables carrying vases of flowers, a lacquered cabinet—and nicely arranged between these antique treasures were sofas, wing-backed armchairs and a variety of tables. The walls were white, the panels picked out with gilt and hung with paintings, mostly portraits, lighted by crystal sconces.

The doctor waved them to chairs amidst this splendour. 'Tea?' he enquired of Mrs Cresswell, unerringly guessing her one strong wish, and at her pleased nod, said something to Lympke who had followed them in. She went away and returned almost at once with a tea tray which she set on a small table by Mrs Cresswell's chair and while the two ladies drank their fill, the doctor gave Willy a glass of lemonade, pouring a whisky for himself.

'You have a very nice home, Pieter,' observed Mrs Cresswell, passing Phyllida her tea. 'I had no idea—you told Ronald that you were a GP and I hardly expected...'

Phyllida stirred uneasily and hoped that the doctor wouldn't take umbrage. He didn't, only saying mildly: 'Well, I do have a surgery here in the house, you know, and quite a few local patients, but I must confess that most of my work is done in den Haag and Leiden, and sometimes abroad.'

'What do you specialise in?'

He smiled very faintly. 'Among other things, hearts.' He was looking at Phyllida, who knew what he was and kept her eyes fixed on a family group on the wall opposite her.

'Now isn't that nice?' asked Mrs Cresswell of the room at

large. Neither of her children answered her because she had a
habit of voicing her thoughts aloud and didn't expect anyone
to reply anyway, but the doctor chose to do so.

'Well, I enjoy it; it's work I'm deeply interested in and it's
a challenge.'

'Yes, of course.' Mrs Cresswell was well away. 'And you,
you poor man, without a wife and children, you must be lonely.'

Phyllida gave her mother a look which that lady ignored,
and the doctor's smile widened. 'I haven't been until now; just
recently I have found that work isn't quite enough, though.'

He was still looking at Phyllida, who felt rather like a rabbit
with the snake's eye upon it. She would have to look at him, she
couldn't help herself; she withdrew her gaze from the family
group, whom she now knew very well indeed, and met his eyes.

'You agree, Phyllida?' he asked blandly, then smiled so brilliantly that she found herself saying fervently:

'Oh, yes, I do! Work's very nice, but it—it...' She had no idea
what she was going to say, but sat there with her pretty mouth
open, praying for some witty, clever remark to come into her
empty head.

It didn't, and his smile became the merest twitch of the lip.

'Would you like to go to your rooms?' He was the perfect
host again. 'We'll dine in an hour's time if that's not too late for
you, but do come down when you would like. I shall be around,
but if I'm not, do make yourselves at home.'

Lympke led the way upstairs, up a handsomely carved staircase at the back of the hall, leading to a wide corridor above.
Phyllida and her mother had adjoining rooms at the side of the
house, while Willy, to his delight, was given a small room at
the back of the house, well away from them. He could just see
the gleam of water from his window even though it was almost
dark now and came running back to tell them so.

'That's where we'll fish,' he told them importantly. 'I'm going
down to talk to Pieter; someone's unpacked for me, so there's
nothing for me to do.'

'You'll wash your face and hands, comb your hair and take a clean handkerchief,' decreed his mother, and when he had gone: 'How beautiful these rooms are, Phylly, and such heavenly bathrooms. Are you going to change your dress?'

'No, I don't think so, just do my face and hair and change my shoes.' Phyllida wandered over to the window and stared out into the evening, although she could see almost nothing by now. She said thoughtfully, 'It's a pity he's rich—I didn't know...' She sighed. 'And not just rich, he's—well...'

'Yes, dear, but he'd be that whether he had money or not, wouldn't he? And remember that your father's family is an old and honoured one.'

'Mother,' Phyllida's voice was rather high, 'I don't know what you're talking about.'

Her mother's reply was placid. 'No, dear, I often don't know either. Shall I back-comb my hair a bit in front? My head's as flat as a snake's after wearing a hat all day.'

They went downstairs presently and found the drawing room empty, but almost at once the fat man they had seen at Calais appeared at the door. 'Aap, madam, miss—the doctor's houseman. If you should want anything I will arrange it.'

They thanked him and Phyllida said: 'What good English you speak, Aap. Have you been in England?'

'Certainly, miss. At times I travel with the doctor, you understand. We also stay there from time to time—the doctor has many friends.' He smiled at them. 'The doctor and your brother have gone to look at the lake. It is now dark but Master Willy wished to see it for himself. It is not large, but there is a canal which leads to the *meer* beyond.'

He crossed to the windows and drew the heavy tapestry curtains, tended the log fire in the wide hearth, begged them to make themselves comfortable, and withdrew.

Mrs Cresswell sank into a deeply cushioned chair and sighed with pleasure. 'The last time I was in a house like this one was when I was ten years old—your Great-Aunt Dora at Weatherby Hall, dear. Such a pity she had to sell it.'

Phyllida had perched herself on a velvet-covered stool near the fire. 'Well, I like our house,' she declared a shade defiantly, 'it's beautiful and old and it's home.'

'Well, of course,' observed the doctor from the doorway, 'but home can be anywhere, can't it? A cottage or a semi-detached or an isolated farm—it's how one feels about it, isn't it?'

She had turned round to face him. 'I'm sorry,' she said quickly, 'I didn't mean to be rude; this is a lovely house and it's home for you, just as my home is for me.'

He smiled slowly. 'I hope that when I marry, my wife will love this house as much as I do. You must explore it one day.'

He had crossed the room to where a tray of drinks stood on a carved and gilded table. 'What will you ladies have to drink?'

He brought them their drinks and went back to get a Coke for Willy and a Jenever for himself. 'I don't need to go to the hospital until after lunch tomorrow,' he told them, 'and surgery should be over by half past nine. Willy and I thought we might do a little fishing, if you don't mind being left to your own devices. Lympke will be delighted to take you over the house and there's plenty to see in the gardens, please go wherever you wish.' He sat down in a great chair opposite Phyllida. 'I thought that we might go to the Keukenhof one day soon, it should be at its best now. It's not far from here and we could leave here after breakfast—I'm afraid I'll have to be back around tea time, though, for any evening patients I may have at my rooms in Leiden.'

They dined presently in a room a good deal smaller than the drawing room but still pretty large. It was furnished in mahogany, gleaming with endless polishing and age, and the table silver and glass almost out shone it. They sat at a round table, large enough to take a dozen people with ease, although they occupied only a part of it, sitting near enough to talk comfortably.

They ate splendidly; caviar for starters, salmon poached in

white wine, chicken cooked in cream with a Madeira sauce. Willy hardly spoke, but ate with the deep pleasure of a growing boy who was hungry; it was left to the other three to carry on an undemanding conversation mostly about gardens and growing vegetables and the difficulties of protecting everything from frost. Phyllida, who was a willing but amateur gardener, marvelled at Pieter, who seemed evenly matched against her mother's expert knowledge. Surely it was enough, she thought a little crossly, that he was apparently a very successful man in his own profession, had a house like a cosy museum and the good looks to turn any girl's head; he didn't have to be a knowledgeable gardener as well.

Even the appearance of a honey and hazelnut bavarois, which tasted even better than it looked, did little to lift her spirits, although she did her best to look intelligent about greenfly and black spot while she ate it. She would excuse herself when they had had their coffee, she decided, on the grounds that she wanted to wash her hair before she went to bed, but in this she was frustrated. Pieter invited her mother to telephone her father, suggested that Willy might like to have an early night so that he would feel fit for a morning's fishing, and invited her to sit down and keep him company.

'For we don't seem to have exchanged more than a dozen words,' he observed pleasantly.

'Well, I'm not mad about gardening,' she said grumpily, and then remembering her manners: 'I'm sorry, I don't know what's the matter with me—I don't mean to be so beastly rude to you. I think...' she paused and looked at him with puzzled blue eyes, like a small girl with a problem. 'I think it's because all this is a surprise. I thought you'd have a house in a village, a bit like ours—and it's not.'

'You don't like it?' he asked in a gentle voice.

'Oh, I do—it's out of this world.' She added shyly: 'I feel as though I'm trespassing.'

'Oh, never that.' She wondered why he looked amused and it

was on the tip of her tongue to ask why when her mother came back into the room, and soon after they went to bed, leaving him standing at the foot of his magnificent staircase. Her mother had already gained the corridor and was out of sight when he called Phyllida back.

'I forgot this,' he told her, and kissed her, hard.

CHAPTER SIX

PHYLLIDA WENT DOWN to breakfast after a somewhat wakeful night. Naturally enough, being a pretty girl and a perfectly normal one, she had received her share—rather more, perhaps—of kisses. She had enjoyed them too, but somehow Pieter had been different from the others. She had told herself several times during the night that it was because he was older and more experienced, but she knew that wasn't the answer. She had given up wondering about it then and gone to sleep.

The doctor wasn't at breakfast, nor was Willy, who had risen early, breakfasted with his host and then taken himself off to spy out the land around the lake. Phyllida assured her mother that she had passed a dreamless night, ate her breakfast under the fatherly eye of Aap and declared that she was going to explore the gardens; for some reason she felt shy about meeting Pieter and the gardens seemed an unlikely place for him to be in at that hour of the day; he had said something about morning surgery...

She had half expected her mother to accompany her, but Mrs Cresswell had found a splendid book on gardening in the library. 'I'll come out later,' she decided, 'when the sun's really warm.'

So Phyllida fetched a cardigan and found her way outside. Now that it was morning, and a bright one even if chilly, and she could see everything clearly, she had to admit that the house was charming; solid and unpretentious despite its size, fitting exactly into the surrounding formal lawns and flower beds and trees beyond. Moreover, everywhere she looked there was a blaze of colour; tulips and hyacinths and scilla and the last of the daffodils. She walked round the side of the house, peering into the wide windows of the wing she was passing. She supposed that it must be a ballroom, for it took up the whole area and its floor was waxed wood. The ceiling was painted, although she couldn't see it very clearly, and from its centre hung a chandelier, its crystals looped and twined into an elaborate pattern.

There were windows on the other side too and she walked on, rounded the wing and found herself facing a formal garden with a square pond bordered by masses of flowers and sheltered by a beech hedge. There was an alley leading from its far end and she went to look at it. It was arched by more beech, trained to form a tunnel, and that in its turn opened into a charming circle of grass, well screened by shrubs and with stone seats here and there. Right in the middle there was a wheelbarrow, loaded with earth and with a spade flung on top of it. It looked as though someone had just that minute left it there, and she looked round to see if there was anyone about, but she saw no one, neither in the alley from whence she had just come, nor on the neat brick path which led away from the grassy plot on its other side. She sat down on one of the seats and blew on her fingers. It might be the end of April, but it was still chilly unless the sun shone.

'It'll be pleasantly warm once the morning mist has gone,' observed the doctor from somewhere behind her.

She jumped. 'I thought you were taking your morning surgery.'

'My dear girl, we keep early hours here; surgery's from eight until nine o'clock and there are seldom more than a dozen patients, often less.'

He sat down beside her and she said doubtfully: 'But I thought you had a practice.'

'Well, I have, but I see most of my patients at my rooms in Leiden—this surgery is just for the villages close by.'

'Oh, I see—and you have beds in a hospital too?'

'In several hospitals.'

She gave him a searching look. 'I think you must be someone quite important.' And when he didn't answer: 'A consultant or a specialist—or do you teach?'

His eyes were smiling. 'Some of all three.' He picked up her hand and held it between his. 'You're cold. We'll walk down to the lake and see if Willy has fallen in, if he hasn't we'll bring him back for coffee before we get down to this business of fishing.'

As they started along the path, he added: 'I wondered if you would all like to come into den Haag this afternoon, you could look at the shops while I'm at the hospital. I shall only be a couple of hours and I'll show you where to go.'

She was very conscious of his hand holding hers; it was firm and warm and impersonal and she wondered again why he had kissed her on the previous evening. 'That sounds nice,' she said, her voice cool because she didn't want to seem too friendly.

They had come to the end of the path and were crossing rough ground at the end of which she could see the lake, and Willy, sitting on a log by it. Pieter had slowed his pace. 'My mother and father are coming to dinner this evening,' he said casually.

'Your mother and father?' Surprise made her repeat his words like an idiot. 'Oh, I didn't know—that is, do they live here?'

'They have a house on the coast near Scheveningen. My father is a doctor but retired now. I have two brothers and two sisters—my sisters are married, both living in Friesland, my youngest brother is in Utrecht, finishing medical school, and Paul, who is a year or so younger than I, is married and lives in Limburg—he's a barrister.'

He hadn't volunteered so much information in such a short

time since they had met. Phyllida digested it slowly. Presently she asked: 'Then why do you live here, all alone in this great house?'

'When my father retired he and my mother went to live on the coast because the house—a charming one—is close to the golf course and he enjoys a game. It was always understood that they would go there eventually and it's like a second home to us all, as we spent our holidays there when we were children.' He sat down beside her. 'And as I'm the eldest son, I took over here. I don't regret it.'

'It's very large for one person.'

His eyes were almost shut. 'Yes, but it's surprising how a clutch of children fills even the largest of houses.'

'But you haven't any children.'

'Something which can be remedied.' He changed the conversation so abruptly that she was startled. 'I think you'll like the shops in den Haag—will Willy be bored?' He turned to look at her. 'I could take him with me; I'll get someone to take him round one or two of the more interesting wards until I'm ready—he's really keen on becoming a doctor, isn't he?'

She agreed, secretly put out. She would have been interested too, and she might have found out something of his life while she was there; his working life, but it seemed that he didn't want her to know. Well, if he wanted to be secretive, let him. 'I said I'd go and find Mother,' she told him.

They had a splendid afternoon wandering round the shops, buying inexpensive trifles to take home, drinking tea in a smart café and then walking back to the spot where Pieter was to pick them up. The journey home was occupied almost exclusively by Willy's observations about what he had seen, the doctor's mild replies and Phyllida's slightly cool ones, which she regretted when he asked her in the friendliest possible manner if she would go with him on the following day in order to choose a birthday present for his younger sister.

'I've no ideas at all,' he assured her, 'and if you would be so kind as to advise me...'

She agreed at once, and the rest of the ride was taken up with a lighthearted discussion between Willy and his host concerning the chances of them landing a good sized pike when next they fished the lake.

Phyllida was a little apprehensive about meeting Pieter's parents; while she dressed she tried to imagine what they would be like and failed; the doctor was an enormous man, probably his parents would be of a similar size, on the other hand, very small women quite often had large sons. She put together a mental picture of his mother, small and dark and terribly smart. She combed her fringe smooth, put on a thin wool dress in a flattering wine shade, and went downstairs.

Her mother and Willy were already there, she could hear their voices through the half open drawing room door—other voices too. Aap, appearing suddenly, opened the door wide, and she went in.

The master of the house was standing against one of the display cabinets, one hand in a pocket, the other holding a glass, his long legs crossed, his shoulders wedged against the dark woodwork. He was talking to a very tall, very large lady, with elegantly dressed white hair, handsome features and what Phyllida described to herself as a presence. Across the room, talking to her mother and brother, was an elderly man, as large and powerfully built as the doctor and just as good-looking. The three of them made a formidable trio, and she wondered briefly if his brothers and sisters were the same size; no wonder they lived in such an enormous house.

The doctor came to meet her, his compelling hand urging her forward to where his mother was standing. That lady surprised her very much by saying mildly, before any introductions had been made: 'My dear, I'm sure Pieter didn't warn you about us—being so large, you know—when the whole family are together I've known people turn pale at the sight of us.'

She laughed, a deep rich chuckle which transformed her austere appearance.

Why, thought Phyllida, taking the offered hand, she's just like Mother, only larger.

Pieter had been standing between them, now he said placidly: 'I don't think Phyllida is easily frightened, Mama.' He smiled a little. 'What will you drink, Phylly?'

He fetched her a sherry and took her to meet his father. It was like talking to Pieter, they were so very alike; the same hooded blue eyes, the same firm mouth and patrician nose, only his hair, still thick, was quite white.

She sat beside him on one of the vast sofas, while the others gathered together on the other side of the hearth, and he talked of nothing much in particular, putting her at her ease, and presently when Aap came to announce dinner, they went, still laughing and talking, to take their places round the beautifully appointed table. Phyllida, sitting beside the elder of the van Sittardts with Willy on her other side and Pieter's mother next to him, noticed with some amusement that her brother was getting on splendidly with his neighbour, which left her mother and Pieter, talking quietly together.

The evening was an unqualified success; the magnificent dinner helped, of course, and the glass or two of claret she drank with it, but even they wouldn't have been of much help without the easy charm of her host and his parents. She found herself quite anxious to meet the rest of the family.

Only one thing marred the evening for her. Sitting round the fire, drinking their coffee, Mevrouw van Sittardt took advantage of a pause in the talk to ask: 'And have you seen Marena yet, Phyllida? I feel sure that you must have, as she spends a great deal of her time here. She and Pieter are very old friends—lifelong, one might say, and he has grown accustomed to be at her beck and call at all times.'

The lady smiled as she spoke, but Phyllida had the strong impression that she would have preferred to have ground her teeth. She said that no, she hadn't met the girl in question yet, and glanced at the doctor, sitting with her mother. He looked as blandly impassive as usual, but she had no doubt that he had heard every single word, for his mother had a clear and ringing voice. She wished very much to ask about this Marena; it seemed strange that if she were such a close friend—perhaps more than a friend—Pieter should never have mentioned her. It wasn't her business anyway, she told herself sternly, and plunged into an account of their shopping expedition that afternoon; probably she would never see the girl.

She was wrong. They met the very next day, after Phyllida and the doctor had returned from a highly successful search for the birthday present. The afternoon had been fun although short, for he had had a number of private patients to see at his rooms in Leiden, and hadn't been able to pick her up until the middle of the afternoon. Nevertheless, the next hour or so had been delightful, especially when she discovered that there was no reasonable limit to the amount he might be called upon to spend. They chose a pendant finally, a dainty thing of gold with a border of rose diamonds, and then had tea before going back home, where Willy had immediately waylaid them and badgered them into a rather wild game with Butch, the nondescript old dog who was Pieter's devoted slave. Phyllida had cast off her jacket the better to run faster and was tearing across the lawn towards the house with Butch in hot pursuit when she saw a girl watching them from the terrace. She was small and slight, with large dark eyes and a pouting mouth, expertly made up; she made Phyllida feel tall and fat and untidy. Untidy she certainly was, for the sun had come out and was shining warmly so that her face was flushed and her hair blew wildly around her head, sadly in need of a comb.

The girl smiled charmingly as she crossed the lawn to join them, but there was malice with the charm and Phyllida sensed that the girl had already decided that there was no competition for her to fear. Her eyes spoke volumes for Phyllida to read—

this guileless outdoor type with great blue eyes and a gentle
mouth and a fringe like a little girl wasn't Pieter's type. The
smile widened as she reached Pieter, tucked an exquisitely cared
for hand under his arm and said in accented English: 'Darling
Pieter, have you missed me very much? And how good it is that
you have friends to amuse you while I am not here.' She gave
his arm a little pat and gave a trill of laughter. 'But now I am.'

He smiled down at her. 'Nice to see you, Marena—how's
the painting?'

She made a charming face. 'Not good, not good at all. I need
your opinion, otherwise I shall destroy all that I have done. Will
you come and look at them?'

'Yes, of course. Still at the studio, are you?' He turned to
Phyllida. 'Phylly, meet Marena. She paints, and she's good at
it, too.' His amused gaze swept over her untidy person and she
flushed. She said politely:

'How interesting. I've never met an artist, it must be wonderful to be able to paint.'

'Anyone can learn,' Marena assured her sweetly, and dismissed her. 'Pieter, can I speak to you for one minute? It is important and private.'

Phyllida was at the door before she had finished speaking;
she could take a hint as well as the next one and Marena clearly
wanted her out of the way. 'I must tidy myself,' she muttered.
'I expect I'll see you again before we leave—so nice meeting
you.' She wrenched open the door and ducked through it, casting a totally meaningless smile over her shoulder as she went.

Willy had melted away as only boys can, and Aap, crossing
the hall as she stood a little uncertainly, offered the information that he and his mother had gone down to the lake to see if
they could find the swan's nest there. There was still plenty of
time before dinner; she flew upstairs and without bothering to
do more than run a comb through her hair, flung on a cardigan,
and using the back stairs, went out of the house. Somehow she
couldn't bear to join the doctor and Marena again—indeed, she

thought it unlikely that they would want her to. A good walk would do her good and if she returned with only enough time to change for the evening, the chance of meeting the girl again would be slight, although she might stay for dinner.

'And why should I care?' asked Phyllida loudly of the trees around her. 'Well, I do, anyway.' And indeed, to be quite honest, she had begun to think that Pieter had fallen a little in love with her, and she, moreover, had fallen a little in love with him. She stopped her brisk walking, struck by a sudden blinding thought. She wasn't a little in love with him; she was head over heels; no one and nothing else mattered in the world. Never to see him again would be a sorrow she wouldn't be able to bear, and it was a sorrow she wouldn't be able to share with anyone, least of all Pieter. At all costs she would have to hide her feelings. They would be going back home in ten days or so and she would have to be very careful. She walked on faster than ever, trying to escape the awful thought that she had allowed him to see that she liked him very much. Well, she could soon put that right. Cool friendliness and steering clear of anything personal when they were talking—that would leave him free to dote on his precious Marena. She ground her splendid teeth at the thought.

She turned for home presently, for she had been out too long already, and reached the garden door just as Pieter came out of it. He was looking preoccupied although he smiled when he saw her.

'Hullo there,' he said easily, and there was a glint of amusement in his eyes as he took in her flyaway appearance. 'You've been out and I thought you were still doing things to your hair. I've just left a message with Aap—I'm afraid I'll have to go out this evening and I do apologise to you all. I doubt if I'll be back until late.'

He held the door for her to go through. 'By the way, Marena wants us all to go over for drinks before you go back—may I tell her that you would like to?'

He was going to spend the evening with the horrid creature. Phyllida said in a cool little voice: 'Why, of course—we shall be delighted. How very kind.' She gave him a bright smile and hurried past him.

Mrs Cresswell made no comment when Phyllida told her that their host would be out for the evening, but Willy asked anxiously: 'Did he say when he'd be back? We're going fishing at four o'clock tomorrow morning.'

'Don't worry, dear,' soothed his mother, 'I'm sure Pieter wouldn't forget anything as important as that.'

But hours later, listening to the stable clock chiming twice, Phyllida wondered if he had, and she was sure of it when half an hour later she heard the Bentley whisper past her windows.

She slept after that, a miserable exhausted sleep which left her heavy-eyed and snappy, and when Berta the housemaid brought her her morning tea, she had no desire to get up. All the same, she went down to breakfast presently and found her mother and brother already there. Her mother wished her good morning and ignored her pale cross face, but Willy was less perceptive. 'I say, Phylly, you do look cross. We had a smashing time...'

'You went fishing? But Pieter...' She stopped herself in time. 'I didn't think Pieter would get up so early.'

'He wanted to,' said Willy simply.

'One can always find time to do what one wants,' observed her mother comfortably. 'Phylly, pass me another of those delicious rolls, will you? It's such a splendid morning, I think I'll take that gardening catalogue Pieter lent me and go and sit in that dear little summer house. What are you two going to do?'

'I'm going to the next village,' said Willy importantly, 'the one you can see across the fields from the side of the house. I have to deliver a note for Pieter; one of his patients has to go into hospital.' He buttered himself some toast with a lavish hand. 'We're all going to the Keukenhof the day after tomorrow, he told me so this morning.' He sighed with content. 'I caught two bream this morning and Pieter got four.' He wolfed down the toast. 'Phylly, are you coming with me?'

She agreed readily. Her own company was something she wished to avoid at all costs, and presently they set off into the bright morning, pleased with each other's company despite the dozen or so years between them, Phyllida rather silent and Willy talking non-stop.

'It was super of Pieter to come this morning,' he told her. 'He's been up most of the night, you know—that case at the hospital in Leiden.'

'What case?' asked Phyllida with instant interest. 'And how do you know?'

Her brother gave her a kindly, impatient look. 'He told me, of course—this boy had a relapse, so he was called in for a consultation. He's very important, you know.'

'Is he?' she asked humbly. 'I didn't know—he never said.'

'Well, of course not,' said Willy with scorn. 'I mean, a man doesn't go around boasting. But he's frightfully brainy—I expect he'd have told you if you'd asked—I did.' His chest swelled with pride. 'He knows I'm going to be a doctor when I'm a man, he says I'm a natural because Father's a doctor anyway and it's in the blood, like it is in his—he says you can't help yourself if it is and that I'll make a jolly good one. He talks to me just as though I'm grown up.'

Pieter loomed large in Willy's life, that was obvious, but then he loomed even larger in hers. She sighed. 'Oh, does he? What exactly does he specialise in, dear?'

They were almost at the village and had slowed their pace.

'Hearts—you heard him say so, didn't you? And leukaemia, didn't you know that either? And you're always talking to him…'

'Am I?' asked Phyllida sadly. But not, it seemed, about anything that really mattered. She wondered what Pieter really thought of her behind that calm, handsome face. Probably nothing much.

Willy discharged his errand and they walked back, having a one-sided conversation about fishing, with him in full spate about lines and hooks and flies and she saying yes and no and really, while she allowed her mind to dwell upon Pieter, so that she followed her brother in through the garden door rather dreamily, to bump almost at once into the master of the house, lying back in a large cane chair in the garden room, his feet on another chair, fast asleep.

They stood and looked at him for a moment and Phyllida saw how weary he was, with lines etched on his face which she hadn't noticed before, a faint frown between his brows. Willy wandered away, but she went on staring and then gave a squeak of surprise when the doctor asked softly: 'Why do you look like that, Phylly?'

'Like what?'

'Motherly and sad.' He unfolded himself and stood up, smiling.

'Oh—oh, I don't know. I'm sorry if we woke you up.'

'I'm not. Let's get Aap to bring some coffee to the summer house. I saw that your mother was there.'

So they all had their coffee together and he didn't say a word about where he had been or why, indeed, he presented the perfect picture of a man of leisure, only presently he went to sleep again and Mrs Cresswell and Willy crept away, leaving Phyllida sitting there with him. She wasn't sure why she wanted to stay, perhaps because it was wonderful just to be there; presently he would go off again and she wouldn't know where, or perhaps Marena would come frisking along to make him laugh. Two large slow tears trickled down her cheeks; she was only half aware of them and didn't bother to do anything about them and there was no one to see.

'Why are you crying?' asked the doctor softly.

She was so vexed with herself that she could hardly speak. She might have guessed that he wasn't asleep, but he had looked so tired. She didn't answer, only looked away from him, wiping the tears away with a finger.

'No job?' he persisted. 'An uncertain future? Not happy here, perhaps?'

'Oh, I am, I am. It's lovely—I thought when I first came that it was all so grand, but now I know just what you meant about it being a home, because it is.' She went on in a muddled way: 'Cats on the chairs and that nice old dog and the way you fling your jacket down on that magnificent table in the hall, and your mother and father...'

The doctor's eyes gleamed beneath their lids, but all he said was: 'Then you must be in love.'

She went red, and then, unable to stop herself: 'Yes, I am—I've only just found out, though I think that I knew days ago. It's funny...'

It was fortunate that she was interrupted, for she had flung caution to the winds and had actually started to tell him that she was in love with him. She froze with horror and for once was glad to see Marena crossing the lawn and smiling with the air of someone who was sure of a welcome. She flung her arms round the doctor's neck and kissed him with what Phyllida considered to be a sickening display of sentiment and then smiled at her. Her voice was gracious.

'Hullo—you look much nicer today, but I do not like your fringe. Fringes are for little girls, are they not? And you are no longer that.'

Phyllida tried to think of a suitable answer to this snide remark, but her head was still full of the things she had so nearly said; she felt sick just remembering them. The doctor answered for her: 'You're wrong, Marena, Phylly isn't grown up at all, not nearly as grown up as you are. And I like the fringe.'

'I am but nineteen,' declared Marena prettily, and perched on the arm of his chair.

'In years, in worldly knowledge, double that.'

She pouted and dropped a kiss on to his head. 'I do not know why I like you so very much, Pieter.'

'Nor I. Without wishing to be inhospitable, I should warn you that I am about to leave for my rooms. What do you want this time?' He sounded amused.

'Darling, I need some money and the bank say no more until my allowance is paid. If I could have five hundred gulden—just till then—I will pay back…'

He put a hand into a pocket and fished out a roll of notes. 'Here you are. A new dress, I suppose.'

Marena took the notes and stuffed them into her handbag, flashing a triumphant look at Phyllida. 'Of course—such a charming one. I shall wear it for you when you come.'

'I look forward to it.' He submitted to another embrace and with a careless wave of the hand for Phyllida, Marena skipped off. A moment later Phyllida heard a car start up and roar away.

'She's the world's worst driver,' murmured the doctor, and closed his eyes again.

Phyllida sat and looked at him, suspicious that he was only foxing again, but presently he snored, very faintly, but still a snore. She gave him ten minutes and then ventured: 'I say, you said you had to leave…'

He opened one eye. 'Did I really say that? Then I made a mistake—I have nothing to do until this evening, when I have to give a lecture at a hospital in Utrecht. You can come with me if you like.'

She sat up very straight. 'May I really—I'd like to.'

'Good. And now shall we finish that very interesting conversation we were having when we were interrupted? You were saying?'

'Nothing.' She couldn't get it out fast enough. 'It wasn't anything, really it wasn't.'

'No?' His tone implied disbelief. 'Ah, well, later on, perhaps.' He smiled at her and her heart bounced so that she caught her breath.

'I thought we might go to the Keukenhof the day after tomorrow,' he told her. 'It should be looking at its best; your mother is anxious to inspect the flowers.'

Phyllida was glad of the change in the conversation. 'Yes, she's a great gardener...' She babbled on for a few minutes and then stopped a bit abruptly; even in her own ears she sounded foolish.

They dined early by reason of the lecture and then drove the forty miles to Utrecht. The evening was fine and the country as they approached the city looked pretty and peaceful. 'But not as pretty as where you live,' declared Phyllida.

'Well, I do agree with you there, but I daresay I'm prejudiced.' He swept the car through the main streets, worked his way through some very narrow lanes and entered the hospital courtyard.

She was given a seat near the back of the lecture hall and made to feel at home by the young doctor who had been asked to look after her. She hadn't given much thought to the lecture. That it was delivered in Dutch really didn't matter; it was bliss just to sit there and stare at Pieter, elegant and assured and presumably amusing, for every now and again there would be a burst of laughter around her. He had a lovely voice, she thought, deep and a bit gravelly and unhurried. She sighed gustily and the young doctor gave her an anxious look which she dispelled with a beaming smile.

On the way home, later, Pieter observed idly: 'It can't have been much fun for you—did you go to sleep? I must have been out of my mind to have asked you in the first place.'

'Oh, but I loved it, and I didn't go to sleep—I listened to every word,' and when he gave a great shout of laughter: 'Well, you know what I mean.'

'I like to think that I do.'

A remark which gave her plenty to think about until they got back.

She saw little of the doctor during the following day, though, surprisingly, Phyllida thought. His mother called in the afternoon and had tea with them, going round the gardens with her mother, enjoying a long talk about flower growing.

'I like her,' declared Mrs Cresswell when Mevrouw van Sittardt had been driven away in an old-fashioned, beautifully kept motor-car. 'She's a bit overpowering, but she's a woman after my own heart.' She added by way of explanation: 'She doesn't cut her roses back either.'

The doctor arrived home in the late afternoon, waved aside offers of tea and disclosed the fact that they were all going to Marena's studio for drinks before dinner. Phyllida instantly went into a flurry of hair brushing and fresh make-up, deploring the fact that the weather had turned quite warm and she really had nothing to wear. It would have to be the thin wool, which meant that after the first drink and with the central heating, she would be as red as a beet in no time at all.

Marena's flat was in the centre of den Haag, high up in a modern block, all black marble entrance and chromium fittings, and her studio was very similar—a vast room with paintings stacked along one wall and an easel under one enormous window. It was furnished in a modern style and its walls hung with Impressionist paintings, a fitting background for Marena who was wearing an outrageous outfit; a tunic slashed to the waist and tight velvet pants. Phyllida eyed her with real envy, wishing she dared to dress like that; it might capture Pieter's attention.

And it did, but not in the way she had expected. He took a long look and said slowly: 'If that's what you borrowed five hundred gulden for, my dear, it's been wasted.'

Phyllida saw the flash of anger in the girl's eyes although she laughed at him. 'It's not for you, Pieter—I've a new boy-friend.' She flashed a look at Phyllida, who looked back at her woodenly.

They drank a concoction in long glasses which Phyllida didn't like but didn't dare to say so, and yet it must have shown on her face, for while Marena was showing Mrs Cresswell her paintings, Pieter crossed the room and took the glass from her and gave her his empty one. He must think her an awful baby, she mused sadly.

They stayed a couple of hours, which gave Phyllida ample time in which to watch Marena at work on Pieter, who was treating her as one might treat a pretty child; goodnaturedly answering her preposterous remarks, praising her paintings, telling her that she was getting prettier each time he saw her. Phyllida, feeling a frump in the woollen dress, registered a firm resolve to go out the very next day and buy some new clothes. It wasn't until they were on the way home that she remembered that they were going to spend the whole of the next day at the Keukenhof.

CHAPTER SEVEN

THE KEUKENHOF WAS beautiful under a cloudless sky, although a chilly wind set the flowers nodding and swaying. They had left the house shortly after breakfast and driven the few miles there in no time at all, so that when they reached the park there were very few people about. They strolled round while the doctor and Mrs Cresswell exchanged Latin names and methods of propagation in an assured manner which left Phyllida and Willy quite at sea. But whatever they were called, the tulips and hyacinths and daffodils were a colourful sight, arranged in glowing patches of colour so that whichever way one turned there was something to delight the eye.

'Mind you,' remarked Mrs Cresswell, 'your own gardens are magnificent and must take a good deal of planning.'

The doctor laughed. 'I must plead guilty to leaving most of the work to Bauke, who has been with the family for so long I can't remember what he looked like as a young man. He's a wizard with flowers—I only study the catalogues and say what I like.'

'Do you ever garden yourself?' asked Phyllida, remembering the wheelbarrow and the spade.

'Oh, yes—the odd hour or so when I have the time; it's good exercise. And you, Phyllida?'

They had paused to allow Willy to investigate a stretch of ornamental water. 'Me? Well, I dig potatoes and pull carrots and cut the flowers if I'm home. What's that building over there?'

'A restaurant and café. If you won't get too chilly we might have coffee on the terrace before we go along to the glass-houses.'

Which they did, sitting near the water in the sunshine, and then wandering on again towards the great greenhouses. The gardens were lovely, but the display in the houses took even Mrs Cresswell's breath. She hurried from one spread of colour to the next, exclaiming over each of them, and: 'Oh, how I wish I could take them all home with me!' she sighed.

'Hardly possible, I'm afraid, but you must allow me to offer you a small memento of your visit—we'll pick out the bulbs you particularly admire and I'll order them—you'll get them in the autumn.'

'Oh, I couldn't!' and then at his gentle smile: 'Well, just one or two, perhaps.' She went happily all the way round again, trying to make up her mind which she would choose. 'Those Kaufmanniana hybrids for the rock garden, perhaps—or should I have that alium Moly, such a lovely colour.' Her eyes wandered to the display of parrot tulips. 'That blue and mauve one—if I might have one or two?'

'Do you care for the Mendel? I have them at home, if you remember—such a good colour in spring, I find.' The doctor was quietly leading her on. 'The clover pink goes so splendidly with the iris danfordiae—an unusual colour scheme, but you must admit that the pink and yellow made a splendid show.'

'Oh, yes—I did admire them in your garden. It's hard to choose—perhaps if I might have a few iris and one or two of the parrot tulips? And thank you very much.'

Mrs Cresswell looked quite flushed with pleasure.

'I'll go across and order them from the office there. Do go on looking around; I shall find you presently.'

Mrs Cresswell pottered off happily enough, pointing out what she would have if only she could afford them. Which gave Phyllida an idea. She would buy some bulbs for her mother too; if she went back to the little rustic hut where they took the orders she would be able to see which ones the doctor had ordered and get something to go with them. She muttered her plan to Willy and slipped away.

The doctor was still there and she was surprised to see the look of guilt on his face when he saw her. She didn't pause to consider this, however, but plunged at once into her idea. 'And if you'll tell me what you've ordered I'll get something else,' she finished.

Something in his face made her transfer her gaze to the clerk holding the order book. A whole page of it was filled and she turned a questioning look upon Pieter, who gave her a calm stare which told her nothing. 'It seems a pity,' he remarked blandly, 'that your mother shouldn't have something of everything she admired; I should like to think of your garden at home filled with flowers—she likes them so much.'

'The whole lot?' she gaped at him.

'Well, not quite all.' He smiled faintly. 'Now you're here, will you help me to decide which of the tulips to have in my own garden? That pink lily flowering one is charming—you were admiring it...'

'I think it's super, but why ask my advice? I mean, you'll be the one to see them, not me. But if I were choosing for my garden, yes, I'd have them. Where will you plant them?'

'In the beds on either side of the front door, under the windows. I'd better have two hundred.'

She gulped. 'That seems an awful lot,' she ventured.

'There's an awful lot of garden,' he pointed out, and took her arm. 'Let's find your mother and Willy—and not a word, mind.'

They had lunch presently in the restaurant and then a last

stroll before driving back. At the house once more, Phyllida, wondering what to do with the rest of her afternoon was over the moon when the doctor suggested casually that she might like to go with him to his rooms.

'I'll be there a couple of hours,' he said. 'You can look round if you're interested and then while away the time at the shops until I'm ready.' He glanced at her mother, happily immersed in a pile of catalogues, and Willy, already on his way across the lawns with the dog. 'I don't think you'll be missed.'

His rooms were in a narrow street of elegant houses, with barely room to park a car before their doors. He stopped the Bentley half way down and got out to open her door. 'If you walk to the end and turn to the right, you'll be in the main shopping centre. This is Finklestraat and I'm at number ten. If you get lost, just ask the way back.'

He was on the ground floor; a richly comfortable waiting room, an office where his secretary sat and a consulting room beyond and beside it a small treatment room. There was a nurse there, a formidable middle-aged woman who greeted the doctor austerely and immediately took him to task for something or other. He listened meekly to her lecture, said something to make her laugh, and led the way into his consulting room. It was of a pleasant size and furnished in soothing shades of grey and soft browns, with comfortable chairs and a large desk. She looked round her slowly. 'You're a very successful man, aren't you, Pieter?'

His lips twitched. 'I work hard, Phylly.'

'Oh, I didn't mean to be rude—I only meant...'

He caught her hand. 'I know that. I wanted you to see where I work for a good deal of my day.' He bent and kissed her lightly. 'Now run along and enjoy yourself. You can have two hours.'

She found herself in the street, her head a muddle of thoughts and dreams. Perhaps he was falling in love with her, on the other hand he could be being just friendly, wanting her to enjoy her holiday. There was no point in brooding about it. She walked briskly to the end of the street and made for the nearest shops.

Egged on by the thought of Marena, she was tempted to enter a boutique presently, and once inside she cast caution to the winds and bought rather more than she had intended; a silk jersey tunic in a dusky pink, a pleated skirt in pale green with a matching jacket and a real silk blouse to go with them, and lastly a cotton jersey shirtwaister in pale amber; she hadn't meant to buy that, but the saleslady had pointed out, quite rightly, that it would be a most useful garment for the rest of the year.

Much lighter in the purse, and in the heart too, Phyllida found her way back to Finklestraat and poked her head round the waiting-room door. The room was empty and she had a sudden pang that everyone had gone home and left her behind; instantly dismissed as absurd, for the Bentley was still standing at the kerb.

She sat down with her packages around her and waited quietly until the nurse came out, followed by the secretary. They both smiled at her and the secretary said: 'The doctor is coming,' as they went out.

Pieter joined her a few minutes later, opened his sleepy eyes wide at the sight of her parcels, observed that she had put her time to good use, swept them up and ushered her out to the car. He seemed disinclined for conversation, so after one or two tentative remarks Phyllida gave up and sat silent until they stopped at his house. There was another car parked on the sweep and as he leaned over to open her door, he observed a little impatiently: 'And now what does Marena want, I wonder? Not another dress so soon?'

Phyllida received her parcels, thanked him for the outing and went ahead of him into the house; if Marena was there she didn't want to see her. Even so, she was illogically put out when the doctor made no attempt to delay her. He watched her make for the stairs, Aap behind with her purchases, before turning away and going into the drawing room.

Once in her room, Phyllida lost no time in trying on everything she had bought. The jersey tunic was certainly stunning. She decided to wear it that evening; it might possibly detract Pieter's interest from Marena. She had heard the car start up and leave, so she would have a clear field.

She went downstairs presently, feeling a little excited, aware that she looked her very best. It was a great pity that Pieter wasn't there. Aap tendered his excuses and begged that they would dine without their host, and offered no further information at all.

Phyllida received her mother's admiration of her new dress with a pleasant calm which concealed rage, carried on a spirited conversation with Willy about the size of the fish he might one day catch, and dinner over, declared that she had a headache and retired to her room, where she threw the new dress into a corner and cried herself to sleep.

The doctor, returning home presently to spend the rest of the evening with his guests, evinced surprise when Mrs Cresswell told him that Phyllida had gone to bed with a headache, but he said nothing beyond murmuring some civility or other, poured himself a whisky and sat down in his chair. Mrs Cresswell, studying him while he exchanged a bantering conversation with Willy, concluded that he looked thoughtful, but not in a worried way; more as though he was mightily pleased about something.

Phyllida went down to her breakfast the next morning with some caution. She didn't want to meet Pieter, not yet, not until her puffy eyelids were normal again. He should be gone, either to his surgery or to one or other of the hospitals he visited. All the same, she approached the breakfast room circumspectly and was about to peer round its half open door when his study door was flung open behind her. His cheerful: 'Ha!' uttered in a booming voice, sent her spinning round to face him.

She managed: 'Oh, good morning—I thought you'd gone?'

He leaned against the door frame, watching her. 'So who were you expecting to jump out on you?'

She had regained her breath and her composure. 'No one. I expect you're just off to the surgery.'

'Indeed I am. But I shall be back. It is unfortunate that I can't take Willy sailing as I'd arranged, but there are a couple of urgent cases I must see. Besides, I fancy this weather isn't going to last and the *meer* can be quite nasty if the wind rises.' He wandered towards her. 'Your headache is quite better?'

'Headache?' She remembered then. 'Oh, yes—yes, thank you—it wasn't a bad one.'

He said with faint mockery: 'I thought it wasn't. A pity that I should have returned home so soon after you had gone to your room.' And when she didn't answer: 'Well, I won't keep you from your breakfast. We shall meet at lunch, I hope.'

Her mother was too wise to ask after the headache. She launched into a rambling chat about a letter she had had from Doctor Cresswell, and Phyllida, listening with half an ear, wondered why Willy looked so glum. She wasn't kept in the dark for long.

'We should have gone sailing,' declared her brother. 'I was looking forward to it no end, and now Pieter says he can't—not today.' He made a hideous face. 'And you'll see, it'll be raining tomorrow and if it's fine he'll have more patients to see…'

'Well, he is a doctor,' Phyllida pointed out reasonably, 'and you've had a lot of fun—fishing and so on.'

Willy buttered toast and spread it with a slice of cheese. 'Yes, I know—it's been super, but there's only another week.'

'Well, let's do something else,' suggested Phyllida. 'Any ideas?'

'I think I'll borrow the bike in the garage and go for a spin.' The look he gave her was so angelic that she instantly suspected that he was up to something, but surely a bike ride was harmless enough.

'OK, I've got some letters to write. How about you, Mother?'

Mrs Cresswell looked vague. 'There was something—Oh, yes, I remember now, Bauke is going to take me round the glasshouses and the kitchen garden. We shan't understand a word each other's saying, but I don't see that it will matter.'

So they all dispersed to their various morning activities and it wasn't until a few minutes before lunch time that Phyllida, wandering into the garden room, wondered where everyone was. Her mother arrived just as she was thinking it and burst at once into an account of the delightful morning she had spent with Bauke. 'A taciturn man,' she observed, 'but a most knowledgeable one. We're going to spend another hour or two together before we go back. Where's Willy, dear?'

Phyllida had one ear cocked for the doctor's firm tread. 'I don't know, Mother—still cycling, I expect.'

'Not at all likely,' remarked his parent sapiently. 'He'll be near home; it's too near lunch time.' She sat down and sighed contentedly. 'See if you can find him, Phylly, he's sure to be grubby.'

There was no sign of him in the gardens near the house. Phyllida went further afield, exploring the shrubbery paths, peering in the summer house and garden sheds, even the garages behind the house. The bike was still there and she frowned at the sight of it and went on down to the lake, its waters ruffled by a chilly little wind coming in gusts, shivering as she went, for the watery blue sky was clouding over rapidly. It took her a minute or two to register the fact that the yacht which had been moored to the jetty by the boathouse wasn't there, and another minute to find Willy's school blazer flung down carelessly beside the path.

He'd taken the yacht. That accounted for the innocence of the look he had given her at breakfast; he had meant to all along. Phyllida ran along the narrow path bordering the lake and then followed it beside the canal which led to the wide *meer* beyond, and presently reached its edge.

Quite close inshore was the yacht, just ahead of her, bowling merrily along—much too fast, she thought—before the blustery wind, and she could see Willy quite clearly in it. As she looked he caught sight of her and shouted something and waved, then turned away so sharply that she thought the boat would heel over. Surely Willy would have enough sense to hold the rudder steady? Apparently he hadn't, for the yacht was careering towards the centre of the *meer* and he was getting further away with every second.

She looked around her, seeking inspiration, trying not to feel frightened. There was a promontory half a mile further along the bank, standing well out into the water. If she could reach it before Willy she might be able to guide him towards it and beach the yacht. It was to be hoped that they could tie the yacht up; she worried for a minute about Pieter's reaction if they damaged it and then dismissed the thought; it was more important to get Willy out of his fix. She began to run, urged on by the rising wind and the first few drops of rain.

She reached the spit of land ahead of Willy, now heading away from it once more, and she hurried to its very edge, filled her lungs and bawled at him to steer towards her. 'Turn the rudder slowly,' she counselled at the top of her lungs, and almost before she had finished the yacht swung violently towards her, its sail almost touching the choppy water. 'Gently!' she called, and waited anxiously as the boat came towards her, much too fast. It wasn't like Willy to behave in such a way; he could do most things well and he had a solid common sense which had got him out of any number of awkward situations. Now he was waving at her and calling, but before she could catch what he was shouting, the yacht careered off again, only to turn in a few moments and come towards her once more, this time within hailing distance.

'What's up?'

'The rudder's broken.' He didn't sound too upset. 'I've got an oar and I'm trying to steer with it, but it's not much good.'

Phyllida had kicked off her shoes and tossed her cardigan onto the grass bank. 'Keep her steady if you can, I'll come out to you.'

She wasn't a strong swimmer and the water was very cold. And worse, Willy wasn't having much success in keeping the yacht on the same course. It was pure luck that the boat swerved towards her, coming so close that she was able to cling to its side, to be hauled aboard with a good deal of difficulty.

She subsided on to the deck, wringing wet, smelling of weed. 'Willy, I'll wring your neck!' she said forcefully, and then: 'What do we do first?'

Willy ignored her threat. 'If we both hang on to the oar—or perhaps we could tie it with something?'

'What?' She looked around her; the yacht was immaculate with everything in its place, but she didn't dare touch the ropes arranged so neatly in case something came adrift and they were worse off than ever.

'We'll hold it,' she decided, 'and try and steer to the bank somehow.' She looked up at the sky, shivering. The wind, freshening fast, had brought the rain with it.

She said suddenly: 'Willy, is there a horn?'

He gaped at her. 'A horn? Yes, of course—it's used when you go through a lock. Why?'

'Can you remember the Morse Code?'

'Yes, of course I can.'

'Well, do it on the horn. Is it three short, three long, three short, or the other way round?'

Her brother gave her a withering look. 'Girls!' he uttered with scorn. 'Can you manage the oar for a bit?'

Her teeth were chattering now; she was already so wet that the rain made no difference, except to make her feel worse.

'I'll have to, won't I? Willy, why did you do it? Have you any idea what Pieter is going to say when he discovers that you've taken his boat?'

'He's going to be angry—I daresay he'll ask us to go home.'

'Oh, you wretched boy! Go and blow that horn, for heaven's sake!'

Mrs Cresswell waited for ten minutes or so and then wandered to the window and looked out. There was no sign of either of her children; it was fortunate that Pieter was late for lunch; they might get back before he did. But after another ten minutes she became uneasy. She drank the sherry Aap had poured for her in an absent-minded fashion and wondered why they were so long—perhaps they could all come in together.

But presently the doctor came in alone, took one look at her face and asked: 'What's worrying you, Mrs Cresswell?'

'Well, I'm not exactly worried. I daresay I'm just being a fussy old woman...' She explained simply, adding: 'Willy did say that he was going to borrow the bike in the garden shed.'

The doctor went to look out of the window. 'We can check that easily enough,' he assured her, and pulled the bell rope by the fireplace, and when Aap came spoke briefly to him.

Aap went away and returned within a few minutes. The bicycle was still in the shed, he reported impassively.

'So he's fishing.'

Aap shook his head. All the rods were in their rightful places; he had looked on his way back from the garages. The doctor frowned, took another look at the rain and wind outside, then opened the french window and glanced around. It was while he was doing this that he became aware of the insistent blast of the horn.

He listened for a moment. 'Someone is sending out what I presume to be an SOS,' then: 'My God, it's the *Mireille*—that young devil's got her out on the *meer*!' He swung round. 'Aap, get me a jacket. Mrs Cresswell, don't worry, I'll be back with Willy and Phyllida very shortly.'

He took the anorak Aap was holding out to him, gave a satisfied grunt when he saw that Aap was putting on a similar garment, and made for the garden. Mrs Cresswell watched the pair of them walking briskly across the lawn, to disappear presently behind the shrubs at the far end.

The moment they were out of sight they broke into a run, the doctor covering the ground with his long legs at a great rate, and Aap, for all his stoutness, close on his heels. They followed the path Phyllida had taken and reached the edge of the *meer* in time to see the yacht veering away towards the opposite shore.

'What the hell...?' began Pieter furiously. 'Aap, I believe they've lost the rudder, and why don't they get the sail down?' His face was coldly ferocious. 'We'll get the speedboat out and get alongside her. Stay here—I'll pick you up.'

He went back, running fast, to the boathouse by the lake, and within a very short time came tearing through the canal, to pick up Aap and then roar out into the choppy water.

Phyllida, wrestling with the oar, watched his rapid approach with mixed feelings—relief, because she didn't want either Willy or herself to drown, and she could see no alternative at the moment, the way they were careering around and the weather getting nastier at every moment—and apprehension as to Pieter's reaction to seeing his lovely yacht exposed to some of the worst handling he might ever witness. Willy, hanging on to the oar beside her, gave a gusty sigh.

'It's like one of the gods coming to wreak vengeance! I'm scared. Are you, Phylly?'

'Not in the least,' she screamed at him above the wind, and felt her insides turn to ice with fright. Pieter, she decided, was going to be far worse than the storm.

It looked as though she were right as the speedboat drew near. The doctor was standing, his face like a thundercloud, tearing off his anorak and then stooping to pick up a rope. If he threw it, she thought miserably, she would never catch it, she was rotten at catching things—Willy would have to do it; presumably they were to be towed in. The yacht, caught in a gust of wind, made a sweeping turn and started off merrily in the opposite direction so that she lost sight of the speedboat. But only for a moment; it roared into view once more, almost alongside, and she gave a gasping shriek as Pieter, the rope in his hand, jumped into the water. He was a powerful swimmer; before the yacht could turn again he had pulled himself on board and was tying the rope, turning to shout to Aap, still in the speedboat, taking no notice at all of her or Willy.

Aap shortened the distance between them and when he was alongside Pieter said: 'Over you go, Willy, into the boat with Aap, and look sharp!'

There was no question of disobeying him; he might be sopping wet, his hair plastered on his head, water dripping off him in great-pools, but that made no difference to his air of command. Willy did exactly as he had been told without so much as a word, landing awkwardly beside Aap, who grinned at him and nodded directions to sit down. Phyllida, expecting to go next, clutched the oar to her as though it were an old familiar friend and had it taken from her, none too gently.

'I would expect Willy to play those schoolboy pranks,' said the doctor in a voice which did nothing to reassure her, 'but you, Phyllida, what the hell possessed you?'

He had dumped her down on the deck and was reefing the sail with swift expertise, and she didn't bother to answer. Let him think what he liked, she thought furiously; she was cold and still frightened and wet and smelly and nothing mattered any more.

Aap was sidling away from the yacht, going ahead of her and turning slowly in the direction of the canal, and presently Phyllida felt the yacht turn too, obedient to the pull of the tow rope. Pieter was hanging over the rudder, examining the break which had caused all the trouble. He turned his head to say: 'Well, you haven't answered my question. Why did you let Willy get on board in the first place?'

She pushed her soaking fringe out of her eyes. 'I didn't,' she raged at him, 'he was already in the middle of the *meer*. I had to swim out to help him.'

She choked at his amused smile. 'Swam, did you? Brave girl!' He turned away to do something to the tow rope and she said angrily to his enormous back: 'I certainly wouldn't have got on to your rotten old boat for any other reason.' Her voice shook. 'I thought Willy would drown!'

The yacht was dancing along through the rough water, the speedboat ahead, and they were almost at the canal. Pieter finished what he was doing and squatted down on the deck beside her. 'Are you very angry?' she asked in a small voice.

He flung a heavy wet arm round her shoulders. 'When I was ten—eleven, I did exactly the same thing, only the rudder didn't break. I got quite a long way before my father caught up with me. I was punished, of course, but the next day he took me out and taught me how to sail a boat.' His rage had gone, the smile he turned on her was very gentle. 'I think we'd better teach Willy how to sail too before he sinks everything in sight.'

'I'm sorry—we'll pay for the damage…' She had forgotten her rage. 'And I didn't mean it—about it being a rotten old boat.'

'I didn't think you did. Can you sail?'

'No.'

'Then I shall have to teach you too.'

'There won't be time.'

He had got to his feet, as they were entering the canal. 'All the time in the world, love.'

They were at the boathouse and he was shortening the tow rope, calling to Aap. 'And don't do that again, Phylly.'

She was on her feet too, relieved to see the jetty and dry land but reluctant to leave him. 'Do what?'

'Terrify me to my very bones.' He said softly: 'You could have drowned.'

He lifted her on to the jetty, fetched a blanket from the boathouse and wrapped her in it. 'Whose idea was it to send an SOS on the horn?' he wanted to know in an ordinary voice.

'Phylly's,' said Willy, 'and I did it.'

'Next time, boy, get it right. OSO isn't quite the same thing, only I happened to recognise the *Mereille's* horn. Off to the house with you, tell your mother you're safe and get dry and into other clothes—you can have fifteen minutes. After lunch you and I have to talk.'

Willy went red but met the doctor's eye bravely enough. 'Yes, you'll want to punish me. I'm sorry I did it.' He darted off, and the doctor spoke to Aap, busy with the boats, and took Phyllida's arm. 'And a hot bath and dry clothes for you, too.' He was walking her along so rapidly that she had to skip to keep up with him.

Steadying her chattering teeth, she asked: 'Am I to be talked to too?'

'There's nothing I should enjoy more,' he assured her, 'but we'll keep that until a more suitable time.' A remark she didn't take seriously.

They lunched at last, the doctor making light of the whole episode so that Mrs Cresswell shouldn't be upset. And afterwards he and Willy went along to the study, leaving Phyllida sitting uneasily with her mother in the drawing room.

'It was most considerate of Pieter to treat the whole thing as a joke,' remarked Mrs Cresswell. 'I hope he's giving Willy the talking-to of his life. Is he angry with you, too, dear?'

Phyllida glanced at her mother. She had thought they had done rather well at lunch, glossing over the whole adventure, but for all her vague ways, her parent was astute. 'I don't think so,' she said slowly.

'I should be very surprised if he were,' observed her mother.

'That girl—what's her name? is coming to tea—I heard Pieter on the telephone while you were upstairs.'

'But Mother, you can't understand Dutch.'

She was treated to a limpid stare. 'No, dear, but I happened to be sitting near him and he's far too well-mannered to speak Dutch when he knows I don't know a word.'

'Mother,' began Phyllida, 'you could have walked away.'

'So I could—I never thought of it. She's coming at four o'clock. Why not go and wash your hair properly, darling? You did it in a great hurry before lunch, I expect. It looks so soft and silky when it's just been done.'

'Mother!' said Phyllida again, then laughed. 'All right, I'll go now.'

She was glad presently that she had taken such pains with her hair and her face and that she had kept on the jersey shirt-waister. Its soft amber gave her a nice glow and contrasted favourably with Marena's flamboyant striped dress. Not that the girl didn't look quite wonderful—how could she help it with looks like hers?

Marena had driven herself over, greeted Pieter effusively, turned her charm on to Mrs Cresswell and smiled at Phyllida, dismissing her as not worth bothering about, just as she ignored Willy. A rather quiet Willy. After tea, when the other three had gone into the garden Phyllida asked him: 'Was he very cross, Willy? Did he suggest that we went back sooner, or anything like that?'

He shook his head. 'No—he gave me a good lecture.' Her brother swallowed. 'He's great, Phylly, and I like him a lot, but he can make you feel an inch high…when he'd finished he said he'd take me on the lake tomorrow if the weather was right and show me how to handle a boat.' He sighed loudly. 'I wish he was my brother.'

'You don't need any more brothers,' declared Phyllida crossly, and added severely: 'And don't you dare do anything else silly!'

The others came back then, Marena with her arm through Pieter's, looking like a sweet little kitten who'd found the cream jug.

They sat about talking for a little while longer and Phyllida did her best not to look at Pieter and Marena. The girl was at her most tiresome, talking about people only the two of them knew, leaning forward to touch his arm, smiling into his face. It was really more than Phyllida could bear. If only something would happen, she mused, something to change Pieter's manner towards her. He had always been friendly and kind and teased her a little, but she had been wrong in thinking that he was even a little in love with her. That had been wishful thinking on her part. Trying not to see Marena's lovely little hand patting Pieter's sleeve while she talked to him, Phyllida guessed that the next few days before they went home weren't going to be either easy or happy ones for her. She pinned a smile on her face now, and listened to Marena being witty about her holiday in Switzerland. To add to everything else, it seemed that she was expert on skis and even better on ice skates, and the horrid girl, drawing Phyllida into the talk, asked her the kind of questions that showed her up as a perfect fool on skates and an ignoramus when it came to skiing.

In the end, sick of the girl's barbed witticisms, Phyllida said a little too loudly: 'I'm no good at anything like that, but at least I can drive a car.' Which was a palpable hit because Marena, when she had arrived that afternoon, had knocked over a stone urn by the sweep, gone into reverse by accident, hit a tree, dented her bumper and then left all her lights on. Everyone had laughed it off at the time, but Phyllida, her gentle nature aroused, didn't see why she should get away with it.

Marena glared at her when she got up to go and ignored her as she said her goodbyes and went to the door with the doctor. When they were out of earshot Mrs Cresswell whispered, 'You were very rude, darling, but she deserved every word!'

Phyllida felt better about it then, but the feeling didn't last long, for when Pieter came back it seemed to her that his manner towards her was a little distant. Not that she cared about that in the very least, she told herself.

CHAPTER EIGHT

IT WAS DISAPPOINTING that Phyllida didn't see Pieter all the next day until the evening. She had been shopping with her mother in the morning, lunching out and shopping again afterwards; they hadn't bought much, small presents for family and friends, but they had spent a good deal of time gazing into the enticing windows. By the time Aap had picked them up at the agreed rendezvous it was late afternoon, but there was no sign of their host as they sank into comfortable chairs in the small sitting room behind the drawing room and drank their tea, soothed by the peace and quiet of the old house.

'Bliss!' observed Mrs Cresswell on a contented sigh. 'I could hear a pin drop.' She took a sip of tea. 'When is Willy coming back?'

'Well, Pieter said he'd be staying to tea at the *dominee's* house.'

Mrs Cresswell ate a biscuit and followed her train of thought.

'Five more days. What a wonderful holiday we're having—I shall never forget it.'

'Nor shall I,' agreed Phyllida; she was going to remember it for the rest of her life, although perhaps not for the same reasons as her mother. 'I wonder where Pieter is—he's usually home just about now.'

Her mother darted her a look over her tea-cup. 'Well, dear, he's a busy man. Besides, he must have any number of friends—after all, we don't know a great deal about his life, do we?' She took another biscuit. 'I shall get fat, but these are so delicious. A pity we aren't likely to meet again once this holiday is over. I expect we shall exchange Christmas cards and I daresay Willy will write to him.' She sighed. 'The world is full of nice people one never gets to know.'

Phyllida, surveying a future without Pieter, felt like weeping. 'The minute I get back,' she told her mother with entirely false enthusiasm, 'I shall start looking for a job. I'll try for something in Bristol, it's not far from home and it'll make a nice change.'

'Yes, dear. Have you heard from Philip since you left?'

'Philip?' Phyllida looked blank. 'Oh, Philip—no, but I didn't expect to.'

Willy came in then, full of his day and all he had done and what he intended to do the next day. He was looking very well; the holiday had done him good at any rate, thought Phyllida; it had done her mother good too—she wasn't sure about herself.

She was pouring second cups when she heard the front door close, a murmur of voices in the hall and then Pieter's firm tread. Her colour was a little high as he sat down beside her mother, although she replied to his enquiries as to her day with composure.

It was her mother who brought up the subject of their return home. 'Ought we to book our places?' she asked, 'and will you tell us which is the best way to go, Pieter?'

He took a large bite of fruit cake. 'With me, of course—in the same way as we came, in the car.'

'Oh, but we couldn't—to take you away from your work...'

He got up and handed his cup to Phyllida, and when she had refilled it, sat down beside her. 'Well, you know, Mrs Cresswell, I am able to arrange my work to suit myself to a large extent, and it so happens that I've been asked by a colleague to see a patient in London within the next week or so. I can combine business with pleasure.'

Mrs Cresswell beamed at him. 'Won't that be nice—and of course you'll stay at least one night with us—longer if you can manage it.'

He glanced sideways at Phyllida's charming profile. 'That depends on circumstances, but I hope that I shall be able to accept your invitation.'

He uttered this formal speech with such blandness that Phyllida looked at him, to be met with a sleepy gaze which told her nothing at all. She occupied herself with the teapot and left him and her mother to make conversation.

But her mother got up presently, with a murmured observation that she was to visit the rockery with Bauke before it got too late, and since Willy was bidden to accompany her, Phyllida was left with the doctor. She sat for a minute or two, thinking up plausible excuses for going away too, and had just settled on the old and tried one of having to wash her hair, when her companion spoke.

'No, Phylly, your hair doesn't need washing, nor do you wish to write letters or take them to the post. Just relax, love, I shan't eat you.'

He lounged back beside her, his eyes half closed, contemplating his well-shod feet. He looked placid and easygoing, and if truth be told, sleepy, and yet Phyllida was aware that underneath all that he was as sharp as a needle, ready to fire awkward questions at her and make remarks she couldn't understand.

'Any plans?' he asked casually.

She hesitated. 'Vague ones—well, not so vague, really. It's time I got back into hospital again.'

'London?'

Her unguarded tongue was too ready with an answer. 'No, Bristol, I thought,' and then, furious with herself for having told him that: 'Probably not—I haven't decided.'

He had moved closer, one arm along the back of the sofa, behind her. 'That's good; I rather wanted to talk about your future, Phylly. We haven't seen as much of each other as I should have wished, all the same...' He paused and she held her breath, her heart thumping nineteen to the dozen while common sense told her that she was being a fool. In a minute she would know...

Aap propelled his cheerful rotundity through the door with a lightness of foot which made the doctor mutter something forceful under his breath.

'A gentleman to see Miss Cresswell,' announced Aap, ignoring the mutter.

Phyllida, brought down from the improbable clouds where she had been perched, said quickly: 'But I don't know any gentlemen,' and Pieter laughed. 'Ask him to come in, Aap,' he said in such a casual voice that she wondered if she had imagined the urgency in his voice not two minutes earlier.

Aap went away, to reappear almost at once, ushering in Philip Mount.

Phyllida caught her breath and jumped to her feet. 'Philip—why ever are you here? How did you find out where I was? What's the matter?'

Philip wasn't a man to be bustled into making hurried answers; he didn't say anything for a moment, only stood in the doorway, looking first at her and then at the doctor, standing beside her. At length he said: 'Hullo.'

The doctor stepped smoothly into the awkward silence. 'A friend of Phyllida's?' he wanted to know pleasantly. 'How delightful.' He crossed the room and shook Philip's hand. 'Pieter van Sittardt. I've heard of you, of course.'

His visitor shook hands cautiously. 'Oh, have you?'

'You'll want to have a talk—I'll get someone to bring in some coffee—do make yourself at home, and I hope you'll stay to dinner.'

He waved Philip to a chair, smiled benignly at him, beamed at Phyllida, standing there as though she were stuffed, and went away so quickly that no one else had a chance to say a word.

Phyllida gnashed her teeth; there had been no need for Pieter
to be quite so hospitable; he had almost flung Philip at her—
perhaps he felt that providence, in the shape of Philip Mount,
had saved him in the nick of time from saying something to her
which he might have regretted. She sat down rather abruptly
and Philip asked sharply:

'Who's he?'

'You heard—our host.' She had found her voice at last. 'Why
on earth are you here?'

He took no notice of her question. 'He said he'd heard of
me—from you?'

'Well, I suppose so.' She felt as though she had been blind-
folded, turned round three times and abandoned. She asked
again: 'Why are you here, Philip?'

'To see you, of course.'

'But why?'

He answered with a smugness which made her seethe. 'I
knew you wouldn't forget me—and you haven't, have you?
talking about me to what's-his-name.'

'Doctor van Sittardt. And I haven't been talking about you.
I may have mentioned you by name, that's all.'

She broke off as Aap came in with the coffee tray, walking
slowly so that he could get a good look at the unexpected guest.
Phyllida poured coffee for them both, asked Philip if he wanted
a biscuit in a snappy voice and waited. Philip had always been
deliberate, now he was maddeningly so.

'I had a few days off,' he told her. 'I telephoned your home
and your sister told me where you were. I've come to take you
back with me.'

'Whatever for? I don't want to go. You're mad, Philip!' She
had got to her feet. 'I'm not staying to listen to any more of
your nonsense!'

He put his coffee cup down and got up too. 'It's not nonsense,
Phyllida; just because you've been living it up for the last few
weeks, you've lost all your good sense. I suppose you think

you're in love with this fellow—well, stop your daydreaming and be your sensible self again. Come back with me and we'll start again.'

'I don't want to start again!' Her voice rose several octaves. 'Can't you understand? I don't want...' He had crossed the room and caught her clumsily in his arms.

'Don't be a silly girl,' he begged her. 'Once you're married to me...'

He was facing the door and she felt his arms slacken around her. Someone had come in, and she knew at once who it was.

'So sorry,' said the doctor with loud cheerfulness. 'I should have remembered. You really must stay to dinner, Mount, and spend the night too.'

Philip's voice sounded stiff and sullen. 'Thanks—I'd like to stay to dinner; I've already booked at an hotel for the night.'

'Splendid!' Pieter smiled, his eyes icily bright beneath their lids. 'Aap shall show you where you can freshen up presently, but while Phyllida changes we'll have a drink. You're a doctor, are you not? What do you specialise in?'

He barely glanced at Phyllida as he opened the door for her, and when she peeped at him, she could see a mocking little smile on his face.

Her mother and Willy weren't to be found. She bathed and dressed in the new tunic, did her hair and face with tremendous care and sat down to wait until the very last minute before dinner. The idea of spending even a few minutes with Philip made her feel quite sick. Somehow she would have to get Pieter alone and explain...

She had no chance; when she eventually went downstairs it was to find not only Pieter with his unexpected guest, but her mother, Willy, Pieter's mother and father and Marena, grouped around the log fire, having what appeared to be a high old time over drinks.

Pieter crossed the room to her as she stood, quite taken aback, just inside the door. The nasty little smile was still there, she saw uneasily, and he observed just as nastily: 'A new dress? Very charming—kept for Philip, I suppose.'

'You suppose wrong,' snapped Phyllida very quietly so that no one else could hear. 'It's a new dress, but I bought it for...' She couldn't tell him that she had bought it for his benefit; she closed her mouth firmly and glared at him.

'You didn't know that he was coming?' His soft voice held incredulity.

'Of course I didn't! Pieter—oh, Pieter...'

'Oh, Phylly!' His voice mocked her. 'What will you have to drink?'

Hemlock would have been a good choice, she thought silently, but aloud she settled for a dry sherry and went to speak to his parents.

Marena was talking to her mother and neither of them looked over-happy. Phyllida smiled emptily at them both and drank her sherry far too quickly, plunging into an animated conversation with Mevrouw van Sittardt and puzzling that lady considerably by answering her questions with a series of random replies, engendered by the sherry and her chaotic thoughts. Out of the corner of her eye she had seen Marena leave her mother and go and stand by Pieter, so close that she was almost in his pocket. No one, she thought bitterly, had warned her that there was to be company for dinner. Which was hardly surprising since the doctor had made lightning telephone calls to his guests at the last minute, intimating that a close friend of Phyllida had arrived to see her and it seemed a good idea to invite a few people to meet him.

His parents had arrived full of curiosity, although to look at their dignified calm, no one would have guessed it; Marena had accepted gleefully, wanting to see Phyllida's close friend. Only Mrs Cresswell had accepted the situation with placid calm, apparently doing nothing about it, merely waiting to see what would happen. She had greeted Philip with well concealed surprise, asked kindly after his well-being and engaged Marena in conversation. But now, seeing her daughter looking quite distracted, Mrs Cresswell wandered over to Pieter and Marena, prised her away from him with a ruthless charm which made his blue eyes sparkle with appreciation, and wandered off again, Marena in tow, beckoning to Philip and talking to Willy as she did so.

'Philip, I don't know if Pieter told you, but Marena is an artist—so clever of her, because she's far too pretty to do anything at all, don't you agree?'

Her listeners swallowed this barefaced flattery with no trouble at all; Marena had such a good opinion of herself that she found it not in the least unusual that other people should share it, and as for Philip, he had been staring at her ever since she had entered the room and had longed to talk to her, something his host hadn't seemed to think he might want to do, for he had stationed Philip in front of him so that he had had no more than a glimpse of her from time to time because the doctor's broad person had quite blocked his view.

Mrs Cresswell, standing between them, listened with interest to Philip, usually so staid, letting himself go. The pair of them, she considered, were ideally suited. She sipped her sherry and glanced around the room, to encounter the doctor's hard stare. She returned it with a vague smile and presently he strolled over and invited her to admire the charming view from the window. They stood for a minute admiring the riot of colour outside.

'Mother love is a wonderful thing,' observed the doctor silkily.

'Oh, indeed, yes,' agreed Mrs Cresswell imperturbably, 'it should never be underestimated.'

'How right, Mrs Cresswell. The pity of it is that it is so often called into action when none is required.'

She turned to look at him. 'Interfering?' she asked. 'Now that's something I never do, Pieter.' She gave him one of her vague, sweet smiles. 'What a lovely girl Marena is.'

He didn't answer her, only smiled a little, and a moment later Aap appeared to bid them to dinner.

Later, during a mostly sleepless night, Phyllida reviewed the evening. It had been pure disaster for her; Philip had been placed next to her at table and Pieter had treated her with the politeness of a good host with whom she was only slightly acquainted, and was bent on giving her every opportunity to be alone with Philip. And the awful thing had been that Philip, although he had stuck to her like a leech, could hardly take his eyes off Marena. And when she had tried to get him alone—really alone where they could talk without anyone overhearing them—it had been impossible; Pieter might have contrived in the most ostentatious manner possible that they should be in each other's company, and yet each time she had sneaked off into a quiet corner with Philip, he had materialised like an evil genie and swept them back with the other guests.

Of one thing she was fairly sure—Philip might have come with the intention of asking her to marry him, under the impression that he loved her, but now that he had actually seen her again, he'd gone off her completely. An arrangement which suited her very well if only Pieter hadn't foiled her every chance to tell Philip that. He had even insisted that Philip should call round on the following morning: 'For I'm rather booked up myself,' he had observed urbanely, 'but do consider yourself at home—I hope to be back for lunch, and I'll see you then.' He had added blandly: 'I had arranged to drive Phyllida back, but if she wants to, by all means take her with you.'

And he hadn't even asked her what she had wanted to do! fumed Phyllida, sitting up in bed, choking with temper at the mere memory. 'If he wants to get rid of me, he can,' she cried loudly, 'then he can spend all the time he wants with his beastly Marena. I can't think why he asked me in the first place...'

She had cried then and gone to sleep with puffy red eyes and a pink nose. Her eyes were still puffy when she went down to breakfast, but she hadn't bothered to find her dark glasses;

Pieter had said he had a busy morning—at the hospital, she supposed, or Marena, of course.

He was occupied with neither. He was sitting at his breakfast table, chatting pleasantly to Mrs Cresswell and discussing the chances of another fishing trip with Willy. He stood up as Phyllida went in, wished her a cheerful good morning, asked her if she had a cold and added: 'Your eyes are puffy,' before begging her to help herself to anything she fancied.

She didn't fancy anything. She crumbled toast on her plate and drank several cups of coffee and had great difficulty in not throwing a plate at his head when he suggested that she should take a couple of Panadol tablets. 'So that you'll feel up to young Mount's company. Have you decided if you are going back with him, Phylly?'

'If Phylly can bear it, I'd much rather she went back with us,' interposed Mrs Cresswell. 'I really cannot manage by myself,' she explained plaintively. She wasn't going to have to lift a finger, everyone knew that, but Phyllida couldn't agree fast enough, the relief in her voice so obvious that Pieter's mouth twitched and his eyes danced with laughter. But all he said, and that seriously, was:

'Of course—I should have remembered that. Mount will be disappointed.'

'No, he won't,' she snapped, tossing her fringe with a pettish shake of her head. 'I can't think why he came in the first place.'

'My dear Phylly,' his voice was very smooth, 'isn't it obvious why he came?'

She went a fiery red, a dozen furious words on her tongue waiting to be uttered, but she had no chance. Willy said in a matter-of-fact voice: 'He's such a saphead I never thought he'd come after you, Phylly—I mean, he's not really stuck on you, is he?' He added with brotherly candour: 'I daresay he fancied you for a bit—you're not bad to look at, you know.'

This remark was received in silence. The doctor's face was impassive and he had dropped the lids over his eyes so that no one could see their expression. Mrs Cresswell buttered a roll with deliberation before remarking: 'I do not like to curb the young, Willy, but I think that you have rather overreached yourself.' And Phyllida stared at him and then burst out laughing, only half way through the laughter changed to tears. Pieter jumped to his feet, but before he could reach her, she had rushed out of the room.

Pieter sat down again. He said thoughtfully, looking at Mrs Cresswell: 'I can but guess at the reason for that; I can only hope that I have guessed correctly.'

Neither of his two companions answered him; Willy for the obvious reason that it might be better to hold his tongue for a while, and his mother because she could see that the doctor required no answer.

He went away presently and as soon as the Bentley had disappeared Philip arrived in the local taxi and Phyllida came downstairs, greeted him quite cheerfully, explained that she was wearing dark glasses because she had a slight headache, and agreed readily to go for a walk.

She had had a good cry upstairs and time to think. She would have to pretend that she intended to marry Philip because that was what Pieter wanted. They had got a little too friendly, but only through force of circumstances; now he wanted to get back to his Marena. She hadn't been able to understand his bad temper of the previous evening, nor guess at what he had been going to say just before Philip arrived, but it couldn't have been what she had hoped and now she would never know. Besides, he had fairly flung her at Philip... She had stopped thinking about it, otherwise she'd cry again, and had allowed her mind to dwell on their first meeting on Madeira. He had been so easy to like...to love...

She took Philip for a long walk, following the narrow brick roads between the canals, carefully pointing out anything of interest as they went. They had walked for more than half an hour before Philip, abandoning the threadbare theme of the weather upon which she had been harping, said: 'You met this fellow on Madeira, didn't you? I suppose he turned your head and now you fancy you're in love with him, just as I was saying when he interrupted us. He's got a girl anyway, that little beauty who came to dinner.' He added, not unkindly: 'You haven't a chance; you're pretty enough in a nice open-air way, but she's gorgeous.'

Phyllida had stopped so that she might steady her breath and answer him with calm. She would have liked to have screamed at him, but that would have done no good—besides, she had realised something in the last few moments.

She said with an entirely false enthusiasm: 'She's terrific, she's known Pieter van Sittardt for simply ages and I suppose they'll marry sooner or later, but I don't know—I'm not sure if she's in love with him, or he with her.' She added distractedly: 'It's hard to tell, isn't it? Philip, all this time while you thought you were in love with me you weren't, you only thought you were, and now you've discovered you aren't. We get on well, I told you that, but you wouldn't listen, and that's not the same as loving someone. I'm not saying you're in love with Marena, but she excites you as I never did, doesn't she? One day you'll find a girl like her.' She stopped because it had just occurred to her that she would never find a man quite like Pieter, even if she searched for the rest of her life.

'She's wonderful,' said Phillip. 'Why can't I meet a girl like that? Clever and stunning to look at...' He went on awkwardly: 'I say, Phylly, I didn't mean to say that—I mean, you're very pretty and no end of a good companion, but you're right—I came over here intending to ask you to marry me, but now...' He paused and she finished for him:

'And now you've seen me, and you don't want to. Well I don't want to either, so don't waste time on me, Philip; there must be hundreds of girls like Marena—you'll just have to look for them. Why don't you ask her out to dinner? She might have sisters or friends or—or someone...'

They had turned for home once more, not hurrying. 'Well, as a matter of fact I did ask her if she'd have dinner with me. I'll have to go back tomorrow some time, but I can catch the night ferry. She wants to show me her paintings.'

Phyllida stifled a giggle. Marena must have heard that one about men asking girls up to see their etchings—only hers were paintings.

Philip gave her a look of suspicion. 'Why are you giggling?'

'Oh, I'm not,' she denied hastily. 'Philip, don't get too serious, will you? It wouldn't be fair to cut out Pieter.'

He gave an angry laugh. 'Good lord, I've never met a man more capable of getting his own way! I thought his mother was a bit of a tartar, too.'

'She's a darling,' said Phyllida warmly, instantly up in arms. 'She's a bit—well, large, but she's kind and—and...'

'Oh dear,' his voice mocked her. 'I had no idea you were so keen on her, but I suppose that's natural.'

They could see the house now, through the trees. 'It's a wonderful place he's got here. We had quite a chat yesterday evening. Can't say that I like him, though.'

She thought it very likely that Pieter didn't like him either, but she didn't say so. There was no point in stirring things up; heaven knew that the muddle was bad enough as it was. But at least she and Philip could part finally and on friendly terms. She would go back home, start all over again and forget Pieter and his family and those nice friends of his on Madeira and the brief period of happiness she had had.

'You're not listening,' complained Philip. 'I was telling you about this new job I've applied for.'

Phyllida said she was sorry and gave her full attention to him prosing on about senior registrars' posts and getting a consulting job in a few years' time and his expectations from an elderly grandparent which was going to make his future a decidedly better one. It lasted until they were within a few yards of the garden room, where they paused.

'I've enjoyed this walk,' said Philip in a voice which implied that he hadn't expected to. 'You're an easy person to talk to, Phylly. You don't mind? Us splitting up, I mean.'

Just as though they hadn't split up weeks ago, only he hadn't accepted it then. 'No, I don't mind, Philip, truly I don't—I hope you find a smashing girl and carve a splendid career for yourself, you've started that already.'

'Yes, I haven't done so badly,' he answered her complacently, and put his hands on her shoulders. 'No hard feelings, then?'

He bent to kiss her just as she became aware that the doctor was standing at the open door of the garden room, watching them.

She wriggled free of Philip, muttering that she must tidy herself for lunch and ran indoors, passing Pieter without looking at him, only to be halted by a large hand on her arm. 'So sorry,' he said softly and sikily, 'I always turn up at the wrong moment, don't I?'

She didn't answer, only ducked her head and rushed across the room and out into the hall, to pound up the staircase as though the devil were after her, not stopping until she had reached her room and shut the door. But there was no time in which to have the good howl she ached to have. She did her face, combed her silky hair and went downstairs again, this time at a sedate pace, to find everyone in the drawing room drinking sherry.

Afterwards, she couldn't remember what she had eaten at lunch, nor did she remember a single word she had spoken; presumably she had been quite normal, as no one had stared at her. And after lunch Philip had gone, but only after the doctor had wished him goodbye and then pointedly swept her mother and Willy out into the garden leaving her and Philip together in the hall. It was a pity that there had been no one there to see them shake hands.

There was just one day left now before they were to return home. She spent the night dithering between wishing that Pieter would spend the whole of it at home, and praying fervently that she wouldn't have to see him again until they left. As a consequence she went downstairs to breakfast in the dark glasses again, with a splitting headache and in a frightful temper.

Pieter was at breakfast, although he left within a few minutes of her arrival at the table. During those few minutes he had been his usual placid self, touching only briefly on their journey and reminding them that they would all be dining with his parents that evening. 'And I'm free for a couple of hours after lunch,' he told Willy. 'We might have a last try at catching a pike.' With which he left them, looking so cheerful and normal that she could have thrown something at him.

She mooned about after breakfast, packing for herself and for Willy, strolling round the garden with her mother, and then at her brother's request, walking down to the village for some last-minute trifles he simply had to have. It seemed an age until lunch time and even Lympke's offer to show her the kitchens, semi-basement but still kitchens which a woman might dream of and never have, wasn't sufficient to take her mind off her own troubles. All the same, she admired their size and old-world charm and all the well-concealed modern gadgets. She hoped that when Marena married Pieter, she would appreciate it all. Somehow she doubted that.

When she went into the drawing room, Pieter was already there although her mother and Willy were nowhere to be seen, which seemed strange because she had heard them go down earlier.

'They're down at the lake,' his voice was disarmingly casual. 'The swans are taking the cygnets for their first swim. What will you drink?'

'Sherry, thank you. Have you had a busy morning?'

'Yes, very. And what have you been doing?' He shot her a glance from under his brows. 'You must miss young Mount.'

She didn't answer that. 'I've been for a walk with Willy and then Lympke took me round the kitchens. They're very—nice,' she finished lamely.

His firm mouth twitched slightly. 'Yes, aren't they? Is there anything you would like to do this afternoon? Shopping? Aap can drive you into Leiden or den Haag.'

They were like two polite strangers and she thought with longing of their easy comradeship. 'No, thank you—I think we've got everything. I expect Mother will want to go round the gardens just once more and I'll go with her, I expect.'

He said carelessly: 'Oh, by all means. Willy and I will be at the lake until tea-time, we don't need to leave for den Haag until seven o'clock.'

He had arranged things very well; she would see almost nothing of him for the rest of the day.

And she didn't, not until the evening, when clad in the jersey tunic, she went downstairs. Pieter and Willy had gone back to the lake after tea and she was reasonably sure that no one would be down yet, as they hadn't returned until almost half past six.

She was wrong. As she reached the hall, Pieter's study door was opened and he came out, dressed for the evening in one of his dark grey, beautifully cut suits; another man entirely from the rubber-booted, sweatered figure which had come hurrying in not half an hour earlier.

He greeted her smilingly and set her teeth on edge with the remark: 'You shouldn't waste that pretty dress on us, you know. What will you drink?'

Phyllida astonished herself and him by asking for whisky, a drink she loathed, but somehow the occasion called for something strong. She sipped it cautiously, trying not to pull a face, and didn't see the amusement in his eyes.

'Was Mount going back today?' asked the doctor casually.

'Yes—on the night ferry. Did you have a busy morning?'

He was kind enough not to remind her that she had asked him that already before lunch, but sketched in his activities at the hospital until Mrs Cresswell and Willy joined them.

The short ride to den Haag was fully taken up with light-hearted talk of the next day's journey, and the other three didn't appear to notice Phyllida's silence. Between her 'yeses' and 'noes' and 'reallys' she was wondering if Marena was going to be there too. Very likely, although it didn't matter any more now. If only she could have had five minutes alone with Pieter while she explained about Philip and herself in the lucid language one always thought of in bed in the dead of night. At least it would clear the air and they could part friends, but he had given her no chance to talk—really talk—while they had been waiting for her mother and Willy, and even if he had, she thought mournfully, she would quite likely have burst into tears.

With an effort she stopped thinking about it and arranged her features into a suitable expression of pleasure at meeting Pieter's parents again.

The evening lasted for ever, with leisurely drinks in the magnificent drawing room, preceding an equally leisurely dinner in the sombre Biedermeier dining room. Marena wasn't there and her name wasn't mentioned until very shortly before they left, when Mevrouw Sittardt asked her son: 'And have you seen Marena, Pieter? She telephoned here earlier today, thinking you might be with us.'

'I saw her this morning, Mama.' Mother and son exchanged a long look and Mevrouw van Sittardt nodded her elegant head, smiling a little. Phyllida, her ears stretched to hear everything Pieter said, had heard the brief conversation but hadn't seen the look. She gazed unseeingly at Pieter's father, telling her a gently meandering tale about something or other, not hearing a word of it, wishing she were anywhere other than where she was; as far away from Pieter as possible, and wishing at the same time that she could stay for the rest of her life near him.

But the doctor appeared to have no such feeling of reluctance at the thought of seeing the last of her. He chatted amiably about her future prospects as he drove home at speed, saw them all safely indoors, bade them a cheerful goodnight and took himself off in the car again.

He got back at two o'clock exactly. Phyllida, who had been lying awake listening for his return, had heard the great Friesian wall clock in the hall boom twice in its majestic voice as Pieter's quiet step mounted the stairs and crossed the corridor to his own room.

Of course he had been with Marena. She stayed awake for another two hours, her imagination running riot, until sheer exhaustion sent her finally to sleep.

CHAPTER NINE

THE RETURN TO England went smoothly. To Phyllida, sitting in the back of the Bentley with her mother, it went far too quickly too. Pieter had hardly spoken to her beyond polite enquiries as to her comfort, observations upon the weather and the remark that she looked tired. It wasn't until they were speeding in the direction of Shaftesbury with the greater part of their journey behind them that she found herself sitting beside him. She wasn't sure how this had happened; they had stopped because Willy had been thirsty and she had found herself propelled gently into the front seat without being able to do much about it. She sat silent, turning just a little sideways, so that she could watch his large capable hands on the wheel. They had covered quite a few miles before he spoke. 'Will you be seeing young Mount?'

'No.' She added hastily: 'Well, not straight away.' It would never do for him to discover that she and Philip, although they had parted friends, were unlikely to meet again.

The doctor grunted. 'It seems a long time since we first met.'

She was breathless. 'Yes, ages.'

'The de Meesters asked after you in their last letter—they would like you to visit them again.'

'That's very kind of them, but I don't suppose I shall ever go back to Madeira.'

'What's happened to us, Phylly?' he asked softly. 'Or rather, what's happened to you?'

It was difficult to get the words out. 'Me? Nothing—what should have happened? I've had a lovely holiday and now I've got to find a job.' She added for good measure: 'I can hardly wait!'

His voice was casual. 'And Philip—he won't mind you working?'

'It's no busi… He won't mind in the least.'

He slid the car past a coach load of tourists. 'I must confess I'm puzzled, Phylly—I understood you to say that you weren't going to marry young Mount. But of course when he turned up unexpectedly like that, you probably realised that you'd made a mistake.'

She muttered something or other, longing to tell him just how she felt, wondering what he would say if she told him that she loved him to distraction. He would be very nice about it, but it was hardly likely that it would alter his feelings for Marena. She sighed, a sad little sound which caused him to glance at her quickly and then again, a little smile lifting the corners of his mouth. When he spoke he sounded very matter-of-fact. 'We shan't be long now—half an hour, I would think.'

Home looked lovely as the car swooped gently down the hill and up the other side, and when they stopped before the door there was Beryl to welcome them and a moment later Doctor Cresswell. Everyone talked at once, unloading luggage, urging the travellers to go indoors, offering refreshment. They all surged into the sitting room finally, still talking and laughing, and Phyllida, watching her family clustered round Pieter, suddenly couldn't bear it any longer. He would be gone soon; she had heard him say only a moment ago that although he had hoped to spend the night with them, he had discovered that it wouldn't be possible after all. She slid out of the room and into the kitchen, where the kettle was boiling its head off beside the waiting teapot. She made the tea, put on the lid and then stood looking at it, willing herself not to cry. She didn't hear Pieter come in and it wasn't until he spoke that she whisked round to face him.

'Well, I must be on my way, Phylly.' He smiled at her and her heart rocked. 'I had hoped…' he paused and sighed gustily. She felt his hands on her shoulders and his light kiss on her cheek.

'I'm not a great lover of poetry,' he told her, 'but there's a verse by John Clare which seems appropriate to the occasion; it goes something like this: "Last April Fair, when I got bold with beer—I loved her long before, but had a fear to speak." I don't know how it ends, but I hope he was luckier than I.'

He had gone as quietly as he had come, out of the room, into the hall, out of the house. Out of her life.

She stood exactly as he had left her for the space of several seconds while the verse rang in her ears. Suddenly she gave a small scream, galloped out of the room in her turn and flung herself at the front door which she banged behind her, to slide to a shaky halt by the Bentley.

Pieter was behind the wheel and the engine was ticking over nicely.

'Pieter—Pieter, don't go. You can't go!' Her voice rose to a wail. 'Can't you see, it's not me and Philip—you thought it was, didn't you? and I pretended it was because I thought it was you and Marena, but it's not, it's you and me, Pieter. Pieter darling!'

He switched off the engine, got out of the car unhurriedly and opened his arms. They were gentle and strong around her, crushing her to his great chest so that it was hard for her to breathe.

'My own dear darling, you've got it right at last.' He smiled down at her and her heart, already doing overtime, leapt into her throat so that she couldn't speak. Not that it mattered. He bent his head and kissed her, soundly and at length, and she kissed him back.

'My darling girl, I love you,' said Pieter in the kind of voice which left her in no doubt about it. And Mrs Cresswell, happening to glance out of her bedroom window at that moment, had no doubts either. She hurried downstairs to tell her husband, talking to herself as she went. 'I thought they never would—at least, Pieter knew, but Phylly—dear child, so dense sometimes!' Her thoughts kept pace with her hurrying feet. 'I shall wear one of those large flowery hats—the bride's mother always does...' She broke off to say to Willy, coming upstairs towards her: 'Wash your hands, dear. I think Pieter and Phylly have just got engaged.'

'Oh, good—now I can go and stay with them and fish. Pieter will like that.'

It was hardly the moment in which to tell the boy that his future brother-in-law might not share his enthusiasm, at least not for the first few months. She said: 'Yes, dear, won't that be nice? Don't forget your hands,' and hurried on down to the study.

Phyllida, being kissed again, found the breath to mutter: 'I thought you were in love with Marena. Oh, Pieter, I'm crazy about you,' and then: 'You were going away.'

She felt his chest heave with laughter. 'No, my dearest girl, I wasn't going away. I thought that if I came and sat in the car you might think that I was...'

She stared at him and then began to laugh. 'Pieter, oh, Pieter!' and then seriously: 'You won't do it again, will you?'

'Leave you? No, my darling, I'll never do that.'

They didn't notice when the milkman stopped his float alongside the Bentley; they didn't notice as he squeezed past them, nor did they hear his cheerful good morning. He left his bottle on the doorstep and wriggled past them once more.

'All I can say is,' said the milkman to no one in particular, 'it's a very good morning for some of us, and that's a fact.'

* * * * *

When May Follows

CHAPTER ONE

THE LONG LOW room gleamed in the firelight and the soft light
from several lamps, giving a patina to the few pieces of well-
polished yew and apple wood and glancing off the beams, black-
ened with age, which supported the ceiling. The room was full
of people; the steady hum of talk and the frequent laughter witness to the success of the gathering.

The two men, latecomers, paused in the doorway to look
around them and the elder of them, a short stout man with a
fringe of grey hair surrounding a bald head, gave a rich chuckle.
'Dear Alice, she only gives two parties a year, you know, and
everyone for miles around comes to one or both of them.'

He turned to look at his companion, a tall man with broad
shoulders but lean nonetheless, elegantly turned out too in a superbly tailored suit, which, while not drawing attention to itself
in any way, caused the discerning to realise that it had cost a
great deal of money. He was a handsome man too, with a narrow face and a wide forehead, dark hair silvered with grey, an
aquiline nose above a firm mouth, and heavily-lidded blue eyes.

He smiled now and said in a rather sleepy voice: 'It was good
of you to bring me—I shall be delighted to meet Mrs Bennett.'

'And her daughters,' finished his companion, and waved to
someone in the room. 'Here's Alice now.'

Mrs Bennett came towards them smiling; she was a small pretty woman in her mid-fifties but looking younger. She planted a kiss on the older man's cheek and said happily: 'Ben, how lovely!' Her eyes took in his companion. 'And you've brought someone with you.'

'Ah, yes, my dear—may I present Professor Baron van Tellerinck,' he added simply: 'His name's Raf.'

'Dutch,' said Mrs Bennett, and beamed at them both. 'On account of the "van", you know. I shall call you Raf.' She shook hands and rambled on: 'You sound very important—are you?'

'Not in the least, Mrs Bennett,' he ignored the other man's look, 'and I shall be delighted if you will call me Raf.'

Mrs Bennett tucked a hand into each of their arms. 'Come and meet a few people,' she invited. 'I've three daughters and they're all here. Ah, Ruth…my youngest—she's just become engaged— so suitably too.'

Her daughter laughed and her mother added: 'This is Raf, dear, he's Dutch and says he's not important, but I don't believe him.'

Ruth shook hands. She was a pretty girl, on the small side, with brown curly hair and large hazel eyes. She said, 'Hullo, Raf, nice to meet you.' She put out a hand and caught hold of a girl on the point of passing them. 'Here's Jane.'

They were very alike: Jane had more vivid colouring, perhaps, but they were the same height and size. The Dutchman shook hands and they stood talking for a few minutes until Mrs Bennett said that he must meet more of her friends. 'Katrina is around somewhere,' she told him vaguely. 'That's my eldest, of course.'

She plunged into a round of introductions, saw that he had a drink and presently left him. She was back within a few minutes a tall, splendidly built girl beside her. 'Here she is; Katrina, this is Raf, he came with Uncle Ben.'

Katrina offered a cool hand and smiled politely, and then the smile turned into a cheerful grin as she saw the look of faint surprise on his face. 'I'm the odd one out,' she told him. 'Five feet ten inches and what's known as a large lady, no one ever believes that I'm one of the family. I take after my father, he was a big man and tall, almost as tall as you.'

She waited for him to speak and when he didn't felt disconcerted.

'Would you like another drink? I'll get…'

'Thank you, no.' His sleepy eyes were on her face, a pretty face with regular features and dark eyes, heavily fringed with long lashes. It made her feel even more disconcerted, so that she turned to the window and looked out, away from him. Outside the chilly March day was giving way to an even chillier evening; the pretty garden already glistening with a light drizzle. Katrina sighed and the Dutchman said: 'Your English spring is unpredictable, isn't it?'

She looked at him over her shoulder. 'Yes, I suppose that's why it's so delightful—though I prefer the autumn.'

His thick brows lifted and she went on, talking at random: 'Bonfires and apples and coming home to tea round the fire. Do you live in the country?'

'Oh yes, and I must agree about the bonfires and the apples; unfortunately we are not addicted as a nation to taking tea round the fire. I shall have to try it.'

She decided that he was difficult to talk to and sought feverishly for another topic of conversation and failed. 'I quite like the spring,' she observed idiotically.

His glance was grave, but she had the strongest suspicion that he was laughing at her. 'Ah, yes—"Oh, to be in England now that April's there". And a much nicer bit about May following…'

'"And after April, when May follows, and the whitethroat builds and all the swallows,"' Katrina quoted.

'You like Browning?'

'Well, yes, though I'm not all that keen on poetry.' She answered warily; if he was going to throw an Anthology of English Verse at her she was sunk. She said quickly: 'Do you have any Dutch poets?'

'Several, but none of them are much good at writing about the weather.'

She saw the smile at the corner of his firm mouth and thanked heaven silently as someone called her from across the room. 'Oh, there's someone…shall I introduce you to…?'

She looked up into his face and saw his eyes twinkling. 'I'm very happy to remain here. I enjoyed our little talk about the weather—to be expected, of course—an English topic and so safe.'

Katrina felt her face pinken and was annoyed; he was laughing at her again and because he was a guest she couldn't tell him what she thought of him. She looked down her beautiful straight nose and said coldly: 'I hope you enjoy the rest of your visit to England, Professor,' and left him, feeling surprise at her feeling of regret that she would never see the tiresome man again. *Just so that I could take him down a peg,* she told herself as she joined a group of young people all talking at once. Their conversation seemed a little brash after the Professor's measured observations, but then of course he was much older; at least thirty-six or seven; she would find out from Uncle Ben.

It was later, when all the guests had gone and they were sitting round the fire drinking tea and eating the left-overs from the party for their supper, that Ruth observed: 'That was quite someone—the man Uncle Ben brought with him. If I weren't engaged to Edward I could go for him—he's a bit old, though.'

Katrina, to her surprise, found herself protesting. 'Not all that old, love. I daresay he's on the wrong side of thirty-five…'

'He's thirty-eight,' said her mother, 'I asked Ben. What were you talking about, Kate?'

'The weather.' Three pairs of blue eyes looked at her in surprise, and she frowned. 'Well,' she muttered, 'I'm so large—men don't chat up big women…'

'But you looked quite small beside him,' comforted her

mother, 'and it must have been very nice for him not to have to bend double in order to talk to someone.' She looked puzzled. 'But the weather, darling?'

'I found him difficult to talk to.' Katrina yawned. 'Let's do the washing up and then I'm for bed; I must be off early in the morning.'

'When is your next holiday, dear?' Her mother piled cups and saucers and smiled across at her.

'Well, I can't be quite certain; Uncle Ben's got a backlog as long as my arm and as fast as there are a couple of beds empty they're filled by emergencies. I expect I'll wait until he's worked off most of his cases and decides to take a holiday himself.'

Katrina got to her feet and carried the tray down the stone-flagged passage to the kitchen where Amy, who had been with the family since she could remember, sat dozing by the Aga. She woke up as Katrina went in and said crossly: 'Now, Miss Kate, there's no call for you to be doing that.' She got out of her chair, a small round person with a sharp nose and small boot-button eyes.

Katrina put the tray down and gave Amy a hug. 'Go on with you!' she declared robustly. 'I've been standing around all the evening; a bit of washing up is just the exercise I need. Go to bed, Amy dear, do, and for heaven's sake call me in good time in the morning.'

Amy made only a token remonstrance. 'And you'll not go before you've had one of my breakfasts,' she declared. She sniffed. 'I daresay they starve you at that hospital.'

Katrina peered down at her splendidly proportioned person. 'Not so's it shows,' she observed.

She left soon after eight o'clock, driving herself in her rather battered Mini. The rain had ceased and it was a chilly morning with a pale sky holding a promise of spring. The house, standing back from the narrow street, looked delightful in the clear light, its grey stone walls softened by the ivy climbing them, its garden showing colour here and there where the daffodils

were beginning to open; Katrina was reluctant to leave it and
still more reluctant to leave her mother and sisters; they had always got on well, doubly so now that her father was dead. She
waved to the various heads hanging from windows and turned
into the street. There was no one much about; she passed the
boys' school and turned into the main street through the town
and presently joined the A30. London wasn't all that distance
away and she had all the morning. She slowed through Shaftesbury and took the Salisbury road; she had done the trip so
often that she knew just where she could push the little car to
its limit and where it was better to slow down. She had time in
hand by the time she reached Salisbury, and once through it,
she stopped at Winterslow and had coffee, and not long after
that she was on the M3, on the last leg of her journey.

Benedict's was an old hospital in name but very modern
in appearance. The original building, empty now and awaiting demolition, lay on the north side of the river, strangled by
narrow streets of ugly little houses, but now it was housed in a
magnificent building, very impressive to look at, and fitted out
with everything modern science could conceive of. It was a pity
that there wasn't enough money left to staff it fully, especially
as the nurses complained that it took them all their time to get
from one part of the building to the other, for its corridors were
endless and staff weren't supposed to use the lifts.

Katrina, in charge of the men's surgical ward on the fourth
floor, glanced up as she swept the Mini into the forecourt and
housed it in the roomy garage to one side. It would be take-in
week in the morning, she remembered: The ward had been full
when she had left two days ago for her days off. Just for a moment she thought longingly of her home in the placid little Dor-
set town, which only bustled into life once a week on market
day, but she had chosen to be a nurse and to train at a London
teaching hospital, and she loved her work enough to stay in the
city even though she disliked its rush and hurry.

She got her bag from the boot and crossed to the side entrance, to climb to the second floor and cross by the covered bridge to the nurses' home. She had a bed-sitting room there in the airy corridor set aside for the ward Sisters with its own door to shut them away from the student nurses, and a tiny kitchen as well as a generous supply of bathrooms, and above all, it held a nice sense of privacy. Katrina unlocked her door and went in. She had time enough to change, time to go to lunch if she wished, but she wasn't hungry; she set about the business of turning herself from a well-dressed young woman to a uniformed ward Sister, and while she did it, thought about the man Uncle Ben had brought with him to last night's party. She hadn't meant to think about him, and it annoyed her that somehow he had managed to pop into her head and wouldn't be dismissed. She forgot him presently, though, going back on duty a little early so that she could have a cup of tea before plunging into the rest of the day's work.

The ward was still full; true, two patients had gone home, but three had been admitted, which meant that there was already one bed in the middle of the ward and with take-in imminent, it would certainly be joined by several more.

Her senior staff nurse, Julie Friend, was on duty and Katrina breathed a sigh of relief; her second staff nurse, Moira Adams, was a tiresome creature, a self-important know-all, who bullied the nurses whenever she had the chance and irritated the patients, Katrina found her much more trying than all the patients put together and had told her so on various occasions, she had told the Senior Nursing Officer too, and that lady, although sympathetic, had pointed out that Adams would be leaving in a couple of months' time to take up a post in a surgical ward and she needed all the experience she could get. Katrina had thrust out her lower lip at that and wanted to know why the girl couldn't be transferred to the female block, only to be told that Adams would ride roughshod over Sister Jenkins. Which was true enough; Jilly Jenkins was a small sweet person and a splendid nurse, but she could be bullied...

Julie Friend was a different kettle of fish entirely. Katrina gave her a wide smile as she came in with the tea tray and put it on the desk, and Julie returned it. She was a pretty girl, good at her job and popular, and saving hard to get married. Katrina, in her rare fits of depression, envied her wholeheartedly; Julie's Bill was a nice young man, a chemist in the hospital pharmacy and neither he nor Julie had any doubts about their future together, whereas Katrina had to admit to herself that she had any number of doubts about her own. She had had the opportunity enough to marry; she was a striking-looking girl and besides that, she had a little money of her own, a wide circle of the right kind of friends, and a comfortable home. She was quite a catch; it was a pity that those who had wanted to catch her were all small men. She hadn't had deep feelings about any of them, but she wondered from time to time if one of them had looked down at her instead of up, if she would have accepted him.

She poured their tea and listened to Julie's careful report, and after that, as Julie tactfully put it, there were one or two things…

They took half an hour to sort out: the laundry cutting up rough about extra sheets; the pharmacy being nasty about a prescription they couldn't read, the CSU calling down doom upon her head because a pair of forceps were missing from one of the dressing packs, and one of the part-time nurses unable to come because of measles at home. Katrina dealt with them all in a calm manner and turned her attention to Julie's report again. Old Mr Crewe, who had been admitted as an emergency hernia four days ago and not quite himself after the operation, had been making both day and night hideous with his noisy demands for beer. Julie had reported that she had allowed him one with his lunch and been told, for her pains, that he had three or four pints at midday and the same again in the evening. Katrina chuckled and then frowned; she would have to think of something. She twitched her cap straight and got up to do a round.

It was one of the quietest times of the day; dinners were over and visitors wouldn't be coming just yet, the men were dozing or reading their papers or carrying on desultory conversations. Katrina went from bed to bed, stopping to chat with their occupants, filling in a pools coupon for a young man who had his right arm heavily bandaged, listening with patience and every appearance of interest while someone read her a long account of startling goings-on as reported in one of the more sensational newspapers; some of the patients were sleeping and two were still not quite round from anaesthetics. She checked their conditions carefully, gave soft-voiced instructions to one of the student nurses, and went on her way unhurriedly. She never appeared to hurry, and yet, as one nurse had observed to another, she was always there when she was needed.

Her round almost over, she tackled Mr Crewe, eyeing her belligerently from his bed. 'And what's all this about beer?' she asked composedly.

She let the old man have his say and then said reasonably: 'Well, you know if you have eight or nine pints of beer each day, we simply can't afford to keep you here. Have you anyone at home to look after you?'

'Me wife.'

'Anyone else?'

'I've got a daughter lives close by. Sensible she is, not like the old girl.'

Katrina thought for a bit. 'Look, let's make a bargain; you can have a pint at dinner time and another with your supper and I'll see if we can get you home a couple of days earlier. Mind you, you'll have to behave yourself.'

His promise was of the piecrust variety, she knew that, but at least it meant temporary peace.

A peace they needed during the next few days; it seemed as though everyone in the vicinity of the hospital was bent on falling off ladders, tripping over pavements or being nudged by buses. Usually there were broken bones involved, but for some reason this week it was cuts and bruises and concussion, so that none of the victims went to the orthopaedic block but arrived with monotonous regularity in the surgical ward.

It was on the last day on take-in, with the cheering prospect of Mr Crewe going home very shortly and a hard week's work behind them all, when things began to go wrong. Julie went off sick for a start, which meant that Katrina wouldn't be able to have her days off and Moira Adams, taking advantage of Julie's absence and Katrina's preoccupation with her patients, began chivvying the junior nurses. Katrina, coming upon a tearful girl behind the sluice door, had to take Moira into her office and rake her down, pointing out as she did so that she was having to waste time which could have been spent to much greater advantage on the patients. Moira pouted and argued until Katrina said sharply, 'That's enough, Staff, you should know better, and you'll never get anyone to work for you if you bully them.' She glanced at her watch and saw with relief that it was after five o'clock and Moira was due off duty—better still, she had days off as well. Katrina felt relief flood through her, but none of it showed; she said with quiet authority: 'Go off duty, Staff.'

It was lucky that she had two second-year student nurses on duty, both good hard-working girls, as well as the tearful little creature who was still apparently in the sluice. Katrina swept through the ward, her eyes everywhere; nothing seemed amiss. She reached the sluice and found Nurse James, washing a red, puffy face under the cold water tap. 'The thing is,' began Katrina without preamble, 'you have to learn not to mind, Nurse James. There'll always be someone you can't see eye to eye with, someone who'll try and upset you. Well, don't let them—you're a very junior nurse at present, but if you work hard you'll be a good one one day and these upsets will have been worth while. Now come into the ward with me; we're going to do the medicine round together.'

The evening went swiftly after that, there was so much to do: cases from the morning's list needing to be settled; dressed in their own pyjamas again, given drinks, gently washed and when they could be, sat up. The four of them had to work hard but by first supper, Katrina was able to send the two senior girls to their meal; there was only one case which bothered her and she had already sent a message to the registrar to come and see the man the moment that he was free. The man had been admitted that morning after an accident in which he had had an arm crushed so badly that it had been amputated. He had come round nicely from the anaesthetic and the surgeon had seen him and pronounced himself satisfied, and although Katrina could see nothing wrong she thought that the man looked far more poorly than he should. It was no joke, losing an arm, but he was a powerfully built young man and healthy. They had settled him nicely against his pillows and he had had a cup of tea and the drip was running well. All the same she was uneasy. Leaving Nurse James to trot round the ward, making sure that the men were comfortable, she went along to write the report in her office, only to go back again to the man's bedside on the pretext of checking his chart. He looked worse, so much so that she drew the curtains around the bed and bent over him with a cheerful: 'Sorry to disturb you, I just want to make sure that your dressing's nice and firm, still.'

The dressing was all right, but there was an ominous red stain seeping through the bandage. There was a tray on the locker by the bed with everything needed for just such a happening. Katrina put on a pad and bandage, binding it firmly and pretended to adjust the drip while she watched. Something was very wrong; already the blood was oozing through the package she had only just put on.

'How do you feel?' she asked the man. 'There's a little bleeding and you may feel a bit faint, but it's nothing to worry about.' She smiled reassuringly at him and called softly: 'Nurse James!'

She was busy re-packing yet again when she heard the girl behind her. 'Go to the office, please, Nurse,' she said in her usual unhurried manner, 'and tell the porter to get Mr Reynolds at once. He must come here immediately. Tell them it's urgent. If he's not available then any house surgeon will do. Be quick and come back as fast as you can.' She hadn't turned round, she heard Nurse James say: 'Yes, Sister,' and added: 'Is the ward OK?'

'Quite OK,' said Uncle Ben from behind her. 'In trouble, Sister?'

She was applying pressure now and didn't look up. Dear Uncle Ben, arriving just when she needed him most. 'An amputation this morning; he recovered well, but his blood pressure has been dropping very slowly. Mr Reynolds came to see him this afternoon and found everything satisfactory. This has just started—five—six minutes ago.'

Uncle Ben gave a little cough. 'Well, we'd better have a quick look—got some forceps handy?'

She turned back the towel covering the tray and was on the point of taking up the scissors when a large hand took them from her.

'That's right, Raf—let's get this off and see the damage. Sister, send your nurse to theatre and tell them I want it ready in five minutes. I shall want four litres of blood too—get on to the Path Lab, will you?'

Nurse James had come back with the news that there was a major accident just in and there was no one available right away. 'Never mind, Nurse—Sir Benjamin is here, so we're all right. Now go to theatre, will you...' She passed on Uncle Ben's wishes and turned back to the patient. He was semi-conscious by now and the bandages and dressing were off. 'Dear, dear,' observed Uncle Ben in his mildest voice. 'Apply pressure, Sister, will you? Raf, can you get at it with the forceps while I swab?'

Professor van Tellerinck, in waistcoat and shirt sleeves, somehow contrived to look elegant despite the messy job he was doing. He was very efficient too; Katrina's head was almost fully occupied with what she was doing, but a tiny corner of it registered that fact, and another one too, that she was pleased to see him again, which seemed strange since she hadn't liked him over-much. Probably it was just relief at his timely help. He hadn't spoken to her, indeed, she wasn't sure that he had even looked at her; in the circumstances that was to be expected. He had found the slipped ligature and had put on a Spencer Wells and the two men were carefully checking that there was no further trouble.

Uncle Ben unbent slowly. 'Something big in the Accident Room, did I hear Nurse say? In that case, Raf, be good enough to give me a hand, will you?'

The theatre trolley and the two student nurses arrived together. Katrina told one of them to go with the patient to theatre and with the help of the other nurse, started to clear up; it took some time to get everything clean and ready for the man's return and it was time for the nurses to go off duty when they had done. Katrina sent them away and greeted the night nurses with the suggestion that they should get started with their evening routine while she got down to the report. She had written it, read it to the night staff nurse and was back in her office when the patient came back, and because the two nurses were changing a dressing and there was no one else available, she saw him safely back into his bed, still groggy from the anaesthetic. She was checking the drip when Uncle Ben arrived and wanted to know why she was still there and when she explained, he gave a snort of impatience and walked off to the Office to telephone.

Katrina hadn't realised that the Professor was there too, standing quietly watching her. His silence was a little unnerving, and, as she knew that despite the fact that she had cleaned herself up as best she could she looked a mess, her pretty features assumed a haughtiness which sat ill upon them.

'I wouldn't have believed it,' observed the Professor suddenly. 'When we met I assumed you to be a young lady of leisure with nothing more on her mind than the latest fashions and the current boy-friend.'

She gave him a cross look and said peevishly: 'Indeed? Just as I was amazed to find that you were a surgeon.'

He looked amused. 'Oh, should I look like one?'

She ignored that. 'I had the strong impression that you did nothing at all.'

'Oh, dear—we seem to have started off on the wrong foot, don't we?'

Several rather pert answers flashed through her tired mind. Luckily she had no opportunity of uttering any of them, for Mr Crewe, his supper pint already forgotten, was demanding more beer. 'Excuse me,' said Katrina austerely, and went into the ward to do battle, telling the junior night nurse to stay with the man until he was quite round from his anaesthetic. She subdued Mr Crewe quietly but briskly, did a quick round to wish her patients goodnight and went back to the Office, where she tidied her desk and thought about the Professor. She had to admit that she had been surprised to discover that he was a surgeon, he had given all the appearance of the man of leisure and she had gained the impression, quite erroneously, as it had turned out, that he was—well, lazy, at least easygoing, but he had done a very neat job without fuss. And so he ought, if he's anything of a surgeon, she muttered to herself as she swept the last lot of papers into a drawer, yawning widely as she did so; it had been a long day.

And not over yet, it seemed. Uncle Ben, coming in as she was on the point of going out, stopped her with a brisk: 'Finished, Kate? You'll have had no supper, I'll be bound—I'll take you back with me for a meal. Go and clean yourself up and be downstairs in ten minutes.'

Professor van Tellerinck had followed her uncle. He was leaning against the wall now, smiling a little, which needled her so much that she said far too quickly. 'That's awfully kind of you, Uncle Ben, but I can get something on my way to the home. It's far too late to bother Aunt Lucy. Will the man do?'

'I think so. We found another slipped ligature, but he's well and truly tied now. By the way, I asked Night Sister to send

someone along to keep an eye on him for a few hours. Now
hurry up, girl, or your aunt will nag me.'

Katrina chuckled. Aunt Lucy was a dear little dumpling of
a woman who had never nagged anyone in her life; she had the
kindest of hearts and a sunny disposition and spoilt Uncle Ben
quite shamelessly.

'All right, I'd love to come if I won't be a nuisance.'

She parted with the two men at the ward doors, sternly rec-
ommended by Uncle Ben not to be more than the time he had
stated, and not quite sure whether she should say goodbye to
his companion or not. She compromised with a social smile
and a little nod.

She showered and changed into a silk blouse and a pleated
skirt and topped them with a thick knitted jacket. With her hair
unpinned from the rather severe style she wore under her cap,
and hanging about her shoulders, she looked prettier than ever,
but she wasted little time on either her face or her hair. With
barely a minute to spare she raced through the hospital to the
front entrance, to find Uncle Ben there and the Dutchman as
well. She wasn't sure if she was pleased or annoyed about that,
but she was given no time to decide. Uncle Ben caught her by
the arm and hurried her across the courtyard to fetch up beside
a Bentley Corniche.

Katrina, breathing rather rapidly because she had had to
hurry, and looking quite magnificent, let out a loud sigh.

'Uncle Ben, is it yours? It's super!'

'Don't be a fool, my dear, it's Raf's.'

She glanced at the Dutchman and found him watching her,
his sleepy eyes alert beneath their lids. She said rather lamely:
'Oh, how nice,' and watched his smile as he opened the door and
ushered her into the front seat. Probably he drove abominably,
she told herself as Uncle Ben made himself comfortable in the
back and the Professor got behind the wheel. But he didn't, he
drove superbly, placidly unconcerned with the traffic around
them, taking advantage of every foot of space, using the big

car's power to slide past everything else. Katrina allowed herself to relax thankfully and just for a moment closed her eyes.

'Never tell me you're tired,' murmured the Professor in a hatefully soft voice, 'a great strapping girl like you.'

'I am not...' began Katrina in a strangled voice, and stopped; he was trying to make her lose her temper, and she wasn't going to. 'You're not exactly a lightweight yourself,' she observed sweetly.

'For which I am profoundly thankful,' he assured her. 'I like to look down on my women.'

'I am not,' said Katrina in a furious rush, 'one of your women!'

'Oh, no, you don't resemble any of the girls I know—they're slim and small and mostly plaintive.'

'I'm not surprised,' she snapped, 'if they know you.'

He had a nice laugh. 'I think we're going to enjoy getting to know each other, Kate.'

They were in Highgate Village now, close to Uncle Ben's house, and as he slowed and stopped before its gate she had what she hoped was the last word. 'Think what you like, Professor van Tellerinck, but I have no wish to get to know you.'

He only laughed again.

CHAPTER TWO

UNCLE BEN'S HOUSE was a Regency villa standing in its own immaculately kept garden, well back from the road. Aunt Lucy flung the door wide as they got out of the car and began to speak almost before they had got within earshot.

'Katrina, how lovely—your supper's waiting for you. Ben dear, how fortunate that it was something I was able to keep hot. Raf, you must be famished!'

She bustled them through the hall and into the sitting-room, furnished with easy chairs and sofas and a number of small tables, loaded down with knitting, books and newspapers. 'Mary's just dishing up—you'll have time for a drink.'

Katrina had her coat whisked from her and was sat in a chair and a drink put into her hand. 'Ben said on the phone that you've had a busy evening,' went on Aunt Lucy, happily unaware of what the business entailed. 'I was a bit put out when the men were called away just as we were about to sit down to table, but this makes up for it. How is your dear mother?'

The men had taken their drinks to the wide french window at the end of the room after responding suitably to Aunt Lucy's greeting, and now she cast them an indulgent glance. 'I suppose they'll mull over whatever it was for the rest of the evening, which means that we can have a nice gossip.'

Aunt Lucy's voice was soothing and the sherry gave Katrina an uplift she badly needed, and by some domestic magic conjured up by the cook, the meal which they sat down to presently was delicious. Katrina, thoroughly famished, fell to with a good appetite, avoiding the Professor's eye and only addressing him directly when he spoke to her.

Which wasn't often, and then with a casual politeness which she found annoying, despite the fact that she had decided that she really didn't like him at all. She was taken completely off guard presently, when, dinner over and coffee drunk in the sitting room, she murmured to her aunt that she would have to go. The two men were standing together, discussing some case or other, but the Professor interrupted what he was saying to observe;

'I'll run you back, Katrina.'

'There's no need, thank you—I'll get a taxi.'

'I have to go back anyway to pick up some instruments.' He spoke blandly, ignoring her reply, and Aunt Lucy at once backed him up.

'Well, of course, if you're really going that way—so much nicer than a taxi at this time of night, Kate—someone to talk to, as well,' she added happily.

Katrina thought of that remark ten minutes later, sitting beside the Professor in the Bentley, trying hard to think of some topic of conversation. She scowled horribly when he observed placidly: 'Considering that it will be April in a few days' time, the evenings are surprisingly chilly.'

'Why are you in England?' asked Katrina, not bothering with the weather.

'Interested? I'm flattered. Your uncle and I are old friends— he knew my father well. When I come to England I like to see him.'

Which hadn't answered her question. 'You're a surgeon, too?'

'Yes.' He turned the car into the hospital yard and parked it.

'No, stay there,' he told her, and got out and opened the door for her. 'Such a pleasant evening,' he murmured. 'Goodnight, Kate.'

She suspected that he was amused about something again. Her goodnight was civil but nothing more. Going slowly up the stairs of the nurses' home to her room, she reflected that she wouldn't see him again and was surprised at her glum feelings about that. She had hoped, with conventional politeness, that he would enjoy the rest of his stay in England, and all he had said was that he was quite sure that he would.

'Oh, well,' she said crossly as she opened her door, 'who cares? I shan't be seeing him again, anyway.'

She saw him the very next afternoon. It had been a simply beastly morning, with Mr Knowles doing a round of his six beds and spinning it out to a quite unnecessary length of time, so that dinners were late, nurses didn't get off duty on time, and Katrina herself had had to be content with cheese sandwiches and a pot of tea in the office. And if that wasn't enough, she had been waylaid by Jack Bentall, one of the house surgeons, and badgered into a reluctant promise to go out to dinner with him in a couple of days' time. Despite the fact that she had never encouraged him, he waylaid her on every possible occasion, making no secret of his feelings, even allowing it to be bruited around that she was quite bowled over by him. Katrina had never lacked for invitations; she was a delightful companion and sufficiently lovely for men to like to be seen out with her, but she had never taken any of them seriously. For one thing, as she had pointed out so many times to her mother and sisters, she was so large...

But Jack Bentall didn't seem to mind that; he was a rather short, thickset young mam, and conceited, and nothing Katrina could say would convince him that she didn't care two straws for him. Usually she fobbed him off, but today she had been tired and put out and had lost some of her fire, and even though she regretted it bitterly already, she was far too honest to invent an excuse at the last minute. But it would be the last time, she promised herself, as she gobbled up the sandwiches and went back to the ward.

The nurses were tidying beds before the visitors were admitted and had prudently left Mr Crewe until the last. They had just reached him as Katrina opened the doors and her ears were assailed at once by his voice raised in anger. 'A pint ain't enough,' he bellowed. 'I wants me usual—'alf an alf an' a couple more ter settle the first pint.'

'You'll be lucky,' observed Katrina,' and I thought you wanted to go home? Here you are lying in bed—if you're not well enough to sit out in your chair, Mr Crewe, then you're not well enough to have a pint of beer. You promised me...'

'Pah,' said Mr Crewe grumpily, 'I want ter go 'ome.'

'Yes, I know that, Mr Crewe, and I promised you that you should go a day or two earlier if you kept your side of the bargain—which you're not.'

Mr Crewe opened his mouth to say, 'Pah,' again and changed it to, 'Oo's that—I see'd 'im yesterday...'

He was staring down the ward, for the moment forgetful of his beer. 'Big chap,' he added, and Katrina's head, before she could stop it, shot round to take a look. Professor Baron van Tellerinck, no less, coming round to take a look down the ward with unhurried calm. He wished her good afternoon gravely, and just as gravely greeted Mr Crewe, who said rudely: "ullo—'oo are you?'

'A colleague of Sir Benjamin,' the Professor told him equably, 'and as I have business with Sister I'm sure you will do as you are asked and sit in your chair and—er—keep quiet.'

And much to Katrina's astonishment, Mr Crewe meekly threw back the bedclothes and got into the dressing gown one of the nurses was holding.

'You wished to see a patient?' asked Katrina, at her most professional.

'Please. Sir Benjamin can't get away from theatre at present, he asked me if I would check up on Mr Miles.'

She liked him for that; so many surgeons came on to the ward and asked: 'Sister, I'd like to see that gastric ulcer you admitted,' or: 'How is that lacerated hand doing?' for all the world as if the ward beds were occupied by various portions of anatomy and not people.

'He's coming along nicely,' she observed, quite forgetting to be stiff. 'His BPs down and he's eating well. We've had him out of bed for a little while this morning.'

The Professor spent five minutes or so with the patient, expressed himself satisfied with his progress, wished him a polite good day, and started up the ward towards the office. 'If I might just write up the notes?' he enquired, and when she opened the door and then turned to go: 'Please stay, Sister.'

So she stayed, waiting silently while he scrawled on the chart, added his initials and then got to his feet. 'Doing anything this evening?' he asked her.

'Me?' she was so surprised that she had no words for a moment. 'I'm off at five o'clock,' she added stupidly.

'Yes, I know that,' and when her eyes looked a question, 'I looked in the off duty book on my way in,' he explained blandly, and waited for her to answer.

'Well...' she paused. 'It's very kind of you, but I'm not sure...'

He interrupted her: 'That's why it would be a good idea if we got to know each other,' he observed placidly. A remark which left her totally bewildered, and before she could answer: 'There's a rather nice place in Ebury Street we might go to—a bistro, perhaps you know of it?'

She shook her head, still trying to think of something to say.

'La Poule au Pot, although you might prefer to go somewhere else?'

She found herself saying just as meekly as Mr Crewe had acted: 'It sounds very nice. Is it a dressy place?'

He smiled, 'No, I think not,' and watched her, still smiling while one corner of her brain was turning over her wardrobe for a suitable dress. 'I'm sure you're thinking that you'll have nothing to wear, women always do, don't they? I'm equally sure that you have. Shall we say seven o'clock at the entrance.'

He smiled again as he left the office, leaving Katrina to wonder if she had actually said that she would go out with him. She didn't think that she had, but it was a little too late for that now.

She got off duty late; it had been that sort of a day, and her nerves were jangling with a desire to allow her ill humour to have full rein, instead of having to present a calm good-tempered face to patients and nurses alike. But a leisurely bath did her a power of good, by the time she had found a dress to her liking—a sapphire blue silk jersey, very simply cut—done her hair in a low roll round her head in an Edwardian hair-style, and got into a pair of high-heeled black patent shoes, she felt quite herself again. She picked up a velvet jacket and took a last look at herself in the mirror. For some reason she wanted to look nice this evening; she had told herself that it was because she didn't like the Professor, which to her at least made sense in a roundabout way, and at least, she told herself as she started downstairs, she could wear high-heeled shoes without being in danger of towering over her escort.

She was ten minutes late, but he was waiting for her with no sign of impatience, only smiled gently as he glanced at her from hooded eyes.

'Ah, the wardrobe wasn't quite empty, I see.'

Katrina found herself smiling too and uttered her thought out loud without thinking. 'You have no idea how nice it is to go out with someone who's taller than I—even in low heels I loom over most people.'

He glanced down at her elegant feet on their three-inch heels. 'I have the same difficulty, only in reverse; I find it so tiresome to bend double each time I want to mutter sweet nothings into my companion's ear.'

'Well, you won't need to worry about that,' declared Katrina sharply.

'Oh, I wasn't,' he told her silkily as he opened the car door. 'I need only bend my head to you, Kate.'

She peeped at him to see if he was laughing, but he looked quite serious and she frowned; it was a remark which she found difficult to answer, so she said nothing, but got into the car, to be instantly lulled by its comfort as they edged into the evening traffic, and her feeling of pleasure increased as they went along; it was decidedly pleasant to be driven in a shining black Bentley towards a good meal. Moreover, the Professor was laying himself out to be pleasant, talking about nothing much in an amusing manner; she almost liked him.

She wondered later, as she got ready for bed, what exactly she had expected of their evening, but whatever it was, it hadn't happened. Her host had been charming in a coolly friendly way and they had talked… She stopped to remember what they had talked about—everything under the sun, and yet she knew nothing about him, for he had taken care not to tell her anything and when she had asked from which part of Holland he came, he had said merely that his family came from the north—Friesland, but he lived within striking distance of Leiden. Whether he was married or no, she had no idea, and although it had been on the tip of her tongue to ask just that, she had stopped herself just in time. She had, she reflected as she brushed her hair, absolutely no reason for wishing to know.

The restaurant had been charming, cosy and warm, with blazing fires at either end of the quite small room and soft candlelight to eat their dinner by. And the food had been delicious; smoked salmon, *noisettes d'agneau Beauharnais* with artichoke hearts and *pommes de terre Berny*, followed by a purée of sweet chestnuts with whipped cream. Katrina smacked her lips at the thought of them and jumped into bed. They had sat over their meal and it was past midnight now, but the evening had flown and when she had said goodbye to him at the hospital entrance, she had felt regret that it couldn't last longer. Perhaps, she mused sleepily, she rather liked him after all. 'Such a pity,' she muttered, 'because I'll never know now; he didn't say he wanted to see me again. I expect he was being polite because he knows Uncle Ben.'

If the Professor was being polite then he was carrying it to excess. He accompanied Uncle Ben on his round the next day and when Katrina escorted them to the ward door and took a formal leavetaking of them, he asked her, with Uncle Ben looking on, if she would care to go to the theatre with him that evening.

Katrina's mouth was forming 'No,' even as her heart sang 'Yes,' but she had no chance to utter, for Uncle Ben said at once: 'What a splendid idea—just what you need, Kate, after a hard day's grind.' He asked the Professor: 'What's on?'

'I've got tickets for *The King and I.*' The hooded eyes were on Katrina's face. 'That is, if Kate would like to see it?'

A show she had wanted to see more than anything else, but how could he possibly know that?

'Going all tarted up?' enquired Uncle Ben with interest.

'Er—I thought we might have supper and perhaps dance afterwards.'

My almost new organza, thought Katrina wildly, and those satin sandals. Aloud she said: 'Well, I don't know…'

'Rubbish,' said Uncle Ben stoutly. 'You know you like dancing, Kate.'

The two of them stared at her without saying anything more, so that in sheer self-defence she said: 'Well, it would be nice… thank you.'

'Half past seven at the entrance,' said the Professor briskly. 'We'll just have time for a drink and a bite to eat before the theatre.'

She asked meekly: 'And am I to come all tarted up?'

'Oh, definitely—that's if you feel like it…' He was laughing at her again, although his face was bland.

'Well, that's settled, then,' declared Uncle Ben. 'Raf, there's that woman I want you to see—the accident that came in during the night…'

Katrina excused herself and left them deep in some surgical problem. She had problems of her own; it was so much simpler to either like or dislike someone, but with the Professor she was unable to make up her mind. Most of the time, she had to admit, she liked him very much, but every now and then he annoyed her excessively. She went back into the ward and found to her annoyance that Jack Bentall had come in through the balcony doors and was doing a round with Julie. He had, he explained carefully, one or two things to write up for Mr Knowles and could he use her office for a few minutes, and as Julie left them: 'You haven't forgotten that we're going out tomorrow evening?' he asked her, looking quite revoltingly smug. She had, but she was too kind-hearted to say so.

He was disposed to linger, hinting at the delights of their evening out so that she had to draw his attention to several jobs awaiting her. He had looked at her like a small spoilt boy and said grumpily: 'Oh, well, don't let me keep you...'

She wished with all her heart that she had refused his invitation in the first place. She had been a fool, but there was no help for it, she would go, but for the last time, she promised herself, and then forgot all about him, going from one patient to the next, adjusting drips, checking dressings, making sure that BPs had been taken on time.

She was a little absentminded at dinner time and her friends wanted to know why, and when she shook her head and denied it, Joan Cox from Women's Surgical said vigorously: 'I bet our Kate's got herself a date with that super man who's doing the rounds with Sir Benjamin,' and the entire table gave a howl of laughter when Katrina went a delicate pink.

'Didn't I say so?' cried Joan triumphantly, and then thoughtfully: 'You went out yesterday evening too.'

'Well, yes, I did—just to a bistro...'

'And is it to be a bistro tonight?' several voices chorused.

'*The King and I.*' Katrina poured tea from the large pot just put on the table.

'And dinner afterwards, I expect, and a spot of dancing?'

'Well, the Professor did say something about it...'

There was another howl of laughter. 'Kate, you don't call him Professor, do you? What's his name—what do you talk about?'

'The weather,' said Katrina guilelessly.

The afternoon went quickly. She handed over to Julie at five o'clock, did a final round to wish the patients goodnight, and went off duty. She had plenty of time, time to lie for ages in the bath, make up her lovely face at her leisure and wind her hair into its intricate chignon before putting on the organza dress. It was a lovely thing, patterned in shades of amber and brown with a square yoke and a waist tied by long satin ribbons, its balloon sleeves ending in tight bands at her elbows. Her slippers were exactly right with it, as was the brown marabou stole she dug out from the back of the wardrobe.

He had said half past seven, and she took care to be on time this evening, even though she was held up for a few minutes by some of her friends who had come to inspect her outfit. Their cheerful teasing voices followed her down the stairs and then were abruptly shut off by the nurses' home door. It was quiet as she went through the hospital corridors: it was visiting time again and nurses would be at first supper while the rest finished the tidying up for the day. The sudden lack of voices worried her. Supposing he wasn't there? Supposing she had made a mistake in the evening—supposing he hadn't meant it? All silly ideas, but all the same they loomed large. Just until she came in sight of the entrance, to see him standing there, enormous, reassuringly calm and very elegant indeed.

His hullo was friendly, as was his: 'How charming you look, Katrina, and punctual too.'

She wondered fleetingly if he said that to all the girls he took out, for undoubtedly there must be girls... She said, 'Thank you,' in a guarded tone, and he laughed and said ruefully: 'It doesn't matter what I say, does it? You see a hidden meaning in every word I utter.'

They were walking to the car, but now she stopped. 'Look, we can't possibly start the evening like this—I—didn't mean… that is, I was only wondering if you said that to all the girls you take out.'

'Would you mind if I said yes?'

She said haughtily: 'Of course not,' and spoilt it by asking: 'Do you go out a great deal?'

They were in the car now, but he hadn't started the engine. 'Yes, quite a bit, but work comes first. What about you, Katrina?'

'Well, I go out—I like my work too,' she added with a bit of a rush.

'We share a common interest, then.' He started the car. 'We have time for a drink if you would like one.'

He took her to the Savoy and gave her a glass of Madeira, and when she confessed that she had had no tea, a dish of salted nuts and another of potato crisps.

She crushed her way very nearly through the lot and then said apologetically: 'I'm making a pig of myself. It was stew for lunch and I got there late.'

His winged nostrils flared. 'Tepid and greasy, no doubt.' He lifted a finger and when the waiter came, asked for sandwiches. She consumed them with the unselfconscious pleasure of a child—smoked salmon and pâté de foie gras and cucumber. But she refused a second glass of Madeira because, as she explained to her companion, she wanted to enjoy every moment of the play.

Which she did, sitting up straight in her seat, her eyes glued to the stage, and the Professor, sitting a little sideways so that he could watch her as well as the stage, allowed himself a faint smile at her obvious pleasure. They went back to the Savoy when it was over and had supper—caviar, poularde Impératrice, and for Katrina a bûche glacée, while the Professor contented himself with Welsh rarebit. And because, as he had gravely pointed out to her at the beginning of the meal, they had both had a tiring day, a bottle of champagne seemed the best thing to drink.

Katrina, her head still full of romantic music, would have happily drunk tap water; as it was, she drank two glasses of champagne and enjoyed them very much. There was a faint worry at the back of her head that she was liking her companion much more than she had intended. Perhaps it was the combination of romance and champagne which had dimmed her good sense, but certainly he seemed really rather nice. When he suggested that they might dance she got up at once. She might be a big girl, but she danced well and was as light as a feather, and the Professor was pretty neat on his feet too. They danced for a long time, going back to drink their coffee and then taking to the floor again. It was past one o'clock when Katrina asked him the time, and gave a small screech when he told her.

'I'm on in the morning, and it's Mr Knowles' round and take-in.'

He didn't try to persuade her to stay but drove her back to the hospital without fuss and saw her to the door, and when she thanked him for her lovely evening, observed placidly that he had enjoyed it too, then he wished her goodnight and opened the door for her.

Katrina went through feeling let down; not so much as a hint that he wanted to see her again, let alone the kiss which she had come to expect at the close of an evening out. The horrid thought that he had asked her out because Uncle Ben had suggested it crossed her mind; Uncle Ben knew how shy she was about going out with men who weren't her size, and here was one who positively towered over her. He hadn't said goodbye, she mused as she tumbled into bed; a clever girl would have known how to find out when and where he was going…and anyway, she asked herself pettishly, why was she worried? She didn't like him, did she? Or did she? She was too sleepy to decide.

The morning began badly with two road accidents being admitted just after eight o'clock, and it got worse as the day wore on, so that when Jack Bentall rather fussily examined Mr Knowles' patients during the afternoon, demanding unnecessary attention and calling for things he didn't really need, she found her patience wearing thin. The urge to cry off the evening's entertainment was very strong, but she was a kind-hearted girl and she had refused to go out with him on so many occasions she couldn't avoid this one without hurting his feelings. Not that she minded about that over-much; he was a young man of unbounded conceit and she doubted if even the severest snub would affect him for more than a few minutes.

She dressed unwillingly and went just as unwillingly to the car park where Jack had asked her to meet him. He drove a souped-up Mini, very battered and uncomfortable and he tended to regard the road as his. She felt a pang of relief as he stopped with a teeth-jarring suddenness in front of a Chinese restaurant in the Tottenham Court Road. It was unfortunate that Katrina didn't like Chinese food and that Jack hadn't thought to ask her. Now if it had been the Professor, with all his faults, she added mentally, he would have made it his business to find out. And even if he hadn't, she mused with surprise, she would have felt quite at liberty to have told him that she loathed sweet and sour pork and could have asked him if they could go somewhere else. But Jack would either laugh at her and tell her that she didn't know good food when she saw it, or worse, sulk.

She ate her way through a great many dishes without once betraying her dislike of them, listening to Jack, carrying on about the other housemen and their inefficiencies, what Mr Knowles had said to him and he had said to Mr Knowles; he droned on and on and Katrina's thoughts turned more and more to the previous evening. Professor van Tellerinck might annoy her, although she wasn't sure why any more—but he didn't bore her. She came out of a flurry of half-formed thoughts to hear Jack say:

'Well, what about it? Everyone else does it these days and getting married seems a bit silly until I've reached the top, and you're not all that keen on it, are you? You can't be—you must have had plenty of chances, but after all, you are twenty-seven.'

She gave him a look of such astonishment that he added querulously: 'Well, you don't have to look like that—I thought we understood each other.'

As well as being astonished she was furiously angry, but she discovered at the same time that she simply couldn't be bothered to explain to him just how wrong he was. She could of course have said: 'I am a clergyman's daughter and old-fashioned in my views about matrimony'; instead she heard herself saying in a reasonable voice: 'I really should have told you sooner, Jack, but I didn't realise...' She left the sentence hanging delicately in mid-air. 'I've resigned—I'm going abroad in a few weeks' time.' She paused, trying to think of a country as far away as possible: 'The Gulf—a lovely job.' Her imagination was working well by now. 'One of those new hospitals, a fabulous salary and a flat of my own...'

He looked at her gobbling with rage. 'Well, you could have told me before we came out to dinner!' he said furiously. He put a hand up for the bill. 'I don't suppose you want coffee.'

They tore back to Benedict's through the almost empty streets and as he came to a squealing halt in the forecourt: 'I hope you get what you deserve!' he hissed at her.

Just as though I'd led him on, thought Katrina as she went into the nurses' home, and giggled. She stopped giggling almost at once, though. She would have to resign in the morning; she had done herself out of a job and banished herself to the Gulf to boot. Jack would tell everyone, he was a noted gossip, and really there was nothing she could do about it but leave; even if she explained to him why she had done it, he wouldn't understand but would merely think that she had been playing hard to get and would pester her more than ever. She lay awake for a long time getting more and more worried, and fell asleep at last with her mind in a dither.

CHAPTER THREE

SHE WAS STILL dithering when she got reluctantly out of bed a few hours later, but by the time she had dressed she knew for a certainty that she would go to the office directly after breakfast and tender her resignation to Miss Bowles. She stopped doing her hair and sat down on the edge of the bed to write out her resignation, then finished dressing in a rush so as to be in time for breakfast. As it was, she was late, which was a blessing for no one had time to ask her any questions.

Miss Bowles asked questions, though. She was a small peppery lady well into her fifties, who ruled the hospital with a rod of iron whatever the National Health Service said. There wasn't much that she approved of, and certainly not Katrina going off to the Gulf. She demanded all the details of the mythical post, too, and Katrina was forced to say firmly that she was still waiting for all the details.

'Well, Sister,' said Miss Bowles, in an ill humour now because one of the best ward Sisters was leaving, 'I hope you know what you're about. You have a good post here and prospects of promotion in the future. I only hope you're not throwing security away for some pipe dream in the desert.'

Katrina longed to tell her that it was a pipe dream, but the repercussions if she did weren't to be contemplated. She would go home for a holiday and then set about getting another job, well away from London. Abroad, perhaps? There was surely no reason why she should think of Holland?

She didn't tell any of her friends straight away; for one thing, she had no opportunity, it was that evening when she went off duty that she told them as they sat around in their sitting-room, mulling over the day among themselves.

'But you can't!' they chorused. 'Kate, why? There must be some reason...'

'I need a change,' she told them, 'I'm going to have a holiday at home and then go abroad. The Gulf,' she added vaguely, mindful of the hospital grapevine and Jack, not to mention Miss Bowles, who in her own dignified manner would allow the news to seep through the upper strata of admin staff.

She had a few days' holiday due to her, which meant that she could leave in just about three weeks' time. She would go home on her next days off and explain to her mother, and until then she would go on with her work in a normal manner. Easier said than done; she worried a good deal about her future, trying to make up her mind just where she wanted to go and she still had to tell Uncle Ben, not a real uncle at all, but he had been her father's closest friend and had kept an eye on them ever since her father's death.

But not just yet, it seemed. Uncle Ben had a severe cold and couldn't operate or do his rounds; his registrar coped in his absence until a nasty traffic accident, full of complications, made it needful for him to call in a consultant.

Katrina supposed she wasn't surprised to see Professor van Tellerinck with the registrar at his heels, come down the ward. She had imagined him back home in his own country, but she had no means of knowing where he was; probably he'd been close at hand all the time. She greeted him civilly, led him to the patient and waited quietly while he went over the man's severe injuries. The leg could be saved, he thought, given a few hours' repair work in theatre, but he wasn't sure about the arm.

He arranged for the man to go to theatre that afternoon, and made his way to the door, the registrar beside him, Katrina, one pace behind, ready to bid him good-day at the ward door.

But once there, he paused, suggested in the nicest possible way that the registrar should go ahead and see Theatre Sister about the case, and when he was out of earshot, asked in a placid voice: 'What's all this about you leaving, Kate?'

'Well, I am,' was all she could find to say.

'For some good reason?' He sounded very persuasive and she found herself saying:

'It seemed a good one.'

'But not any more,' he finished for her. 'You're off this evening? Good, we shall have dinner somewhere and you can tell me all about it.' And when she hesitated: 'Well, you can tell me, can't you? It's easy talking to a stranger—besides, I'm no gossip.' He didn't give her time to prevaricate. 'I'll wait for you at the entrance—about seven o'clock suit you?'

Katrina found herself looking forward to the evening; it was quite true one could often tell things to a stranger that one wouldn't dream of discussing with one's nearest and dearest. Her mind shied away from the fact that he had described himself as a stranger, though. But why should he be anything else? She went off duty late because the accident case had gone to the theatre later than had been planned. He was in the ICU when she enquired just before she left the ward, and likely to pull through. A marvellous job on the leg, Margaret Cross, the theatre Sister, told her enthusiastically; as for the arm, although it would never be the same again, it would be better than no arm at all. 'Quite a genius, our Dutch honorary,' she went on happily, 'and marvellous to work for. What's he like on the ward?'

'Very nice,' said Katrina sedately.

She wore the blue jersey again and spent time on her hair and face. The Professor had said somewhere quiet and she hoped she would do; in any case, she didn't much care. Life had gone sour on her and it was her own fault; she should have listened more carefully to Jack, then she could have stopped him from making his preposterous suggestion. If only he hadn't taken her to that Chinese place, if only... She reached the entrance and walked through the door, to find the Professor deep in conversation with Margaret. They both turned to look at her as she went towards them and Margaret said: 'Hullo—you look smashing, Kate, have a lovely evening.' She rolled fine blue eyes heavenwards. 'More than I shall! Bill and I are going to distemper the kitchen.'

'But think of the fun of being in your very own kitchen in a few weeks' time,' observed Katrina. She smiled at the Professor as she spoke and wished him a good evening rather sedately, wondering if she should have come after all; she didn't feel all that good company, and he might find her dull...

He seemed to have no doubts, at any rate; she was popped into the car and they were out of the forecourt before she had time to think up something to say. 'I said somewhere quiet,' he remarked placidly. 'How about the Waterside at Bray? Nice and peaceful by the river and there shouldn't be too many people there so early in the evening. They're keeping a table for us, but if there's somewhere else you'd prefer, do say so.'

Katrina didn't know whether to laugh or cry. 'It—it sounds lovely, but anywhere will do as long as it's not a Chinese restaurant.' Her voice was high and had a little shake in it.

'The reason for you leaving?' enquired the Professor, at his most tranquil.

'Yes, I suppose it is in a way.'

She waited for him to ask more questions, but he didn't, only embarked on a rambling small talk about nothing in particular and just sufficiently amusing to hold her attention.

By the time they reached Bray she was so soothed by it that she was ready and willing to pour out the whole miserable story, but he gave her no chance; she was seated at a table overlooking the river, given a drink and then the menu. With a little gentle prompting from her host she decided on *soufflé*

Eleonora, followed by *filets de barbue au champagne* and obediently drank the excellent sherry she was offered. It was presently, when she had sampled these delights and rounded them off with a heavenly pudding, and the whole washed down by an excellent white wine, that the Professor paused in his lighthearted conversation.

'And now supposing that you tell me all about it, Katrina.'

'It'll bore you...'

'No,' and funnily enough she believed him.

It was difficult to begin, and she was still hesitating when he prompted: 'Why not start with the Chinese food?'

It all came pouring out, a frightful muddle of Jack Bentall, the disadvantages of being a big girl, sweet and sour pork and the utter stupidity of letting it be known that she was leaving to take up another post. 'In the Gulf, too,' she said bitterly. 'It's a part of the world I've never really wanted to visit.'

'Well, you don't have to go, you know,' observed the Professor in a soothing voice.

'No, but I've resigned, don't you see? I've no job—I'll have to find one, there's nothing else for it.'

A small smile tugged at the corners of the Professor's firm mouth. 'Yes, there is, but not just now, I think.'

Katrina opened her mouth to protest and thought better of it. He looked as placid as usual, but somehow she felt she would get nowhere if she started to argue with him. She said instead: 'I've been very silly.'

'Oh, no! If you had allowed—this—what is his name? Jack Bentall, to ride roughshod over you, telling you what to eat and arranging your life to suit himself, then you would have been a very silly girl. It was perhaps a little imaginative of you to get yourself a job in the Gulf, but it can always fall through at the last minute, you know.' He smiled at her. 'And now we won't talk about it any more. Are you on duty in the morning? Yes? Then I had better drive you back.'

And although she made one or two attempts to re-open the conversation, he skilfully prevented her.

It was a splendid evening, with a full moon and a sky crowded with stars, and when he advised her in a friendly fashion to forget her worries and enjoy the lovely night, she said quietly: 'I'm sorry, I'm being a bore. It is a lovely night—what a pity one can see so little of it from the nurses' home at Benedict's.'

'Not the pleasantest part of London,' conceded the Professor, 'but then the older hospitals so seldom are—it is the same in Holland, although the modern buildings are excellently sited.'

She would have liked to have learned more, but he was already turning into the forecourt. It was at the entrance, when she had thanked him for her evening and wished him good night, that he said matter-of-factly: 'I'm glad that you enjoyed it. I did. We have a good deal in common, and not only our size, Kate.'

She said a little shyly: 'Well, it is much nicer...' and paused, for the remark struck her as fatuous.

'In Friesland, which is my home land,' observed the Professor, 'both men and women are tall and well-built—you would go unnoticed there, Kate.' He gave a sudden crack of laughter. 'No, that's not true—you would never go unnoticed, Katrina.'

She looked at him, searching for a suitable answer to the quite unexpected compliment, but before she could think of anything to say, he had opened the door for her and she found herself inside, with the door shut firmly behind her.

It was two days before she saw him again. Uncle Ben came for his usual round, gave it his opinion that on the whole it might be a good thing if Katrina gave up her job at Benedicts. 'Otherwise you'll be here for the rest of your life,' he admonished her. 'You know how it is, you get into a rut and there you stay until you wake-up to find that you're retiring next year...'

Katrina, who had been a little apprehensive about telling him her news, was relieved to hear this speech. 'Of course I'm not going to the Gulf,' she told him as he sat in her office drinking coffee before going on to the Women's Surgical. 'I thought I'd have a week or two at home and decide what to do.'

Uncle Ben gave her a thoughtful glance. 'Yes, you do that, my dear. You never know what may turn up.'

The Professor came early the following day, walking silently into the dressings room where Katrina was checking the sterile dressing packs. For a wonder it was fairly quiet on the ward; moreover, she had both Julie and Moira on duty, which meant that she could do several small chores at her leisure. She had her back to the door as he went in and supposing it to be Julie, spoke without turning round.

'Ask Moira to go to coffee, will you, Julie and she can take Nurse Jeffs with her—when they come back send the others, we'll have coffee in the office.' She closed a drawer and opened another. 'Oh, and I'll take a look at Johnny Clark's dressing when it's down...'

'Good morning, Katrina,' said the Professor quietly, and she dropped the dressing pack she was holding and shot round to face him.

'Oh, it's you,' she observed, her usual serenity ruffled. 'Good morning. Did you want to see someone?'

'You. From your remarks I take it that you're not too busy to spare me ten minutes.'

She asked a little breathlessly: 'Oh, have you thought of something? I've been a bit worried, although Uncle Ben seems to think it's a good idea if I leave. I haven't told Mother yet and I haven't an idea what I'm going to do...'

He held the door wide for her to go past him. 'That is what I've come to see you about.'

'Yes, well...' She felt nervous and did her best to cover it up.

'I think I should say what I have to say first,' said the Professor blandly, and ushered her into her office, closing the door firmly behind him.

He looked so businesslike that Katrina didn't sit down behind her desk, but stood in front of it facing him. 'Have you heard of a job?' she asked hopefully.

He shook his head. 'I haven't made any attempt to look for one. If you will sit down, I will tell you what I have in mind.'

She sat, her hands clasped loosely in her lap, her head a little on one side, watching him. She wished he would sit himself, for he loomed enormous in the little room so that for once she wasn't so conscious of her own magnificent proportions. But he remained standing, leaning against the door, so that if anyone wanted to come in, they wouldn't be able to. He wasn't smiling either; it must be something which required serious discussion—she couldn't imagine what, but she was prepared to listen carefully: she was secretly worried about her future, although she had concealed her worry well enough from her friends; she was beginning to think that any likely solution would be welcome.

She gave him a questioning glance and he smiled a little. 'Would you consider marrying me?' asked Professor van Tellerinck.

Katrina's beautiful eyes goggled at him, her soft curving mouth fell open. 'Marry...?' she began.

'I should like a wife,' went on the Professor, in much the tone of voice of one wishing for a new pair of shoes or the latest good book. 'I have considered it for some time, but until I met you I had not given it really serious thought.'

Katrina drew breath and uttered a sound which could have been anything at all, but she was ignored. 'I realise that we know very little about each other and in the normal course of events I would have suggested that we became engaged for several months so that we might remedy that, but since you find yourself—er—without employment and without definite ideas as to your future, it seems sensible to marry as soon as possible, don't you agree?' He didn't give her a chance to speak, but went on blandly: 'I suggest that we regard the first few months of marriage as a trial period. Will you marry me, Kate?'

She stared at him, her eyes enormous, her mouth still open. When she didn't answer, he prompted: 'Well—you don't answer...'

'I'm flabbergasted!'

His expression didn't alter, only his eyebrows rose a little so that she went pink. 'You're so surprised, then, Kate?'

'Yes—Oh, yes. I'm sorry, I didn't intend to be rude, only... well, I didn't like you very much when we met and I didn't think you liked me and I can't help wondering why...is it because I'm more your size?'

His eyes were almost hidden beneath their lids, but his smile was kind. 'I have never found you...' He stopped and began again. 'I had thought that you were beginning to like me just a little.'

'Well, yes, I am—I mean I do.' She swallowed and hurried on: 'But you don't love me.'

His voice was very placid. 'You are twenty-seven, Kate, and I am more than ten years older than you. Have we not reached an age where the first fine rapture of love is a little unlikely? It seems to me that a liking for the same things and a mutual regard for each other is more likely to make for a happy marriage.'

'Yes, I suppose so.' He was right, of course, but it was hard to fling romance away without a backward glance. 'But do you like me—I mean enough to want to marry me?'

'Yes, Kate, I like you.' He sounded reassuringly friendly and normal, and quite suddenly the whole thing didn't seem preposterous at all.

'Yes, well...if I could have time to think about it...'

The Professor contrived to look wistful and worried at the same time.

'Now that is the difficulty. I have to go to Edinburgh—a series of lectures—in a month's time. It would be convenient if we could marry before then. We might have a few days' holiday in Scotland before returning to Holland.' He went on smoothly: 'And I'm sure you will agree with me that we should take our time in getting to know each other so that we may make sure of our feelings before we assume a deeper relationship. I have no wish to rush you into anything.'

He sounded a little old-fashioned, rather like a professor in fact, but Katrina didn't like him the less for that, she was inclined to be old-fashioned herself. If she did marry him she would need time to get adjusted to the idea although now, being honest with herself, she had to admit that she liked him; perhaps she had liked him all the time, she wasn't sure about that. They might even be very happy together in a mild kind of way; the wistful thought that he didn't expect more than that crossed her mind, but she dismissed it. 'I haven't even decided,' she said out loud.

'You have your days off tomorrow,' observed the Professor, cutting into her musing. 'May I not drive you home?'

She searched his face. 'I don't know a thing about you,' she said.

'Soon told, but not now, I think. I'll tell you as we go.'

'Will you stay?' she asked him. 'Even if I... Perhaps I won't have made up my mind...'

'I should like to stay, if your mother has no objection.' He looked very relaxed and sure of himself, almost as though she had already decided. She was about to utter another disclaimer when the telephone shrilled, and she lifted the receiver.

'It's for you,' she said, and sat silent while he listened, gave terse instructions and then put the receiver down. 'I have to go, I'll see you later.'

She was left alone, wondering what later meant, still bemused.

She should have been off duty that evening, but the case the Professor had been called away to see was admitted to the ward just before dinner time and went to theatre an hour later. Intensive Care handed him back to the ward about four o'clock and he was still far too ill for her to go off duty; Moira was on that evening, but Katrina, who would have handed over to Julie quite happily, hesitated to leave him with her. She decided to stay until the night staff came on at half past eight. She wasn't doing anything anyway she told herself, there had been no sight of the Professor either.

In this she was proved wrong, for he turned up around six o'clock to take a look at his patient. 'A very nasty perforated ulcer,' he observed, 'but he should do. Who is looking after him?'

'I am,' said Katrina, 'just until the night staff come on duty.'

He didn't waste time asking questions, only nodded. 'Well, we'll have a meal,' he told her. 'Somewhere close by, though. There's a pub down the street, isn't there? The Lamb and Fleece. It's not five minutes' walk away, we could have something in the basket.'

Katrina, whose dinner had been sketchy, agreed at once. 'I'm famished,' she told him, and then added hesitantly: 'I meant to drive down this evening, but it'll be too late...'

'I'd rather not go until the morning; suppose we leave about eight o'clock? Could you manage that? Sir Benjamin isn't taking over until midnight and anything could happen between now and then.'

She nodded. 'Yes, of course. I'll be ready at eight. Are you sure you want to go out this evening? I'm not off until around nine o'clock.'

His eyes searched her face sleepily. 'You should have been off for the evening?'

'Well, yes, but I thought I'd stay on and give a hand for a while...'

He nodded, taking it for granted that she forfeited her free time willingly. 'Shall we say a quarter past nine, then? Put a coat on over your uniform, no one will notice.'

Katrina was tired by the time they met and although she had tidied herself she hadn't bothered much with make-up, only flung a coat on as he had suggested. As she glanced at herself in the mirror in her room, ready to leave, she thought it was a good opportunity for him to see what she looked like when she was weary and careless of her appearance. And far too tired to give a thought to his proposals as to her future. If he started on that, she told herself as she ran down the stairs, she would most likely turn the whole thing down flat.

The Professor was too clever for that; he walked her to the pub, found a small table in its crowded saloon bar, put a glass of sherry before her, refreshed himself with beer and offered the menu.

The food was homely; they spent a few minutes debating the merits of beans and fried eggs or fish and chips in a basket, and presently Katrina settled for the fish and chips and her companion ordered the same, and while they were waiting for it, embarked upon an account of the case that morning. He could be amusing as well as interesting; they passed from that to a general survey of surgery and from that to some lighthearted reminiscences of his student days. They followed their supper with cups of coffee and they were still sitting over them when closing time was called.

As they strolled the short distance back to Benedict's they were for the most part silent. Pleasantly silent, thought Katrina, like two old friends who didn't have to talk unless they wanted to. They were just inside the door when the night porter came to meet them. 'I was just going to buzz you, sir—you're wanted in the Accident Room.'

The Professor's goodnight had been brisk, almost business-like; his crisp; 'Eight o'clock in the car park' was equally so, Katrina flung some clothes into a case before she got into bed and remembered that she hadn't telephoned her mother. Well, it was too late now, and her parent, thank heaven, wasn't a woman to fuss over unexpected guests.

Contrary to her expectations she went to sleep the moment her head touched the pillow, and she didn't wake until her alarm clock roused her.

She took longer than usual dressing; it was going to be a lovely day, that was obvious even at such an early hour in the heart of London. She decided to wear an Italian knitted suit in a shade of almond green and her new Raynes shoes. The outfit called for extra care with her hair and face, so that there was barely time to make a cup of tea in the tiny pantry at the end of the corridor before she left.

And even though she was punctual to the minute, the Professor was there before her, leaning against the Bentley's gleaming bonnet, lost in contemplation of the chimney pots on the opposite side of the street. He came to meet her as soon as he saw her, however, took her case and put it in the boot and opened the car door.

'You look nice,' he told her. 'It's going to be a beautiful day, too. Have you breakfasted? Do say no, because, I haven't.'

She laughed, 'I haven't either.'

'We'll use the A3 and then stop at the Hog's Back on the other side of Guildford—the A31, isn't it?'

'Yes, I forgot to telephone Mother. She won't mind in the least, you may have to take pot luck for lunch.'

They breakfasted with splendid appetites and set off again through a perfect April morning, and once they had passed Farnham and were racing along the A31 towards the Alton roundabout and Alresford, Katrina broke their companionable silence: 'You were going to tell me something about yourself,' she suggested.

'Ah, yes. Where to begin? I live in the country, to the north of Leiden, but my family came from Friesland originally, a small village not so far from Leeuwarden. I have a housekeeper and a houseman—an elderly couple who look after things for me. I'm away a good deal; I have beds in Leiden hospitals as well as in den Haag and Amsterdam. I have no family.'

She turned her head to look at him. 'No father or mother?'

His profile was all at once bleak. 'They—died a month or so before the war ended.'

She had seen the bleakness. 'Died?' she asked softly.

'They were shot by the Germans for helping someone to escape.'

She caught at his sleeve with a hand. 'Oh, Raf, how terrible, and how sad! Do you remember them at all?'

'Oh, yes. I was getting on for four years old. Caspel and his wife—they are with me still—took me to Friesland, walking all the way, to my grandparents who had a house there. It was my home until they died and in the meantime my father's property was restored to me. Once I had qualified I went to live there.'

'All alone,' said Katrina in a sad voice.

'Quite alone, Kate.'

'Oh, I'm sorry,' she told him, 'though what's the good of being sorry? But you must feel proud too, to have had such a Father and Mother, bearing their name.' Her lovely eyes filled with tears. 'You were such a little boy...'

'Don't forget that at least I had grandparents, many children had no one at all.'

'Yes, but now you're all alone.'

'Don't tempt me to use that as an argument for you to marry me, Kate.'

'Oh, I hadn't thought of that. But you wouldn't would you?'

'No. How about stopping for a coffee?'

It was while they were drinking it that she asked: 'Just supposing I did marry you, would you like me to go on working—a lot of wives do.'

His eyes danced with amusement beneath their heavy lids but he answered seriously enough. 'Oh, I don't think so. I've plenty for two and I'm sure you'll find things to do around the house, and there's the garden. I have a number of friends too; there would be the occasional dinner party and function to attend.'

'Do you have a secretary or a receptionist?'

'At my consulting rooms, yes, but I can always do well with help at home—most of the post goes there, you see, and it does pile up.'

Katrina brightened at the prospect of making herself useful, and he added: 'I shall enjoy having company, Kate—someone I can talk to and discuss the day's work with, someone, moreover, who will understand what I'm talking about.'

She looked up and caught his eyes looking at her so intently that she said quite sharply: 'I haven't made up my mind…'

She changed it a dozen times during the rest of their journey. When Sherborne came in sight at last she still couldn't make up her mind; childishly, she hoped that there would be some omen to make it up for her. It would have to be soon, too. She tried to imagine what it would be like if she did refuse and chose not to see Raf ever again, and had to admit that she wouldn't like it at all. He grew on one, she mused, sitting silent beside him, in a placid kind of way, only every now and then he wasn't placid at all.

CHAPTER FOUR

IT WASN'T ONE of Sherborne's busy days. The Professor drove the Bentley slowly through the town, turned down a side street, skirted the boys' school and gentled the big car into the quiet little backwater where Katrina lived.

The house looked charming, its garden a riot of colour, its latticed windows open. They went up the flagged path side by side, and the door was found open before they reached it.

'Darling, what a lovely surprise!' exclaimed Mrs Bennett happily, 'and Raf too.' She nodded her head in a satisfied way. 'You'll stay, of course.' And then, with all the disconcerting simplicity of a child: 'Why?'

'Mother dear,' began Katrina, and stopped, not quite sure how to go on, but the Professor didn't beat about the bush.

'I've asked Katrina to marry me,' he said matter-of-factly, 'and she thought she would like to come home and think about it.'

'Splendid!' Mrs Bennett beamed at him, 'I was only thinking the other day that really Katrina should be the first to marry, being the eldest, you know.' She waved an arm. 'Come in, my dears, and tell me all about it—I do love a wedding. It's a cold lunch, will you mind? And Raf can have the guest room…'

Ten minutes later, over their sherry, Mrs Bennett asked: 'Is it to be a white wedding, Kate? Satin, dear, cut very simply; you've such a good figure.' She turned to the Professor. 'Hasn't she, Raf?'

Katrina went pink. 'Mother, I've not said I'll get married yet...' She glanced at Raf and saw the twinkle in his eyes and suddenly she didn't feel awkward any more. Not even when he agreed with her mother with a good deal of warmth.

'Would you like to be married in satin?' he asked interestedly.

Katrina thought for a minute. 'Well, neither of us have large families and your friends won't want to come all this way, will they? I think it should be quiet; just us and Uncle Ben and—and anyone you wanted to ask.' The pink which hadn't quite subsided glowed crimson. 'Not that I've said...'

'No, no,' agreed the Professor soothingly, 'it was merely a hypothetical question.'

Mrs Bennett had picked up some knitting. 'That would be nice,' she mused. 'We could come back here for a luncheon party afterwards. Where will you live?'

'My home and my work are in Holland,' explained the Professor, his voice placid, 'but I do come to England very frequently and of course Kate would come with me.'

'It's all so suitable.' She stopped knitting to look at them both in turn. 'Well, Kate darling, you can sit in the garden after lunch and make your mind up while I show Raf the Abbey.'

Which wasn't quite what Katrina had intended, but perhaps it wasn't such a bad idea after all, for it was very peaceful sitting in one of the elderly deck chairs, with Mrs Mogg, the family cat, curled up on her lap. Left to herself after casual goodbyes from her mother and the Professor, Katrina relaxed. She relaxed so well that she went to sleep in no time at all.

When she woke up, an hour later, it was to find the Professor sitting on the chopping block, facing her, and to her great surprise, although she hadn't given a thought to her problem, it seemed to have solved itself while she was sleeping, because she said without any hesitation at all:

'Yes, of course I'll marry you, Raf, that's if you still want me to.'

He smiled faintly. 'Yes, I want you to, Kate.' He got to his feet and caught hold of her hands and pulled her up. 'Shall we go and tell your mother? She's getting the tea and sent me to find you, but I hadn't the heart to wake you up.'

'I wasn't snoring?'

He tucked a hand under her arm. 'Not so that you'd notice. I liked the Abbey, do you suppose we could be married in one of the chapels?'

'I don't see why not. I mean, with Father having been there... and we know everyone quite well. I'd like that if you would.'

They went in through the side door and met Mrs Bennett with the teapot in her hand. 'We'll have a cup now,' she told them. 'The other two will be home at five o'clock, we can have another cup with them.' She threw Katrina a sharp glance. 'So you've decided,' she declared happily. And when Katrina looked surprised: 'Well, you wouldn't be walking arm-in-arm otherwise, would you?' she observed.

The rest of the day passed in a pleasant dream, with Ruth and Jane showering congratulations on them both, and plunging at once into the vital question of what they should wear at the wedding. The Professor didn't say much, only when there was a pause in the conversation, suggested diffidently that he and Katrina might stroll round and see whoever it was they had to see about the licence, and when that had been done, settled with the least possible fuss by Raf, they went on walking through the quiet little town and she discovered that he had a solution, offered in the most matter-of-fact way, to each and every of her small doubts and problems. It was almost as though he had planned everything days before and had an answer ready for any contingency. But that was absurd, she told herself.

They wandered back presently to drink the champagne Raf had thoughtfully brought with him in the car, and eat the rather special dinner Mrs Bennett and Mary had conjured up, and later, just as she was falling asleep, Katrina was suddenly sure that she was doing the right thing. Unexpected and rather sudden, but right. She turned over and went to sleep on the thought.

She and Raf went for a walk before breakfast the following day—a suggestion he had made the previous evening. 'So that we can get the date settled,' he had suggested placidly, 'and the time...'

They agreed on ten o'clock in the morning, in three weeks' time; they could return to her home for an hour after the wedding and then leave for Scotland, spending a night on the way. 'We'll be there for a week, at least. I shall be lecturing for that time. I thought that if you would like to, we might spend a few days travelling around before we go back to Holland.'

Katrina agreed happily; it would give them a chance to get used to each other and time to learn about his home and way of life. A busy one, by all accounts, but he hadn't told her much so far.

'Do you go to Friesland often?' she wanted to know.

'Oh, frequently—the farm is managed by a remote cousin of mine, but I like to go there as often as I can.' He turned to smile at her. 'You like farming?'

'I don't know a great deal about it, but I'm sure I shall love it. Is there a garden?' she added.

'Yes, a very pleasant one—you will be able to potter there as much as you like.'

'And your home? What's it like?'

'Oh, old and square with a steep tiled roof—like so many other Dutch houses.'

She had to be content with that; Raf started talking about something else and she found it impossible, without being downright rude, to ask more questions.

It was after breakfast when she had supposed him safely telephoning someone or other, and had slipped into the garden to hang the washing on the carefully concealed line behind the lilac bushes, that he came to join her. She threw him a glance over her shoulder and spoke first.

'Mother and Ruth and Jane are too small,' she explained matter-of-factly, 'so when I'm home I always do it.' She tossed a sheet over the line with effortless grace and stretched her magnificent proportions to peg it.

Raf stood watching her. 'Penthesilea,' he murmured.

Katrina frowned, shook out a pillow case and then said smugly: 'I know—Queen of the Amazons, wasn't she? Came to a sticky end, too.'

'I wasn't thinking of her end,' observed the Professor mildly, so really, Katrina told herself crossly, there was no reason why she should blush. She made a great work of pegging a table-cloth and hurried on: 'Father was interested in mythology; he read Latin and Greek like I read the *Telegraph*, he used to let me sit with him as long as I didn't disturb him—over the years I worked my way through Beeton's Classical Dictionary.'

'Do you read Greek and Latin as well?'

She picked up the laundry basket and he took it from her. 'Heavens, no, but it was much more exciting than Grimm's Fairy Tales.' And when he laughed: 'I suppose you do…?'

He sounded almost apologetic. 'Well, yes, I do—not avidly, though: I shan't object to you interrupting me when I do.'

He gave her a hard stare and she looked back at him, faintly bewildered by it. It was like having a spell cast over one, she thought childishly, and then, even more bewildered, a spell she didn't mind about. But before she could think about it he said in an ordinary voice:

'I wondered if we might dine out this evening—all of us; Ruth's fiancé and Jane's current boy-friend and your mother, naturally.'

'That would be fun. Where?'

'Sir Benjamin told me of a good place at Wincanton—Hol-brook House.'

'Oh, lovely! We've been there once or twice—birthdays and that sort of thing.'

'Would it be an idea if we went round to see your vicar, Mr Thomas?—he's not married, I understand—to make up the numbers?'

He sounded as if he had just thought of it, but later, making beds, Katrina wondered if he hadn't laid his plans beforehand, knowing quite well that everyone would fall in with them as long as he proposed them at the right time. Would it be like that when they were married? she wondered uneasily, and then rejected the idea, he had a caustic tongue upon occasion, but on the whole he was a placid man, not easily put out—or put upon, she added thoughtfully.

Mr Thomas would be delighted. They took the opportunity to discuss the details of the wedding while they were there and then strolled into the town's main street, looking at the shop windows. It was Katrina who deliberately didn't look in the jeweller's; an engagement ring hadn't been mentioned—perhaps she wasn't to have one. She looked away as they reached the best one in town, but Raf caught her hand and stopped her. 'I'll bring the ring with me,' he told her. 'It's been in the family for quite some time—a little old-fashioned, but I hope you won't mind.'

She didn't know how her eyes sparkled. 'Oh—how nice! I shall love it. When are you going back to Holland?'

'Tomorrow evening—I've some lectures to give, but I'll be back within a week. I promised Sir Benjamin that I'd give him a hand with that arterial graft—he hasn't quite decided whether to do a thrombo-endarterectomy and core out the lining...'

'Oh, you're talking about Mr Parsons who came in yesterday—does it have to be surgery?'

'Oh, yes, I'm afraid so...' The talk turned to surgery in general and kept them occupied until they reached home once more. Not quite the kind of conversation one would have expected between two newly engaged people, perhaps, and as they entered the house Raf paused in the doorway to say: 'I teased you once—when we met—because we talked about the weather, and now I have been boring on for hours about something you must be only too glad to escape once in a while.'

Katrina eyed him gravely. 'Usually I am, but I enjoyed it, really I did.' She hesitated. 'You don't know me very well, Raf. I'm not—not frivolous, I mean, I'm not very amusing company and I'm not witty or anything like that. I like clothes, but I don't worry about them, if you know what I mean. I can cook and sew and do the washing if the machine breaks down, but I haven't any—any...'

'Parlour tricks? My dear, I've seen all of those. I think you may rest assured that we shall suit very well' He grinned wickedly. 'I hope at any rate that you will find me a shade better than the Gulf!'

Katrina chuckled. 'Wasn't I a fool? The things one says when one is unprepared!'

They spent the afternoon in the garden, Raf mowing the lawn with beautiful precision while Katrina weeded under her mother's eye. Mrs Bennett had started off weeding too, but had declared herself tired to death and made herself comfortable in a deck chair, opening an eye every now and then to point out the odd groundsel or blade of grass which her daughter had overlooked. But presently she dropped off to sleep and the Professor, finished with his mowing, made short work of the rest of the weeds, pulled Katrina to her feet and suggested that they should sit under the lilacs at the end of the garden. It was warm there, sheltered from the wind, and they didn't bother to talk much. Katrina, covertly eyeing her companion, stretched out beside her with his eyes closed, found it somehow reassuring that they could be together and not need to talk.

'You're very restful,' said the Professor suddenly, and opened an eye. 'When I've finished my lecturing in Edinburgh, shall we go to the west coast? A small place called Ledaig, there's a delightful hotel there—you cross a bridge to reach it; it's on an island only a short distance from the shore. I think you might like it, Kate. I was there a couple of years ago and I enjoyed it enormously. No cinema or dancing or shops, just fields and the sea and animals and delicious food. If we need the bright lights Oban is no distance away.'

'It sounds super, and I don't suppose I'll need any bright lights. I'll have time to read and look at the birds. Do you fish?'

'Yes, but I won't—it's rather dull for the non-fisher.'

'I'm willing to learn, but I don't think I'd like the worms and hooks.'

He smiled up at her. 'I won't fish. I shall probably lie down all day doing absolutely nothing.'

'Is that all the holiday you'll get this year?'

'Good lord, no—I snatch a day here and a day there and most weekends.'

'But you have hospital rounds,' she persisted, 'and a practice?'

'Oh, yes, of course. I'm afraid I have rather a full day's work, but being a nurse you'll understand that—and I'm often away from home.'

'Your lectures… Do you visit interesting places?' She was angry with herself for saying that; it sounded as though she wanted to go too. So she added with a touch of pettishness: 'That sounds as though I want to go too, but I don't.'

'What a pity.' His tone was light, so she wasn't sure if he were joking or meant it. She asked hastily: 'Do you fly?'

'Always, unless it's in Holland or perhaps Belgium.'

Katrina seemed unable to stop the questions tripping off her tongue.

'Are you important?' she asked.

'My dear girl, what is importance? A housewife is important in her kitchen, but only because she knows what to do there— if I'm important, which I doubt, it's because I know what to do with a scalpel when I'm handed one.'

She wasn't getting anywhere; she had asked several questions and the answers had been clear and concise and had told her virtually nothing. She said crossly: 'Now if Father were alive he would ask you all sorts of questions and you'd answer...'

'How much do I earn and can I support you in a manner to which you are accustomed? Isn't that right? Well, my dear, I have sufficient to do that...'

'Now you've made me sound like a prying harpy!'

Raf's huge shoulders shook. 'My dear Kate, have you any idea what exactly a harpy is?'

'Well, no—I don't think I have...'

'A fabulous winged monster, quite ravenous and filthy dirty, with the body of a woman, a face pale from hunger, and large wings. Somehow you don't quite fit the bill.'

Katrina got slowly to her feet. 'The trouble is,' she said thoughtfully, 'I'm never sure when to take you seriously.'

The dinner party was a resounding success; the hotel had at one time been a country house set in charming parkland and the owners had managed to keep its original atmosphere, merely adding good food and excellent service. Katrina, who had dug deep into the old oak clothes closet in her room, had found a cotton voile dress in tawny colours which she had had for at least two years and had intended to throw away, to discover when she tried it on that it was undeniably becoming and to all but the very discerning, quite fashionable. At any rate the Professor had declared that she had looked charming, adding with a decided twinkle in his eyes that he knew very little about girls' clothes: 'Although I must say that some fashions do seem rather peculiar.'

Katrina, pushing a comb into her hair, looked at him in the mirror. 'I expect you've had a lot of girl-friends,' she said.

The twinkle became a gleam. 'Oh, naturally—one must have company from time to time,' he explained, and smiled with great charm.

Katrina tugged the comb out and stuck it in again rather painfully. 'Well, you won't need them any more, you'll have me,' she reminded him with something of a snap.

'Yes, I had thought of that,' said the Professor placidly. 'That comb looked very nice where it was before, why didn't you leave it there?'

He took it gently out again and slid it expertly into its original place, then bent to kiss her cheek. 'I never asked any of the other girl-friends to marry me,' he told her gently.

Katrina enjoyed her evening very much after that.

They went back to London early the next morning because Katrina was on duty after one o'clock dinner. Usually she didn't mind too much, getting back into uniform and plunging back into the hustle and bustle of a big ward, but today, for some reason, she did. Perhaps because she wouldn't see Raf for a few days. She hadn't seen much of him at the hospital, but she had known that he was around somewhere and that he might pop in. It struck her that she had looked forward to their unexpected meetings. And anyone would think, she mused, sitting quietly beside him as they drove back, that I was never going to see him again, whereas in a couple of weeks I shall see him every day… She went pink at the idea, and Raf, throwing her a quick sidelong glance, asked with interest: 'What are you blushing about, Kate?' He added thoughtfully. 'I've not said anything—I wasn't even thinking…'

Katrina giggled. 'Don't be absurd—and you don't have to sound aggrieved, because you never are. I—I was just thinking that I'd see more of you after we're married.'

His fine mouth quivered. 'It would be rather extraordinary if you didn't. But I must warn you, Kate, that I am a busy man, and if the day's gone badly, an ill-tempered one too.'

'In which case I shall go somewhere quiet with a good book,' said Kate.

They stopped for lunch at the Castle in Sunbury and he delivered her neatly to the nurses' home door with half an hour to spare. There were plenty of people about; she supposed that was why he parted from her with a casual: 'I'll see you in a few days, Kate,' and a wave as he drove off.

It seemed the right moment to discount the fiction of her job in the Gulf; she had only to tell one or two friends, pass the news on to Julie during the afternoon's work and ask for an interview at the office and by teatime the entire hospital knew that she was the lucky girl who was going to marry the handsome Dutchman that the unattached female staff had secretly hoped to capture for themselves. Inevitably, Jack bearded her in her office as she wrote the report that evening.

'That was a pack of lies you told me,' he began, gobbling with indignation.

Katrina held her pen poised over the Cardex. She looked down demurely and murmured: 'I had no idea when I told you about the job in the Gulf that I was going to marry Professor van Telerinck.' Which was perfectly true. 'It all happened rather suddenly.'

'You can say that again—he's only been an honorary consultant for a few weeks.' His eyes narrowed. 'I suppose he's filthy rich?'

Katrina wrote a few words. 'You're being very rude—and I might add that it's none of your business.'

She wrote busily and after a moment or two he grunted something under his breath and went away. She finished her report and then, with five minutes to spare until the night staff came on duty, sat back to think. Jack hadn't worried her at all and she didn't give him a second thought, but a small niggling idea at the back of her head needed to be brought out into the open and aired. Was Raf rich, and how was she to find out anyway? He had always parried her questions very smoothly when she had asked him, and was it quite the done thing for a girl to ask her future husband what his income was? She supposed it was; in these hard times it was essential that they knew exactly what they were letting themselves in for. He had assured her that he had enough money to provide for her and at the time the answer had contented her; she wasn't greedy or extravagant and she was a good manager, she had no doubt at all that she would be able to manage very well with whatever he gave her for the household expenses. She frowned and pushed her cap back on her head. That wasn't quite it; if he were a very rich man—and after all, he did run a Bentley—she wasn't sure that she would have said she would marry him, but she had, and it was too late to go back on her promise now. Anyway, she admitted, she didn't want to; Raf was much much nicer than she had thought he would be. Besides, she was fast reaching the conclusion that being with someone you liked and trusted was far more comfortable than loving someone to distraction and not being quite sure of him. She went to bed and slept dreamlessly after an uproarious hour with her friends, discussing wedding clothes.

She had told herself that she wouldn't buy anything at all until Raf came again, but the next day, with an afternoon off duty, it seemed a pity not to at least do a little window shopping. Rosina, the junior theatre Sister, and Delia, in charge of the Accident Room, were both off duty too, and the three of them took a bus to Regent Street where Katrina bought a pair of strappy sandals at Raynes in champagne kid and a leghorn hat swathed with a chiffon scarf in a rich cream. A most sensible beginning to the buying of wedding clothes, she was assured by her friends, and back in her room, with the hat poised on top of her rich brown hair, she was inclined to agree with them. She would have to find a suit or a dress which would go with it, but it would have to be something she could wear later.

She was on duty all day for the next two days so that shopping was out of the question, but on the day after that she was to have a morning off; she had some hours owing to her and both staff nurses on duty, so she had the whole morning free until one o'clock.

She went out immediately after breakfast and began painstakingly to search. Several times she found something which she liked and each time the size was wrong, so she was forced to reject them in turn. She was beginning to lose heart when she found exactly what she wanted—a sleeveless dress and little jacket in a thick slub silk, its colour an exact match of the chiffon in the hat. What was more, it fitted. Katrina, studying herself carefully in the pier glass, beamed at the sales lady, who beamed back and forgot to be aloof. 'Modom is a big girl,' she observed in a voice of ultra-refinement, 'but Modom has the figure to carry off the beautiful lines of the dress—such an exquisite cut...'

The price was exquisite too; Katrina had come prepared to be extravagant, but this was ridiculous. She got out her cheque book and paid without protest.

It had all taken a long time, of course. She was tearing across the forecourt, intent on getting to her room, when she ran full tilt into Raf. A man of lesser bulk might have been bowled over, but all he did was to clamp her round the waist, take her dress box from her and remark: 'Shopping, I see. The wedding dress, I hope? Where can we go for a moment?'

'Nowhere,' said Katrina, a little breathless and not altogether from hurrying either. 'I mean, I'm on duty in twenty minutes—and do take care of that box,' and then: 'How nice to see you.'

'I should have said that first, shouldn't I? I know somewhere we can go.'

He hurried her through the entrance, across the hall and into a wide corridor where she did her best to come to a halt; a quite useless effort anyway, although she did protest in a hissing whisper as he opened a door. 'Raf, you can't—not in here—it's where the consultants come...'

'I'm a consultant, aren't I? And there's no one here, is there?' He smiled at her in his sleepy fashion. 'Don't fuss, Kate.' He put the box down on the old-fashioned central table, and still holding her by the arm, fished a box out of a pocket. 'Open it,' he suggested.

She blinked at the ring inside—a great sapphire, flanked by smaller ones on either side and all three surrounded by rose diamonds. 'My goodness!' gasped Katrina. 'It's—it's absolutely super—I'll never dare to wear it!'

For answer Raf took the ring from her and slipped it on her finger, where it looked exactly right; what was more, it fitted.

Katrina held up her hand and looked at the jewel from every angle. 'It's magnificent—oh, I'll take such care of it! Thank you very much, Raf.'

She looked at him a little uncertainly and he read her thoughts unerringly. 'Shall we not kiss and seal our pact?' he suggested in such a matter-of-fact voice that she forgot to feel awkward and flung her arms round his neck and kissed him with the spontaneous pleasure of a child. She drew back almost at once; his kiss had been brief and friendly, like hundreds of other kisses from hundreds of other people; there was no reason why she should have felt unhappy about it, but she did, and made haste to cover it up.

'So sorry,' she told him brightly. 'I got carried away—it must be the effect of having sapphires offered to one before lunch,' and before he could answer: 'That reminds me—I've about five minutes in which to change and get on duty—I simply have to go.'

It was more than five minutes, but it wasn't long enough for her to brood over his cool reception of her kiss; she'd think about that later. It was much later when she finally left the ward. The afternoon and evening had proved even busier than usual, and Uncle Ben had been to see a new case of his, so had Jack Bentall and a variety of other people—path lab technicians, the lady from CSR, fussing about some packs which had gone astray, the dietitian, who wasted a lot of valuable time fretting over steamed fish. Katrina, who had her mind on other things, wished her and her fish a thousand miles away.

She said good night thankfully to the night staff and went yawning down the stairs. She had intended to try on the new outfit, but now she was tired, more so because she was hungry too. She was rounding the dark corner at the bottom when she bumped into something very solid, Raf's massive waistcoated chest, and she was so delighted that she put out a hand and grabbed at it, babbling, 'Oh, I'm so glad... I wasn't looking, I'm sorry,' and then, like a child: 'I'm tired!'

Just for a moment he held her close. 'Go and get your coat, we're going to your uncle's—you need a stiff drink and something decent to eat and half an hour to unwind.'

It was nice to have someone arranging everything for her, but she protested all the same: 'I'm a bit bad-tempered too—not fit company.'

'Do as I say,' said Raf quietly, and disentangled her from his chest with kind impersonal hands, so that she said: 'Very well,' at once and hurried to her room. She had irritated him, whining about being tired and then clinging to him like a leech. She must be careful never to do that again...

Uncle Ben and Aunt Lucy were so kind. The ring was admired while Raf got them all drinks, and when she had relaxed under the influence of the Madeira he had given her, they sat down to supper; one of Katrina's aunt's light-as-air omelettes and a bowl of salad. They sat for a short while afterwards, talking, and Katrina became aware that Raf was rather quiet; perhaps he was annoyed because she had sprawled all over his waistcoat and moaned about being tired, perhaps he was having second thoughts about marrying her.

It was a relief to hear him presently, discussing the wedding with Uncle Ben. She listened unashamedly while Aunt Lucy rambled on happily about white satin and orange blossom, although Katrina had pointed out to her several times that for the bride to float down the aisle in all the traditional wedding finery with barely a dozen people in the church to admire her seemed a bit foolish. She caught Raf's eye presently and they got up to go, and although he said very little on the short drive back, he kissed her lightly as they said good night and urged her to sleep well in a kind voice. In bed, on the point of sleep, she remembered that he hadn't said when they were to meet again.

CHAPTER FIVE

THE NEXT TWO weeks went in a flash. Katrina, caught up in the business of handing over the ward to Julie, had no time to do more than smile and murmur at Raf when he came, either alone or with Uncle Ben to see their patients. True, they had managed to have dinner together twice before Raf went back to Holland, but they had talked about the wedding in a rather businesslike way, getting the times right, checking the travelling arrangements, and when he had said goodbye and gone, she wished with all her heart that she could have seen more of him; it would have made the wedding day seem more real. But there was no time to waste upon her vague doubts; she smothered them with a bout of shopping and then went home for her last days off before she left Benedict's for good.

Her mother welcomed her with open arms and a list of things to be done or decided upon. It was to be a very small wedding, but nonetheless Mrs Bennett had consoled herself for the lack of satin and orange blossom by arranging for an elegant luncheon party after the ceremony, and the purchase of a decidedly becoming outfit for the occasion. Katrina, who hadn't got around to thinking about wedding cakes and flowers, agreed to everything, surprised to hear that Raf had sent a case of cham-

pagne from London and that the flowers were already ordered.
So that was why he had stopped on their way back from dinner and studied a florist's window so carefully, asking her if
she liked roses, and how charming lilies of the valley were. To
her great astonishment too, he had brought with him on that
same evening, a pocket full of wedding rings, because, as he
had pointed out, there was no chance of them going to a jeweller's and choosing one. She had decided on a plain gold one and
rather shyly asked if she might give him one as well. He already
wore a heavy signet ring and she hadn't been sure if he would
like the idea, but he agreed readily, scooped the rings back into
a careless heap, and promised her lightly that he wouldn't forget to bring them with him.

Her mother had given her a Gucci travelling case for a present, and Ruth and Jane had contributed a matching beauty case.
Katrina spent a good deal of time packing these, for she was to
leave Benedict's the day before she was to be married, which
left precious little time. Indeed, her mother, sitting on the bed
with her sisters, watching her fold her new outfits, bemoaned
the fact at some length. 'No hairdresser, and no time for a manicure or something for your face…'

Katrina flew to the dressing table. 'Have I got spots?' she
demanded.

'No, dear, of course not, you have a lovely skin and such
pretty hair too…it's just that you seem to be being pitchforked
into marriage with barely a good night's sleep as preparation.'

Katrina gave up looking for the mythical spot and went to
hug her mother. 'Darling, don't worry, I'll have clean nails and
a powdered nose, and it's only a very small affair, you know,
Raf's only got a couple of his friends coming—I haven't even
met them, and there'll be ten of us for lunch, no more. Besides,
we have to leave by two o'clock.'

'Will you have time to come and see us before you go over
to Holland?'

'I don't think so; Raf's got a full programme ahead of him—lectures, you know, but he's coming over to London in about six weeks and I'm to come too and we'll come and see you then.'

'Yes, dear. Katrina, I do hope...'

'We're going to be very happy,' said Katrina firmly.

It was surely wedding day weather, thought Katrina, creeping from her bed very early to peer out at the bright May morning. She glanced at her wedding hat, lying in splendour on the table under the window, and then jumped back into bed as she heard feet on the stairs.

'I thought I heard you up, Miss Kate,' said Mary severely. 'Don't you know better than to get out of bed before your breakfast on your wedding day. Now drink up this nice cup of tea and I'll be up in no time with a good nourishing meal.'

Just as though Raf intends to starve me for the rest of my life, thought Katrina, giggling, and then stopped because this really was her wedding day and she ought to be serious about it. It was too late now to wonder if she had done the right thing. Perhaps she hadn't; she was marrying Raf for several good reasons, but none of the usual ones; she admired and respected him, though, and that was surely important, and he was just about the handsomest man she had ever set eyes on; and she liked being with him. She hoped that he felt the same towards her, because if he did, they would probably make a success of their life together. All the same, marriage was a big risk...

Raf appeared to have no such doubts. As Katrina went into the Abbey and reached the little side chapel, he turned to look at her, his face calm and very assured so that at the sight of him, her mouth curved into a smile. Perhaps it wasn't quite the thing to think about clothes in church, but she knew that she looked her best and very feminine, despite the fact that she towered over Uncle Ben. She clutched the exquisite bouquet rather more tightly and glanced down at it: creamy roses, lilies of the valley, delicate pink orchids and carnations—all the flowers she had imagined, and admired. It was nice to think he had remembered and taken the trouble to get them.

There was a tall man standing beside Raf; the best man she hadn't met, and just beyond him, two more men, big and burly, faultlessly turned out, going elegantly grey at the temples, as selfassured as Raf. There were three youngish women there too, smartly dressed. Wives, thought Katrina; let's hope there's enough lunch—and why didn't Raf let us know?

She glanced at him and saw that he was looking at her with a half smile, probably guessing her thoughts. She looked at him gravely then; she was here to get married and anything else, for the moment, didn't matter.

The ceremony was very short. She hadn't really realised that it was all over before they had signed the register and she was walking out of the Abbey doors, the organ booming triumphantly in the empty Abbey and her hand tucked into Raf's arm. The bells were ringing too and she glanced at him in surprise. 'Because you are your father's daughter,' he said softly, 'they wanted to do it.'

They started down the path towards the Bentley and for a moment her steps faltered. 'Oh, Raf, how kind…' her voice shook a little because she had loved her father very much, and Raf glanced down at her face.

'I thought you were going to bawl me out for bringing unexpected guests,' he said cheerfully, and made her laugh. 'Your mother knew—I told her last night.'

'You telephoned?'

'I called, but you were already in bed.'

Someone was holding the car door open and she got in. 'Oh, why didn't you wake me?' she wanted to know. 'There were lots of things I wanted to say…'

He turned to look at her before he started the engine. 'And all the time in the world to say them, Kate.'

'Yes, isn't it funny…? I do hope…'

'You mean you know, Kate. What a pity it's such a short

drive, only just time to tell you that you look very lovely; I feel very proud of you, my dear.'

She pinkened charmingly. 'The flowers are beautiful. Thank you.'

And there was no time for more. They had reached the house and there was Mary, who had rushed back from the Abbey ahead of them, waiting by the open door.

The sitting room looked delightful, crammed with flowers, its slightly shabby appearance making for comfort. They paused inside the door, and Katrina said quickly: 'Everyone's to come here first—drinks and gossip, you know, and then the food.'

'Thank God! I couldn't eat my breakfast.'

'Why ever not? It's the bride who's nervous.'

'Well, here's a bridegroom who didn't conform—I imagined you not turning up.'

'Raf—Raf, you're joking! I wouldn't do a thing like that, ever.'

He picked up her hand and kissed it. 'I know that. Before everyone comes, I've a wedding present for you.'

The box he produced was long and slender and velvet-covered; it looked old too. Inside was a pearl necklace with a diamond and sapphire clasp.

'Raf!' Katrina let out a great sigh of delight. 'It's beautiful—they're real...' she added in something like awe.

'Yes, and very old. They're handed down to the family brides, not to be put away in a safe, but to be worn. There's a rather nice little story attached to them, I'll tell you one day.'

'Please, and thank you, Raf.' She leant up and kissed his cheek just as the first of the wedding guests came through the door.

The best man was a Dutchman, an old friend of Raf's, he assured Katrina gravely, married to one of the three women who had been at the wedding. The youngest and prettiest, too, as well as tall and well built.

'Jake and Britannia,' Raf had introduced them. 'I've known Jake for a long long time.'

He looked nice, thought Katrina, with grizzled hair and bright blue eyes which never left his wife's face for long, and she, offering a hand, confided: 'I did hope you wouldn't mind—all of us coming uninvited, you know. But Jake did promise to be best man if ever Raf married, and we do like to do everything together—so we packed up the babies and Nanny and came with him.'

Katrina beamed at her, liking her instantly. 'Of course I don't mind—I think it's lovely. But where are they—the babies?

'At my mother's—near Wareham. Twins, you know. You must come and see them, we don't live far away from Raf. I say, I do love your hat, it's quite stunning—you're just right for Raf.'

'Thank you, Britannia,' smiled Katrina. 'Who are the other ladies?'

'Partners' wives—I expect you forgot. Raf has got two—partners, that is. They're nice. How do you like being a baroness?'

'Me?' Katrina looked astonished and then added lamely: 'Oh, I quite forgot—I always think of Raf as a professor.'

Britannia blinked. 'Well, I don't suppose you do all the time. I'm one too,' she grinned, and added disarmingly: 'I was Miss Smith.'

Katrina watched her join the others at the end of the room and felt suddenly quite lighthearted at the idea of having a new friend ready and waiting when she got to Holland. 'I like your best man and his wife,' she told Raf quietly, and held out a hand to his partners and their wives, prepared to like them too.

And less than two hours after that, she found herself sitting beside Raf in the Bentley, waving goodbye to the little group of people at the gate. Everything had happened much too quickly; she had cut the cake, but she couldn't remember eating anything, although she had had at least two glasses of champagne before going upstairs to change into the pale green knitted dress and jacket she had most extravagantly bought. She had consoled herself at the time that as she wouldn't be wearing a hat, she could afford it, and the kid sandals which went with it so well. Now, their well-wishers out of sight, she sat back for a moment, her eyes closed, and repeated her thoughts aloud.

'Everything happened much too quickly—it's like a dream.'

'Quite a nice one, I thought,' observed Raf easily, 'even though it was reality. You made a charming bride, Kate.'

They discussed their wedding at some length as they travelled north, stopping for tea presently and reaching the hotel where they were to stay the night in good time for dinner.

They were well on their way now, in Cumbria, having travelled over three hundred miles, but the Bentley had made light of it and for the greater part of the time Raf had kept to the motorway, but now they were in charming country, with Bassenthwaite Lake on one side of them and Thornwaite Forest on the other, and the old coaching inn showing welcoming lights as they stopped before its door.

Katrina got out of the car and looked around her. 'Raf, however did you discover this place? It's out of this world!'

'I stayed here once, years ago. I hope it hasn't changed.'

They went inside and presently, her face and hair carefully done, Katrina joined Raf in the bar. It was still early enough in the season for the hotel to be only half full, but that, for Katrina, didn't matter at all; they ate their dinner at a table in a window, with a log fire smouldering in the hearth, and soft candlelight in place of lamps. And afterwards they had their coffee in the drawing room, sitting in easy chairs with the table between them, talking about whatever came into their heads. Katrina, nicely tired by now and made even more so by the champagne she had drunk, found her lids drooping and was thankful when Raf said, half laughing: 'Bed for you, my girl, before you're out cold.'

He pulled her to her feet, dropped a light kiss on her cheek and wished her goodnight. 'Breakfast at eight?' he wanted to know. 'Or is that too early?'

'Not a bit, but I'll have to be called.'

'I'll arrange that. Off you go.'

So she went upstairs to the delightful room on the first floor, made short work of undressing and bathing, and tumbled into bed. Just before she went to sleep she heard Raf's footsteps pass her door.

She was called just after seven o'clock and skipped out of bed to look out on to the lake and the mountains while she drank her tea. It was going to be a lovely day, too. She switched on the radio and whistled an accompaniment while she dressed.

Raf was already downstairs when she went to investigate, sitting outside in the sunshine, reading the newspaper, but he got up with a smile as she joined him, wished her good morning and expressed the hope that she had slept.

'Like a top. It was quite a long day, wasn't it?' She perched beside him. 'This is very nice.'

'I think so too. A pity we can't stay for a few days, but we'll come back some time if you like. I thought we'd take the Moffat road from Carlisle, we can pick up the 701 there and stop for lunch at Cringletie House just north of Peebles, there's a good restaurant there. We can go on at our leisure and get to Edinburgh in the late afternoon.'

'Are we staying near the hospital?'

'In Princes Street, at the Caledonian—not small and quiet as the Pheasant Inn was, I'm afraid, but there are conference rooms there, which makes it convenient for the various meetings, and so on. I'm afraid I shall be busy most of the time, Kate, but there's a good deal to see and some splendid shops.'

'Oh, don't worry about me, I'll do fine,' she assured him, and thought uneasily of the not very large sum of money in her purse. It seemed strange, now that she came to think about it, but they had never discussed money. Beyond assuring her that he had enough to live on in comfort, Raf had told her nothing.

But he must have read her thoughts. 'There are a great
many things to discuss still, aren't there?' He glanced at her
and smiled. 'If we had had a longer engagement we could have
settled everything then, as it is we shall have to talk things over
as we go along. You'll have an allowance, Katrina. For conve-
nience you can draw on the account I've opened for you at my
bank here. When we get home, you will have an account at my
Dutch bank. Nothing to do with housekeeping…'

'I've a little money of my own,' she began.

'You're my wife now, Katrina, it will be my pleasure to provide for you.'

'Oh, well, thank you. I'm not extravagant.'

He didn't answer, only smiled slowly. 'Let's have breakfast.'

They had time enough to reach Edinburgh and Raf didn't
hurry through the Lakes, keeping to the smaller roads until
they had gone through Carlisle, but once through that city he
speeded up, only slowing again to allow Katrina to look at the
famous forge at Gretna Green. But they stopped at Beattock
for coffee before taking the Tweedsmuir road and then making
their way along country roads to Peebles.

'Heavens,' observed Katrina, seeing a signpost, 'we're not
far from Edinburgh!'

'Twenty minutes, but we are going to have lunch first.'

He turned the car off the road and into a winding drive, pleasantly wooded on either side, and presently reached his goal,
Cringletie House, a turreted mansion of some charm.

As Katrina got out she stared round her appreciatively. 'I say,
Raf, you do know a lot of delightful places!'

He took her arm and they strolled towards the house. 'I was
told of this place when I was up here last year and dined here
with friends.'

What friends? Kate's mind wanted to know, but she didn't
like to ask. He must have any number of friends, and some of
them women. She sighed unknowingly and he said: 'Tired after
all the scenery? We won't hurry over our lunch.'

And they didn't indeed; it was getting on for three o'clock before they were back on the main road once again, heading for Edinburgh.

They entered the city from the south, through the Lothian Road and so into Princes Street. The hotel was on a corner, with Arthur's Seat easily to be seen high on the hill, and below it, in Victorian grandeur, was the imposing pile of the Royal Infirmary.

'Gosh, we're right in the middle, aren't we?' said Katrina. 'Just look at the castle, did you ever see anything so absolutely splendid?'

'Magnificent, isn't it? I hope we'll have the chance to see everything. There's the Palace of Holyroodhouse too, you'll know more about that than I.'

'But I don't. Oh, I shall enjoy being here.' She turned a beaming face to him as they went into the hotel.

They had rooms on the first floor and Katrina, prowling round hers, decided that it was the height of luxury. She unpacked slowly and when Raf tapped on the door, wanted to know if she should unpack for him too. 'And what lovely rooms,' she went on happily. 'It's an enormous hotel, isn't it—I've never much fancied staying in such a vast place, but I see I was mistaken.'

Raf had gone to look out of the window. 'You prefer small hotels?' he asked carelessly.

'Yes, I think so—and the country.' She hastened to add, in case he thought that she was complaining, 'But it's nice getting the chance to explore. When do you have your lectures?'

'Nine in the morning and then again after lunch, two o'clock until half past four.' He turned to look at her. 'Oh, and on two evenings in the week there will be a conference here in this hotel. I'm afraid you won't be able to come.'

'If I see half the sights I'm sure there are to see, I'll be too tired to want to do anything in the evening.' She saw the quick frown on his face. 'Not with you, of course.'

They had tea then and went for a stroll along Princes Street and Katrina spent a blissful hour peering at the shop windows. She would certainly do some shopping, she told herself happily.

But she found that, even with so many tempting shops and visits to almost every museum in the city, she was lonely. She saw Raf briefly at breakfast and then again at lunch, but then he was preoccupied with the afternoon's work ahead of him so that conversation, although easy enough, was at a minimum. But he always enquired after her morning and listened apparently with interest to her carefully pruned accounts of the places she had visited. She took care not to chat, though, and was rewarded after a few days by his: 'I can see that I have married a treasure—not so much as a tiny moan from you, and I've left you alone for several days now.'

'We have our evenings,' she pointed out.

He smiled at her. 'Indeed we have, and very nice they are, too.'

Katrina agreed with him silently; they dined and danced each evening, sometimes at the hotel but once or twice at hotels a little way from the city's heart—Prestonfield House, which she liked very much, and the Inn at Cramond, where they dined in an oak-beamed room, close to the harbour.

It was on their last day in Edinburgh that she asked him, a little diffidently, if she might attend his lecture.

Raf looked taken aback. 'My dear girl, whatever for? You'll be bored to tears in half an hour. You'll enjoy yourself far more doing some last minute shopping.'

She had agreed with him quietly and then gone out and spent a good deal of money in a reckless fashion on shoes which she didn't really want and a silk trouser suit which she was sure she would never wear. And when Raf asked her at lunch time what she had done with herself, she told him, not mincing her words.

'You told me to go shopping, so I did. I bought some wildly expensive shoes that don't go with anything I've got, and I bought a trouser suit—blue silk with flowers all over it. I can't think when I shall ever wear it.'

'Why, at home in the evenings, I hope, to cheer me up when I come home tired.' He was smiling a little and it annoyed her.

'I didn't think of that,' she told him. 'I bought it because I just wanted to waste your money; it would have cost you far less to have let me come to the lecture.'

His eyebrows shot up. 'Ah, here we have it. Am I to understand that each time I—er—decline your company you will rush to the nearest shop and buy unsuitable clothes out of revenge?'

'Yes, if you like to put it that way—and I dare say,' added Katrina with some heat, 'my wardrobe will be bulging in no time at all!'

He spoke smoothly. 'Are we having our first quarrel, Katrina?'

She looked at him bewildered. 'No—no, of course not. I snapped, and I'm sorry. It's just that I want to know more about you.' She didn't see the sudden gleam in his eyes. When he spoke his voice was kind and understanding.

'Then you will attend one of my lectures in Holland—that's a promise.' He hesitated. 'I'm sorry, but there's a final short meeting this evening—here at the hotel. Will you be all right on your own? It's at eight o'clock and should last no more than an hour.'

Katrina had promised herself that she would make him a good wife. She said brightly: 'Of course. Shall we dine early or would you rather wait until it's over.'

'Oh, before I think, don't you?' He glanced at his watch. 'I must be off—I should be back around four o'clock. We might stroll round the shops.'

'That would be nice.' She smiled him a cheerful goodbye.

They had tea out, at a dear little teashop, all chintz and flowered china, a fitting background for the paper-thin sandwiches and cakes oozing cream.

'I ought not to,' said Katrina, having a second one.

Raf eyed her across the little table. 'Why not? You don't have to starve yourself on my account. I like curves.'

She went a delicate pink. 'Yes, well…' she began uncertainly. 'It's bad enough being so big, I don't want to get fat.'

'You won't. Besides, we shall walk miles during the next few days, you'll need all your strength.'

They wandered down Princes Street, pausing to look at everything which caught their eye, and when Katrina remarked on a handbag, displayed in unpriced state on a length of velvet, Raf walked her into the shop and bought it for her, and when she thanked him and protested at his extravagance he remarked easily: 'Ah, but it's an investment—it will last you a lifetime.'

She brightened. 'So it will—I'll take great care of it, Raf.'

They left Edinburgh early the next morning, taking the motorway to Stirling and then on to Callender and so to Lochearnhead, where they stopped for lunch. They were in the Highlands now, and Katrina was loving every moment of it. 'I could go on for ever like this,' she told Raf. 'There couldn't be anything more beautiful.'

'Wait until you see the Isle of Eriska,' he promised her.

They reached it, not having hurried, in the late afternoon, crossing the small bridge from the mainland and following the track, bordered by shrubs and conifers, to the hotel.

It didn't look in the least like a hotel; it had battlements and turrets and gabled windows and inside it was warmly welcoming with tea in the library, where a log fire burned cheerfully and the proprietor joined them briefly, chatting about Raf's last visit, recommending some walks they might like to take and then handing them over to a pleasant girl who took them to their rooms and offered to unpack for them—an offer Katrina declined, happily putting her things away and then going through to Raf's room to see if she could do the same for him.

They dined off fresh salmon, a magnificent salad and apricot brulée, and joined the other guests for coffee in the library, and presently tired with her exciting day, Katrina said goodnight and went upstairs. Raf had gone to the door with her and stood a moment holding it open.

'We might try one of those walks tomorrow,' he suggested. 'I'm told the weather is going to be good for a few days at least.'

'Lovely. It's beautiful here, Raf—what a marvellous holiday!'

His mouth twitched faintly as he wished her goodnight.

They had five days there, and every one better than the last, thought Katrina on their last evening. They had walked, picnicked and fished, sat in the sun and read and talked unendingly. At last she felt that she was beginning to know Raf, although there was a great deal more she still had to discover. That they were happy in each other's company was a solid fact upon which she felt they would build a happy marriage, and they were friends, too, and if once or twice she found herself wishing that Raf behaved rather more like a husband and less like a lifelong friend, she didn't allow herself to brood over it. After all, he had to get to know her too.

They left quite early in the morning, the Bentley making light work of the run down to Carlisle and then on to Crooklands where they spent the night; a country inn in Cumbria, peaceful and quiet but near enough to the M6 to make it a matter of minutes before they joined it.

It was a long trip to London and Raf kept to the motorway, leaving it for a short time south of Stoke-on-Trent so that they might have coffee and then again, once they were through Birmingham, for lunch at a village inn before getting on to the M1.

'Tired?' he wanted to know, as he started the car. 'It's only just over a hundred miles now.'

Katrina wasn't tired, the Bentley was too comfortable and Raf drove superbly, so that she was completely relaxed. 'You didn't say where we're spending the night,' she observed. 'In London?'

'Yes, at my flat.'

She turned to look at him. 'Your flat? Have you got one there?'

'Well, I come over to England quite a lot, you know.'

'No, I didn't', said Katrina a shade tartly. 'I supposed you stayed with Uncle Ben.'

'It quite slipped my mind.' Raf sounded so meek that she looked at him again, but he was staring ahead, his profile as calm as always. 'It's only small, but I have a good housekeeper. She'll have a meal ready for us.'

She longed to ask more questions, but although she was his wife she didn't want to be nosey, and after all, they would be there within an hour or so and she would see for herself.

It took some time to penetrate London: the rush hour was just starting and it was a little while before she saw that Raf was working his way towards Hyde Park Corner and then turned north of Piccadilly into one of the quiet streets there, to stop at last before a town house of some size with an important porch and flower boxes at the windows.

Inside it was cool and very quiet, with a door on either side of the wide hall, but Raf ignored them and went up the staircase between them, taking her with him. On the landing he took out a key and opened one of the doors and ushered her inside, and she realised at once that his idea of small was hardly hers. The hall was narrow, it was true, thickly carpeted and pleasantly lighted; it led to a sitting-room of a size and height which she described to herself as vast, although charmingly furnished, but before she could say a word an elderly woman joined them to be greeted by the professor with: 'Ah, Mrs Thomas, Katrina, my dear, this is Mrs Thomas, our housekeeper. I expect you'd like to see your room first, wouldn't you? There'll be time for a drink before dinner.'

Katrina went with Mrs Thomas, still not having uttered a word, feeling at a disadvantage. He could have told her about the flat; they'd been married almost two weeks and heaven knew they'd had plenty of time to talk. She tidied herself in the charming room she had been taken to and hurried back to the sitting-room.

'You could have told me,' she said crossly, and when he asked mildly: 'Told you what my dear?' snapped: 'About this flat, of course.'

He said casually: 'It didn't seem important to me—to you, either.'

'Yes, but don't you see? It's—it's like having secrets...'

He came across the room and took her hands in his. 'Kate, if I have any secrets from you, they're harmless ones. After all, if we had had a long engagement, you wouldn't have discovered all there was to know about me in a couple of weeks, would you?'

She saw that this was a reasonable remark. 'Well, no. I'm sorry if I made a fuss.'

He gave her back her hands and walked away from her to a sofa table holding a tray of drinks. 'And now what will you drink?'

So they weren't to talk about it any more, she thought; perhaps it was early days for them to be quite—she was at a loss for a word.

The dinner was excellent, served in a much smaller room, elegantly furnished, and after an hour's gentle conversation, mostly on the part of Raf, Katrina went to bed. Her teeth clenched on the numerous questions she was dying to ask. Was the flat rented? she wondered, and did Mrs Thomas live there all the time? Wasn't that rather extravagant when Raf only came to London every so often? She thought uneasily of the Bentley and his handmade shoes and silk shirts and beautifully tailored clothes—perhaps he was rich, not just comfortably off but really rich, in which case why couldn't he have said so? Or was he waiting for her to ask him outright? Sleepy though she was, she began trying out various ways of putting the question. Should she baldly ask: 'Are you rich, Raf?' or put it more politely: 'I suppose you've got a lot of money?' or even try a round-about way: 'Are you sure you can afford to run a Bentley?' None of them sounded right; she gave up and went to sleep.

CHAPTER SIX

RAF HAD AN appointment at Benedict's in the morning and it had been arranged that he should drive Katrina to Aunt Lucy's house and join her there for lunch, bringing Uncle Ben with him. Katrina, left on her own with Aunt Lucy, drank coffee, answered a great many questions and gave a detailed account of their stay in Scotland.

'A pity you haven't been able to see your dear mother,' commented her companion, 'but of course, Raf is a busy man. Did you like his partners, dear?'

Katrina said that she did, their wives too, 'And his best man—I thought his wife was a dear—I hope we'll see something of each other in Holland.'

Aunt Lucy murmured comfortably and went on to discuss the wedding at some length. She was still explaining, rather vaguely, why she had chosen a grey outfit for the occasion when the men came in and Katrina found herself with Uncle Ben, listening to his pithy account of his morning rounds. 'There was this terrible Staff Nurse—Adams, I think she's called, queening it round the place—she didn't seem very popular. It needs you there to get them into line, Kate...'

'Over my dead body,' observed Raf without heat, and Uncle Ben laughed and added:

'I keep forgetting that you two are married.' He looked at Katrina. 'You enjoyed Scotland, Raf tells me.'

Katrina plunged into her second time round account of their holiday, and it lasted nicely through drinks and the first part of lunch. The second part was largely taken up with a discussion between the two men as to the exact date of a seminar they both wished to attend.

'Well, if it's to be in Birmingham,' said Uncle Ben, finally, 'you can bring Kate over with you.' He beamed at them both. 'You're going on the Harwich night boat, I suppose?'

They went back to the flat later, and Katrina busied herself repacking her case with the things the housekeeper had washed and pressed for her. She had another case too, of clothes she hadn't needed to take to Scotland; she disposed of those in her neat fashion, and enquired of Raf if she should do the same for him, but it seemed that Mrs Thomas had already done that, so there was nothing more for her to do but sit quietly. Raf had gone to his study down the hall, saying in the nicest possible way that he didn't want to be disturbed; she leafed through a pile of magazines and tried not to get agitated at the thought of going to a new house in another country. Supposing she hated it, supposing they found they couldn't get on together, supposing… She called a halt; she was a grown woman, used to dealing with emergencies, difficult people, running a ward successfully and surely not so poor-spirited that she couldn't make a success of their marriage. After all, she had gone into it with her eyes open and with a mind clear of infatuation. She reviewed the number of her friends and acquaintances who had married for love on the spur of the moment and come a cropper. Well, she had married on the spur of the moment, too, but in full possession of her senses, thank heaven, and as for Raf, she couldn't imagine him anything but placid; even when he was annoying her, he was calm about it.

They left London in the early evening, dined on the way to Harwich and went on board just before the ferry was due to sail. Katrina, inspecting her cabin, was impressed by its comfort although she wasn't sure if she was going to sleep soundly, but a brisk walk round the deck with Raf and a drink in the bar made her change her mind; besides, she had to be up early in the morning and look her best. She got into her narrow bed and closed her eyes determinedly and was asleep within minutes.

In the early morning light, the Hoek van Holland looked very like Harwich, only the people around her were speaking another language, even Raf, who switched from one language to the other without effort.

Sitting beside him in the Bentley, she was suddenly shaken by doubts again, and turned a bewildered face to his, to be instantly reassured by his understanding smile and a firm hand on her own two, lying tense in her lap.

'We'll soon be home, my dear,' he said placidly, and everything was normal once more.

He took the road to Den Haag, turning away from that city on its southern outskirts and taking a lesser road to join the motorway to Leiden, but before they reached the first of its houses, Raf turned away from the road again on to a narrow sandy road which led them within minutes to a small village. After the rush of traffic on the motorway barely a mile away, the rural quiet was pleasant and when Raf slowed and stopped outside the village café and she looked questioningly at him, he said: 'I thought a cup of coffee...no tea, I'm afraid, but the coffee's good.'

The narrow street was empty of people, it was still so early and there was nothing to break the stillness except the birds. 'Oh, a cuckoo!' exclaimed Katrina. 'It's...'

'And after April, when May follows,' interrupted Raf. 'That's almost the first thing we said to each other.'

'Yes—I didn't think...that is, I would never have guessed that by May we would be married, would you?'

He didn't answer her, but she didn't notice because a jolly old man had opened the café door and called something.

'He's telling us that the coffee is ready and waiting,' said Raf, and ushered her inside.

They went back on to the motorway presently, allowing Katrina only a glimpse of Leiden on their left, but as they reached the last houses of the small city Raf left the motorway for a minor road and this in its turn became a narrow country lane. 'We're almost there,' he told her. 'If you look to your left you'll see Warmond and in the other direction is Rijpwetering, large villages both of them. The water ahead of us is the Kager Plassen, there's a good deal of sailing in the summer and if it freezes hard enough, skating in the winter.'

Katrina stared round her. The country was flat and gentle; water meadows with cattle standing quietly. They were on a dyke road now, with a narrow canal on either side and a mile ahead she could see the lake quite clearly, ringed with shrubs and clusters of trees. 'It's nice,' she said. 'Do you know, I've not thought much about your home—you said it was in the country, but I hadn't pictured it in my mind. Is there a village?'

'In the trees close to the lake—a very small one, but there's a shop and a church and a school for the small children—the others go to Warmond.'

'You live in the village?'

She wondered why he hesitated. 'On the fringe.'

The village came into view a moment later, a cluster of neat cottages with a church, much too large for them, in the centre of an open grassed square. There were several people about now, and they smiled and nodded at Raf, who lifted a hand in greeting as he slowed the car round the church. Katrina, looking about her, tried to decide which house was his. There were two or three villas in between the cottages, but none of them really looked like a doctor's house; besides, he had said he lived on the edge of the village. The road straightened out on the other side of the square with tall trees on either side of it and thick shrubs behind which she glimpsed high old-fashioned iron railings. And round the bend there were high wrought iron gates, opening on to a sanded drive and at the end of it, a house.

'This isn't...' began Katrina, eyeing its solid white plastered walls and high shuttered windows with utter surprise. 'It can't be...'

'Yes, it is.'

She looked again; it wasn't of great architectural beauty, perhaps, but it looked just right, standing as it did with trees in a semicircle behind it and a formal garden in front. Its steep roof was grey-slated and every window gleamed in the morning sun. She counted them; there were twenty of them, and up in the roof there were small shuttered windows, the shutters painted red and white and green, each of them crowned with a kind of tiled frill. 'You should have told me,' she muttered.

'Are you disappointed, Kate?'

'Disappointed? Of course not!' Her voice rose a little. 'It's beautiful, but it's so enormous—I didn't know—I'll make a mess of it, being your wife and living in a place like this,' she added, quite worked up by now, 'and I suppose you're stinking rich as well!'

Raf stopped the car and turned to look at her. 'Now you see why I didn't tell you, my dear. You would have shied away like a startled pony, gone to the Gulf and probably become a dedicated spinster. There is no possible reason for you to worry about making—er—a mess of living here, you will be welcomed and liked by everyone.' He sounded matter-of-fact and a little amused. 'And I am stinking rich!'

'Oh,' said Katrina, 'I'm sorry, I shouldn't have said that—it's none of my business...'

He gave a crack of laughter. 'It is, you know—you'll have to learn all the business of the estate so that if I'm away for any reason, you can carry on.'

'But it's all Dutch!' She was horrified.

'You'll learn very quickly—Caspel speaks a little English,

so does the *dominee* in the village and the schoolteacher. And Nanny, of course.'

'You make it sound so easy!'

'And you, my dear, are making a great fuss about nothing.' He spoke pleasantly, but she blushed scarlet.

'I'll not make a fuss again, I promise you,' she told him in a wooden voice.

She would have liked to burst into tears, boxed his ears and then been soothed to calmness again; as it was she took a deep breath and remarked in an over-bright voice: 'How very pretty it is—I expect the garden runs down to the lake on that side?'

'Yes, there is a boat-house there and a small landing stage.' Nothing in his voice gave her a clue as to what he was thinking. He was going to be impossible to quarrel with, she thought pettishly, and then pulled herself up sharply. This was no way in which to begin life in her new home; she would do everything to conform to Raf's idea of a good wife. And the first thing was to accept everything without question, learn the language, and learn to run his home as he wanted it.

He started the car again and drove the last hundred yards or so to where Caspel was standing by the open door.

And not just Caspel. As she walked up the steps beside Raf, Katrina saw several other people standing beside him. Raf greeted them and then introduced her; Caspel, his wife Berthe, Wibrich and Jildou, the two young maids, Franz the gardener, and someone called Mevrouw Boot, whose position in the household was rather vague. Nanny was in her room and after a welcoming speech from Caspel on behalf of the others, and which she couldn't understand anyway, Katrina was taken to see her.

The hall they were standing in was large and square, with heavy side tables and several large chairs. There were portraits on its white walls and an enormous chandelier overhead. Katrina would have liked time to examine it, but Raf had a hand on her arm, leading her down a short passage at the back of the hall, to the side of the curving staircase.

Nanny, being old, lived on the ground floor. 'She suffers from arthritis,' explained Raf, 'but hates to be shut away, and here she gets visited by anyone who happens to be passing.'

He knocked on a door at the end of the passage and went in, taking Katrina with him.

The room was a surprise, it was so very English, with cretonne covers on the chairs, and matching curtains at the window, a table in the centre with an old-fashioned serge cloth on it and a great many shelves and little tables, all crammed with photos and china ornaments—the kind of ornaments friends are prone to give when they've been on holiday. And in the middle of this sat Nanny, small and bony and bent. But she had a sweet face and bright blue eyes, as guileless as a child's.

Raf hugged her gently and kissed her. 'Well, Nanny, here she is—my wife, Katrina,' he had gone back to take her hand, 'I hope that you and Nanny will be friends, just as she and I have been friends.'

Katrina put out a hand. 'May I call you Nanny?' she asked. 'I'm so glad you're here, I don't know anything about Holland and I'll be so happy to have your help and advice.'

Nanny pushed her glasses up her nose. 'Freely given, Baroness. You just come along and talk to Nanny whenever you want to. You're a bonny girl, too—just right for Master Raf. We'll have a nice little chat one day soon.'

Outside the door, Katrina said: 'What a darling old lady, and she looks so happy and content—those poor hands, all knotted up.'

'Not so old either—seventy-three, but she's suffered a good deal. She was away from my home when they came for my parents, and when she found out what had happened and that the Caspels were already on the way to my grandparents, she decided to follow. Only she was caught on the way—she would have been sent to a prison camp, but it just so happened that some official or other was taken ill and she knew what to do for him. They let her stay alive then, working in the hospital half starved and sleeping in a damp cellar. I can just remember the fuss I made because she had disappeared from my world too. Once the war was over my grandfather set about finding her; it took a long time.'

'And has she been with you ever since?'

'Of course, and will stay.'

He looked a little grim, so she didn't say any more, only agreed pleasantly when he suggested that she might like to see her room.

Berthe took her upstairs, moving slowly because she was on the stout side, which gave Katrina time to look around her. The stairs swept up one side of the hall to curve into a gallery above. They walked along one side of it to the front of the house and Berthe opened a pair of doors in the centre of the wide corridor. The room was quite beautiful, with a high ceiling covered with intricate plaster work and deeply carpeted in a thick cream pile. The bed had a mahogany headboard inlaid with a marquetry of flowers and fruit in woods of all colours; its spread of cream silk had a pattern of blue birds and pale pink roses and was quilted, matching the curtains at the high, wide windows. There was a sofa table in one corner with a triple mirror on it and a tallboy, its bowed front covered with the same marquetry as on the bed. The chairs were covered in a pale blue velvet and the walls were hung with striped cream silk with groups of small flower paintings hung here and there, the whole lighted by rose-tinted lamps.

Katrina drew a long breath. It was the loveliest room she had ever seen, and it seemed that it was to be hers.

Berthe, watching her, smiled and nodded and crossed the room to open a door in the opposite wall; a bathroom, blue and white, with a thickly carpeted floor and glass shelves stacked with blue and white towels. There would be blue soap, thought Katrina, and went to look. There was.

There was no sign of her luggage; she would unpack later. She smiled dismissal of Berthe and went to sit before the mirror, noticing for the first time that the table was gleaming with silver—brushes and comb, mirror and small silver and cut glass bowls. She picked up the brush, plain silver, initialled in the centre. Her eyes widened. Coincidence, of course, but the initials were hers.

She tidied her hair, did things to her face, and went downstairs to find Raf waiting for her in the hall.

'The luggage will be taken up while we lunch,' he told her, 'and someone will unpack for you. I hope you like your room?'

'It's beautiful,' she assured him, 'quite the most beautiful I've ever seen.'

He turned away. 'The things on the dressing table are a wedding present, the pearls have been in the family for a long time. I wanted to give you something I had chosen myself.'

She hurried across the tiled floor. 'Raf, they're absolutely lovely—thank you very much. When I saw then I wondered...' she smiled rather shyly. 'I thought perhaps they were your mother's and by some coincidence we had the same initials.'

'She had a Friese name, Jikkemien; she was christened Jacomina, but it was quickly changed to the Friese form.'

'And very pretty it sounds, although I like Jacomina, too. Was your father called Raf?'

'Yes, and his father before him—a Dutch custom, fast dying out.' He smiled at her. 'There would be old Raf and young Raf; very confusing.'

'But nice to keep the name in the family.' She looked up and saw his eyes upon her and looked away quickly; probably he thought that she was being a bit sloppy and sentimental. 'I heard a dog barking while I was upstairs,' she observed brightly.

He seemed content to change the conversation. 'That is Boots—a black labrador. I have another dog, too—a Corgi called Vondel.'

'But I thought he was a Dutch poet...'

'So he was—I found Vondel in Vondel Park, tied to a tree: he was a very small puppy.'

'Oh, how beastly; I'm glad you found him—and Boots? Don't tell me you found him too?'

Raf laughed. 'Well, yes—lying in the doorway of a chemist's shop in Den Haag.' He took her arm. 'Come and meet them.'

After the initial surprise it seemed to Katrina that she had lived all her life in Huis Tellerinck. For one thing she was accepted at once, smoothly integrated into the house, helped enormously by Caspel and Berthe, who unobtrusively showed her the routine of the household, indicated which tasks she might be expected to do; the flowers, the morning visit to the roomy kitchen, the inspecting of the linen cupboards, and what was most important, Raf's likes and dislikes. He wasn't a fussy man, she discovered, but he liked things just so and the house was geared so that when he returned home in the evening or late afternoon, it welcomed him with its gleaming furniture, its bowls of flowers and its air of peace.

And Katrina welcomed him too, surprised to find herself looking forward to his return each day, taking trouble with her hair and face and putting on a pretty dress, learning within a few days to read his face as he came in and being careful to adjust her own mood to his. It was on the fourth evening after they were back that she asked him a little diffidently if he never came home for lunch. She had been occupied with some needlework and hadn't given him more than a quick glance, so that she missed the long thoughtful look he gave her and his slow smile.

'Would you like me to come home during the day?' he asked her.

Katrina bit off her thread. 'Oh, yes—I'm not lonely, you know, but it would be nice to hear how your day's going, only I can quite see that you might not want to; it must be convenient to lunch in hospital or—or wherever you are.'

His smile widened. 'Where else might I be, Kate?'

She was untangling a skein of silk. 'Well, I don't know that, do I? Friends—perhaps...' A vivid picture of him lunching with some beautiful girl-friend from his bachelor days made her scowl.

'I always found it a little lonely lunching alone at home,' he said placidly, 'and I thought that you might prefer to have the day to yourself...'

'Raf, whatever made you think that? I'd love you to come to lunch at home, only I thought, when you stayed away the first day, that it was what you always did and I didn't want to interfere...'

'I can't imagine that you would do that.' His calm voice soothed her ruffled feelings. 'I said before we married, Kate, that we would have to get to know each other.'

'Yes, I know.' She wanted to add that there was a great deal she would like to know about him: his friends, if he had ever been engaged or been in love...he must have been. She wondered where the girl was now—perhaps more than one girl. She pricked her finger and sucked it; it would be nice when they were sufficiently old friends to be able to ask these things. She didn't quite have the courage to question him now; he would treat her to a bland look and one of those smiles which meant that he was amused at her.

She said into the small silence: 'So you'll come for lunch when you can?'

'Certainly—I should manage to get home about half past twelve; if I can't I'll telephone.'

She wasn't sure what made her ask: 'And breakfast? I expect you like to be alone then?'

'I've had my breakfast alone for a number of years, Katrina,' he reminded her, 'and rather early—half past seven most mornings, but if you don't mind getting up early, I should enjoy your company very much. I can't guarantee to have much conversation, though.'

She felt out of all proportion delighted. 'Oh, I'll not say a word unless you actually speak,' she promised him.

And it worked very well; it was surprising what a difference it made to her days too, even though Raf, for the most part, sat frowning over papers or his post while he ate his breakfast she didn't mind, for every so often he would look up and smile and once or twice he remarked on something she was wearing. But lunchtime was even better; she took care to have a drink waiting for him and lunch ready to be served, carefully thought out food which he could eat quickly if he had an early appointment after lunch. At the end of ten days, Katrina had found her feet. She had inspected the house from cellar to attics and loved every inch of it, she had wrestled with menus and grocery lists under the kindly eye of Berthe, she had even picked up a few useful words in Dutch, although it still sounded nonsense in her ears.

She hadn't done badly, she considered, sitting in the drawing-room waiting for Raf to come home from his day's work. She had put on one of her new dresses, a pale green crepe very simply made and she knew she looked nice, sitting there, her embroidery in her hand, the evening sun lighting up the charming room with its beautiful furnishings. She hoped she was proving to be the kind of wife Raf had wanted. There was a lot to learn still, of course, and the rather frightening prospect of meeting his friends—if they were half as nice as Britannia and Jake then everything would be all right.

An invitation had come that very morning from Britannia, asking them to go over to dinner in four days' time; she would show it to Raf when he got in. He agreed at once, but she hadn't expected otherwise. Moreover, he suggested that since he was free for the weekend, they should go to the sea the next day. 'You've not had much fun, have you?' he observed, 'and I've had my nose to the grindstone and my hand on the scalpel... we'll go to Katwijk-aan-Zee, early in the morning, and drive up the coast. At least, we'll park the car just outside the town and walk along the dunes and take the road again when we're tired. Would you like that?'

'Oh, yes—lovely.' A whole day with him, a day in which to

learn a lot more about him, his work, for instance, and his life before they married, and his friends…especially did she want to know about them. She wasn't jealous, she told herself as she got ready for bed, that would be absurd, only curious. She would wear the blue and white striped separates, then if it got really warm she could leave the jacket in the car…and her new sandals, the ones with the low heels.

They left the house really early after breakfast and they were there, standing on the wide golden sands within half an hour. There was no one around, the sea stretched away to the horizon, a choppy sea, whipped up by the sharp wind which was freshening at every minute. It took Katrina's hair and tossed it round her shoulders, and when she would have stopped and tied it back, Raf said, 'No, leave it,' and flung an arm round her shoulders as they walked. He was relaxed, placid almost to the point of sleepiness, and in his linen slacks and cotton sweater, he looked younger. They didn't bother to talk a great deal, odds and ends of gossip, arrangements for going to Britannia's home during the week, tentative suggestions for a small dinner party, the possibility of Katrina visiting the hospital in Leiden. They were discussing this when Raf paused and then stopped dead.

'There's a yacht…' he said thoughtfully. 'I noticed it just now—whoever is sailing it is a fool, the red flag's out and he must have seen it—there's quite a current along here, and the wind is pretty strong.' He stared out to sea, his arm still round Katrina. 'He's coming much too far inshore.'

As he spoke the yacht veered into the wind, racing off on a different course, only to veer again, sailing towards them again.

'Perhaps there's no one on board,' suggested Katrina, and then cried: 'Oh, but there is—there's a child crying!'

A small screaming voice could be faintly heard as the yacht drew nearer and Raf said unhurriedly: 'I'll just take a look—no one in their senses would sail like that, and if they're in trouble why don't they shout?'

He took off his shoes and walked into the water without another word. The yacht was going out to sea again and Katrina reckoned that it was roughly a quarter of a mile away. Raf was swimming now and without further ado she took off her own sandals and went in after him; she was a strong swimmer and could do a mile in a calm sea. But this sea was decidedly choppy and before she had gone very far she encountered the current Raf had mentioned. Just for a moment she felt panicky, but the yacht was coming inshore once more and wasn't all that way off now. She rested briefly and went on, swimming strongly. She hadn't seen Raf get on board, but he would be there by now.

She reached the yacht presently and heaved herself untidily on to its deck, streaming water and shivering a little now. The child was still screaming and she got to her feet, staggering a little with the boat's movement, and went below. There was a child all right, three years old perhaps, a boy, bawling his small head off, sitting in one of the bunks watching Raf bending over someone lying on the floor of the cabin.

'Hullo,' said Katrina, not knowing what else to say and Raf looked up.

'Ah, just the girl I wanted—concussion and a smashed leg. Find a broom handle or something, will you, and bring them here and then hang on while I get it splinted. I think I've got it in alignment.'

His voice was almost casual and he evinced no surprise at her appearance; she said nothing at all, but began her search. There was a child's wooden spade lying in one corner, and in the kitchen a handled mop; Katrina couldn't get the mop off, so she took it to Raf and offered it with the spade. 'Splendid,' he said, 'and something to tie them with.'

She took the sopping tie belt from her waist—the dress was ruined anyway—sawed it in half with a knife from the galley and handed the pieces to him.

'Very nice, my dear. Now come here and take the leg from me—you'll need to keep a good pull on it.'

She applied traction while he applied the makeshift splints.

They looked peculiar when he had finished, but at least they were doing their work.

'Leave him here,' said Raf, and put a cushion gently under the unconscious head. 'I'm going up to see if I can sail this boat in, you see if you can pacify that unhappy scrap.'

He had gone, leaving her to cover the man with a blanket and then take the weeping child on her wet knee and soothe it to quietness, wondering as she did so what would have happened if she hadn't been able to swim. The boy quietened presently and quite soon worn out with fright, dropped off to sleep. Katrina tucked him up securely, took a look at the man, and took his pulse, and went on deck.

Raf was at the rudder, working the boat slowly towards the shore. 'We're going to end up at Noordwijk,' he told her cheerfully. 'Everything quiet below?'

'The little boy's asleep, the man's still unconscious—his pulse isn't too bad—just over a hundred, but it's quite steady.'

He nodded, smiling at her. 'You're wet—it suits you.' He looked away from her, towards the nearing shore.

Was this all she was to get for her pains? She had, after all, swum a considerable distance in a nasty sea, ruined a dress, produced splints when asked for them, suffered aching arms from pulling on a large and very heavy broken leg, soothed a child when she badly needed soothing herself…he was indifferent to her, arrogant, thoughtless, overbearing. Katrina, normally a mild-tempered girl, was possessed of a splendid rage, then in a twinkling of an eye it had evaporated because at that precise moment she became aware that she was head over heels in love with Raf.

She stood, the blue and white stripes clinging wetly to her magnificent figure, quite unaware of the delightful picture she made, and gaped at him. There was an awful lot she wanted to say, but her thoughts were in such a jumble she was unable to put them into words—and anyway, she wasn't given the chance.

Raf looked at her for a long moment, his eyes almost hidden beneath their lids and then he looked away again.

'We're almost in,' he said in a detached voice. 'Would you like to go below and rouse the little one?'

She didn't trust herself to speak, and as she slipped and slithered into the cabin she thanked heaven that she had held her tongue.

CHAPTER SEVEN

RAF HAD MADE for a jetty in the small harbour at the end of the little town. He tied up neatly, shouted to a man lounging over the rail watching them and went below.

Katrina had had a few minutes in which to pull herself together; she felt lightheaded, excited and at the same time ready to burst into tears; all the same, she had roused the little boy and was tidying him up as Raf joined them. He said something to the child and went to look at the man. 'I've asked someone to fetch the police and an ambulance,' he said. 'The quicker this man's in hospital the better.'

For something to say, Katrina asked: 'Is there a hospital here?'

'They'll take him to Leiden, it's the nearest, if he goes to Katwijk he'll probably be transferred. I wonder who he is?'

'The child?' She was quick to understand him.

'The police will look after him while they get his mother.' He lifted his head. 'Here they are now.'

The police car and the ambulance arrived together and it was at once apparent that the police and the ambulance men knew Raf. They listened to his brief story and then the ambulance men, under his guidance, re-splintered the injured man's leg and carried him to the ambulance while the police carred a surprisingly docile little boy to their car. They knew the man, they even knew where he lived, and a message was sent out to fetch the mother while the senior officer wrote in his notebook.

Katrina sat on the side of the jetty, watching. To all intents and purposes, she might not have been there. The men had saluted her politely and then ignored her and beyond a brief: 'OK, Kate?' Raf hadn't looked at her once. A pity I'm not a dainty mouse of a creature, prone to fainting, she thought crossly as she watched her husband dealing with the situation in his calm way. And finally, when the constable had at last put his notebook away, Raf said something to him which sent him to the car's radio. Only then did Raf join her.

'They'll drive us back to Katwijk,' he told her. 'We'll have to go back home and change our clothes.' Just for a moment he rested a hand on her knee. 'I'm sorry, my dear, but there really wasn't anything else to do.'

Her heart was thudding away, making such a noise in her ears that she was afraid that he would hear it too. 'Of course not—thank heaven you were there to help.'

'And thank heaven you were there, Kate. I don't know why, but I took it for granted that you would be right beside me, and you were.'

The pink crept into her cheeks. She was going to say something about wives helping their husbands; she might even have said more than that, only he answered her with a prosaic: 'I expect it's your hospital training—once a nurse, always a nurse.'

She looked away, choking back a strong desire to burst into tears. After a moment she said in a brittle voice: 'Here's another police car coming.'

Raf was watching her; he looked thoughtful and at the same time pleased, as he said casually: 'A pity about the dress, it was charming. We'll have to get another one exactly like it.' He got to his feet and pulled her to hers. 'I'll just have a final word—jump in, my dear.'

A moment later he got in beside the driver and turned to

speak to her. 'The mother's on the way. I'll telephone the hospital when we get home.'

Her lovely day was ruined. Raf would spend the rest of it in Leiden, she supposed. Well, she would get into a swimsuit and spend an hour in the swimming pool behind the house, then she would go for a good long walk and try and sort things out. There was a lot of thinking to be done. The thought uppermost in her head at the moment was that Raf must never guess that she loved him. She would have to go on just as always, good friends and companions with each other, and she learning to be a good hostess and manager of his home, and perhaps in time he would learn to love her too—just a little would do…

The journey was a brief one, they transferred themselves into the Bentley and drove home, not talking much. Once there, Raf explained what had happened with no fuss and in the shortest space of time and then bore Katrina off to the library where Caspel followed them with hot coffee and brandy.

'But we'll ruin the furniture,' objected Katrina. 'I'm still damp and so are you.'

But her objections were ignored; she was given coffee to drink with a stiff dose of brandy in it and then told to go and have a hot bath and put on dry clothing. 'Half an hour,' suggested Raf 'We'll drive into Leiden and if I have to stay more than a few minutes at the hospital you shall go on a tour of inspection, but I don't expect to. We'll go back to Noordwijk for lunch, there's a rather nice hotel, Huis ter Duin, overlooking the sea. We can drive on up the coast as far as Alkmaar and come home along the inner road.'

Katrina was on her feet, starting for the door. 'Oh, that sounds heavenly!' She suddenly remembered that she must stay friendly and nothing more. 'That's if you would like to too.'

Raf had reached the door and was opening it for her. 'I can think of nothing I'd like better,' he told her. He stood looking down at her, smiling a little. 'Quite an adventure, wasn't it? It didn't upset you?'

'Me, upset? No, of course not—it all happened rather quickly, didn't it?'

'Indeed, yes—one rarely has forewarning of the more dramatic moments in life. Have you found that too?'

A bit near the bone; in another moment she would be telling him that she had had a dramatic moment when she discovered that she loved him, not two hours ago. She muttered 'Yes' as she passed him, but he put out a leisurely arm and held her for a moment, to kiss her on her surprised mouth.

She didn't allow herself to think while she bathed and dressed. There wasn't much time, anyway, for she had her hair to wash too. She had no leisure to fuss over it, leaving it, very clean and shining to swing round her shoulders. It was a pity about the blue and white striped dress, she thought as she got into a cotton voile, lemon and lime stripes on a white ground, and just in case it should turn chilly, she snatched up a white blazer before she ran downstairs.

The rest of the day was heaven. Raf spent no more than fifteen minutes at the hospital, looking at X-rays, giving instructions for his latest patient's treatment, and while he was away, Katrina was entertained by the Directrice, a rather formidable lady whose excellent command of English allowed her to ask polite but searching questions of her while she drank a cup of coffee she didn't want.

Raf, coming to fetch her, smiled very faintly at Katrina's determined but polite efforts not to answer any questions at all, and stood listening with a bland face while she thanked the Directrice and said that yes, she'd love to come again and spend an hour or two over a cup of coffee.

He had told her about the man as they drove to Noordwijk and she had been careful to be interested and ask all the right questions and laugh with him over their early morning swim. And at the hotel they lunched off lobster and an enormous salad while Katrina took care to keep their talk light and impersonal, and still keeping it up as he drove north, leaving the main road each time a signpost showed the way to the sea and another small seaside resort, with the wide sands stretching as far as the eye could see and the sea, very blue beyond. The freak wind had died down and it was pleasantly warm, and at Egmont-aan-zee they stopped to eat ices on the terrace of the lido restaurant and then, as a concession to Katrina being English, had tea as well. They were on the coast road now and stayed on it until they reached Alkmaar, where they lingered to look at the magnificent church and inspect the cheese market and the Waagge-bouw, where the cheeses were weighed each Friday market day, and since it was a sight not to be missed, they waited until the hour struck so that she might see the gilded figures prancing round the clock tower.

Katrina, very much taken by all that she had seen, chatted lightheartedly on as Raf drove across the polderland to join the main road running down to Amsterdam; the Ijsselmeer on one side of them, the neat farms on the other, but he didn't go to Amsterdam, skirting it and taking the motorway between the city and Haarlem until they reached Leiden. The quiet little country road at the end of their journey was quite empty of traffic and serene under the clear early evening sky. The house looked just as serene as they went up the drive and Katrina said suddenly after a quite long silence:

'What a beautiful home you have, Raf. How you must love coming back to it each time you go away.'

He sounded very casual. 'Yes, and more so than ever before.'

She kept her own voice casual too. 'Oh, why's that?'

She was disappointed at his: 'I'm getting older, I feel the need to put down roots.'

They were getting out of the car when he stopped to add: 'It's your home too, Kate.'

She hadn't known what she had hoped he would say, so she couldn't quite understand why she should feel so forlorn. She told herself angrily that she would have to do better than that if their future was to be the pleasant calm life Raf so obviously expected, and—patience, she cautioned herself; even though he may never love you he may grow fond of you over the months—years, perhaps.

They went indoors and presently had dinner together and then spent an hour or so playing the record player. Katrina, curled up in a deep chair, listened to Sibelius's Symphony Number 5, and Prokofiev's *Romeo and Juliet*, found them almost more than she could bear; that kind of music always made her feel sentimental, full of longing for something or other, sad… She watched Raf, sitting in his chair, legs stretched out before him, smoking a cigar with his eyes shut, or at least she wasn't quite sure if they were shut or not.

They weren't, for presently he asked: 'Why are you looking at me, Kate?'

She became flustered at once. 'Oh, was I? Not looking at you, really, just—just…'

'I happened to be in the way?' he suggested placidly.

'Yes, that's it.' She rushed on feverishly: 'What a lovely day it's been—thank you for taking me, Raf.' And when he smiled: 'I had no idea that the coast was so lovely—all that sand—and Alkmaar, and—and the farms…' She paused, aware that she was babbling.

'I'm glad you enjoyed it. It hardly began well. We must do better next time.'

Her heart lifted at the prospect of a next time. 'Do you often get days free or weekends?'

'When I can fit them in—I haven't bothered too much about them, but now that you are here we must get around a little. I've neglected my friends. When do we go to Britannia's?'

'On Tuesday evening.'

'I've a couple of lectures next week—Amsterdam and Utrecht, would you like to come along? You could have a look round and meet me for lunch—they're both in the morning.'

Katrina tried not to sound eager. 'I'd like that very much, but you promised that I might go to one of your lectures.'

'Did I? Won't you be bored? I lecture in Dutch, you know.'

'I don't mind—it's just that I'd like to be there, if you wouldn't mind.'

'Why should I mind?' He didn't sound very interested and she hurried on, afraid that she was being too interested. 'I'd like to start learning Dutch—is there someone I could go to? Nanny's been a dear, telling me what I ought to say and when, but I expect I ought to have a teacher.'

'I'll see about someone—would you like them to come here or will you drive in to Leiden?'

She had used the Mini, parked in the big garage between the Bentley and a Saab Turbo Jet, and she had been surprised how quickly she had adjusted to the right-hand traffic. 'I'll drive in.'

Raf nodded. 'Good, I must see about getting you a car of your own.'

Katrina looked shocked. 'Raf, there are three in the garage!'

'But none of them yours, Kate.' He smiled at her. 'Would you like a Mini?'

'Oh, yes, please, but really I could use the one that's already there...'

He frowned faintly. 'There's one thing we've never talked about in depth,' he observed, 'money. We must make time to go and see my solicitor so that you understand about the estate and so forth—there are several trusts...'

Katrina said weakly: 'Oh, are there?' and wondered just what a trust was. She had often wondered, but had never bothered to find out—why should she? She wasn't likely to be involved in one, but now it seemed that she was.

'I'll give you a bird's eye view, though. I have a lot of money, Kate. A good deal of it I inherited, the rest I earn. I own this house, the house in Friesland and a charming little cottage just outside Den Haag—oh, and the flat in London, of course.'

'Good grief!' exclaimed Katrina. 'You must be rich. Not a millionaire?'

'Well, yes.' He had never looked so bland.

'Why didn't you tell me?'

'You asked me that once before and I answered you. Do you find it so very disturbing, Katrina?'

She was honest enough to admit that no, she didn't. 'In fact, it must be quite fun, though I expect you're quite used to it, Raf; you can have everything you want.'

He was examining his shoes carefully. 'Not quite everything,' he said softly. She thought she knew what he meant.

'Oh, Raf, I'm sorry—of course not. No mother and father and brothers and sisters, and no cousins or aunts and uncles— how could I be so thoughtless?' She got up and went to stand in front of him. 'I'm not the same, but I'll do my best to fill the gap, at least, a little of it. And you can share my family.'

He stood up and took her hands in his. 'What a dear girl you are, Kate.' He was staring down at her and she waited for him to go on talking, but after a moment he dropped her hands and said in a quite different voice: 'I've some telephoning to do.'

She was quick to answer her cue. 'And I'm off to bed—all that fresh air,' she spoke gaily, 'and I promised Berthe that I'd inspect the jams and pickles in the morning.'

And what that has to do with it, I don't know, she thought as she went upstairs, but I had to say something, didn't I?

They left at about six o'clock on the Tuesday to drive to Jake and Britannia's home in the Veluwe, near the little town of Hoenderloo.

Katrina, wishing to look her best, had chosen to wear a crêpe-de-chine dress, a honey-coloured pattern on a creamy background; the pearls went very nicely with it. Raf, waiting for her in the drawing-room, gave her a long look. 'Very nice,' he remarked, 'but why have you put your hair up?'

She was surprised. 'Well, I only had it down the other day because I hadn't time to do anything with it. Don't you like it?'

'It's delightful, but a pity to tuck it all away. Are you ready? It's roughly two hours' driving, but I daresay we shall do it in less time.'

It was well within that time as they came in sight of their friends' house. It was a charming gabled place, surrounded by groups of trees and encircled by a wall, and before they reached it its great door was opened and Jake came out to meet them.

Sitting sleepily by Raf some four hours later, on the way home again, Katrina thought about the evening. It had been delightful. Britannia had come hurrying out to meet them in the hall, a square apartment, tiled underfoot and with a branched staircase at the far end, embraced her with every sign of pleasure, kissed Raf and then led the way into the drawing-room. 'We'll have a drink,' she had declared, 'and then we'll go up and see the twins before dinner.'

Katrina had been surprised at their smallness. They looked like two dolls in their cots, but despite their lack of size, they had inherited their parents' good looks. She had been quite unaware of the wistful expression on her face as she bent over them, nor had she seen Raf's eyes watching her so intently.

The evening had been lighthearted and the dinner delicious, Katrina and Britannia, leaving the men to their port, went back to the drawing-room to chat cosily about babies, the beauty of their houses, their splendid husbands, the clothes they intended to buy and then back to babies. The men joined them presently and they had talked about everything under the sun and when they at last got up to go, Katrina did so with regret, mitigated by the prospect of seeing her new friends again very soon; Raf had suggested a dinner party; it was time, he said, that they had a few friends for the evening and if Jake and Britannia came it would make things easier for Katrina. When he had mentioned it earlier, she had supposed that they would invite two or three of his closest friends, now it seemed there were to be twelve at least. She thought about it on their way home, already worrying about the food and what she should wear and not knowing anyone except the Lutingh van Thiens, but she was too sleepy to talk to Raf about it; tomorrow she would get a list of who was to come and when, from him, and he would have to tell her about them.

It was the evening before she saw him again. When she got down to breakfast the next morning it was to find that he had left an hour earlier; something urgent at the hospital in Leiden, Caspel thought, and he would try to telephone her during the day. It was a brief call when it came, though, merely saying that he was sorry that he had to leave early and that she wasn't to expect him to lunch and that he was bringing an old friend back for dinner.

Katrina went happily enough through her day. There were the dogs to walk, the flowers to do, a visit to the village shop to buy postcards, letters to write and a long afternoon in the pool and then sunbathing.

She went to change in good time. Raf usually came home about six o'clock, but perhaps this evening he would be early. She put on a cream silk jersey dress, sleeveless and simply cut. It was a splendid foil for the pearls and her ring and because Raf had said that he liked it she washed her hair and allowed it to hang loose, curling on to her shoulders. Pleased with her appearance and feeling happy, she went downstairs to wait in the drawing-room, and because she was impatient to see Raf she went to sit in one of the wide window seats, so that she could get a good look at him as he came into the house.

She was looking forward to the evening; she had arranged a delightful dinner, seen to it that the table in the dining-room shone with glass and silver and the white napery Raf liked and made sure that the drinks were ready on the sofa table in the drawing-room: Raf would see to the wine when he got in. She let out a little sigh of pure pleasure as the Bentley came up the drive and got to her feet.

Raf got out and rather to her surprise went round to the other door and opened it. A woman got out; a slim willowy creature, not too tall and beautifully proportioned, her golden hair dressed in an elaborate coil on the top of her head, laughing up at Raf as she stood beside him. She was wearing black, some soft stuff which floated about her and made her more willowy than ever. Katrina stood staring, temper rising slowly. Raf could have warned her that it was a woman guest, given her some idea whom she was to expect. But he hadn't, had he? Her head was already full of half-formed thoughts. Was this the reason why he hadn't come home to lunch or for that matter why he had left so early that morning? Katrina left the window and turned a welcoming, smiling face in the general direction of the door.

They came in together, smiling and at ease and obviously liking each other's company, and Katrina crossed the room to meet them, her lovely eyes glittering with anger. She turned a cheek to receive Raf's casual kiss, said: 'Hullo, dear,' a little too loudly and turned to their guest.

Older than I am, she thought, but loaded with charm, and held out a hand.

'Katrina, this is Beyke. We've known each other for most of our lives, but don't often meet.' He turned to Beyke. 'Two years, is it? How time flies! She landed at Schipol at seven o'clock this morning and the least I could do was meet her.'

Beyke laughed gently and he added: 'This is Katrina, my wife.'

The two shook hands and murmured the usual nothings. She wasn't pretty, Katrina decided, but very, very attractive, which was worse. Her clothes were beautiful too and she made Katrina feel too large. In Raf's company she tended to forget her size because he was much bigger, anyway; and why hadn't he said that he was going to collect a friend from the airport? Why all the secrecy? Her thoughts, behind a smiling face, were hidden, but Raf, watching her, knowing her better than she knew herself, smiled faintly.

'Beyke is just back from the States,' he observed. 'You've been away too long, Beyke.'

Beyke shot him a look which seemed to imply that she agreed

with him, and Katrina looked away, feeling murderous. The woman had a lovely voice too, soft and very beguiling...

'Well, that's obvious, isn't it? Marrying behind my back, Raf!' She added something in Dutch and Raf laughed and then as though he had just remembered that Katrina was there too and didn't understand Dutch, translated:

'Beyke says that if she had known I was going to settle down at last, she would have come back sooner.'

Katrina, wishing to crown her husband with something suitably heavy, achieved a bright smile. 'Well, it's nice that you're here now, Beyke—I hope we'll see a lot of you,' she added mendaciously. And while Raf was getting their drinks: 'You must have such a lot to talk about. Your English is marvellous, but do speak Dutch if you'd rather, I don't mind in the least.'

'You see what a paragon I have married,' observed Raf blandly as he came back with the drinks. 'She not only swims like a fish, runs the house like clockwork, shares my breakfast each day, but likes all my friends on sight. Was ever a man so blessed?'

Beyke said something softly in Dutch and he grinned and said: 'I shan't translate that, Katrina, you might get a swelled head.'

She smiled her empty smile again, wishing with all her heart that she could understand Dutch.

They went into dinner presently and Katrina laid herself out to be a superb hostess; it was amazing what one could do when one tried, she mused, listening with every sign of interest to Beyke's witty talk. She might be the wrong side of thirty, but that was the only thing against her, and probably that didn't matter. Raf was thirty-eight...

She poured coffee in the drawing-room with a steady hand and then strolled round the garden with their guest while Raf made some telephone calls. They had reached the swimming pool when Beyke observed: 'I had every intention of marrying Raf, but I was offered this terrific job in the States and I went—

you see, he seemed to be a more or less confirmed bachelor and I thought he would be safe to leave for a couple of years.' She made a delightful face and then laughed. 'That'll teach me, won't it? All of a sudden he sees you and here I am, left high and dry.' She sighed so heavily that Katrina felt bound to ask: 'Do you love him very much?'

Beyke shrugged. 'Oh, I'll get over it. It is a pity that he is a man who takes marriage seriously, otherwise I might prise him loose.' She gave a trill of laughter and Katrina, at boiling point, laughed too, and then asked in what she hoped was a pleasant friendly voice: 'Where do you live? Raf didn't say…'

'Oh, Den Haag—I have a flat there. You must come and see it—Raf knows the way. I haven't got a car yet, such a nuisance, but Raf will drive me back.'

The Hague was no distance away, so why was Raf two hours getting there and back? Katrina lay in bed, fuming until she heard the car go past under her windows. She heard Raf come upstairs presently and go to his room, but she had no desire to sleep, instead she bunched her pillows comfortably and sat back, going over the evening. She hoped she had behaved exactly as Raf would expect. Of course, he hadn't heard all the things that wretched woman had said and his manner towards her had been that of an old friend; Katrina wasn't sure if he had been pleased when she had invited Beyke to join them at the dinner party. She had explained that she didn't know who was coming yet, but she was sure that Beyke would like to meet the other guests, and when she had urged Raf to persuade Beyke to come, he had done so with every appearance of pleasure. All the same, she fancied he had been taken by surprise.

She greeted him briskly the next morning, her cheerful voice belying her pale face, bearing all the obvious hallmarks of no sleep, and as soon as she had sat down with her coffee she cut ruthlessly into the reading of his letters.

'Raf, may I have a list of guests for the dinner party? You did suggest the end of next week and they ought to be invited…'

He lifted his eyes from the letter in his hand. 'I'll let you have it at lunchtime, Katrina. Will that do? They're all old friends and won't mind short notice. We'll have to find a man for Beyke...'

Katrina scalded her tongue on her coffee and put the cup down carefully.

'Find a man for me,' she suggested, keeping her voice down with an effort, 'then Beyke can have you all to herself.'

She picked up the cup again and burnt her tongue once more, for Raf had put his letter down and was looking at her so ferociously that she felt the stirrings of fright. 'And what exactly do you mean by that, Katrina?' His voice was so suave and soft that just for a moment she imagined she had dreamed the fierce look on his face. But only for a moment; he was looking at her steadily, and just for once he had lifted his lids so that she saw how bright blue his eyes were and how cold.

She said weakly: 'Well, nothing really—just...'

'A joke?' he prompted. 'If it was, it was in very poor taste.' He picked up his letters and got up. 'I've just remembered, I shan't be able to come home to lunch after all, and I'll probably be late home this evening.'

Katrina could think of nothing to say; she'd been a fool, but she mustn't make it worse. Silence is golden and all that, and on no account cry.

She said to his retreating back: 'It's the lecture tomorrow morning, Raf, the one you said I might attend.'

He had stopped and turned round to look at her. 'I hadn't forgotten. Amsterdam at nine o'clock at the Binnenhof. We shall have to leave here at eight-fifteen, it's only thirty miles, but we may get held up by the traffic.'

'I'll be ready,' said Katrina meekly.

She spent a wretched day doing all the things she had learned to enjoy and now found quite pointless—taking dogs for a walk, arranging a bowl of flowers in the hall, talking to Berthe about food, swimming in the pool, a little gossip with Nanny... The day was endless, and at eight o'clock with no sign of Raf and no message either, she sat down to a solitary dinner. It was a couple of hours later, as she sat pretending to read a book, that Raf came home. He looked tired and out of temper, greeted her abruptly and went to get himself a drink.

'Would you like dinner?' asked Katrina. 'I asked Berthe…'

'Thanks, no—I had a sandwich. You've had a pleasant day?' He had flung himself into his chair.

'Me?' She reflected on its arid wasted hours. 'Oh, very nice, thank you. You've been busy?'

'Yes,' he fished in his pocket. 'Here is the list of people I thought we might invite—I got my secretary to type it out. She's enclosed an invitation written in Dutch for you to copy.'

'How thoughtful of her. Will you thank her from me?'

He said suddenly: 'Katrina, about last night—Beyke…'

She wouldn't be able to bear it; the creature had been on her mind all day and now he wanted to talk about her. It was too much. She got up so suddenly that her book slipped on to the floor. 'Raf, I'm so sorry, but I've got a headache—I would have gone to bed early, but I wanted to be here when you got home, just in case there was anything you needed.'

He said blandly: 'But, my dear, there are servants enough to see to my needs.' He stood up. 'Don't let me keep you a moment longer. Will your headache prevent you coming in the morning?'

She beat a retreat to the door and found him beside her. 'No—no, it will be perfectly all right by then. Goodnight, Raf.'

He didn't wish her goodnight, but said something in Dutch, and it sounded as though he were laughing.

CHAPTER EIGHT

KATRINA WAS EARLY for breakfast, but Raf was already there. He wished her good morning and hoped that her headache had gone and she told him mendaciously that yes, thank you, it had, reflecting the while that one's sins always found one out; on the previous evening she had pleaded a headache she hadn't got and now she had a bad one, the result of a poor night's sleep, and had to deny it. Several cups of coffee helped and once they were in the car, driving through the clear sunny morning, she began to feel better. It was going to be a warm day, and she was wearing the striped voile again, high-heeled sandals and their matching shoulder bag. Getting into the car, she had a moment of doubt; Raf was wearing a grey suit, silk shirt and a richly subdued tie; he looked every inch the professor, self-assured, a little aloof, brilliantly clever but modest about it…

'Should I have worn a hat and gloves and sensible shoes?' Katrina glanced down at the green kid sandals.

Raf's eyebrows rose. 'I can't think why, but do tell me.'

'Well, you—you look just as a professor of surgery should look—clever and confident and beautifully tailored…'

He said smoothly and without conceit; 'But I am all those things. Why the hat?'

'Well, wouldn't it be more suitable—the professor's wife, you know.'

'Am I to understand that I am a suitable partner for a female in a hat and sensible shoes? Is my image so staid and middle-aged?'

'Of course not!' She hurried to answer him: she had made it sound all wrong, somehow. 'You're neither and you must know it. What I meant was that I'm not elegant enough for you.' Despite herself the words came tumbling out. 'It ought to be someone like—like Beyke.'

'Beyke seems to be rather on your mind.' His voice was silky.

'Well, she's not, but she's on yours...you wanted to talk about her yesterday evening, but I don't want to know.' She added snappily: 'And I have no wish to quarrel.'

Raf said very evenly: 'In any case, I'm afraid we haven't the time—I don't like to keep the students waiting.'

If Katrina could have had her way, she would have sat silent for the whole journey, but Raf talked as though nothing had happened, making himself agreeable with remote courtesy; as though she were someone he didn't know very well and didn't like over-much, to be tolerated because good manners demanded it.

She sat almost silent, wishing that the day could begin again, that she could unsay the things she had said. And they had been doing so well, too, even before she discovered that she loved him, she had felt happy and content, determined to make a success of things. She wondered miserably if she hadn't fallen in love with him, if she would have minded Beyke turning up. Probably not. The least she could have done would have been to listen to what he had had to say on the previous evening, now he knew her for a jealous ill-tempered creature; probably he already felt resentful that he was tied to her for the rest of his life. After all, he had never said that he loved her; indeed, he had told her that he believed he was past falling in love— the first fine rapture of love, he had said, and he had included her, too. But that wasn't to say that he hadn't been in love, still loved—but for some reason couldn't marry and decided on the second best; an amiable wife, a comfortable relationship with someone who was just as glad as he was to settle for deep liking and compatibility…

She would have to get back on to their original friendly footing and bury her love so deep that no one would ever know it. And she would start now, this very minute. 'Raf—' she began in a small voice.

She was cut short by his cheerful: 'Here we are, and there is my registrar waiting for us—he'll look after you.'

She was being ushered out of the car before she could utter another word, introduced to Hans Penningvester, told that she would be picked up after the lecture, and left, to watch Raf disappear through a side door of the hospital.

The registrar was very careful of her, rather as though she were made of something easily broken. He escorted her to a seat in the middle of the lecture hall, but not too near the front, and in his turn introduced her to an older man, whose name she didn't catch.

'I'm so sorry,' she said as she settled in her chair, 'I didn't get your name,' she added apologetically: 'I find Dutch names a bit difficult.'

'Klaus von Donegan, Baroness.' He had a nice rugged face and a friendly smile. 'Do you want me to translate the Professor's lecture, or can you understand Dutch?'

'Almost nothing, but it doesn't matter, I just wanted to come along and hear him.' She gave him a brilliant smile and turned to the registrar. 'May I call you Hans?' she asked him. 'And what happens after the lecture?'

'I take you to the consultants' room, Baroness, and the Professor will be there.'

'Oh, good. He hasn't got any rounds or anything?'

He looked a little surprised and she realised that very likely a husband would tell his wife things like that, so she added: 'I expect the Professor told me, but I've forgotten.'

'No rounds today, but I believe he has private patients this afternoon.'

Katrina looked as though she already knew that. 'Oh, yes, I'd forgotten that too.'

She took a quick look round the hall. It was full now and even as she looked everyone got to their feet and Raf walked on to the platform. She almost burst with pride and love at the sight of him; she wanted to wave and shout that she was there, watching him, but instead she sat primly down with everyone else in the respectful hush.

The registrar whispered that he was lecturing on end-to-end anastomosis and then sat back, his arms folded across his chest, the picture of attention. Katrina stole a glance at her neighbour on her other side. He was obviously going to give whatever Raf had to say, his closest attention too. Katrina put on a listening face and hoped she looked intelligent.

But it was wonderful just listening to Raf's voice delivering whatever he was delivering in succinct phrases and in tones which compelled attention. She listened to every word and didn't understand one of them.

And afterwards, when the clapping had ceased and Raf had gone, she allowed herself to be led through the hospital to the consultants' room, where she, outwardly composed and never mind how she felt inside, was introduced to half a dozen learned-looking gentlemen who chatted to her in a dignified way, hoped that they would have the pleasure of meeting her frequently, and expressed the opinion that Raf was a lucky devil. A pity Raf didn't seem to feel that he was.

He came to her presently and said in just the right tone: 'We should be going, my dear—I'm afraid that I have several patients to see this afternoon, and if we're going to lunch...'

Katrina made her adieux gracefully and finding Hans and

Klaus van Donegan in the entrance hall, stopped to thank them for their services before getting into the Bentley with Raf.

'I enjoyed the lecture,' she told him brightly as the car swept through the gateway into the main street.

He gave her a sidelong glance. 'Indeed? Without understanding a word of it? Or did Klaus translate?'

'No—I just enjoyed it.'

He didn't pursue the matter further. 'We'll have to have a quick lunch, I'm afraid,' he observed. 'I've several patients to see this afternoon. I'm sorry.'

He didn't sound particularly sorry, but she murmured that of course it didn't matter in the least, and would he rather drive straight back home, or better still, could she not catch a train or something.

He didn't bother to explain the trains to her, merely said that no, he had ample time to drive her back provided they didn't linger over their meal.

He took her to Dikker en Thijs—the Café du Centre—where they had a delicious and very expensive lunch, served with unobtrusive speed, and then he drove her back, talking pleasantly to her in much the same manner, she guessed, in which he would talk to someone he hadn't met before and wasn't likely to meet again. Peeping at his grave, handsome profile, she decided that she was a little in awe of him. He did everything so well; gave lectures as though he had delivered them since the day he was born, drove a car through thick traffic without so much as tutting once, and despite his prominence in the profession, was almost retiring in his manner. It was the same when they ate out, she had discovered. Waiters rushed to serve him and when he ordered wine, he knew exactly what he wanted; its name, the year...and she, who had been reared in a household where the sherry, though a good one, was seldom produced unless there were guests and where claret was served with Sunday lunch and never on a weekday, found it nothing less than miraculous that he should have such a vast knowledge of wines and never boast about it. But he didn't boast, not about anything; if she hadn't attended his lecture that morning she would never have known how important he was.

He didn't get out of the car when they arrived at the house, merely leant across her and opened the door and told her that he hoped to be home about tea time, so she thanked him quickly and went indoors at once as the car rushed back down the drive. Probably, if Raf hadn't said that he would take her to lunch in Amsterdam, he would have brought her home sooner, but he wasn't a man to break his word, even for a lunch which neither of them had really enjoyed.

Katrina felt restless once she was indoors; she took the dogs for a run in the garden and then went to tap on Nanny's door. They had become friends already. Katrina went each day to see how the old lady did, taking care to go during the day, for she knew that Raf spent half an hour with Nanny each evening and he had never suggested that they might go together. Nanny was glad to see her. Her rooms opened on to the verandah which in turn led down easy steps to the garden, and today she was sitting in an upright chair at the top of the steps. Katrina perched on the top of them and began to tell the old lady about the lecture.

Nanny nodded her old head in a satisfied way, 'I always knew he'd be a success,' she said breathily. 'Such a clever boy, he was, and so determined. He used to say to me: "Nanny, am I like my papa?" and I'd say, "Yes, just the same," and he'd be happy.' Nanny cast a quick glance at Katrina. 'I was getting to think he'd never marry, my dear.'

'Well, he must have had lots of opportunities,' Katrina hurried on in what she hoped was a casual manner. 'That lady who came last evening—Beyke something or other—she's so beautiful, Nanny, and an old friend. If I were a man, I'm sure I'd fall for her.'

'Oh, well, I suppose he did, just for a little while,' said Nanny comfortably, 'years ago, that was, and he soon came round, though I'm not so sure about her. Scheming baggage,' Nanny added darkly.

'But I expect she's married since then,' suggested Katrina cunningly.

'That she had, and divorced the poor man—someone from foreign parts, it was. That's why she's back in Holland—looking for someone else to get her claws into, I've no doubt. A good thing Master Raf's married, he'd be just what she's looking for—handsome and successful and more money than he knows what to do with.' She smiled at Katrina. 'He couldn't have chosen a better wife—such a handsome pair you make. I'll be too old to nanny the children, of course, but it'll be nice to see them. And that reminds me, ma'am, I've a niece, not so young, neither, been a nanny until she married and now she's widowed and none of her own—she'd do very well for you once you get started on a family.'

Katrina looked away across the garden with its wide lawns and beds bright with flowers—splendid garden for children, safe and wide, and the swimming pool enclosed with a good stoutgate to keep little people out. Little Rafs with their father's good looks and powerful noses, plaguing the lives out of their little sisters...

'That would be ideal, Nanny,' she said dreamily.

'A family,' went on Nanny, happily. 'There's nothing like it—Master Raf never had the chance, poor boy, all the more reason to make up for it with children of his own.' She shot a quick glance at Katrina. 'Of course, you've only been married for a few weeks.'

Katrina turned to face the old lady and achieved a smile. 'Yes—it seems longer than that, somehow. Nanny, you're tired, aren't you? Shall I help you indoors and ring for tea?'

She had tea with Nanny, listening to her talking about Raf when he was a very little boy and how good he had been to her after the war when she had been traced at last. Katrina listened to every word while at the back of her mind she was rehearsing what she would say to Raf when he got home.

But she had no chance to utter any of her carefully planned speeches. Raf didn't come home, instead there was a message to say that he had gone to Utrecht to see an urgent case and would she not wait dinner for him. So she ate alone and then went to read a book until it grew so late that she was forced to go to bed. Caspel, wishing her goodnight, assured her that he would remain up for another hour and if the Professor wasn't back by then, he would see that a tray with suitable refreshments was left out. But long after the old man went to bed, Katrina lay awake. It was the early hours of the morning before she heard Raf's quiet tread on the stairs. Only then did she allow herself to go to sleep.

She tried, during the next couple of days, to talk to Raf. She wanted to apologise for the things she had said about Beyke, she wanted to tell him that she hadn't meant to vex him, that she hoped that they could resume their easygoing relationship and forget all about it, and she wanted to say, too, that she had no intention of prying into things that were no concern of hers. Which wasn't quite true, but anything to penetrate the placid politeness with which he now treated her.

He gave her no chance, and she was no match for him either. He had the ability, she discovered, of being able to avoid talking about something in such a way that there was no getting round it. She didn't even know if he was annoyed with her, but of one thing she was sure: he had put a barrier between them.

Everyone who had been invited to dinner had accepted. Katrina, anxious to have everything perfect, spent a good deal of time with Berthe with Caspel translating for them both, discussing the all-important question of food. She settled for consommé Madrilène, salmon cutlets Mornay, crown roast of lamb with saffron rice and then, since strawberries were to be had, a meringue gateau, topped with lashings of cream. And this being settled to her satisfaction, she spent the rest of the morning arranging the flowers for the dining-room; a great Delft bowl full of pink roses on a side table and a smaller silver rose bowl cunningly heaped with honeysuckle, lilies of the valley, roses in various shades of pink and pale coloured stocks, spiced with rosemary and sprigs of mint. It looked charming and smelled delicious. The heavy candelabrum, in the baroque style and fashioned in silver-gilt, had been polished to perfection by Caspel, as had the table silver, and Katrina, mindful of Raf's preference for white linen, had searched the great linen cupboard until she found a damask cloth and matching napkins, and then, her heart in her mouth in case something was smashed, decided on using the Weesp porcelain dinner service, preserved intact since the end of the eighteenth century. Caspel, helping her to sort out what was needed, told her that it hadn't been used for some time—special occasions, he said, weddings and christenings and so on.

'Well,' said Katrina a shade defiantly, 'I consider this is an important occasion—our first dinner party! And Caspel, don't let anyone wash the dishes, will you? When everyone's gone, I'll come down to the kitchens and do them. You can dry, if you like, but I'll take the responsibility.'

'But, Baroness, you must not...' began Caspel.

'No one need know,' she told him bracingly.

She went to dress in good time. Raf, who should have been home about five o'clock, hadn't yet returned, nor had he telephoned. Katrina pondered the advisability of telephoning the hospital and decided against it; it smacked of fussing, something which she knew he couldn't tolerate. Something urgent would have held him up, but obviously he would be able to get home in time, otherwise he would surely have let her know.

She didn't allow herself to worry about it as she dressed. She had taken the Mini in to Leiden on the previous day and bought a new dress—piece of extravagance which took—for a brief period at any rate—her mind off her troubles. It was a misty blue and green pattern in organza with a wide neckline and long tight sleeves, and she knew that she looked good in it. And since it was an important occasion, to her at any rate, she wore the pearls and put her hair up into a chignon.

The house was quiet when she went downstairs and into the drawing-room. She sat down and picked up her needlework, wondering if a drink would help her to get rid of the apprehension she was feeling. She went over the dinner arrangements once more and found them quite perfect. She hadn't missed a single detail, of that she was quite sure, so the scary feeling must be something to do with Raf.

It was. She hadn't been sitting for more than five minutes when she heard the Bentley sweeping up the drive. She flung down her work and went to one of the windows, just in time to see Raf get out of the car and go round to open the door for his passenger. Katrina knew who it was before the door was fully opened—Beyke, looking glamorous in black chiffon and looking up at Raf as though she were sharing some delightful secret... Katrina ground her teeth and went back to her chair. She was stitching with apparent calm when the door opened and Raf and Beyke came in. The look of surprise she gave them was very well done, even though it didn't deceive Raf for one moment. He smiled at her gently, looking at her through half shut eyes. 'Hullo, my dear—I'm very late, but I really couldn't get away earlier—and since I was so delayed it seemed a good idea to fetch Beyke on the way.'

'Why, of course.' Katrina exchanged a social kiss with her guest. 'What a good idea. Do come and sit down—we'll have a drink while Raf's changing.'

Raf went to the sofa table. 'Whisky for you, Beyke? Sherry for you, Katrina?' He had a hand on the decanter when she said quickly:

'I'll have a whisky too, thank you, Raf.'

She never drank the stuff, but she needed a stiff drink. Raf, bringing them their glasses, hid a smile behind his placid face. 'I'll take mine with me,' he observed. 'I'll be fifteen minutes.'

It seemed like fifteen hours to Katrina, chatting brightly about clothes and the weather and Beyke's numerous men friends. 'None of them can equal Raf, of course,' she said carelessly, 'but I suppose I'll have to make do. Some of us have been planning a couple of weeks on the Riviera, and I suggested that you both might like to join us. Raf's got a couple of weeks free at the end of August—it shouldn't be too bad then, although the spring is the best time to go, don't you agree?'

'I wouldn't know. I've never been.'

Beyke's eyebrows rose. 'No? My dear, what can you have been doing with yourself all these years?'

'Working in London. I always went home for holidays, it made a nice change.'

'You poor dear!' The smile was a charming one and as cold as ice. 'Could I have another whisky?'

Katrina gave herself another one too. The first had gone to her head straight away, heaven alone knew what the second one would do—send her flat on her face, probably. Not that it would matter, she had no doubt that her companion would step into her shoes and play the hostess with grace and charm. She turned a slightly flushed face to her husband as he came into the room. 'Beyke's been telling me about this scheme for a holiday on the Riviera...'

If the whisky hadn't had such a peculiar effect upon her, she might have noticed the look of surprise, instantly gone, on his face, and if she had looked at their guest, she would have seen the sudden dismay on that lady's beautiful features. It was perhaps fortunate that the great door bell clanged at that moment and Raf went into the hall to meet the first of their guests.

Outwardly, the evening was a success. The dinner was excellent, and Katrina, still slightly woolly from the whisky, nevertheless played her part well. It was Britannia who came to sit with her for a few moments in the drawing-room after dinner, and whispered: 'Your eyes are glittering—are you in a rage?'

'Yes—oh, dear, does it show?'

'No, everyone is saying how lovely you are and what a marvellous hostess...' Britannia paused and went on in a much louder voice: 'It's such a lovely colour, Katrina—just right with your colouring. Where did you get it?'

One of the partners' wives had joined them, a pleasant little woman with not much to say for herself, but she had a sweet face and a complete lack of ill-nature. The three of them talked clothes until the men joined them.

Everyone began to leave about eleven o'clock, showing a flattering reluctance to do so. Britannia and Jake were getting into their car when Beyke swam into the hall, a filmy wrap over her dress. She stood on the steps between Raf and Katrina, watching them, and Jake, on the point of getting in, said: 'Would you like a lift? We can drop you off.'

Beyke tucked an arm into Raf's. 'How sweet of you, but Raf's taking me.'

Katrina didn't look, but stood smiling woodenly at Britannia, which was a pity, for if she had done so, she would have seen Raf gently remove Beyke's hand.

Raf didn't go back into the house. 'I'll get the car,' he said cheerfully, and walked off round the side of the house in the direction of the garage, leaving Katrina to make bright conversation until he returned, ushered Beyke into the seat beside him and with a casual salute, drove off.

Katrina went back into the house then, suppressing a desire to bolt the doors so that Raf wouldn't be able to get in when he got back. And when would that be? she wondered. She was halfway up the stairs when she remembered that she had promised to wash the Weesp china.

Caspel was waiting for her in the kitchen, and what was more, he had thoughtfully made a pot of tea for her. 'Caspel, you're an angel,' she told him. 'How did you know?'

'The Professor told me that you very much liked your tea, Baroness, and it seemed to me that a cup might refresh you.'

Katrina kicked off her slippers and drank two cups and then, wrapped in one of Berthe's aprons, started on the china, washing each piece with the utmost care and laying it on a thick cloth to drain. She was on the last few pieces when the kitchen door opened and Raf asked mildly: 'Now why are you doing that, Kate?'

She put down the plate in her hand very carefully. 'I wasn't sure if you would mind me using the Weesp dinner service,' she told him in a voice she strove to keep matter-of-fact, 'and it seemed only fair to wash it up myself, then if I smashed any of it, you could blame me.'

'Something I would never do, Kate. It was an inspiration to use it, the table looked delightful.' He strolled over to where Caspel stood, tea towel in hand, and took it from him. 'Caspel, go to bed, and thank you. I'll help the Baroness and if we smash anything, we can share the blame.'

Caspel wrung his elderly hands. 'It is not possible,' he began, 'that you should wash the dishes. It is not fitting...'

'It makes a nice change, Caspel—and thank Berthe for her splendid cooking, will you? Everything was delicious.' Raf picked up a small dish. 'Goodnight, Caspel.'

And, 'Goodnight, Caspel,' echoed Katrina. She washed the last plate, emptied the sinks, wiped them clean, and went over to the big scrubbed table and began to stack the porcelain carefully on to two trays, and while she did it she tried to think of something to say.

'If you go ahead and open the cabinet doors, I'll bring the trays up,' observed Raf pleasantly.

The cabinet was in one of the long wide corridors on the ground floor, a huge walnut piece, with bow-fronted glass doors. She had them open as Raf appeared with the first of the trays. It took them ten minutes to house the precious stuff and when Raf closed the door and locked it Katrina let out a sigh of relief. 'I've been on tenterhooks the whole evening,' she admitted, 'in case something got smashed.'

'Is that why you drank two whiskies before dinner?' asked Raf silkily.

She was too tired to think of a clever answer. It was ironic that now, when they were alone together, undisturbed, she found herself unable to say any of the things she would have liked to. She said merely: 'I was nervous—it was my first dinner party and I wanted it to be a success.' She found herself hoping that he would praise her and perhaps even say that her dress had been pretty.

'I can't imagine why it should have been anything else but a success.' He was leaning against the cabinet, his hands in his pockets, looking at her. 'You're a very capable girl and you have plenty of help.' He turned away. 'I think we had better go to bed, don't you?'

Katrina stayed where she was choked with rage. 'Yes, I do.' She took a breath. 'I'm surprised you're back so quickly.'

He had turned to look at her. 'I had no reason to loiter,' he said evenly.

She was beside herself, not really caring what she said now. 'No, I don't suppose you had, you had had plenty of time to tell Beyke how lovely she looked in that dress and how pretty her hair was...'

She took a step backwards because Raf was suddenly close to her, his hands on her shoulders. 'And is that what you want of me?' he asked. 'That I should tell you that you were the loveliest woman in the room? That none of them could hold a candle to you? That your hair shone like silk in the candlelight? And if I did, would you believe me?'

Katrina felt the tears prick her eyes. 'Raf, why didn't you tell me about Beyke?' And then seeing his face, bland once more: 'No, it doesn't matter.' She turned and ran down the corridor, out into the hall and up the stairs, into her room. Her slippers were still in the kitchen, but she hadn't given them a thought; indeed, she wasn't thinking at all, she was too unhappy.

CHAPTER NINE

KATRINA MIGHT BE UNHAPPY, but she wasn't a coward. She got up at the usual time and went down to breakfast, pale and heavy-eyed but quite in command of herself again.

Raf's good morning was pleasant. He looked exactly as he always did, calm and self-contained. He passed her the toast, remarked upon the splendour of the morning and went back to his letters. Only as he was gathering these together prepara-tory to leaving did he say: 'I find I have a day free this week. I thought we might go up to Friesland and I could show you the house at Waaxburen. I've some business to attend to there as well, but that shouldn't take too long.'

She was so surprised that she stammered a little. 'Oh—I'd like to go v-very much. I won't be in the way?'

She couldn't understand the look he gave her, questioning, amused and something else. 'No, Kate. Would directly after breakfast tomorrow suit you? We'll take the dogs with us, they enjoy the ride.'

Later that morning Katrina went along to see Nanny; the old lady would like to hear about the dinner party, what the women wore, what they ate. She recounted it all faithfully to Nanny and she sighed with pleasure. 'Master Raf, he's a good boy, always tells me everything, but he's no good with dresses and suchlike, not that he doesn't like to see women well dressed. Berthe told me that the evening was a great success and that you looked like a dream. You shouldn't have done the dishes, though, ma'am dear—baronesses shouldn't wash up.'

'Well, here's one that does. What's more, the Baron helped.'

Nanny's old eyes gleamed. 'Did he now? Well, I never did! That was after he took Mevrouw van Teule home, no doubt.'

'Yes.' Katrina didn't want to talk about that. Nothing would have been nicer than to have sat at Nanny's feet and poured out the whole story, but being a wife meant being loyal too. She said cheerfully: 'We're going to the house in Friesland tomorrow. Such a funny name—Waaxburen. Have you been there, Nanny?'

'Oh, yes, and very nice it is too, quite different from this house, of course and very countrified. Master Raf does a good bit of sailing in the summer; it's close to the sea.'

'And a farm too?' prompted Katrina, wanting to know more.

Nanny nodded. 'Friesian cows, sheep and those giant horses—percherons, as well as Friese *ruiters*, I think they're called. It's a big place—not a large farmhouse, but plenty of land. You'll like it there, ma'am dear.'

Perhaps, thought Katrina wistfully, she would have a chance to talk to Raf while they were there; peace and quiet, away from everyone. She couldn't tell him that she loved him, of course, but she could let him see that she really wanted to make their marriage work. Even if it meant accepting Beyke as a friend... She looked so fierce that Nanny asked her if she was feeling all right.

She did her best at lunch time, trying not to notice Raf's cool courtesy, chatting brightly about the farm and getting brief polite replies. He would be later home that evening, he told her as he went; he had private patients to see and she need not expect him before six o'clock. As an afterthought he asked her what she was doing that afternoon, and she was able to tell him with perfect truth that she was having tea with the partners' wives.

She drove herself in the Mini to Leiden, where they both

lived, and spent an hour or two drinking milkless tea and nibbling wafer thin sweet biscuits, listening to their friendly chatter. They were two nice young women, anxious to make her feel at home, laughingly correcting her Dutch when she tried out a sentence or two. She left them about five o'clock and since Raf wasn't coming home until six o'clock, she drove towards the sea and when she reached Noordwijk, parked the car and walked down to the beach.

It was a warm day, but the breeze was strong and she shivered a little as she watched the sun-spangled sea, dotted by sailing boats. It had been exciting, rescuing the injured man and the child. Raf seemed to have forgotten all about it and she had consoled herself by telephoning her mother and telling her the whole story. It had been nice to be praised a little and exclaimed over, just as Nanny, bless her heart, had done—all the same, Raf might have said something, not taken her for granted. Next time there was a crisis, she told herself, she would take care to faint or scream or do something else entirely feminine.

After a while she turned away from the sea, got back into the car, and drove home, to find Raf already there. He was with Franz, in front of the house, examining the lawns, but when he saw the Mini he came to meet her. 'I finished rather sooner than I expected,' he greeted her. 'I rang Greta's house, but she said that you had already left.' He didn't ask her where she'd been, but she heard the faint question all the same.

'I drove to Noordwijk and had a look at the sea. It was full of sailing boats, and sparkling in the sun…' Her voice died away. She wasn't looking at him, but remembering how she had climbed on board the yacht and seen him there, dripping water all over the place, not in the least surprised to see her, demanding splints…

'Rather different from our little adventure,' he observed placidly. 'Did I ever tell you how magnificent you were, Kate?'

She felt the tears crowding her throat. 'No, you told me I was wet.'

He glanced at her and saw her eyes bright with tears. 'That sounds a little inadequate.'

She had turned away from him. 'No, not in the least—it was quite true.' She had swallowed the tears now and went on: 'I'm going in—I promised Nanny I'd have a chat after tea.'

She didn't care if Raf believed her or not; it was an excuse to get away from him.

Perhaps it was a good thing that he was called out that evening halfway through dinner. An accident near Utrecht and the two victims had been taken to the hospital there, both needing expert surgery. As he left the table he said quietly: 'I'll try not to be late, my dear, but it sounds like a long business. Don't wait up.'

Katrina went to bed early. The great house seemed so empty without Raf. She wandered through the splendid rooms, loving them, wondering if she would ever feel as though she belonged there. In time, she supposed, if she could come to terms with her new life.

She had been asleep for some hours when she heard the car coming up the drive. It was almost three o'clock; Raf would be tired out and probably hungry. She got out of bed, put on a dressing gown and slippers and went silently downstairs to meet him as he opened the great front door.

'What's the matter?' he asked sharply. 'Are you ill, Katrina?'

She hesitated on the bottom step. 'No, I heard the car and I wondered if you wanted a hot drink and something to eat.'

He was already on his way across the hall, going to his study. 'I had something at the hospital. It was kind of you, but there was no need to come down. Go back to bed and finish your sleep.' He glanced at her briefly. 'Goodnight, Kate.'

She turned without a word and went back to her room, to sit up in bed and worry. There was something not right between them; she had offered such a small service and been thoroughly snubbed—very nicely, of course, but snubbed. And he had said before they married that he liked her—enjoyed her company, that they were compatible. They were nothing of the sort; she cried a little then and presently fell asleep, to wake heavy-eyed when her morning tea arrived.

But very little of her worries showed on her face when she went down to breakfast, thanks to make-up and a determination not to let Raf see that she was hurt. She wished him a serene good morning and took a good look at him. He might not have slept, but excepting for the tired lines of his face, no one would have guessed it. Fortified by a cup of hot coffee, she asked: 'Do you have to go back to Utrecht today, Raf?'

He shook his head. 'No, my registrar can deal with anything. Both the men who were injured stand a good chance of recovery.'

'Oh, good. What was wrong?'

He told her while they breakfasted and then gathered up his letters. 'I'll leave these for Juffrouw Kats to deal with. Can you be ready in ten minutes?'

She had taken the precaution of seeing Berthe the evening before, so that the meals for the day had been decided upon. 'Yes. If I could know roughly what time we'll be back, so that I can let Berthe know about dinner...'

'We'll dine at Waaxburen, that will give us more time there.'

The journey was just over a hundred miles and most of it on motorways, with a brief pause for coffee at Wieringerwerf, they were across the Afsluitdijk and tearing along the Friesland countryside well before noon. Raf had turned away from the main road at Franeker, going towards the coast now, through farmland, dotted by farmhouses, their barns built against their back walls, looming high above them. Presently he turned on to a narrow *dijk* road, which wound through two small villages and then disappeared into a belt of trees. The trees opened out presently, on to green fields, surrounded on all sides by more trees, and fenced by tall iron palings. Katrina could see the farmhouse now, standing well back within the protecting circle of trees. There were cattle in the fields surrounding it, and horses, but she lost sight of it all for a moment while Raf turned the car between two great stone pillars almost hidden by trees and shrubs. But on the other side she had a clear view again and she exclaimed with delight.

'Raf, it's beautiful, all those trees and the fields are so green. How you must love it!'

'I do. If I hadn't become a surgeon, I would have chosen to be a farmer.'

'But you like being a surgeon?'

'Oh, yes, I couldn't be anything else—it's in my blood, but I love this place.'

He had stopped the car before the front of the farmhouse and got out. As he opened Katrina's door, a man came out to meet them; a tall sturdy man with greying hair and the same aquiline features as Raf.

The two men shook hands and Raf turned to Katrina. 'My cousin Seles.' He smiled at the man. 'This is my wife, Katrina.'

'I'm so glad to meet you, Katrina.' He had a nice smile. 'I am a cousin, but not a close one, you understand—we are separated by many uncles and cousins, all, alas, dead.'

'But we bear the same name,' said Raf. 'He took Katrina's arm and led her indoors, into a square hall, panelled in wood, and a little on the dark side. It was furnished with an old cloak chest, a couple of high-backed chairs, and a wall table with a great deal of carving on it, the whole made cheerful by the copper bowls filled with flowers. The stairs were in one corner, uncarpeted and narrow, polished with age and beautifully carved too. There were three doors leading from the hall and the room they entered was obviously the sitting-room, a large, high-ceilinged room, running from the front of the house to the back and with windows at each end. It was most comfortably furnished with outsize chairs and sofas, covered in tapestry, a number of tables scattered around, shelves of books against one wall, and a variety of paintings on its plain whitewashed walls. There were flowers here too, and Raf said easily: 'I see that

Mieke is still as artistic as ever,' to be answered by the woman who had just joined them.

She was not young any more and not pretty, but she had lovely eyes and a sweet smile and she went straight to Katrina. 'You don't have to tell me who this is,' she said to Raf. 'I'd have known her from your description, only she's ten times prettier.' She took Katrina's hand. 'It's lovely to meet you—I'm Mieke, but you'll have guessed that.' She drew Katrina down on to a massive sofa as she spoke. 'Shall we have coffee first, then you two men can talk business and I'll show Katrina the house.'

The men didn't linger, but drank their coffee and left the two of them chatting happily. Mieke had spent several years in England and her English was fluent; they had a son there now, she told Katrina, at one of the agricultural colleges. 'Our other son is still at school, he intends to be a doctor,' she added. 'He'll go to Leiden, of course, and Pieter, the eldest, is going to farm in Groningen. Raf has a small farm there too—I expect you know that, he promised it to Pieter some years ago, good kind generous man that he is. This farm isn't ours, you see, it's Raf's, but we've lived here for years now and run it for him. He comes here a great deal and takes a great interest in it, but it's ours for our lifetime. Between us we've made a great success of it, I think. Come and see the house.'

There was a dining-room across the hall, furnished ponderously in the Beidermeier style but bright with chintz and flowers, and the kitchen, a large room with a great table in its centre, an Aga cooker and rows of copper pans against one of the walls. There was an old-fashioned dresser too, filled with rows of beautiful old plates and saucers, their matching cups hanging on little brass hooks. There was a door into the garden and another door which led straight into the barn, with its rows of spotless stalls and scrubbed floor. And upstairs there were a number of bedrooms, all furnished with taste and in great comfort, and still higher, up a tiny staircase like a ladder, was a loft running right across the house. There was a table at one end, a darts board on the wall, and a train set arranged on the floor, as well as several comfortable chairs, a TV set, a record player and a pile of skates, fishing rods and tennis rackets.

'This was—is—the boys' room. When they're home they come up here and make all the noise they like. I leave it like this because it'll do for your boys when they come up here to stay.' She twinkled at Katrina. 'A bit soon, I know, but here it is ready and waiting.'

Katrina smiled and nodded, thinking sadly that as far as she could see it would go on waiting. 'What's it like in the winter?' she asked, anxious to change the subject.

'Well, cold. We get a good deal of snow and there's usually a chance to skate for at least a few weeks, sometimes longer. Raf always comes just before Christmas, so you'll be able to see it for yourself. Only wear lots of woollies.'

They went back to the sitting room presently and the men joined them for drinks before lunch, a substantial meal of smoked eel, chicken casserole and fruit salad and cream. Katrina, who possessed a good appetite, found that she had none at all, probably because Raf, while treating her with his usual pleasant good manners, somehow contrived to make her feel like a stranger. Perhaps it was something she was imagining, though, for the other two laughed and talked as though she had been in the family for ages.

She wasn't alone with Raf for one single moment for the rest of the day; he was out and about all the afternoon, coming in briefly for a cup of tea and going off again to look at the horses. Katrina, listening to Mieke's cheerful voice, remembered that she had supposed she and Raf would be alone all day. Perhaps on the drive back...

They left about nine o'clock after a bountiful dinner and, in Katrina's case, a little bit too much to drink. It had made her feel pot-valiant and once they had waved their last goodbyes and the farm was out of sight she began: 'Raf, there are lots of things I want to say to you, and you must listen. I thought we'd be alone at the farm and I'd made up my mind...' She was suddenly overcome with sleep.

She woke up again as they were coming off the Afsluitdijk and turning on to the E10 going down to Amsterdam. 'Oh, where are we?' she wanted to know, her wits still woolly.

'Back in north Holland, just off the Dijk. You've been asleep for almost an hour.' Raf sounded amused.

'Oh, I'm sorry, I didn't mean to go to sleep—dinner was rather much and I had three glasses of claret.'

'You were saying before you slept...' Raf's voice was dry.

Katrina sat up and looked around her, gathering courage. The country was pretty in the late evening dusk, but they were rushing along so fast she couldn't see much of it. She glanced at Raf, but their was nothing to learn from his profile. 'I just want to say,' she began carefully, 'that something's gone wrong—I know what it is, you're angry because I—I said that about Beyke. I expect you think I'm jealous, but I'm not.' Her voice shook a little over the lie, but she went on steadily: 'When we married I knew that you must have friends of your own, people you'd known long before you met me.' She took a deep breath and rushed on: 'I don't know why...that is, I expect if you'd known Beyke wasn't married any more you wouldn't have married me. You told me that you wanted a wife—well, a companion really, and I thought that you were lonely and—and just wanted—well, a companion, like I said, but of course you wanted to forget Beyke, and then she turned up and you could have married her after all.' She added in a very small voice indeed: 'I don't know if you want a divorce.'

Raf didn't answer; he was driving very fast now, tearing down the road, passing everything ahead of him. Presently Katrina said admonishingly: 'You're not frightening me, going fast.'

His harsh laugh made her jump 'Frightened? Which of us is supposed to be frightened?'

Which left her wondering what he had to be frightened about.

He slowed as they reached the outskirts of Amsterdam and then wound through its streets until they joined the motorway to Leiden, less than thirty miles away. It was quite dark now and she couldn't see his face. At last she ventured: 'You haven't said anything.'

'What exactly did Beyke tell you?' he asked in a voice which held no expression at all.

'That you were going to marry, only she went to America and got married there, and when she got back you—you'd married me...'

'And of course you believed her.' He sounded quite friendly again.

'Yes, yes, I think I did. You see, when you brought her home...you knew each other so well... Only I wish you'd told me, Raf.'

He said thoughtfully: 'What difference would it make? When I asked you to marry me I made it plain what I wanted, did I not? You can hardly say you lost me, for you are so sure that you never had me.'

Katrina said slowly: 'That's true.'

She was glad of the dark when he spoke again. 'Do you love me, Kate?'

'No, no, I don't.' She spoke too loudly and too quickly. 'So you see it's quite all right for us to be friends again, and I'll do anything you want about Beyke.'

He said very quietly: 'Have we given ourselves a chance, Kate? We've been married such a short time...'

'Yes, I know, but when we married we didn't know about Beyke—that's altered everything...' She tried to make her voice eager.

'It seems so.' He had heard the eagerness. He said impassively: 'Perhaps we should allow ourselves a little more time to consider.' He was tooling the car along the narrow road leading to their home. 'I have to go to Vienna tomorrow morning, perhaps we could let the matter stand until I get back.'

'How long will you be gone?'

'Two days. Kate, are you quite sure you don't love me—just a little? It would make all the difference.'

Of course it would. If she said yes, he would turn his back on Beyke and spend the rest of his life being a good husband. 'No, no, I don't.' She added to clinch the matter: 'I like you very much though.'

'Thanks.' Raf stopped the car before their door and Caspel, although it was long past his bedtime, opened it with a soft-voiced welcome and the offer of hot coffee in the smaller sitting-room. To rush upstairs to her room wouldn't do at all, so Katrina said, 'Oh, Caspel, how thoughtful of you,' and added: 'I'd love a cup.'

They drank their coffee in the pleasant little room, discussing their day just as though their talk in the car hadn't been. Katrina didn't notice that she had burnt her tongue with the scalding coffee, she was so miserable that nothing seemed real; she heard her own voice answering Raf and it sounded quite normal in her ears. She got up presently, thanked him for her lovely day and tried not to see the bitter little smile on his face, wished him goodnight and asked: 'Are you going very early?'

'I'll leave about six o'clock.'

'Oh—then I hope you have a good trip. I'll—I'll see you when you get back.'

Raf stood up too. He looked angry and remote and very tired. It was all the more surprising that he should suddenly be close to her, wrap her in his arms and kiss her hard and long.

The moment he let her go, Katrina flew from the room and up the staircase. She'd never been kissed like that before; she supposed it was a farewell kiss to their brief marriage. Whatever it was, she wouldn't forget it in a hurry.

She got into bed and cried her eyes out and at last fell asleep, not to wake until Juldou roused her long after eight o'clock with her morning tea. She drank the pot dry, thinking of Raf, already in the air, going miles away from her.

She spent an aimless morning, exercising the dogs, patiently listening to Franz, explaining in basic Dutch so that she could understand him why the peach trees, espaliered on the old brick wall at the end of the kitchen garden, were being sprayed with Bordeaux mixture to destroy peach leaf curl, and then going to the kitchen to tell Berthe that she would have something on a tray for her lunch and would be out for tea. She had no idea where she was going; she would take the Mini and go somewhere—anywhere—away from her unhappy thoughts.

She was pecking at her lunch and listening to the news on the radio when there was a sudden break and another urgent voice took over. There had been a bad plane crash, it said, somewhere in Austria. A morning flight out of Schiphol. The voice gave the flight number and added that as far as was known there were some survivors. Katrina hadn't understood every word, but enough. She flew out of the sitting-room and into Raf's study; when he was away he always left the details of his journey on his desk. The flight number on the memo pad was the same, it seemed to leap from the paper and blind her. She was running back across the hall when she met Caspel, white-faced.

'Caspel, you heard? It's the Professor's flight. Oh, Caspel!' She put a hand on his old arm and just for a moment was swamped by black despair. But only for a moment. 'I'll ring Schiphol, they may know something.' It took a long time to get through, probably the wires were jammed with people as anxious as she was. Finally there was a voice, a kind voice, answering her questions. Yes, there had been a plane crash, there was a possibility that there were survivors, and when Katrina asked from a dry mouth if Professor Baron van Tellerinck had been on the passenger list, the voice became kinder than ever, and said that yes, he had, and asked if further information as it came in should be telephoned through.

Katrina felt very calm now. 'No, thank you. I'm driving to Schiphol now—if my husband is one of the survivors, I'll be able to get a flight to him without delay.'

She stood for a long moment, pushing panic and fear and a terrible grief on one side so that she might think clearly. She would need her passport, money, the car. She turned to Caspel standing by her. 'There may be survivors.' Her eyes begged him to believe that. 'I'm going to Schiphol—if necessary I'll get a flight to wherever it is. I could charter a plane... Caspel, get the Mini round for me, will you? I'll be five minutes.'

Her eyes filled with tears, but she dashed them away and ran upstairs to return within minutes with a jacket, shoulder bag and passport. Caspel was standing at the open door, and everyone else who had anything to do with the house was standing behind him.

'Perhaps it's not true,' he said, and his eyes searched her face like a trusting old dog.

'We'll pray it's not, Caspel. I'm not sure if I'm doing the right thing, but I can't just sit here and wait. If there are any messages let me know. If—if I need to fly there I'll telephone you.' She took his hand and squeezed it, then remembered at the last minute to fly along to Nanny's room, to find the old lady sitting in her chair, staring blankly before her.

'It's all right Nanny,' Katrina spoke with false cheerfulness. 'I'm driving over to Schiphol now—they say there are some survivors, so we mustn't give up hope.' She gave her a quick hug. 'Oh, Nanny dear, he must be safe—we all love him so.'

Nanny's face broke into an uncertain smile. 'That's right, dearie. You'll let us know...?'

'At once, Nanny.' Katrina dropped a kiss on the elderly cheek and hurried back to the hall. She was conscious of sympathetic voices as she went out of the door and got into the Mini, and she remembered to wave to them all before she stormed down the drive.

The first part of the journey was along a narrow country lane running between water meadows, and there was almost no traffic. Katrina slowed through the village and then sent the little car tearing along the dyke road until a huge farm wagon, lumbering ahead of her, blocked it completely. She crept along behind it, her nerves screaming, shaking with impatience, until it turned into an open gateway and she was able to pass it at last and speed on again until she reached the next village. She was almost at the motorway now; one more village first, though. She could see it ahead of her, a couple of miles away, clearly visible in the flat landscape. She was driving too fast, but she would have to slow down again and the first few cottages were at hand already. The road had a bend in it as she entered the long street of the village and there was a good deal of stationary traffic drawn up on it. Which was why she didn't see the Bentley surging towards her to pass in a flash while she was crawling round an awkwardly parked van.

Raf saw her, though. He had brought the car to a halt, turned it smoothly and was on her tail as she reached the centre of the village. The road curved here, round the church, then straightened out again beyond it, and here it was empty of traffic and quiet as Raf shot the Bentley alongside the Mini and then deliberately crowded the little car on to the grass verge.

Katrina, anxious to pick up speed but vaguely aware that there was a car creeping steadily past her, slowed and shot an impatient glance sideways to see the Bentley's sleek nose alongside with Raf at the wheel. She didn't believe what she saw, not for a second or two, but in that time he had drawn ahead of her, crawling to a stop so that she had to brake hard; even so the Mini crunched into the Bentley's stately back. And before she could move Raf had opened the door, switched off the engine, undone her seat belt and plucked her out of the Mini.

It was when she felt his great arms around her that she began to cry; great gulping sniffs and sobs which he didn't try to stop, only held her close.

'They said you were on the plane,' mumbled Katrina into his shirt front. 'Oh, Raf, I thought you'd been killed and I never told you that I love you, and it doesn't matter if you know now,

I don't care any more even though you don't love me. I'll never say it again, I promise I won't, only let me stay with you...'

A small number of people, pleased to have something out of the ordinary to stare at, had formed a ragged circle around them but Katrina hadn't noticed, and as for Raf, he didn't care.

'My darling girl, I hope you will say it repeatedly for the rest of our lives together.'

Katrina stopped snivelling. 'Raf—Raf, you don't mind? You want me to love you?' She lifted a sodden face to his and he smiled at her, a slow tender smile to make her poor scared insides glow.

'Why, of course, my dearest darling. If you hadn't been quite so anxious to keep everything on a friendly footing between us, you might have noticed that I've been in love with you since that day we met. What other reason could I have had for marrying you?'

'Yes, but you said...'

He bent to kiss her. 'It seemed the quickest way to get you.'

'I didn't love you—not at first.'

'I know that; I began to despair that you ever would, and I was angry too.'

'Because of Beyke?'

'Yes, my love, because you thought that I could treat you in such a way. I went out of my way deliberately to make you think that there was something between us. There never was, you know. Beyke puffed up a mild flirtation ten years ago into an affair because she rather enjoys making mischief. And just for a time I thought it might scare you into realising that you loved me.' He kissed her again and she said dreamily:

'It was on that yacht.'

'My brave girl!' He paused to look at a policeman, getting off his bike and coming towards them. 'Yes, Coulsma?'

'Oh, it's you, Baron.' The man beamed at them both. 'A small accident, perhaps?'

Raf explained while the onlookers murmured sympathy.

'I'll see about the little car, Baron—you'll be wanting to take the Baroness home.'

In an atmosphere of the utmost goodwill, Katrina was helped into the Bentley. She must look a perfect fright, she thought distractedly, but everyone was looking at her so kindly while they told each other what had happened and smiled and waved as Raf started the car. She looked at him too and encountered a look of such love that she almost burst into tears again.

'Everyone's so kind,' she gulped, 'and that nice policeman, too.' And then remembering: 'Raf darling, why didn't you go to Vienna?'

He smiled at her. 'I found I couldn't leave you like that; I couldn't wait two days before seeing you again. I cancelled my lectures and came home determined to make you see that I loved you.' He picked up her hand and kissed it gently and an old lady looking on clapped her hands with delight. 'Let us go home, my darling.' He raised a polite hand in farewell to their audience and drove round the church, back on to the road which would take them home.

The various members of the household, who had been standing about aimlessly, too shocked to do much, had come running at Caspel's news that the Bentley was coming up the drive. They all watched with deep pleasure as the Baron got out of the car, helped his Baroness out, kissed her with great satisfaction, and then led her up the steps to the open door. They surged forward then, uttering a wild welcome, shaking hands, exclaiming delightedly that of course they had known all along the Professor was safe.

Raf thanked them all in his calm way, then to Caspel: 'We shall take a stroll in the gardens, and perhaps tea in half an hour, Caspel,' then tucked Katrina's arm under his and went out of doors again.

'I must look awful,' said Katrina, lagging behind a little. 'I must do my face.'

'I like it like that,' declared Raf, 'covered in tears for me.'

All the same, he paused long enough to mop them up for her with his handkerchief.

Caspel, Berthe and Nanny watched them strolling away to the shelter of the trees. Nanny spoke first. 'I knew it would be all right, I saw four magpies this morning.' Her Dutch was fluent but terrible.

'Magpies? What have magpies to do with it?' asked Caspel.

His companions gave him a pitying look. 'Four for a boy,' they explained carefully, and smiled at each other, mentally getting out their knitting needles, infusing raspberry leaf tea and airing the christening robes stored so carefully in tissue paper.

Caspel looked down his old nose at them both. 'Tea in half an hour, the Baron said. It's a lovely afternoon for a stroll.'

Which was exactly what Raf was saying to his Kate, well away from the house by now and she wrapped securely in his arms, being kissed and loved and happy at last.

* * * * *

MILLS & BOON
Book Club

Why not try a Mills & Boon subscription? Get your favourite series delivered to your door every month!

Use code ROMANCE2021 to get 50% off the first month of your chosen subscription PLUS free delivery.

Visit **millsandboon.com.au/pages/print-subscriptions**
or call Customer Service on
AUS **1300 659 500** or NZ **0800 265 546**

No Lock-in Contracts

Free Postage

Exclusive Offers

For full terms and conditions go to millsandboon.com.au
Offer expires 31st Feb 2022

These independent women may not be looking for love, but when the right man comes along, will they go all the way and marry?

Available in-store and online February 2022.

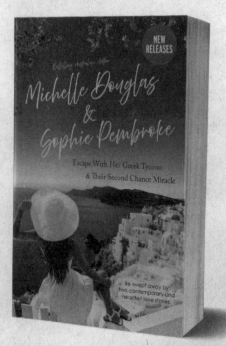

NEW YORK TIMES BESTSELLING AUTHOR

JULIA LONDON

opens her sparkling, witty, sexy new series, A Royal Match,
with a young future queen in the market for a husband, and
the charming — and opinionated — Scottish lord tasked to
introduce her to the ton's most eligible bachelors.

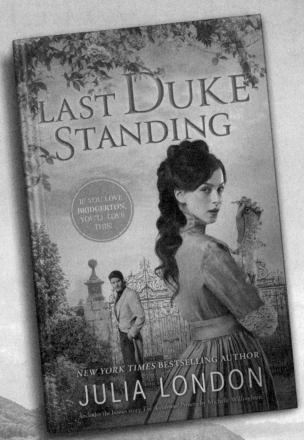

Available in-store and online March 2022.

MILLS & BOON

millsandboon.com.au

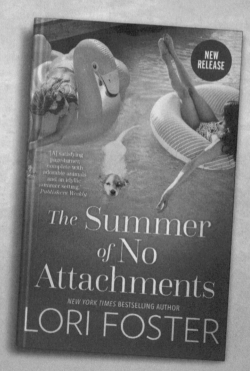